The Dire Wolf Alliance

A Native American Saga

PHYLLIS A. FAST

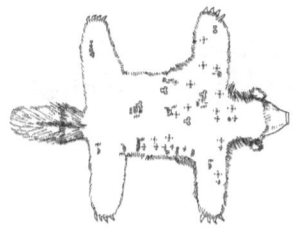

The Dire Wolf Alliance: A Native American Saga

Fast, Phyllis A.

ISBN: 978-0-9974977-6-2 (trade paperback)
ISBN: 978-0-9974977-7-9 (ebook)
ISBN: 978-1979992930 (Library edition)

This book is a work of fiction. All of the characters, organizations, and events portrayed in this novel are either the products of the author's imagination or are used fictitiously.

Cover painting "Indigenous DeManned" by Phyllis A. Fast, acrylic, 2016.

Book design and prepress services by Kate Weisel (weiselcreative.com)

DEDICATION

Richard J. Fast

ACKNOWLEDGEMENTS

Richard J. Fast, both a loyal brother and talented fellow writer, argued with me tirelessly over many plot points. Because of his greater knowledge of how a story works better with both timing and humor, *The Dire Wolf Alliance* is far easier to read than I could have imagined. Jane E. Harper, a fabulous writing partner, spent hours reading *The Dire Wolf Alliance,* and much more time helping me get back to the point. With gratitude, I relied heavily on Paula Desoto's pithy remarks and practical points to make *The Dire Wolf Alliance* a more youth-friendly book, and to avoid boring anthropological sentences. Thanks to Paula, I added several sections to let 21st-century Deloo ask questions that younger Americans might ask. Kate Weisel, a tireless pre-press specialist, reminded me that people always ought to know where the ancient past fits in the world they know. Others who have helped me along the way include my sister, Esther Fast, and my cousins, Michael C. Harper and Johanna L. Harper. Like my brother, Richard, they share my indigenous ancestry, and know far more about working in tense Alaska Native political meetings. I also thank Marilyn Griffin and Carmen Bydalek, who agreed to read early versions of *The Dire Wolf Alliance.*

CAST OF CHARACTERS

Contemporary Characters (story tellers)

Name   (Age at time of novel)

Baasee'   (14,000 years of age, or so)   Deloo's spirit guide

Deloo Goode (21)   Mortal guided by Baasee', widow

Grandfather Kwaiikit   (14,000 and more)   Baasee's grandfather, the Naan's nephew, Tuudzaado, one of several original members of the Dire Wolf Alliance

Also mentioned

Great Aunt Pauline   (70)   Deloo's great aunt, can see Baasee'

Taale Denaa Harper   (41)   Deloo's mother, recently married to Frank Harper

* * *

Primary Ancient Characters (in alphabetic order)

Name   (Age at time of novel)

Chebucto   (16)   Son of Njootlan and Malu

Dagoli   (12)   Zaandan's and Jenda's daughter

Joot   (40)   Malu's husband, Chebucto's father, Hutlan

Kenduu   (20)   Zaandan's adopted son, Duna's husband, Nightstalker heritage

Keyo   (15)   Zaandan and Jenda's youngest son

Mala   (32)   Chebucto's mother, Njootlan's wife, Jenda's sister, Datherd (Southern Tuudzaado)

the Naan   (50)   Zaandan's mother, Hlairen's aunt, Tuudzaado, one of several original members of the Dire Wolf Alliance

Ping   (24)   Tuudzaado, son of Reega, North Face

Rastuk   (35)   Black Sun Warrior, son of Slana (Tuudzaado) and Ryx (Dotson)

Zaandan   (34)   Tuudzaado, the Naan's son, Jenda's husband, children: Keyo, Dagoli, and adopted son, Kenduu

* * *

Secondary Characters (in alphabetic order)

Name   (Age at time of novel)   Clan, and other features

Aadso' (10)   Hutlan boy captured in west and died at Falls Creek

Arg'etan (deceased)   Zaandan's adoptive father (Hutlan)

Clarvu (11)   Kwaiikit's second daughter, Red Paint Woman

Duna (18)   Kenduu's wife, mother of Masi, Hutlan

Garantu (25)   Kwaiikit's first daughter, mother is Memree

Iglan (40)   Tuudzaado of Uplands, father of Nazu, killed by Jis

Jenda (31)   Zaandan's wife, Datherd

Jis (20)   Dotson who killed Iglan, Mysfet's husband

Kejimkujik (70+)   Tuudzaado, one of several original members of the Dire Wolf Alliance

Memree (deceased)   Kwaiikit's first wife, member of core group of Dire Wolf Alliance

Mysfet (24)   North Face Hutlan, sister of Lo

Nazu (15)   Iglan's son, abducted and enslaved, Tuudzaado

Old medicine man (71)   Hutlan relative of Njootlan who lives on North Face

Reega (38)   Ping's mother, Tuudzaado

Skritforce (40)   Hutlan, Dire Wolf Alliance secret ally in the Grotto

Stal (5)   A slave boy with Hutlan mother and Dotson father

Var (41)   Tuudzaado, guard of the West Face

TERMS USED IN THE DIRE WOLF ALLIANCE

Places

Zana

Area on the east of the glaciers before 10,000 BP (before the present era), most of which is now under the Atlantic Ocean east of Nova Scotia. There are two climate areas: the uplands (the Dzagh) and the lowlands along two glacial rivers. Chebucto's father takes him to the lowlands in the north. Later, his cousin Kenduu was abducted and taken to the lowlands in the south. Home for Chebucto is the Dzagh.

Broken Jaw

An area of Zana along the southern side of the coast. In Kwaiikit's youth, it was a thriving population of many kinds of people who came there to trade, to meet, and to celebrate summer solstice.

Dzagh

The uplands inhabited by a mixture of Hutlan and Tuudzaado, composed of steep ridges and occupied by widely scattered family encampments. The houses are primarily made of sod, rock slabs, and fallen logs built atop two or three feet of soil that covers glacier ice. Food (meat and roots) is stored in ice pits.

Falls Creek

A sprawling community of scattered homesites along the inland (northside only) bank of the glacial river that bordered Zana on the south side. Kenduu was imprisoned here near a complex of abandoned adobe buildings whose original builders are unknown. It is on the banks of a glacial river south of the Dzagh. At the time of the novel the Dotson (strangers from the west) use it for fishing and imprisoning slaves. In Kwaiikit's era, it was noticeable only when the glaciers were melting in the spring and summer. By his granddaughter's (Baasee's) era, it flooded more and more each year.

People of The Dzagh

Death Runners

The Dotson trainees are called Death Runners because they seek human victims to kill. Those who survive are expected to return home to Dotshon.

Dotson

People from a place they call Dotshon in the west and south of the glaciers who are known by their hair stiffened by tree pitch or animal fat. Otherwise, they look like the Hutlan, and speak a similar language. They train their youth be sending them on training raids into Zana (see Death Runners).

Hutlan

Short people who use spoken languages. They are the most numerous. They have developed a religious system about the spirit animals who protect the grazing animals favored by the Hutlan in hunts. It is this religious training that Joot wants his son, Chebucto to learn. Joot, Mysfet, and Duna among others are Hutlan.

Tuudzaado

Extremely tall people who use both a telepathic or mental language as well as the Hutlan spoken languages. While resembling Hutlan in other respects, they differed in eye-color, as they had changeable hazel eyes rather than dark brown eyes of the Hutlan. The Tuudzaado hunt by inter-species telepathy. In that system, Tuudzaado hunters learn to communicate with grazing animals in order to learn which grazers are deemed ready to be killed, and what those the families of the selected creatures will take in return. Zaandan expected his sons, Keyo and Kenduu, to learn this system. Most of the members of the Dire Wolf Alliance were Tuudzaado people.

Hunting Tools Used On The Dzagh

Bola

Throwing weapon made of rope (usually one or more strips of rawhide, or braided grasses or tree bark). The hunter tied rope-bound rocks to each end of the main rope. Sometimes they linked two or more strips together to increase the grabbing power of the bola. The technique called for gripping the main rope in the center, getting the rock to rotate in opposing circles around the hunter's fist. Hunters learned quickly to develop tight wrist action in order to get the rocks to make even circles. Once their rocks were making even circles, the hunter aimed the bola toward his target (birds and land animals) and released the rope. Experienced hunters usually got what they needed on the first try. Bola hunters usually made new bolas a day or so before hunting, but talented bola hunters could make a new one in a few minutes. In the twenty-first century, Inuit and Inupiat people refer to bolas as the Eskimo yo-yo.

Hunting spears

A rock sharpened by chipping shards from a larger stone. When its size met the hunter's need, they attached the non-sharpened ending to a stick using strips of hide, often reinforced by tree pitch. This tool was useful for poking, but the technology of spear-making never developed on the Dzagh like it did elsewhere.

Knives

Both men and women of the Dzagh knew how to chip stones in order to make the tools needed, and both men and woman used knives, however women tended to own more knives for more uses than did men. Most people favored igneous rock such as the many kinds of crystals of the Dzagh. The uses varied from slicing meat for searing, surgery for cleaning minor wounds, and preparing raw hides for each stage of making garments.

Animals (Birds and Mammals) of Zana

Dire Wolf

Now extinct, the most common of the canine (dog) species of the era. It was known for having larger teeth than its modern wolf species counterparts. In this novel the dire wolf was the most important spirit animal of the Tuudzaado people.

Moschid

An extinct ungulate (related to moose), was one of the many large deer species of Zana, and a favorite game animal because of its huge size. Zaandan preferred to hunt Moschid in the Dzagh.

Rynchotherid

Now-extinct species of proboscid. Modern proboscids include the African and Asian elephants. The Rynchotherids had spiraling upper tusks and downward pointing lower tusks.

Scimitar Cat

Now extinct, it is a member of the Homotherium or saber-toothed cats. They were known for their immense size and large incisors.

Teretornis

Now extinct, predatory birds with long necks. They were bigger than modern condors, and thought to be related to swans because of their long necks. They flew in pairs (life-long male/ female mates) and lived on the cliffs overlooking the southern side of Zana.

For more information about animals of this era, see *Evolution of Tertiary Mammals of North America*, edited by Christine M. Janis, Kathleen M. Scott and Louis L. Jacobs, 1998, Cambridge University Press.

PROLOGUE

Deloo studied the chipped quartz blades in a museum display and wrinkled her forehead. "Baasee'?"

I let out a gust of air. Sometimes a glorious spirit guide with over fourteen thousand years under her aura has to invent ways to shell out wisdom. Deloo had begun to "hear" me a little over a year ago, we had come to rely on each other to figure out who had killed her late husband and why. I thought about that day. It had been a long time since any mortal had known I existed, not to mention that I might have something important to tell them. We did all that and more. Now, at last, I would help her with an ordinary spirit-guide issue: Sex among the elderly. Her mother, a pretty Athabascan woman of forty-five or so, had recently married Frank Harper, a detective with the Fairbanks police department. To my young Deloo, her mother was too old for sex or romance. I smothered Deloo with a cloud of tenderness, and preened.

"Baasee'," Deloo stared at a display of meat cutting tools mislabeled as neolithic spear points. "Are these really hunting knives?"

"Good question, my brilliant detective. No. Those," I pointed to the slightly wider chipped quartz, "were women's knives used in slicing meat into small, thin pieces so that they cooked quickly on an open-stone fire. Men used the narrower flaked stones to slice meat into the big pieces their wives later cut smaller." I, Baasee' the incredible, was about to remind her that many women, and I was one, ended up being the main hunter of orphans and widows, when she interrupted.

"Arthur used to say things like that to his students." Deloo took a breath and turned to me and communed *Baasee', back in your time, did anyone ever try to run a safe neighborhood for women and children the way Great Aunt Pauline does with Little Tanana?*

It was a dodge to avoid the sex topic, but a fair one. I pretended to fold my brilliant lecture into my invisible jacket while I answered in the silent way we had developed over a year ago. *Yes. There was a small group called The Dire Wolf Alliance. Grandfather Kwaiikit was one of them. It was mostly run by Tuudzaado people.*

"What's Tuudzaado?" Deloo asked aloud.

Grandfather Kwaiikit is Tuudzaado. I referred to him as my grandfather although he had adopted my mother and later me. *They were tall and skinny and very rarely used their mouths to talk. I had to learn it to understand him and to talk to him.*

Did you call me, Granddaughter, my illustrious and equally invisible grandfather communed.

If I had a body, I, the ever sane Baasee', would have jumped. Instead, I thought-chided, *Grandfather!*

Deloo thought-demanded, *Is that the weird guy, Baasee'? Grandfather Kwakiit?*

I sighed. It was Deloo's plight not to be able to see us, and mine to have to deal with my snoopy grandfather. Even so, she was being rude. It was obvious that my spirit-guiding hadn't been as successful as I hoped.

Yes, Grandfather, I was about to tell her about the Dire Wolf Alliance.

Ah, yes, my grandfather blew me a smile and thought-said to Deloo, *the Dire Wolf Alliance was my aunt's idea. I was one of her first rescued children. She was my aunt, so it was easy to be with her after my mother was killed. We were Tuudzaado people.*

Round-eyed, Deloo stared into the air where she thought Grandfather was. *What's a dire wolf. Are you a wolf?*

Both my grandfather and I chuckled in our spirit guide way, and I supplied my little charge, *No, my dear Deloo, Grandfather Kwaiikit and I are both human, like you. The name, Dire Wolf Alliance, came from the wolves, themselves. They formed alliances with humans and other species. They helped us to take care of the many people whose parents died during the invasion of the Dotson people of the west.*

Grandfather Kwaiikit piped up silently, *Let me tell the story.*

One

A small group of men stole out of the Falls Creek grotto in southern Zana. Jogging in single file, the men moved quietly along a well-trodden trail toward the West Face. They moved silently and with a practiced pace, pausing only when they neared the swamps where the poisonous giant salamanders often used wide paths to sunbath. Salamanders never attacked their prey since a single touch of the slime that oozed from their skins killed most creatures. Thick-skinned tapirs seemed immune to the poison, but humans never survived. Giant salamanders were among the few predators that Dotson men allowed themselves to fear. They were proud of overcoming their bodily functions. Not one of them dared stop even to urinate.

* * *

High in the hilly country north of Falls Creek in a place called the Dzagh two boys skidded past the boulders that marked the entryway and scrambled across the trail that edged the ravine. Urgency propelled their hands and feet over familiar stones. Wind ruffled their short-cropped hair and rain struck their faces just as lightening flashed in the north.

"What do you want to do?" A blast of air stole the sound from Chebucto's mouth almost before it reached Keyo.

"I want to see your father's knife."

Chebucto sneered. "Nothing will happen, as usual," he panted, breathless because of the wind. "Why don't you give up? It's been three years."

"It talks to me," Keyo grunted. "It talked to me last night."

"What?!" Chebucto rolled his eyes. "What did it say?"

"Hurry," Keyo responded.

In moments they were inside Chebucto's home. The pair ran straight for his parents' hide-covered sleeping quarters, and to a place on the rear wall where they stored their most precious belongings. Chebucto and Keyo had played with every object on that wall since they were toddlers. On this day their objective was Joot's amethyst knife. The smells in his parents' house suddenly made Chebucto ill, and midway he turned back. Keyo stood in his way. Chebucto collided with him.

"What's the matter with you?" Keyo complained. "Get it!"

Trapped, Chebucto went to the far wall and in the darkness felt among the objects. When his fingers felt the hard, cool surface, he grabbed it and whirled around. Dashing out the entryway he pushed Keyo aside. Keyo plunged after him and grabbed the amethyst knife out of its sheath. Keyo held it for a moment before letting it slip from his fingers.

"Why did you drop it?" Chebucto complained. He reached for it, but Keyo stopped him.

"I saw blood," Keyo whispered, "blood all over me."

Chebucto stared at Keyo, who suddenly sprinted away. Chebucto called "Keyo! Stop!" But his cousin was deaf to everything but the screams in his mind. Springing into action, Chebucto jumped Keyo from behind. The force and angle of Chebucto's weight brought both of them to the ground.

What happened to you? Chebucto asked in the silent language. *What happened in there?!*

"Stop doing that," Keyo said angrily. "You know I don't understand it very well."

Chebucto examined Keyo. "You're bleeding!" He wiped blood from Keyo's face.

Keyo stared at the smear of blood on his cousin's hand and felt his own face for a cut or gash. Finding none, he burst out, "It's my blood, but I'm not bleeding."

Suspicious, Chebucto led his cousin to a dribbling spring. The rain, heavier now, combined with water from the spring to clean Keyo. Chebucto asked again "what happened?"

Blood spatters across Keyo's face, his hair and clothing had lost shape and color in the rain. Chebucto sniffed, thinking of his father's many lessons about scent. "Learn the difference between nose blood, arm blood, and blood from a woman, Son. Learn all of them. It could save your life one day." Chebucto thought about the day his father's message first made sense. He had been four when his mother had gone to her private hut. The smell of her menstrual blood was strong, but Chebucto did little more than sense it. While he helped his father on that long-ago day, Chebucto's nose began to bleed, giving him two kinds of blood to smell at once. From then on, Chebucto could tell the difference between his own blood and anyone else's.

Bringing himself to the present, Chebucto noted this blood was indeed Keyo's. Chebucto stared at the blood, wondering if Keyo had cut himself as a joke. It wouldn't be the first time. Each of them had devised many elaborate schemes to fool the other. Once again suspicious,

Chebucto dabbed at the spots still untouched by rain. Chebucto asked again, "What happened back there?"

"Blood spurted out of me," Keyo said, his voice oddly still. "I was on the ground. I was dead but I could see myself looking down from above the trees."

Chebucto's hands shook a little as he continued working the blood out of Keyo's hair and clothing. "We should tell your mother."

Keyo looked hopeful. "Yes. She'll know what it means."

Chebucto finished cleaning his cousin, and the two boys left. Of the squall, so noisy on Chebucto's side of the ravine, there was no sign on the other. Their mothers were busy putting the finishing touches on a new drying rack. When Jenda spotted her son, she called them to help. Soon both boys were busy cutting raw meat and draping it on the willow branches of a new rack; a smudge fire burned below.

Where Chebucto's father, Joot, had created a Hutlan world on his side of the ravine, Keyo's father, Zaandan, had created a typical Tuudzaado household on his. The former was tidily arranged with tiny, hide-covered structures that served as sleeping quarters, work areas, and storage bins. By contrast, Zaandan's compound was equally tidy, but rigidly defended against weather and enemies through the use of stones and sod. Only Keyo's sleeping area looked out of place. He had built it himself to look like Chebucto's modest, hide-covered lean-to. Although Zaandan had offered to help him build a "real" house, Keyo repeatedly declined, happy with his own handiwork.

Chebucto thought of the way Keyo's face had brightened when Joot slapped his nephew on the back and barked, "Looks like we've got a real Hutlan in this compound!"

Chebucto glanced at Keyo's dark face, understanding that his cousin hadn't mentioned the blood to his mother, Chebucto shrugged inwardly. Perhaps the smoke was too dense in the small space to allow conversation. Perhaps it was Keyo's gloomy mood that prevented either of them from speaking. Whatever the case, Chebucto and his mother returned to their home in early evening without hearing about Keyo's blood or Joot's amethyst knife.

Much later that evening Chebucto crawled into his own narrow, hide-covered lean-to. He had positioned it to face east, giving him privacy from his parents as well as passers-by. There was another advantage. By turning it just so, the length of his lean-to lined up with Mala's cooking pit, and heat from her roasting fires warmed his spine throughout the night. Ordinarily Chebucto luxuriated in the soft lynx pelt that awaited him, but thought's of Keyo's blood haunted him. He shifted restlessly in his lean-to, unable to sleep. Mala retired to her own bed, and soon Chebucto heard her even breathing. After a while the sound lulled him to sleep.

* * *

Someone crept toward an unwary man. The attacker yanked the unsuspecting man's head toward him with one arm and slit his throat with the other. Blood shot out so far and fast that drops hit Chebucto in the face. The killer then felled a woman who toppled onto the man's corpse. Chebucto saw someone else moving toward Nazu.

"Watch behind you!" Chebucto shouted.

Chebucto ran toward them, but his legs wouldn't move. He heard screams and tried harder to run.

"Son! You're dreaming." Mala shook the wall of his lean-to. "Son! Wake up."

The sharp tang of fresh blood filled Chebucto's nostrils and dripped from his face. It took a while to realize that the woman speaking was not the dead pair, but Mala, his mother. Mala tugged Chebucto out of his lean-to and mopped sweat from his face with a scrap of hide. Chebucto realized with relief he had confused the taste of sweat with blood.

"Tell me quickly, Son, before your dream fades."

"Two people got killed," Chebucto rasped between choking sobs. "There's blood everywhere."

Do you see who did it? Mala asked, switching to the Tuudzaado silent mode.

Yes. I see his face, Mother, Chebucto communed in return, now fully awake. *I don't know who he is, but I see he is Dotson by his stiff hair. His tunic is marked with the sign of the Wind.*

Mala projected a mental image, but Chebucto's skills in the Tuudzaado silent language were insufficient to receive it. Switching tactics, she cupped her son's right hand in her left and traced a bent cross shape on his open palm. *Is that it?* She communed silently, adding the projected image again to reinforce yet another language lesson.

Yes.

Mala lifted her chin in the dark as an invisible sign of assent. *The Dotson think of it as the symbol for the Sun. We Tuudzaado say it represents the Wind, the Sacred Forces of the Wind. The four bent lines look to us as if the wind has blown against grass. I suppose the Dotson see them as sunbeams.*

I remember. Yes, it's their sign for the Sun, Chebucto communed in silent agreement.

Mala cradled her son against her bony chest as he described the man who killed their friend, Iglan. *What about your father? Did you see him, too?*

Father! Chebucto's heart raced. Joot had gone to the wedding. *No, Mother. I saw the dead man's silvery eyes staring at me for a long time. I saw Nazu but not Father. Mother, do you think it was real? Do you think something bad has happened to Father? Maybe I should go after him.*

Mala hesitated a little too long. Chebucto felt anger roiling in his stomach even before she responded. Finally she communed, *Son, sometimes these are just nightmares. You've had quite a few strange dreams since you were a little boy. The only one ever to come true was about the old Prayer Woman dying—and she did die, but not for two moons. If something calls you to your father, you will know it yourself. Do you feel called?*

Chebucto wanted to shout out loud, "you never believe me," but controlled himself. He closed his eyes and took several deep breaths to feel for a call. Nothing happened. He wondered if it would help to touch the amethyst knife, but discarded the idea as foolish in his mother's presence. Finally he gathered his wits and communed, *You are right, Mother. My dreams never come true.*

Mala relaxed and nudged Chebucto. *You should get some sleep.* A gust of wind shifted the hide on his lean-to. *It's going to rain again. If you have another vision, call me.*

* * *

"Were those people Tuudzaado? Why did you call them Dotson? Do you mean dotson like the raven? How big are salamanders? You made them sound huge." Deloo's voice rose to a shout.

Bathing her in soothing golden thought, I thought-shushed her. *Remember to THINK your questions to us. Grandfather Kwaiikit forgot that you are in Alaska, not where we were from. Tell her, Grandfather, about the Dotson and salamanders.*

Grandfather held back a grouchy thought-sound and answered *I am a Tuudzaado man. The runners were short Hutlan people from the west. They didn't know the silent language, just the tongue languages. They called themselves Raven people, and I used your Denaakk'e Koyukon word, Dotson, so that you would understand me better. The Dotson were our enemies. As for salamanders, those of Zana were gigantic and looked a little like crocodiles. May I continue?*

Deloo shook her head, and thought-asked timidly, *Where did all this happen?*

I could see Grandfather Kwaiikit grimace, and answered for him, *it's that place I tried to show you last year. Remember? It's off the coast of Nova Scotia, but many years ago it was swamped by the melting glaciers.*

"Oh," Deloo smiled apologetically, and continued silently. *Of course I remember. Sorry. Please go on, Grandfather Kwaiikit.*

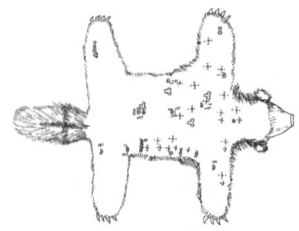

Two

A short man shuffled nervously from foot to foot. A messenger had run ahead of the Hutlan, or short people of Zana, to announce the impending arrival of his bride-to-be. His parents were proud because the groom had entered each of the first three stages of Hutlan adulthood by or before the age of ten. The rules for a first kill were to feed at least three adults without leaving any of them hungry for more. Starting at age ten, the Hutlan groom brought home a long-nosed peccary, big enough to feed all twelve of the people in their household, including himself. The rule for the second stage of manhood was to have a vision that came true. For instance, the Hutlan groom had a vision about a weasel with double white patches over each eye. The very next day his mother brought home a weasel with two tiny white spots over each eye, very unusual in the summer. The rule for the third stage was to fast for three days while others ate in order to prove self-sacrificing strength. Thus, the groom fasted for five days and would have continued if his father had not intervened to declare his son a fully mature adult.

Now, facing a lifetime with a total stranger, the groom couldn't remember any of these feats of maturity. For the first time in years he wished he could run to his mother. Suddenly he felt something move softly against his right palm. He glanced around, but no one was close enough to have touched him. Nazu's jaw tightened against the force of a shiver that swept across his shoulders. His mother had died four years ago when he was eleven.

Suddenly the bride entered the glade first. The groom's heart leaped. She was the most beautiful girl he had ever seen. Dressed in white doe-skin from her head cover to her moccasins, her dark eyes locked with his. The groom took a step forward without waiting for his father to make the customary greetings. Suddenly someone leaped from behind an outcropping of rocks, grabbed the bride with one hand and did something to the back of her head that seemed to make everything burst out the front. The groom froze in horror as hands pulled him to the ground. He felt a blow against his back but not the pain of it, and the last thing he remembered was the feel of wet soil on his lips.

* * *

Chebucto awoke again, sweating, but fully aware. He didn't call his mother as he had done earlier. This time he understood more. As always, he dream-knew the man was Hutlan, and something always made him thing the dream-man was about to marry. This time was different. Chebucto allowed himself to realize the dream had just come true, and knew that one day he would find out who they were and why he was to know about it.

I felt Deloo's confusion swell through the room. Used to her impatience, I held still, knowing that she'd get control of herself. She did so by wailing out loud.

"Wait! I'm confused. Why is the first dream was about a Dotson and this one is about a Hutlan. I thought they were two kinds of people. What happened?"

Grandfather was beside me and spirit-grinning, which I have always hated. I let him answer. *Very good, great-granddaughter. Just remember that there were short people called Hutlan and tall people called Tuudzaado. The Hutlans in the west were our enemies, known as Dotson. Dotson also had stiff hair. Hutlan people had soft, dark hair that wasn't stiff, and were our friends in the east and north..*

Deloo turned away from the museum's big flaked stoke displays, and murmured, "I'm short with soft, dark hair. Am I Hutlan?"

This time I cut in. *Maybe, but the main difference was that the tall, skinny people like Grandfather Kwaiikit have a silent language, which we have called communing with each other.*

"But you talk to each other in that silent language. I thought you said you were a Hutlan," Deloo shrugged sullenly.

You are right as always, my gentle Deloo. It is not uncommon for anyone to commune. People who have been together a long time commune even when they don't know that's what they are doing. Tuudzaado people communed, could float rather than walk, and were also different in other ways. For instance, Grandfather and his kind were VERY tall. He and others like him were at least a meter taller than us shorter Hutlan. Their hands very long too. Grandfather's feet were so big he didn't use footgear because it was a waste of hide and because he could float.

"Float? What do you mean? Did he fly like Superman?" Deloo asked in a loud voice. I reminded her to use her silent voice.

Deloo turned back to the display case, "it sounds like he was some kind of Superman. Was he?"

I, the eternally patiently Baasee', enveloped Deloo in a cloud of love and said silently, *He was my superman. Maybe for others, too. He's ready to tell you more.*

Wait, Deloo thought-wailed, *how come you both use thought language. Was it like that when you were alive?*

I managed an apologetic look toward Grandfather, and communed to my irritating mortal, *I had to learn it or die. You'll learn all about that later. Ready, Grandfather?*

Grandfather Kwaiikit shimmered and then said in the silent language, *the next part of the story is about the man who murdered his mother. His name in Rastuk. He was half Tuudzaado, and therefore taller than most. I suppose he could float as well, but I never saw him try. Like we said, before, he only murdered his mother because he was required to do so by the Dotson. She was the one who had the argument that he could do so if he went on a Death Run to Zana.*

"Death Run?" Deloo blurted loudly, and commune-asked, *what's that?*

Grandfather Kwaiikit answered, *that means he was to go alone to the country of his mother to prove his manhood as a Dotson Black Sun Warrior, meaning he had to prove he was ruthless killer, knowledgeable about all ways to survive and to lead others. He had to follow one rule, which meant to kill any Hutlan or Tuudzaado who got in his way. There were no other rules, since few Dotson ever made it back to the Dotson homeland alive.*

I sensed Deloo's many questions, and shushed her with my superwoman's gentle force, *He'll explain it as he tells is. Be patient. The first part is about getting to the center of Zana, which is a place called Blue Rock. This part of the story takes place in what we call the Peccary Moon, which started on the day summer ended, or what we would call late September.*

* * *

Rastuk labored over the first knoll past Blue Rock. As usual the first run of the day caused every joint to ache. He knew it would pass and he forced himself to quicken his pace. A sea of dry, late summer grass met his eyes and filled his nose when he reached the top of the knoll. The grass swallowed him whole. Suddenly in darkness, the grass itself dragged him to a stop. He pulled a triangle of rawhide over his face to keep the dust out of his eyes and nose. He took in the shape of the west side of the hillock with all of his senses. Carefully, he lifted the scrap of rawhide to add more odors to the inventory. Satisfied, he pushed slowly into the grass. A coyote hunting nearby was the largest mammal on the slope besides himself. Countless small birds and insects swarmed in the upper level while even more insects, lizards and small mammals crawled at his feet. Rastuk ignored them all, worried only about crevasses and large cobbles. Reaching open air on the other side came as a welcome shock. Ripping away the rawhide kerchief, he glanced around and saw his mistake. A well-beaten path edged the grass a few steps away. Rastuk grimaced but didn't move until he had studied the terrain again. Finally assured that no other human was near, he trotted to the path and resumed running, feeling the muscles moving along his bones the way they used to do when he was a boy.

However, by the time the sun reached its second quarter, Rastuk no longer felt his legs or lungs. His eyes seemed to be the only part of him that actually moved, always darting across the horizon, always aware of the slightest movement. He would have smiled if smiling had ever been a part of his life. With his attention fixed in constant mobility, Rastuk allowed his inner thoughts to roam. First his mother's long-lashed eyes flared at him, laughed at him while a two-year-old Rastuk tumbled after her, always a little too far away to catch her outstretched arms. Rastuk's belly cramped as it had not done for years. Without slowing his pace, he forced himself to breathe shallow gulps of air. Bile flooded his belly. Rastuk opened his mouth as wide as possible to clear his throat. Even before the spasm passed, he forced his mind to follow his feet as they moved without hesitation over the trail. In a few moments, the pain quieted. He relaxed. Another unbidden image flowed into him, first in grey tones, then color: his father's severe face, averted, backlit by a dimming sun.

Rastuk spat, daring his mind to betray any other weaknesses. As it hit the dust and grass, something large slithered across his path. To avoid it, Rastuk hopped awkwardly back a step and nearly fell. The bright eyes of a big prairie dog caught his before it disappeared into a clump of uprooted grass. Righting himself, Rastuk caught a westerly breeze. A human, sweating female odors labored ahead. He slowed his pace to learn more. He felt in his mind for knowledge of the earth and air. When he detected basalt and tide water he recognized Falls Creek. He wiped his forehead with the same scrap of rawhide he'd used before and adapted his gait to a long walking stride, the almost-saunter he had seen men of Zana use. His legs were used to running, he hoped the stride didn't look as clumsy as it felt. When he tucked the scrap of rawhide around his belt, he saw a flash of white and glanced at the hide more carefully. A single shaft of stiff white hair glistened in the sunlight. He twirled the hair between thumb and forefinger, lifted a brow and tossed it aside, wondering if it was his imagination that not only was he losing more hair lately, but a lot of it was white.

The sun climaxed at midday when the Dotson men arrived at their destination on the twenty-third day of the Peccary Moon. Still far behind them, Rastuk reached the area just north of the slab of wood that crossed Falls Creek near the falls themselves. He stopped on the slab and stared at the maze of rocks on the west side of the falls. He was about to give up when he spotted a hand emerge from within a thicket of aspens. The fingers flickered an intricate signal and disappeared. Rastuk moved his own fingers in a quick series of movements and walked gingerly across the slippery wood. Once past the creek, Rastuk broke into a run. He caught the first waft of Dotson passage beside the salamander swamp and paused briefly, then ran harder than ever.

* * *

An old medicine man on the North Face awoke and called to his granddaughter. "Send for Ping," he said. "Tell him to bring his men."

Just before dawn the following day Ping moved silently to the rear of the old medicine man's household whistling softly. He received a signal to enter and emerged from the shadows, crossed the short space and sat cross-legged beside the old medicine man without any apparent transition from absence to presence.

The old medicine man didn't turn his head. His eyes seemed fascinated by something in front of him. "It's good to see the Marten again." He murmured. "Nephew, your grandfather would have been proud to see you with the marten *yeege*. Instead, it is I am who glad to see you have come so quickly." The old medicine man waved a hand. By the customs of Zana, he used the honorific "Nephew" on all young men who earned his favor. He didn't tolerate others. "Eat with us. Then I will explain what I saw."

* * *

Beside me, the beleaguered Baasee', Deloo thought-whispered, *What's a yeege?*

It's from your own language. I see you haven't touched that Denaakk'e dictionary in a while, I, the Magnificent Baasee', have fully mastered all of it!

Deloo glared at me with a sour smile. *Sorry. What does yeege mean?*

Grandfather Kwaiikit intervened, *a spirit. Here it is the marten spirit.*

Deloo ducked her head sheepishly, or dare I think *yeegishly,* and thought toward us, *Thanks.*

Grandfather Kwaiikit hid a spirit-grin, and continued.

* * *

Ping looked at the wooden platters laden with food and lifted an inquiring eyebrow toward the old medicine man's pretty, young granddaughter.

"I greet you, Agra," Ping said. "You are as radiant as the sun this morning."

The young woman's blush darkened her dusty brown face to nearly black. She dimpled. An odd quirk in Ping's eyebrows seemed to ask for more than food. Suddenly breathless, she forced herself to breathe slowly before answering. "Look! This is for all of you. Bring them in as well." She kept her eyes steadily on the tall visitor.

Ping emitted a short, loud whistle. Four young Hutlan men also entered the old medicine man's household. They immediately surrounded the young woman, sitting much closer to her than the old medicine man thought necessary. He watched Agra's bright eyes, heard her playful retorts and sighed but said nothing. Ping, on the other hand, was not so tolerant. He coughed once, slid his black eyes along the chin or forehead of each of his men, and tilted his head to the side. Amid muffled snickers and lustful grins, they moved a little away from the young woman.

The old medicine man contemplated the looks that passed between his granddaughter and Ping. After a moment, he, too coughed. Ping smiled at the old medicine man who tilted his head toward the food. He waited until Ping selected some food before taking the lean young man aside to explain what he needed.

"I saw the Nightstalker. Dead."

"Var?" Ping interrupted. Nightstalker was the role that defined him. "How?"

"Murder. A man stands near him. He is not the killer, but he knows who did it and why. I called you, Nephew, for two reasons. First, find out if my vision is true. Second, find out who that man is. He looks Tuudzaado in some ways but he has that Dotson hair. And a scar." The old medicine man drew something in the dirt near Ping's feet. "It's on his forehead." The old medicine man looked closely at Ping. "Does that mean anything to you?"

Ping stared at the drawing. It was a simplified face. A zigzag crossed the forehead twice starting from the upper left side to the bridge of the nose. "It looks familiar, but I don't remember why."

The old medicine man tipped his head upward. "You were very young at the time. I never met the man who killed your father but I had a vision of him, too. That man had a scar like this." He tapped his drawing. "Chegwet told me about it afterward. I want you to find out who this man is. I think it is important to your family, indeed, to all of Zana."

Ping thanked the old medicine man and called to his men. With a wink to their hostess he loped away.

"He's Tuudzaado," the old medicine man said when they were out of sight. "Some of them are just like us Hutlan people, but Ping has to follow his grandfather's way."

His granddaughter blushed again, but said nothing. *Grandfather always knows what I think,* she thought. *He knows, but he can't stop how I feel.*

"His life is going to change in a terrible way soon. So will all of our lives."

His granddaughter stared at him, mouth agape. "How?"

"My visions for Ping are not clear. He will not die soon. But others do." The old medicine man shifted, trying to find a less bony part of his old rear end. His granddaughter continued staring and then dropped her gaze. Neither of them spoke until much later, and then only about life's simple things, such as food.

* * *

At dawn on the twenty-sixth day of the Peccary Moon, a Dotson Black Sun Warrior explained what he wanted. "None of your fancy marks on the bodies this time. I want it to look as it could have been done by anyone."

One of the Dotson men growled low in his throat but tipped his chin upward when the Black Sun Warrior loomed toward him, lips tightly compressed. The ugly zigzag scar on his forehead seemed to ooze with malevolence. "What about our odors? They might know us by our scent."

"Just do as I have said," the Black Sun Warrior snapped and turned on his heel.

* * *

As soon as he saw the solid wall of glaciers bordering the West Face, Rastuk sensed he was too late. The trail from where he stopped was barely visible along the gravelly moraine that extended a full day's run from the base of the steppes on the west side of the Dzagh to the glaciers ahead. With no cover to hide his progress Rastuk decided to rest while he tried to remember the region. By habit he sank into a crouch and listened to the birds. His father had taught him the basics of bird communication. Several birds flew straight upward and then downward at an angle a short distance away. Rastuk knew that something large and predatory had entered their territory, and they were attempting to chase the invader away. His theory was confirmed when they repeated the pattern, this time with strident squawks. The birds continued diving and screaming, each time aiming their attacks a little farther along an invisible northerly trail. Rastuk followed the birds north. He reached a small knoll that allowed him to see above the tall prairie grass. He stopped to study the birds again, this time to determine how far away he was from the Tuudzaado household he had visited only days before. He spotted the unusually shaped orange and green boulder that marked the eastern point of the compound. Of the Dotson men he was following, he saw nothing.

Instead, he saw a column of men ran toward the Tuudzaado household from the north. Normally, Rastuk would have held back, waiting for more information. Instead, he began loping toward the household himself. He kept his pace slow to allow the strangers to reach the compound ahead of him. They were Hutlan men. They stopped and waited. Rastuk stopped as well. He hoped he had not been seen, but one of the Hutlan men pointed in his direction, so Rastuk ran toward them, choosing a moderately fast pace. When he was a short distance away, he came to a halt to wait for a signal to approach. Rastuk felt the warning hairs along his neck rise, but ignored it. None of the Hutlan men seemed inclined to acknowledge his existence. Rastuk contemplated taking the initiative when he heard a soft sound to his left. Donning an unconcerned air, Rastuk turned toward the noise. He was surprised to see a man standing almost within reach. The stranger had bright black eyes set close together, nearly hidden by a thatch of dark eyelashes. The man smiled. His remarkably white teeth created an air of friendliness. The two stared at each other. Neither moved.

"Who are you?" Rastuk asked.

"Ping," the other smiled.

Rastuk frowned, unsure which was more disarming, the name or the white teeth. "I am Rastuk," he supplied after a moment.

"Why are you going toward Var's house?" Ping asked, smiling evenly. He glanced once at the scar. It was exactly like the one drawn by the old medicine man.

Rastuk considered and dismissed the usefulness of insolent silence and instead answered pleasantly, "They are my relatives. I visited them a few days ago and thought I would pay my respects now that I am back here. What about you?"

"Our respects? I'm afraid it's too late for that," the tall man said. "My friend, Var, is dead." The Hutlan men moved into a semi-circle around Rastuk. "So are his wife and daughter."

A scowl blackened Rastuk's face as he stared toward the stone household. "No! I was just here. What could have happened?" He turned toward Ping, but the man was no longer present. A wall of prairie grass met his eyes. He glanced at the bent grass marking the spot from which he had himself emerged moments ago. A quick visual and olfactory survey told him that Ping had not gone that way. As he puzzled, a distant shout called his attention back to Var's household. The Hutlan men were gone as well. Suspicious, Rastuk moved toward Var's household compound. He could smell human blood several strides before he reached the place and slowed.

A slight rustling behind him was his warning, and he whipped around to find Ping facing him, looking at something out of Rastuk's sight. Rastuk again looked around, and caught scurried movement. Although Rastuk didn't see Ping's signal but he knew obedience when he saw it in motion. The four Hutlan men had split into pairs, one heading to the left of the compound, the other to the right. Ping moved into the compound slowly. Showing no interest in Rastuk, he prowled first to the exterior of the main sod house, then to each of the eight smaller structures scattered around the compound. Rastuk decided to hold back and watch. His nose told him the main source of blood was not in the compound, but behind it. He heard a Hutlan shout.

"Dead?" Ping shouted in return.

"Two women."

"Leave them," Ping called out and continued prowling.

Ping's search was for the thoughts left in the ground, the air, and the minds of the compound's occupants. A mental phrase lingered in the space around Kat's work area.... *short, stiff braids, I can tell they are Dotson. The braids are brownish red, like this old blood....* Ping looked at Rastuk's reddish hair, plaited firmly into two stiff braids. It gave away his Dotson heritage more as easily as the rest of him did.

Ping paused at the entrance to Kat's house. He spotted a singed area near the top of the structure, but there were no other signs of fire. The main dwelling, a semi-subterranean sod house, was too low for him to stand upright so he entered on his knees. Much like his mother's house, it was dug deep into the ground with a long entry tunnel. Ping crawled into the main chamber. He could feel Rastuk's body heat directly behind him and forced himself to concentrate on the messages left behind. As he moved, he realized that he was the only man to have entered the dwelling by this opening besides Var. He stopped before entering the main chamber. Like most Tuudzaado dwellings, a woman's lamp hung on the left side and several furs were coiled and hung from two rafters above. Ping waited until he gathered as much information as he could, but Rastuk's presence behind him rattled his concentration. Irritably, Ping crawled into the primary sleeping quarters. His nostrils told him that Var and Kat had slept in the center of the room while their daughter had slept against a wall on the north side. A light smell of smoke hung in the air despite the draft coming in from what remained of the smoke hole. He moved toward it. A vision of Kat, a woman he had met five times, came to him. He saw her tearing at the stones with her fingers. A thin membrane from a scimitar cat's stomach, now badly torn, had covered the smoke hole until she'd ripped it out.

My husband, they intend to murder Veetu and me.

The urgent message hung in the air. Ping couldn't tell if Var had responded. He sensed Var was already dead by the time Kat communed her panic. An image of their daughter, Veetu, wavered briefly in Ping's mind. He remembered Veetu. He had seen her a year ago when she was about twelve. Her body had been almost skeletal, typical of a Tuudzaado child. Ping wondered why Kat tried to escape when the Dotson had not reached the tunnel and then he turned to look toward the entryway and understood. They must have threatened to burn it—one of the greatest perils of sod houses was that enemies could block the entryway with a fire, leaving the occupants to suffocate inside.

Ping examined the widened smoke hole and tested his weight on the root of a juniper tree near the top. It held, so Ping swung forward and up, legs tucked close to his chest. He used the momentum to roll to the side and onto his feet, pivoting quickly to face the smoke hole. Rastuk climbed out more carefully. Once again in the light, Ping examined the man. Bright shafts of white hair shot through the stiff Dotson hair. He must be more than thirty, possibly even forty by the look of him, Ping thought, satisfied his own twenty-four years made gave him an edge against a man so much older. The juniper root broke under Rastuk's weight, forcing him to drag himself out with his back toward Ping. Ping suppressed a sudden shudder and blinked his eyes a couple of times. If Rastuk's hair had not been so stiff and reddish, Ping could easily take him for Tuudzaado.

Are you Tuudzaado? Ping asked, testing the man with the silent language.

Rastuk turned to Ping with interest. *Yes.*

Ping hesitated and then communed, *They spent time with you in the family area outside. Why?*

Rastuk lifted his heavy brows and communed, *Kat was related to my mother.* He looked at the bloody remains of Veetu just beyond them. *I'm sorry I wasn't here to stop this.*

Ping didn't answer. As clearly as if she said had whispered it into his ears, Ping felt/heard Kat's mental communication to her daughter, *Veetu, you must crawl to the edge and hide in the thicket. Along with her words,* she had projected an image of foliage.

Ping followed their trail. Against her mother's order, Veetu had slithered out of the thicket and rushed toward a path that led to the menstrual hut farther up the drumlin side of the compound. A well-marked trail led toward the hut. They had made a tunnel by weaving nettles along the sides and tops to keep unwanted viewers away—something for the ordinary days when they had the luxury of life ahead of them. In his vision, Ping saw them wedged against each other inside. The menstrual hut was meant for one woman at a time, not two. Ping both heard and felt the brittle echoing of fear still radiating from Kat's mind. He saw that Kat then pushed her daughter into a deep thicket and crawled away. Veetu's body was still partially hidden in the shrubbery her mother had hoped would hide her. A horrible vision suddenly came to Ping. Through Kat's eyes he saw the Dotson face of her murderer. Through her eyes Ping watched the man raise his stone club and strike her. Ping pulled himself away from the vision and looked at Kat's body. It was obvious from what little remained of her head the man had struck her again and again.

At that moment one of the Hutlan men came toward Ping and whispered something in his ear. Ping said something in return, and moments later all four of the Hutlan men returned with Var's body suspended between them. Ping signaled for them to place the body beside the main cooking pit. In a while all three bodies were together. Ping and the Hutlan men gathered firewood with amazing speed. It took Rastuk little time to realize that they were preparing a funeral pyre. He covered his confusion by gathering what seemed to Rastuk an enormous waste of good wood with the others. Suddenly the Hutlan men disappeared.

"Where did they go?"

Ping turned to him. Although it was past sunset by then, there was no mistaking the lack of friendship in Ping's face. "We'll take care of the rest ourselves."

Hundreds of questions came to Rastuk's mind, but he carefully maintained an even expression. "Certainly. What would you like me to do?"

"We'll start with a prayer for their First Walk of Death and then wait until they are completely consumed by the fire. We'll have plenty of time to get to know each other better while they burn," Ping peered at his companion more intently. "Don't you agree?"

Rastuk stumbled through the first prayer, hoping his mumbled words sounded something like what Ping expected. He was glad he had kept the red ochre pouch his mother had owned. Dutifully, he smeared all three heads with the powder in the same way that Ping did. After Ping lit the fire, the younger man incanted a powerful, incomprehensible, silent song. Rastuk didn't understand a single bit of it but he marveled at the sensations pulsating along his spine in chilling circles. As it happened, Ping had composed the song with great care. It was an ancient Tuudzaado song of grief in which Ping had embedded a coded message that he knew would reach only the people for whom it was intended.

Then Ping began to dance. Rastuk watched first with discomfort, then a strangely familiar feeling came to him. It looked as if something had come into Ping from the earth itself. Rastuk smiled inwardly. His mother and he had argued once about what she called the Sacred Forces. Afterward she refused to teach him anything else about the Tuudzaado religion because he would not say that the Sacred Forces were in the Wind, the Earth, the Ocean and the Sky. He could not. The Dotson religion was very clear. They believed the only Sacred Forces were the Sun itself. Agreeing with her on Tuudzaado beliefs was the only thing he could not force himself to do.

Ping's odd prayer ended and he turned to Rastuk. "Shall we make fire?"

Rastuk lifted his chin in agreement and found himself standing opposite the gaunt man with the pile of wood between them. Ping used a fire bow with quick dexterity to ignite a blaze. In a few moments, a hot fire snapped with sudden surges of flames. Rastuk stared at the fire, thinking of Kat's odd, green eyes and easy smile. He had asked where her husband was, and she replied that he was a Nightstalker with a shrug as if that explained everything. It had not.

"What is a Nightstalker?"

Kat had regarded him with sudden doubt and didn't answer. Rastuk tried to find a way back to the mystery of her husband, but she seemed to anticipate his questions, and moved smoothly through many stories about their mutual family members. At last Rastuk asked the right question: "How did you meet your husband?"

Veetu, who had been silent all night, burst into laughter and trilled happily, "he left her presents every day for a moon. Tell him, Mother."

Kat shushed her daughter and tried to change the subject again, but Rastuk persisted. "What did he bring you?"

Kat tilted her head back and thought about that time long ago. "The first gift was a bright blue feather. He left it on the big rock that is in front of my mother's house." She chuckled. I had never seen such a pretty feather, so I picked it up and put it in my hair. When my mother saw it, she smiled and said she had wondered if he would ever get enough courage to give me something. She said he'd been prowling around our house for three moons.

Rastuk's imagination was captured. "Had you seen him?"

Veetu bounced to her knees and said, "we never see Father. It's against the rules. He always leaves before dawn and doesn't come into the house unless he's sure we are both asleep. Once, I tried to stay awake all night when I heard him come in, but I fell asleep."

"Veetu!" her mother said reprovingly. "You shouldn't talk so much."

"How many gifts did he bring to you?"

"Mmmm. I don't remember. He brought a lot of meat for us. That went on for more than a moon. One day he left a beautiful shell; it must come from the ocean. It is the most beautiful thing I've ever seen."

"A shell?" Rastuk was curious. "What does it look like? Do you still have it?"

"Mamma sewed into Father's belt," Veetu shrilled, bouncing happily on her knees. "It took her the whole moon to make the belt, Father has it on all the time. I know because I hear it rattling once in a while when he's outside when he's here. We're not supposed to go out when he's there except tonight because you are visiting."

Rastuk heard the rattling and smiled at Kat. She smiled shyly and peered at Rastuk through thick eyelashes. Rastuk, now seeing flames licking at her body, found himself swaying and stomping in a way he had never done in his life. His legs seemed to be possessed by something Rastuk again seemed to recognize. He opened his mouth and began to chant loudly using words he didn't know but felt with confidence they belonged to this funeral and to the people he had been with for so short a time. When he finished, he turned to find Ping staring at him, mouth agape. The younger man closed his mouth and lifted his chin as if in acknowledgment of something that had passed between them.

"I haven't heard that prayer since my father died," Ping murmured.

Rastuk thought about his mother's determination to teach him all the prayers. "My mother taught me many things," he replied, wanting to add, but not daring to with a stranger, *but never any funeral songs.*

* * *

Grandfather Kwaiikit paused and asked Deloo, *Questions?*

Deloo looked up at her usual spot on the ceiling where she thought I lived, smiled and said, "It's all making sense so far. Please go on, Grandfather Kwaiikit." She dimpled with her single dimple. "I probably have lots more questions that haven't yelled at me yet."

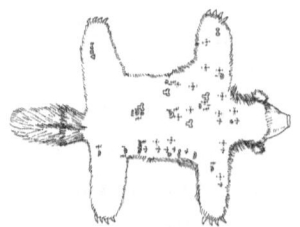

Three

The Naan had been navigating a particularly tricky ascent along the eastern ridges of the Dzagh when Ping began his silent prayer. Although she didn't know who was calling, by its phrasing she knew another of the original six members of the Dire Wolf Alliance secret council was dead. She shivered, not wanting to learn which of the four remaining was gone, including Kwaiikit's wife. Kwaiikit wanted their group to take a lead in ending the slavery and murders committed by the Dotson. The rest agreed and named their group the Dire Wolf Alliance.

It took a few moments to reach a stable outcropping where she could attend to the song in full. Despite the ice the platform, she found meditation worked best if she sat cross-legged. This time she couldn't find comfort in any position. Perhaps it was her age. She disregarded the irritating thought and arranged herself to receive the message. In moments she saw two strangers, one Tuudzaado and another who looked Dotson. The zigzag on the Dotson man's forehead appeared slowly to her. She pondered its shape, then recalled that if the scar started in the upper left as the stranger's did, he was a Black Sun Warrior. If the scar had stretched toward the upper right, he would have been a Red Sun Warrior. Zana had become home to many Red Sun Warriors and recently to one Black Sun Warrior. The woman in her observed his body, approved of his manly figure. Despite the scar, his face was evenly shaped. She smiled at a private joke and watched more closely as the Black Sun Warrior began to chant, using a voiced prayer instead of the silent prayers. Nonetheless, the words came to her.

The Naan's eyebrows lifted in surprise. Her mother had taught her that prayer decades ago, but the Naan had never used it herself. It was a prayer of vigilance and war. The power of Var's Nightstalker *yeege* or spirit force appeared before the Naan and rose upward. It was the signal that Var was dead. A deep shudder rolled across her shoulders and caused her to break contact with both the Black Sun Warrior and the unknown Tuudzaado man. Immediately after she ended the vision another came unbidden toward her. She greeted it with warm pleasure. It had been too many years since she had seen the sign of the marten. She hoped, although her visions were not always reliable, that the marten was with the unidentified Tuudzaado man.

The Naan didn't waste any time moving toward the eastern side of the big gorge. She knew she would find Kwaiikit, Garantu, and Kejimkujik—the last of the Dire Wolf Alliance's original members.

* * *

Later Ping and Rastuk tore apart the stone roof and pulled the family possessions out of the house, tossing them to the fire. Rastuk was relieved that despite the huge fire and chanting, the rest of the funeral customs mirrored those of Dotson. They destroyed everything owned by the deceased, it was burned rather than distributed to others. He wondered if the Tuudzaado believed, as they did in Dotson, that keeping any object out of the fire might insult the spirit of the dead, giving him or her reason to return. He fingered his mother's red ochre pouch once again.

Finally, Ping signaled Rastuk with a tap on the shoulder and tilt of the chin to go to the high boulder behind the newly shattered house. Rastuk stiffened his spine, forcing away a sense of malaise, and followed the taller man into the darkness of a nearly moonless night. Following the gaunt Tuudzaado man reminded him of the night he spent with Kat and Veetu. Var invited him to the top of the boulder, and after his conversation with Kat, Rastuk was not surprised when the Nightstalker didn't join him. Nightstalkers had mental gifts that only they had, one of which was a yeege, or spirit force, that only worked with Nightstalkers. On that earlier evening Rastuk had stood a while to take in the feel of the area. The boulder was the most logical place for an evening look out before retiring. The boulder was almost above the average height of the local prairie grass so that if they had seen enemies approach, he could stay flat against the rock's surface while getting more information, such as odors. Dotson odors were distinctively different from either Tuudzaado or Hutlan. Rastuk's mother always told him he smelled like a Tuudzaado. Ryx, his father, would laugh and tell him he smelled like a real Dotson man. The boulders were short enough so that a man could assume a squat-like position, thus ready to move in almost any direction at a moment's notice. Even so, astute enemies would approach from the downwind side, safe at least from one of the ordinary senses.

* * *

"Who are you?" a voice had asked when Rastuk first stood outside their compound. Rastuk looked for the speaker, frustrated that all he knew was the speaker was male with an odd turn of language. Despite the unusual method of greeting a stranger, Rastuk smiled. It was exactly the question he hoped to hear. His story was accurate and honest with one exception: he told Var that his father was a man from the country east of Dotson, rather than of Dotson itself. The people looked like Dotson, but were known to be far more peaceable. The rest of the story was true. Rastuk's father had abducted a Tuudzaado woman and taken her out of Zana to a place south of the blue glaciers. Eventually the Tuudzaado woman gave birth to Rastuk and died when he was fifteen.

Rastuk said, "I want to find my Tuudzaado relatives. Someone told me to ask here."

While Var remained out of sight, Kat, had stepped forward to listen to his story. When he was finished, she had knotted her brows and said, "Bina. I think I remember someone named Bina. How is she your relative?"

"My mother's mother," Rastuk answered with a hopeful smile.

Kat closed her eyes while she thought about the name and then opened them. Rastuk admired her large eyes with their widely arching eyebrows. "She was my mother's mother's sister. I have heard about the massacre all my life. What happened to your mother?"

Rastuk relaxed and replied, "My mother was very young at the time. My father was allowed to keep her as a wife. He was expected to kill her when I was able to walk, but he couldn't. My mother wanted to come back to warn people, but it was never possible. She always waited for a chance to get away with me, but it never happened. She wanted me to come, but until now I didn't have a reason. After she died, I was ashamed that I didn't really know anything that she taught me about her relatives when I was a child. She had me recite those names from the time I was able to talk." Rastuk came to a halt, shocked at how much he had said in one moment. *That's more talking than I've done in a year,* he mused.

Did you learn to talk this way? Var asked silently, challenging their visitor.

Yes, Rastuk answered. *I learned as much as I could, but only Mother talked this way with me. She's been dead a long time.*

Kat smiled and communed, *you learned well, but it is obvious that you learned from a woman. Men have a different way to say things.*

Rastuk was thunderstruck. "I didn't know that," he said aloud and continued silently, *Mother never said anything about it.*

* * *

"Why are you here?" Ping asked once they were settled near the top of the same boulder that Var had invited him to use when he visited before.

The question pierced Rastuk's reverie. He didn't respond.

Ping waited. Finally, he asked, "who are you?"

Rastuk sighed, and murmured, "I've told you my name. You've told me yours. I have just lost my relatives. You have dug through everything they owned. It is I who wants to know why you are here, but I am not as insolent as you are."

Stymied, Ping didn't say anything for a while. "You are right. I have made an assumption that you are the outsider and that I am the one who had the right to investigate their horrible deaths. I apologize."

"Not necessary. I have lost my newly found Tuudzaado relatives. I didn't know them well, but I found that we shared some common knowledge and..." Rastuk stopped speaking. Ping waited patiently in the style of Zana. Rastuk began again, "At least in you I have met another Tuudzaado person. My mother told me to look for..." Rastuk's voice drifted away again.

Ping tossed a pebble into the blaze. The pebble caused a small avalanche of charred wood. Ping glanced toward the Dotson man. Light flickered from black eyes in a night-blackened face. "Why do you have that scar?"

Rastuk shrugged irritably and glanced at the other man. "It's the emblem of a Black Sun Warrior."

Ping waited expectantly, suddenly profoundly aware that this was his first conversation with a Dotson man. After a decent interval of silence, he ventured, "how did you come to learn the Hutlan language so well? Didn't you say you've just arrived?"

Rastuk shrugged again and decided against using the fiction of being from another place than Dotshon. He said, "It's not that different from the Dotson language. My mother and father spoke this Hutlan language rather than Dotson." *She taught both of us to speak this way,* he communed. Suddenly he laughed aloud, the sound seemed to shake the flames even though at that moment Rastuk's face had turned away from the fire in his continuous, habitual scanning of what little he could see.

"What's so funny?" Ping asked aloud, his own head turning gently in nearly the same rhythm as he, too, kept up a habitual search for danger.

Rastuk responded in the silent language, explaining how he learned from Var and Kat about what his mother taught him. Not waiting for confirmation from Ping, Rastuk launched into a silent communing of his mother's family names. When he finished, he sat, head rotating slowly, waiting for Ping's eventual response.

Rastuk's family names meant nothing to Ping, but something else in Rastuk's story did. "Please explain why you are here."

Rastuk dropped his chin to his chest to control sudden fury. When he was ready he said, "I came to Var hoping he would lead me to the Dzagh. Most of my mother's family came from there. She called it the Dzagh, but Var called it the uplands," he said aloud. "I want to meet them." Ping was clearly waiting for more, so he pressed on, "my mother told me that to ask the Tuudzaado at the West Face for help."

Why? Ping communed in the silent way.

Rastuk turned his face and didn't answer.

Ping turned his face toward Rastuk. Backlit by the fire, it was impossible to see the North Face man's expression. Ping asked aloud, "Why did she tell you to go to Var?"

"I don't know. He was Tuudzaado, the first one I ever met besides Mother. They were the only Tuudzaado family I have ever met, and as I hoped, they were my relatives. Now I have met you."

"Where is your homeland?" Ping asked

"In the west. Dotshon."

"Where in the West?" Ping persisted. "I see nothing but blue ice over there."

Rastuk glanced toward the blackened mountain of glaciers and chuckled. "It's south and then west of those mountains. There's a narrow pass between the ocean and the glaciers that leads from here to there."

While Ping mused about Dotshon, he felt the tug of lethargy on his eyelids. More to keep himself awake than to satisfy a need to know he asked, "and how far is Dotshon from here?"

"Far. It takes the cavalcades two moons because others set up caches along the way. Single travelers like me have to hunt fairly often. It took us, that is, it took about three moons to get here."

"Us?" Ping resisted the overwhelming urge to sleep away while he wrestled with the word. It was important, but even as he listened to Rastuk stumble through another explanation, the older man's seemed to jumble together.

"… others … traveled … ahead … "

The effort to focus became too difficult. Ping forced himself to stand and said, "The fire is out. Let's rest. Tomorrow we will go to Falls Creek."

"Falls Creek?" Rastuk repeated, stunned. "Why there?"

"There's someone I want you to meet. We'll leave at dawn, we are expected tomorrow at the beginning of night's second quarter."

* * *

Deloo was so still I, the Ever Alert Baasee', thought she let museum fatigue get to her, and was about to touch her with a silent alarm when Deloo glanced at a window and thought/said toward both me and Grandfather Kwaiikit, *They just sounded the five minute warning that the museum closes in five minutes. Does that mean that our night's second quarter is about to start?*

I knew she was joking, but one look at my puzzled grandfather told me otherwise. *No, Oh-Wise-and-Wonderful Deloo, second quarter begins around nine p.m. in the normal part of the world. Here in the Arctic...*

"Subarctic" Deloo corrected me without interest. Outsiders always made that mistake.

I continued, *why don't we go back to your mother's house. It's time for supper.* We all, mortal and floating immortals, followed Deloo to her car. Back in Little Tanana, Grandfather Kwaiikit resumed his story.

He announced, *Yes, this next part is in the mountain area we call the Dzagh. Joot, his wife Mala, and Chebucto lived there.*

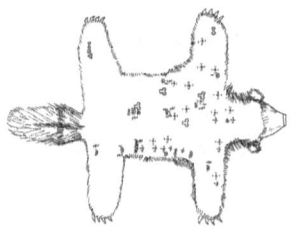

Four

Mala caught three grouse and prepared them for storage. As she worked, she kept herself from looking at Chebucto's small dwelling. Mala cherished her only child but still wished for more children. She envied Jenda's fertility. *Of course,* she reasoned to herself, *Zaandan's children are half Tuudzaado through him half Hutlan by his wife just like my Chebucto is. They are not all Hutlan like my Joot. That makes a difference for some reason. The Naan warned me about it, and of course, she is an example, herself. She had only one child by her all-Hutlan husband.*

Mala shook her head, feeling the hair sliding from one side of her back to the other. *Chebucto is a good son although he still needs to be reminded of his obligations from time to time. He is a thinker. When he doesn't understand a rule, he will think it through until he realizes why the rule is necessary. It will take a while, but eventually he will understand that he has to find a wife.*

Mala's mind always turned to this particular imaginary future, a future in which everything happened the way it was intended, and that she was recognized for her hard work in making it so. In her perfect world her son, Chebucto, would continue to live with Joot and her after he married—if he married. Chebucto was sixteen now. There was plenty of time for that. Even so, Mala looked forward to building a compound in the tradition of the Tuudzaado people of Broken Jaw, just as Jenda was doing with Zaandan. *It's true,* she pondered the issue objectively, *my son now refuses to contemplate marriage because of what happened.*

The woman had been more than twice Chebucto's age. Four years ago, long after Chebucto's first kill—a ground squirrel when he was three-and-a-half—he proved his qualities as hunter more than capable of feeding at least three adults when he brought home five ducks and a small opossum. Joot arranged a marriage with the widow of one of his Hutlan cousins over in the Wind Side Hill area. Mala had been very uncertain about a marriage between a thirty-year-old woman and a twelve-year-old boy. That would have given her a daughter-in-law who was her age. Not surprisingly, Chebucto resisted, but Joot told him it was his obligation and invited the family to visit.

My husband has a talent for that, Mala thought in the secret way she had learned over time. Unlike the usual Tuudzaado communing system that allowed anyone who could do "listen" in, she knew how to block out spies. She continued in the same way, look how easily he pulled Nazu's marriage together. My husband is good at arranging marriages, but Chebucto will never let us try again. Not after what happened to his bride-to-be.

More than a moon after their expected arrival the bodies of the woman's father and oldest son were found not far away from their own home on Wind Side Hill. Of Chebucto's future bride there was no sign. Mala shuddered when an unbidden image came to her: a tiny sealskin bag. Joot brought it home shortly before the bodies were found.

Seal.

No one in the Dzagh had sealskin. It was a coastal fur, not a mountain fur. She asked him where he got it, but Joot changed the subject. He gave it to her, but Mala wouldn't use it. After a while he put some of his stone spear heads in it and began to carry it on his inner belt. One evening when they were feeling particularly cozy with each other, he began to remove his clothing and the bag slipped off the belt. When Mala saw him pick it up the following morning their eyes met. Joot opened his mouth to speak, but the suddenly stiffened air in the small house seemed to block all words. After a long moment he emptied the pouch and hung it on the rear wall. One day she searched through her husband's gear, but she didn't find it. She never saw it again.

Closing herself away from the memory, Mala mused, more and more women have been abducted on the way to the homes of their future husbands, Mala thought. I hope my lost daughter-in-law was not enslaved by the Dotson at Broken Jaw. Jenda and I were lucky to escape from there.

Mala and Jenda's parents along with four other big Tuudzaado families were forced out of their homes in the west in a land they called Datherd. The Datherd people settled on the south side of the Red River in Zana. Their parents had been children at the time, each from a different family. Eventually they grew up, married, and soon gave birth to first Mala, then two years later to Jenda. Their new home on the south side of the Red River faced the ocean. The Datherds, or southern Tuudzaado, learned to fish and hunt for seals, but they were used to hunting land animals on the plains. Food was scarce. Every hot summer when the water was low and the river seemed to be dry, one or two people tried to move to the north side of the river. None of them ever came back, leaving their families to wonder if they had drowned or killed by the Dotson.

The year the girls were seven and five years old was the worst. Everyone was starving. Their parents took a chance and crossed the Red River. They reached the other side where they found other Datherd people, Tuudzaado who came from Datherd, but not those who disappeared. The north side of the river was called Broken Jaw and lots of people lived there. Some were from Datherd and some were the Tuudzaado who had always lived there. Hutlan and Dotson people also lived in Broken Jaw.

Mala remembered the first time the Naan came to visit her parents. The Naan was the tallest person Mala had ever seen, and the kindest. She helped Mala and Jenda learn to hunt small game animals with a five-stone bola and taught her parents to hunt together for larger animals, like tapirs and peccaries. Sometimes she brought a skinny young man with her. It was her nephew, Kwaiikit, who was fifteen when Mala first met him. Mala thought they were Datherds and tried to speak to Kwaiikit in her language, but he didn't understand. He tried to commune with her, and she almost understood him, but he used too many Tuudzaado mental quirks she couldn't follow. She enjoyed those special moments when Kwaiikit practiced the Datherd silent language with her. Jenda accused Mala of being in love with Kwaiikit, but she wasn't. She didn't like the hard look she often saw in Kwaiikit's eyes. It reminded her of the way her father and one of the old southern Tuudzaado men of Datherd who looked when they thought they were communing in secret. Mala always paid attention to them whenever the old Datherd man was there because they talked about finding a way to fight the Dotson. She wanted to help even when she was little.

Her favorite person was Memree, her cousin who had grown up in Broken Jaw. Memree was beautiful and funny. She had a crush on Kwaiikit, and every time she heard the Naan was coming to visit Mala's family, Memree would happen along. Memree learned to commune in Tuudzaado. Always copying Memree, Mala did so as well. One day Kwaiikit surprised her by communing in decent southern Tuudzaado of Datherd. They called it the Datherd language. That was when Mala finally understood why he had been so determined to practice the Datherd language with her. He had fallen in love with Memree, and they married a year or two later. Mala felt smug about her part in their romance.

Memree often brought their infant daughter for Mala and Jenda to admire and cuddle. Sometimes Memree asked Mala to watch baby

Garantu while she went hunting or did other things with Kwaiikit. Mala loved playing with Garantu, and was happy to oblige when, as Garantu grew old enough to wean, Memree asked to leave her overnight and eventually for days at a time. Mala watched Garantu make all of the discoveries of childhood with an avid greed that troubled Mala's mother.

"She's not your baby, Mala," her mother would caution. "Remember that Memree is the one who will teach her how to commune, not you."

Her mother's words had the opposite effect, as Mala was greedy about Memree as well. She offered to watch over Garantu even when Memree was at home just so she could "listen" to the many things that Memree communed with invisible others. In that way, Mala learned about the resistance group that Kwaiikit and Memree formed with the Naan and a few others. She didn't realize until years later the same small group of Tuudzaado and Datherds created the Dire Wolf Alliance, and that she had been spying on their early discussions about how to make it work.

She wasn't the only one who could spy on them. She never learned his name, but as her spying techniques improved she frequently encountered signs of someone else. She knew he didn't know much about Tuudzaado communing because she sensed his confusion whenever the Naan or others began using their high-speed Tuudzaado communion. Thanks to her silent language lessons with Kwaiikit, Mala understood them perfectly. After a while it occurred to Mala that she should let Memree know there was a spy, but doing so would reveal her own guilt, so she didn't. Instead, she tried to find out who the other spy was, and couldn't.

She learned he was male. Eventually she realized that he actually thought in the Datherd silent language. Evidently no one ever told him how to keep his inner thoughts secret. He didn't do it all the time—only after spying on Memree and the others. For a little while afterward the secret group meetings he would think in Datherd while he planned what to say to someone else. After a while she realized that he was always rehearsing what to say to someone in the Dotson language rather than southern Tuudzaado Datherd as Mala had thought at first. Mala didn't know Dotson. She had learned Hutlan well enough to understand the local people, but she was far more used to communing in Datherd than speaking out loud. The other spy did what Mala tried to do when she had to speak Hutlan. He would think the phrase in Datherd's silent language, then speak it in Dotson. Once Mala realized who his audience was, she realized with horror that the other spy was giving away all of Memree's secrets. Without waiting for another quarter of the sun to pass, Mala ran to Memree's little house.

"You've got to listen to me!" Mala said to Memree. "There's someone spying on you and he heard you tell them when you are taking the next group of escapees out of Broken Jaw."

Memree tried to shush her cousin by communing, but Mala put an immediate stop to that. "Don't ever use Datherd's silent language again, Cousin. Don't use spoken southern Tuudzaado either. Everything you have been communing to the others has been too easy for me to understand." Forcing away knowledge that Memree would despise her for being a spy, Mala told her everything she knew.

Over the course of the following day Mala explained it again first to Kwaiikit and then to the Naan. Far from being angry with her, Mala discovered they saw her as a new asset for their resistance group. Instead of stopping Memree from using Datherd while the others used the Tuudzaado silent language, they decided to use an even older, faster version of the Tuudzaado silent language and have Memree use Datherd only to give wrong information to the other spy.

Meanwhile, Mala was to continue trying to find out who he was. With Memree's help, she discovered she had a weakness having to do with distance. Memree's house was only a few steps away from Mala's— close enough so that anything Memree communed, Mala received. Memree tried communing from Left Moon Sleeve, almost directly east of Broken Jaw and Mala received it with no difficulty. When Memree went to Right Moon Sleeve to the south and a little farther away, Mala picked out a few words and nuances, but not the full meaning. She hoped the spy man had the same weakness she had.

The group surmised the male spy was a southern Tuudzaado man of Datherd who now lived in Broken Jaw. So did a lot of other people. There were over fifty Datherd men in Broken Jaw. Mala spent all of her spare time trying to find out who he was, but for every new trick she devised with the help of the group, the spy always outwitted her. The next four years went by so quickly that Mala still had trouble trying to remember what led up to the day she got caught.

They didn't know which of the sisters was the true culprit and took both Mala and Jenda to Kultprist's compound. Kultprist was not merely a Dotson, but the senior Red Sun Warrior in Broken Jaw. Both girls were beaten, raped, and starved. Their captors assumed that Jenda was faking ignorance and beat her even more than they did Mala.

One day their father's body was thrown into the compound. Then, using a typical Dotson strategy to force their enemies to obey, the Dotson took the girls with them to the beach and forced them to watch as scavengers fought over her father's remains. The sisters still refused to tell them who belonged to the secret group, so the Dotson brought in their mother and butchered her before the girls' eyes. Jenda screamed until there was nothing left of her voice but a rasp. Mala didn't close her eyes for nearly three days because each time she did so, she saw her mother's soft mouth vomiting horrors.

That night the Naan blackened her hair and body and ran into Kultprist's compound, scooped up the girls, and took them out of Broken Jaw before the Dotson had time to organize a hunt. Ten days later, after wandering with the Naan across the Zana all the way to the West Face, they were housed by a Nightstalker's family. The Naan had taken them there because she had heard about a recent increase of attacks on Nightstalkers. She left Mala and Jenda with the family while she went to visit someone. Inside the stranger's house Mala "listened" to the high-speed communing between the Naan and someone from the secret resistance group. The Naan came back with a little boy named Kenduu and took all three of them to the upper Dzagh and to her son, Zaandan.

The Naan had encouraged marriage between her son and Jenda, and likewise marriage between Mala and Joot. Mala cherished the Naan and went without a qualm into a marriage with the Hutlan man, Joot. Thinking about those days, Mala shrugged her powerful shoulders and shook out her hair. She was tall even for a Tuudzaado woman, more than two heads taller than her Hutlan husband. Joot never seemed to mind her extra height. She knew from the first moment she saw him staring at her hair that he was transfixed in the same way that Kwaiikit was by Memree. Mala guessed it was because Hutlan women always bound their hair so that not even one strand came loose. Tuudzaado women rarely did more than bind the top third or so to keep the hair out of their eyes. Joot still had trouble taking his eyes and hands away from Mala's luxurious hair even after all these years.

Mala felt lucky as a woman without family support to marry a good provider like Joot. Between Joot, Chebucto and herself, they could provide easily for their own needs and donated extra whenever the Hutlan Prayer Women called upon them. Unlike other men, Joot had married only once and preferred to sleep with Mala in her house rather than go to the trouble of building and sleeping in separate quarters as other men did. This both pleased Mala and alarmed her. Failing the advent of other children, especially daughters, she needed another woman to help her. If Chebucto did not bring her a daughter-in-law, she would face old age without someone to cook, twist willows, or clean. An alternate solution was very obvious to her, if not to Joot. When Chebucto steadily refused to consider another arranged marriage, Mala began to hint to her husband that he should consider taking a second wife.

Joot, at first amused, reminded his wife that no one had ever sought him out as a husband except the Naan on Mala's behalf. He agreed, however, that she was right. They needed extra help, but he didn't know how to do it. Privately he resented her constant nagging about it. His Tuudzaado wife never seemed to understand what marrying her had done to his reputation and social life. He was outcast by other Hutlan.

Before Mala came into his life, he had been a respected Hutlan hunter and member the Hutlan Bola Society. Until his marriage, each moon had required his ceremonial participation on the north side of the ritual grounds as Joot filled the role of the ancestral home of all Hutlan—the North Face. After Mala came to him, he was no longer invited him to ceremonies, he was shunned. The Prayer Women came to him only when they needed extra food to help impoverished Hutlan families. The first time he went to a Bola Society ceremony after their marriage, the other men openly jeered at him; no one had to explain why. He had been warned that his long friendship with Zaandan troubled other Hutlan people. Marriage to a Tuudzaado woman was simply not tolerated.

Joot often tried to explain it to Mala, thinking his words were enough to quell her zeal for a bigger household, but Mala thought he exaggerated. She didn't like Hutlan women, so it didn't matter to her that she had no Hutlan friends, but the Prayer Women were usually polite to her. She thought her husband was just a little shy. Mala's imagination quickly incorporated Joot's diffidence into her perfect world.

I will make the arrangements, she thought. *There are lots of Tuudzaado women who need a safe family. I will tell the Naan about my plans.*

With such a small barrier between herself as the eternal slave to her own household and envisioning herself as a proud overseer of others, a few moons earlier Mala had begun preparations to bring in a second wife. Among these were attempts to stimulate better relations with the Hutlan people. She joined Joot in giving extra meat to the Bola Society Prayer Women. If he returned with an empty game bag, she often filled hers and donated it in his name. She was proud when the Prayer Women asked for a little help and smothered her resentment about the way they looked at her. They must have realized that Mala was the one who dried, smoked, or froze all of the extra food from their household. Over the years she had helped over a dozen Hutlan families through terrible times of crisis. It bothered her that none of the families came to thank her, but she understood the shame of poverty. After all, she and Jenda had come to the Dzagh as complete beggars, lucky to get good husbands. Mala had pieced together a theory about the reason for continuing to be generous in spite of unrelenting snubbing by the Hutlan. She thought that the Sacred Forces preferred her to work in subtle ways rather than through the flamboyant rituals of the Bola Society. *So, I am to always be a subtle helper*, became a rote thought every time she felt the jabs of Hutlan insults.

Now staring at her son's sleeping quarters a mental voice, silent, gently seductive approached her. *Not a solitary woman Nicoleena like the Naan? Isn't that what you really want? Someone a little more like you—yet not Joot?*

Mala froze at the thought and then pushed it violently away. *All that is over. It's not for me, the wife of a Hutlan man. Even though I am tall and skinny like a Nicoleena, I do not live alone. I have no time for such nonsense anymore.*

* * *

Filled with sadness, Joot made his way back home from Iglan's compound where he and the Naan and two survivors of the massacre had built a funeral pyre and demolished the compound following both Hutlan and Tuudzaado customs after a death. At midday Joot passed one of his favorite hunting places, an area that attracted a turkey-sized deer species. The small deer were easy to carry on one shoulder. Joot appreciated they had chosen to live on his side of the ravine rather than on Zaandan's side. Joot never bothered to hunt along game trails. That was a waste of time. Joot's hunting visions came to him often because of his gift to receive and then to study what he saw. Only those deer given by the Sacred Forces in a hunting vision would come to the place shown in the vision. In the old days Joot would wait for as much as a long morning, but lately the waiting stretched into days. Mala and he worried, but dared not talk to each other about it.

I wish Chebucto could hunt deer with me, Joot thought. Chebucto had never had a hunting vision, and Joot would not let him come along because he didn't want a visionless hunter to ruin his success

"You haven't earned the privilege," Joot growled the last time Chebucto had asked, annoyed that at the advanced age of sixteen his son should have had hunting visions long ago instead of sixteen and nothing. Joot allowed Chebucto to hunt only small game without a hunting vision.

Joot stopped stewing about Chebucto when it occurred to him that his thoughts had wandered in every direction except the massacre of twelve people. Who had done this? How had they known to ambush Iglan at that time? The Hutlan would not butcher their own. Nor would the Tuudzaado. While it's likely to have been a Dotson ambush, only a Tuudzaado or Hutlan person could have brought them to Iglan's sequestered compound.

Joot grimaced at the pale yellow sky. The sun was well into the fourth quarter. The chill of early autumn should have cooled him, anger kept him from feeling it.

Mala thought of the Naan, who had given her life to the Dire Wolf Alliance in order to stop the Dotson from killing both Hutlan and Tuudzaado people. She even gave up living in peace with her husband and Zaandan in order to do it. He thought, she has seen too many bodies mutilated and murdered by the Dotson. I have stayed away from all of that, thinking that hunting is enough. Friendship does nothing to stop this butchery of human life.

While Joot mourned over his dead friend, he couldn't know that his wife's relentless thoughts followed a similar route with a different history and a different outcome. Mala paced around the cooking arbor, kicking loose pieces of shale as she moved. An image swelled, letting her imagine the bodies of the father and son who died while escorting Chebucto's never-to-be bride. Mala saw them in a vision, a vision that continued to fester in her mind years after they were killed. Disquieting as was the first vision, it was less alarming than the one that always followed: her future daughter-in-law, a faceless shape wearing a skin strap on her head marked in charcoal with a bent cross, the mark of the Dotson sun.

A violent tremble in Mala's right hand brought her back to the present. She looked at the hand, shocked to see a bead of blood oozing from her knotted fist. At some point in her pacing she had picked up a stone and squeezed it hard enough to cut her palm. Mala dropped the stone and looked for dried clubmoss. Carefully she applied just enough.

As she waited for the blood to clot, Mala thought, I know too much and too little. Her massive shoulders sagged. We don't know she actually died, since no one found her body, and yet I know that she couldn't have survived. Jenda and I almost died when those butchers had us! In some ways, Jenda is already dead. Such cruelty can't go on. Mala continued pacing but no solution came to her.

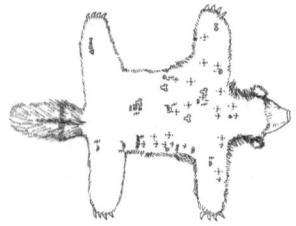

Five

Joot was surprised to see one of the local Prayer Women talking to Mala. They usually waited until he was at home in order to avoid his wife.

"It was Dotson!"

The weirdling sound that only Hutlan Prayer Women voiced sent shivers running across Joot's back. A bit like the whip-poor-will, it had a high-pitched throb. Each Prayer Woman had a different prayer voice that came to her young in life. At that crystalline moment in her life, mysterious songs flowed into the new Prayer Woman. She would also know at that moment precisely which direction of the Sacred Winds she represented. Over the years Joot and Mala had snickered when others seemed amazed that the appointed direction exactly matched the one recently vacated by a dead Prayer Woman.

Joot stared at the Prayer Woman standing outside his compound. He heard Mala attempt to converse with her. Despite eighteen years in the Dzagh, his wife had still not mastered the Hutlan tongue language. He saw the Prayer Woman's rising irritation. What little respect he had for her evaporated when he noticed the Hutlan's muddy grey eyes fixed on his wife's head. With mixed feelings, he observed she didn't pretend to like the way Mala's hair shimmered as it drifted along her shoulders with every move.

"Did you say there is a new family up here?" Mala asked.

"I don't understand you," the Prayer Woman's voice grated, totally unlike her prayer voice.

"What happened?" Joot asked.

Startled, the Prayer Woman whirled and patted the tethers binding her hair. She coughed and said, "some people were ambushed by Dotson. She," the Prayer Woman said with an insolent shrug toward Mala, "doesn't understand."

"It's true," Joot said calmly. "I was hoping to help celebrate a wedding. Instead, I found their bodies. It was a terrible sight."

"Horrible!" the Prayer Woman's tongue couldn't quite bring the sounds together. Shrugging, she left without asking for any details.

"No! Not again," Mala whispered. She stared at the woman's departing back and slowly turned toward her husband. Wordlessly she searched his face. Joot shifted uneasily in his tracks.

"I hate that woman!" Chebucto said from behind his parents. "I hate all of them. Why is she so rude to us? Why are all those Bola Society people so mean to Mother especially?!"

"It's the way of the world, my son. We can't change them," Joot said, encircling his son with his arm. Chebucto stiffened and then allowed his father's arm to remain.

"Keyo says his father is doing things to change them. Zaandan and his mother have been rescuing Hutlan people for years with no thanks for what they have accomplished. I know they need help. Why can't we join the Dire Wolf Alliance, too?"

Joot's arm tightened on his son's shoulders. "Zaandan." Joot grimaced. "He wants a lot of things lately." He met Mala's eyes, this time without flinching. "First, let me tell you about the deaths." Mala and Chebucto stared at Joot, hungry for details. Their faces were nearly invisible in the deep twilight by the time he finished telling them what happened.

"Was Zaandan there?" Mala asked.

Joot's lips tightened and he took a deep breath before answering. "No. His mother was there, of course, but ever since he told everyone that Hutlan and Tuudzaado should keep apart, I haven't seen him." Joot stood up, knocking over a rack of baskets as he did so. He helped Mala set the baskets right before he continued into the darkness. "Zaandan and I made the marriage agreement between Lo and Nazu. I think something happened to him after he agreed to take a Dotson wife..." Joot broke into a patently false coughing spell.

"Father, what Dotson wife?"

"What do you mean, Nazu took a Dotson wife? Or do you mean Zaandan? Does my sister know about her? She hasn't mentioned it at all. Has Jenda mentioned it to you, Son?" Mala turned to Chebucto.

Chebucto shrugged, backlit by the small fire.

"I promised I wouldn't tell anyone," Joot muttered. "But Zaandan hasn't talked to me since he first told me." Joot slammed his hand on the cutting stone. "We've been friends for years, and suddenly he ducks out of sight when he sees me coming."

"Husband, I'm sorry he's treating you this way. Now, please tell me about this new wife. Where is she?"

"I don't know much more than what I said. Her father asked him if he would accept an alliance through his oldest daughter, and Zaandan said yes. She lives at Falls Creek."

"Father!" Chebucto stood and paced. "What about the Dire Wolf Alliance? I was hoping we could join it. If Uncle Zaandan married a Dotson woman, can there be a Dire Wolf Alliance anymore?"

Joot held his silence for such a long time that Chebucto wondered if he could speak again, or if he still had to wait. A small cough from Chebucto's mother stilled his impatience. He took a deep breath and dug a two-finger hole in the soil beside his leg on the far side of the fire where his mother couldn't see what he was doing.

Mala glanced at Joot and said quietly, "Zaandan is important but he is not the only one in the Dire Wolf Alliance. Even so, you would not be able to join it, at least not yet."

Chebucto, profoundly disturbed that his mother knew anything about the Dire Wolf Alliance, snapped, "why not?"

Simultaneously one parent said, "Son!" while the other communed, *don't speak to me that way.* Mala continued with a complicated silent explanation that for the most part escaped Chebucto's Tuudzaado language ability. He caught and kept a single visual image of Zaandan's dire wolf pelt. He turned, suddenly quiet, and said, "I'm sorry, Mother. Could you please explain it to me again?"

It would have been quicker and more complete to tell him in the silent language, but for Joot's sake Mala continued in Hutlan. "They call it the Dire Wolf Alliance after alliances that have happened over the years between dire wolves and humans the wolves. Zaandan happens to be such a human. When a dire wolf pack matures, sometimes they take an interest in human affairs. When that happens, they select a likely person, usually young Tuudzaado men, but others have been selected as well. I've heard stories about three Hutlan women who are active with their dire wolf packs. I've often thought one of you could have been chosen if we lived closer to the plains. Zaandan finally told me why you, my husband, will not be taken by dire wolves."

Joot coughed and started a fire. Something about his posture forbade any conversation until he directed them to sit. Finally, Joot said in a quiet voice, "when he first came home one day with his dire wolf pelt, Zaandan told me about a great dire wolf leaping on him. I was too young to ask what else it involved, and ever since we grew up things have changed and I've been reluctant to ask." Joot stopped again, but resumed, directing a question to his wife. "Why does he hunt for them? Why doesn't he stay home and hunt for his own family? Dire wolves don't live in the Dzagh. They like the prairies and plains."

With a careful eye on her husband, Mala lifted her chin. "Zaandan has to hunt with his dire wolf pack at least once a moon. There are a lot of giant herd animals that humans can trap that dire wolves can't. In return, they help him and the Dire Wolf alliance."

"Is that why he always has cuts of meat from those giant animals? Last year they had some mammoth roast. It tastes very sour," Chebucto said. His brows twisted as he added, "how does he get any of the meat? Those wolves are huge. They might like to eat him instead."

Mala laughed. "It's part of the agreement the wolves make with their humans. They let Zaandan cut the first piece, then they go in."

"Zaandan got his pelt when he was just a boy," Joot said. "I was about Chebucto's age when that happened. Zaandan would have been ten or eleven." He looked at Mala. "Zaandan is well over thirty now. How long do dire wolves live?"

Chebucto interrupted, "You grew up on the North Face where there are prairies. You must have seen dire wolves there."

Joot grunted, "I used to see them on the North Face, but I was a child when the Naan adopted me and took me up here to her home. I've never spent enough time there to watch any dire wolf grow up or grow old." He paused and cocked his jaw toward his wife. "Did you ever see an old one, my wife?"

"Yes, once. She was from my father's pack. She died a little before he was murdered by the Dotson." She sighed heavily. "He told me she was Jenda's age, a couple of years younger than I. So she was about fifteen when she died. My father let me bring her a special treat when I killed my first beaver. It was one of the small beavers. I took the heart to her and she ate it in one gulp. She licked my hands."

Mala's pause was long enough for Chebucto to dig yet another two-finger hole in the cool soil beside his leg. The soil was sandy. By the time he finished the second hole, the first had collapsed inward on itself. He patted the ground flat over both holes while he waited.

Finally his mother resumed, "Zaandan's pack has had four dire wolf leaders since he started. Each wolf pack leader has different rules. He complains to Jenda about it, saying he doesn't like the new one because he's bitten Zaandan twice. The most recent pack leader expects to go hunting with his human exactly at full moon, but because of all the recent trouble with the Dotson, Zaandan has missed one hunt and was two days late for another. Zaandan spent most of the Peccary Moon trying to find a home for one little boy. Just as he left Falls Creek he found a widow who agreed to help him hide the escapees. She had already adopted a child from an earlier run. It was new moon, days away from when the big dire wolf expected him. Zaandan told Jenda that he didn't know what else to do but hunt for the widow, so he left the new escapees there and ran to find his dire wolf pack any way. He was a long way from his usual place to meet them but he thought it was worth the effort since with a pack he could get a lot of meat for the widow. He got to a tall grass prairie halfway between Falls Creek and Broken Jaw—and there he saw his pack, lounging around as if they had been waiting there for a year." Mala broke into a merry laugh. "They were a half a day away from the usual place that Zaandan hunts with them. That prairie is not a good place for dire wolves to hunt since a scimitar cat ranges there, but the wolves seemed to know what Zaandan needed. In less than a quarter sun they brought down a giant red-meat peccary. Do you know the kind I mean? They have a lot of meat on their shoulders and very skinny legs."

Joot lifted his chin. "I've seen them. It would take a lot of men to haul the meat from one of those creatures."

"How much meat did Uncle Zaandan get?" Chebucto asked.

"The widow needed a lot of meat, so he cut two big pieces, far too much for one man to carry in one load. He dragged the first piece away from the kill and the pack leader followed him. Zaandan stared at the wolf for a long time before rushing back to get the second piece. The leader stayed beside the first piece to keep the other wolves away. Zaandan wrapped the first piece onto a couple of aspen poles and hauled it back to the widow. He didn't wait to talk to her. He just raced back to the wolves. He was surprised to find the pack leader waiting beside the second cut of meat. None of the wolves had touched it."

She shifted her weight and muttered, "At least, that's what he told Jenda. Now," she tipped her head toward Joot, "I wonder if that so-called Hutlan widow was actually his new wife!"

Joot shrugged. "I believe him. He and the Naan always spent a lot of time hunting for others. I used to give my extra meat to them, too. At least I did until the Prayer Women started asking me for help. Things have changed a lot around here because of the Dotson."

Chebucto barely heard his father, his mind still envisioning his uncle's dire wolf pack. He whistled softly. "Keyo must hear these stories but he's never mentioned it."

Mala said, "Keyo doesn't know much about it for the same reason that you don't, son. With the help of the Sacred Forces we have to keep our Dire Wolf Alliance a secret. If anyone asks you about it, tell them that only hunters who have proven themselves are ever chosen for the Dire Wolf Alliance. The truth is the Naan and a few others choose new members based on three qualities. First, they have had at least one big kill. Second, they must be willing to sacrifice their lives for others. Finally, they have visions of people and animals in danger and then go to help. Zaandan had done all of that by the time he was eleven."

Chebucto studied the toes of his moccasins, avoiding the eyes of both parents. "Why are you telling me? I haven't done any of that."

Mala looked inquiringly at her husband, but he flicked his face to the side, indicating he wanted her to continue. "Son, neither you nor Keyo have made a big kill yet, even though you are well beyond the age to do so. But now I have great hope for you, because at last you have had a vision of importance."

Joot cleared his throat. Mala glanced at him and raised her eyebrows. He spoke, "Hunting visions are part of this. Animals tell us when they are in trouble or ready to die. That's the way that I get my large kills. By way of visions I have also been called to help a doe when she had trouble giving birth. It was before I met your mother. I knew the Sacred Forces were with her fawn and so did the doe. Even though I had never helped anyone at a birth before, my hands seemed to know exactly where to be and what to do. The fawn seemed very healthy and was able to walk within a few moments. I was happy about that for a long time."

Mala smiled tenderly at her husband. "That's exactly what Zaandan told me. You can never be part of a dire wolf pack because the *yeege* of those deer have selected you, my husband, through the power of the Sacred Forces. The dire wolves will always honor that kind of arrangement and leave you alone so that you can continue to help the deer. The deer will avoid a man who smells of dire wolf."

Chebucto stared at his father, surprised. "I didn't know about the doe, Father."

The important thing is that finally you have received a true vision, Mala communed, returning her attention to Chebucto. *This time something kept you from going to your father and Iglan, but that may change. Keyo never seems to get visions. I have never told you about the dire wolves or the Dire Wolf Alliance because it's not something you can do without the help of the Sacred Forces.*

Chebucto's stomach churned. Fueled by doubt and anger, he communed, *You didn't think I should go to Nazu.*

Mala lifted her chin and stared at her son through slitted eyes, exasperated. She didn't know how her son could be so indifferent to the power of the Sacred Forces. When he didn't say anything, she communed, *You told me you didn't feel called to go to your father.*

I wasn't... Boiling rage overpowered him. Chebucto leaped to his feet and flung himself onto the trail outside the compound.

Joot studied his wife casually and when Chebucto was well out of earshot communed, *What about this vision?*

Why don't you ever answer me in the silent language when I need your help? She communed, kicking him playfully on the shins.

"Ow!" Joot moaned, pretending to be in pain, and answered aloud, "It takes me a while to piece things together. By that time, you've already asked out loud at least six times." He reached out and tugged her onto his lap. "Tell me about this vision."

They both kept their attention on the entryway to the main trail while Mala told her husband about Chebucto's vision. "You were already gone," she finished, "but he could have caught up. There was plenty of time for a young runner like him to reach Iglan's household in time."

"It was raining. I had to wait it out as would Chebucto have done, but you are right, he could have tried," Joot said. "Come, I'm tired. It's time to get some sleep."

"I'll clean up my work area first," Mala said.

Joot crept into their sleeping quarters and began his methodical preparations for sleep. As was his habit, he touched each object on his side of the rear wall to make sure it was secure and in place. Shocked to find the empty spot where he kept the amethyst knife, Joot examined the hides that covered the ground below their bedding. His fingers found the sheath under the hide nearest the dangling objects above it and the amethyst knife a short distance away. The knife must have bounced after he dropped it, Joot thought. He sniffed the sheath carefully and amended, after they dropped it.

Joot made his way out of the hide-covered shelter, unsheathed knife in hand. He held it up to show Mala just as Chebucto stepped off the trail into their compound, lower lip protruding. The amethyst stone seemed to glimmer. As he stared, a beam of light stretched out of it. Father and son locked eyes in its eerie light. Chebucto's glare lost momentum and slowly he lowered his eyes to the knife.

Joot relaxed his stance and said conversationally to Mala, "What you have said, my wife, is important. We have lost many people in the past few years; giving our extra food to those in need is good. Even if our son doesn't try to help others with his visions, he could become a better hunter if he worked with simple hunting dreams. I have tried to teach him, but he won't learn from me. No hunting visions means none of the larger creatures, such as deer or peccary, have decided to give themselves to him. It's time for our son to learn more about the ways of becoming a good provider."

"Keyo doesn't have hunting visions," Chebucto interjected, "because Uncle Zaandan doesn't believe in them. Uncle Zaandan says there are better ways to hunt."

Joot bit his lip. "Your uncle and I differ on several things, including how to hunt, he and I agree on this: to become a good provider, a man has to bring home at least one animal big enough to feed three people. Neither you nor Keyo have accomplished that goal, although you are clever and do so with small game. I'm going to take you somewhere I know you will learn these lessons."

Chebucto slumped. He and Keyo had worried about their hunting failures for as long as he could recall. After a long silence, he looked up and asked, "where am I to go?" It was his deepest fear. "Am I being banished?" Chebucto had heard stories of how banishments happened—mostly from Keyo. The banished were always abandoned in unfamiliar territory where they were sure to die. Thoughts racing, he didn't understand his father's reply but the words hung in the evening air.

"We will go to one of my relatives on the North Face."

Chebucto gaped at his father. "The North Face?"

"The North Face?" Mala echoed. "Isn't there any place closer? What about the glacial floods? They happen more often there than anywhere else in Zana."

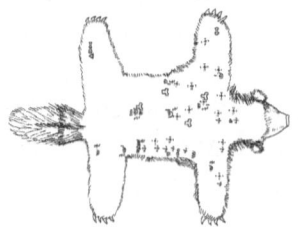

Six

Joot waited until silence was restored before continuing. "I know it is unusual to travel at this time of year, but as I said before, my wife, our son has to learn responsibility. I haven't been successful in teaching him the most important lessons about hunting or becoming a good provider. He must go to someone who can. If he learns from my relative, he will be able to help others. Besides, we all know there are more animals to hunt on the North Face. They survive, and so did my family."

Mala stared at her husband in horror. "But if you die in the glacial floods, how will that help anyone? Especially me?"

She had never been to the North Face and imagined its alluvial plains flooded every day. It was called the North Face because it was north of the wide flood plains. The north side consisted of a high impassable wall of many glaciers that edged the plains on the north and west. The plains were hot, windy, and dry much of the time. The glaciers had unpredictable melting patterns and calved huge icebergs without warning, releasing large quantities of water. When that happened, the plains became chaotic with flash floods, tumbling boulders, and fleeing animals. Most flooding occurred from spring through the summer and into the fall season, or whenever there was a long stretch of heat.

While the sun rarely gave the upper levels of the Dzagh much warmth, the people in the uplands above could see the impact of a hot season by the color of the prairie grasses below. During that past summer, Mala had watched the bright green of the Elderberry Moon deepen into darker green by the middle of the Moon of the Short-Faced Bear cycle, well before leaves open in the Dzagh. Joot's favorite weather prediction was 'dark green in the Short-Faced Bear Moon always led to flash floods for the rest of the year.' Mala had been glad when Joot decided not to escort Lo and her family to Iglan's home site because she feared the floods and he had been there often enough that year. Now she was afraid that his plans to take her only child down to the alluvial plains would lead to one or both to drown.

After arguing, begging, weeping, and offering several impractical and original alternatives, Mala sighed. The time she had been dreading had finally arrived. Joot had told her many times he wanted to send their son to a famous Hutlan medicine man at the North Face who was known to turn boys into men within twelve moons. She hoped he could do something with her son—but sooner. Then she remembered there was a Dotson training area on the North Face and began another barrage of counter suggestions, all which Joot steadfastly refuted.

Worn down at last, she asked, "when will you go?"

"If my son is willing, we leave tomorrow before dawn."

Chebucto had been hugging his skinny legs to his chest ever since his father mentioned the North Face. He, too, knew what it meant, he had heard about the Hutlan medicine man most of his life. Even Keyo had heard of him, neither of them had heard anything good. Chebucto rested his forehead on his knees, bedeviled by conflicted feelings. Eventually he realized that both of his parents were waiting for him. Words came out of his mouth before he realized he was speaking. "I'm ready, Father. I'll go tomorrow." The sound of his voice rang loudly in the night air. No one moved, his words had become invisible enemies.

"Good! Before dawn then," Joot spoke at last. He signaled for his son to follow him to their dark work space. They would have to make sure they had the right spear points and other tools to last a moon or more. The two worked in silence each tense with private thoughts. Chebucto sorted through all his tethers, making sure he had wound each of them tightly and neatly around carrying sticks or other tools. As he worked, he pictured the wild alluvial plains his father had described so many times.

While Joot had been born there as well, he left it when he was a child and didn't learn much about its history until later. Small wonder he knew so little, for his departure had been sudden and traumatic. Joot glanced at his son, wondering if Chebucto was in the right mood to hear yet another of his father's stories.

"Did I ever tell you when my best friend was killed by Dotson?"

Chebucto recognized the story but held back the acrid reply hovering in his mind. Instead he said, "Was that when you still lived down there?"

Joot lifted his jaw and thought about the day when death runners suddenly appeared in front of Joot and his friend. "Haavro was bigger than I and they wanted someone fat and weak. I was skinny, so they shoved me onto a pile of rocks. Then one of them pointed to the trail and nodded at Haavro, I knew what that signal meant. "A death run, the Dotson have a training camp over there. They trained boys your age or even younger by forcing them to chase other boys whom they felt were weak until the victim is too weak to move any more. When the boy falls, the death runners beat him to death. It was punishment for being weak. It didn't matter to the Dotson who the boy was, only that they killed as instructed without emotion. I didn't know what to do after they left me. I was too small to do anything but I had to try. I ran along the trail after Haavro, hoping for a miracle. I didn't know that the death runners would feel the blood of the kill and be glad to run me down after they killed Haavro."

As his father talked, Chebucto remembered the story. It had been his favorite when he was ten. Suddenly, Chebucto felt ten years old again.

"What happened then, Father?"

Joot sighed. "I knew that Haavro was slowing down. I almost caught up to them when a tall, thin woman stepped onto the trail in front of me. She scared me more than the death runners did. I could hardly breathe when she held me against her chest. I fought as hard as possible, and she just stood there waiting for me to calm down. Finally, I stopped fighting and waited for her to do what she was going to do anyway, Kill me. That's when a boy stepped onto the trail beside her. He was about my size, so I thought he was my age."

"When the boy spoke, I knew he was much younger than I. His voice was high and he talked like a boy of five or six."

"He said to me. 'It's no use, they will kill him, we can't stop them, there are too many, they will come back for you and you had better come with us—now!'"

"She was the Naan and the boy was her son, Zaandan. She didn't talk much then, so Zaandan did all the talking. He told me the Dotson death runners never allowed a victim to get away. 'Not unless they are all dead themselves.' He thought they would have come back to find me. They had my scent." Joot looked back into a space Chebucto could not see. "Since then we've learned differently. If a person gets away from a death run, the Dotson believe the victim is blessed by the sun and aren't supposed to be chased again. We didn't know that until much later."

Zaandan believed those stories and told me, 'They will kill anyone who tries to hide you. That's why you have to come with us.' So they bought me to the Naan's household far away from the Dotson. At first I ached for my mother and father, I missed everyone so much I got sick for a while. I knew my new friend was right but I always wonder if I could have gone back. I wish I had sometimes."

Joot sighed, "My father used to tell me the same thing but he liked the Dotson. My father was proud that the North Face Hutlan were so well protected by the Dotson. He thought the Dotson were making life safer for Hutlan people."

"What happened to my grandfather?" Chebucto asked.

"He is dead now. One of the lucky ones because he died at an old age. The Dotson killed many of our people but not my father. I think he must have been working for them, because he was never harmed. Your grandmother died two years after I came up here. I think they killed her. Because she probably wouldn't do some of the things they expect of women."

"What things, Father?" Chebucto had asked before, but both his father and mother would change the subject or promise to tell him later. Chebucto sensed he might finally hear the rest of the story tonight. Joot didn't say anything for a long time, so Chebucto prompted him, "Father? I'll be on my own over there. I think it's time for me to know the truth."

Joot sighed and clapped his son on the shoulder. "You are right. You should know this now. The Dotson have no respect for women, you'll see as you grow up. When I was young there are no Dotson women in Zana, only Dotson men. In the last few years they've brought Dotson women from wherever they come from a place I believe it is called Dotshon. They don't come up here, at least I haven't seen any myself. Dotson men are brutal to Hutlan women unless they get pregnant by any of them. Only then they leave her alone until the child is born. They kill the female children because they want only men, they let the Hutlan women keep their sons. As long as the woman gets pregnant every other year, they let her live. If she has two female children in a row, they kill her. That's what your mother said happened at Broken Jaw, I don't know how they treat their own women."

"What about cooking and making clothes? Do they make our women do that?"

Joot frowned. "Yes. The slaves they put to work on food or clothes have to wear a stiff piece of hide with the mark of the Dotson on it, that's the way they do it at Broken Jaw."

"It must be better to be a cook than to be a woman who could be killed for having a girl child," Chebucto said.

"They beat the slaves, cooks or not," said Mala, coming up to them from behind. "Jenda and I were whipped with straps, hit with fists, and raped almost every day. The older women, women who survived for more than a year were often beaten with clubs."

Chebucto turned to his mother, mouth agape. "How did you survive?"

"As happened to your father, the Naan rescued both of us. Actually, it wasn't just the Naan. There's a great man down there. I think he has become part of the Dire Wolf Alliance. When I lived there he was trying to do things to help Kwaiikit and the Naan. His name is Urd. He set up a plan. Once a moon he sent a Datherd woman into the slave areas at night to help them escape. Women who were still strong enough went with her to a cave beside Right Moon Sleeve. There is a winding tunnel on the south side of Broken Jaw that leads to a cave. It was safe, but difficult to endure because the runaways had to stay in the dark for such a long time. They had to get strong enough for the trek to their homes."

Joot put his arm around his wife's waist, and asked, "Did the Naan bring you out herself?"

"Yes, but that's another story for another time. The Naan took Jenda and me up here." Mala leaned into Joot, "and that's where I met your father."

"What happened to that weak boy?" Chebucto persisted.

They stood in silence for a while, and then Joot resumed his own story. "One day the Naan told me that all the Dotson who killed Haavro were dead. I could have gone home, but by then I didn't want to leave Zaandan and the Naan. I'm glad we're going to North Face together, Son. I enjoy the look and feel of the rolling heaps of the gravel deposits of the moraines. When I was a child I heard elders talking about the glaciers that used to be on the plain and on the rolling hills beyond. Once in a while someone would show me ice lenses that poked through the gravel on the moraines. They explained the shimmering blue and white hills beyond the North Face were more than rock. They are mountains of ice. Those elders say the Nicoleena knew how to walk the glaciers in safety. They also say the Nicoleena had white hair all over their bodies."

"Like the Naan," exclaimed Chebucto.

"Yes, like the Naan," smiled Joot. "But don't believe everything old people tell you. They also said the Nicoleena have special powers. I was convinced the Naan was a Nicoleena. The Naan can do anything just as the Nicoleena do in the legends, but she laughed at me about my ideas. Enough of these stories for now, Son," Joot said. "We need to rest." He crawled into the hide covered shelter with Mala. Mala stretched, loosening her stiff back.

* * *

Deloo settled into her favorite chair in her mother's home and managed a silent question that combined whining, barking and sighing all in one silent moment. *Baasee', what is a Nicoleena? Is she Superwoman? Or a bigfoot? Is that what bigfoots or bigfeet are? Are you one?*

I rolled my gorgeous, ephemeral eyes at Grandfather Kwaiikit and created a pair of big feet to try the part. *No, my dear. Neither my grandfather nor I are Nicoleena. She wasn't a superwoman, exactly, but she always managed to show up when Zaandan or Grandfather Kwaiikit needed help. Now, let's get back to Grandfather's story. In some ways, your Great Aunt Pauline is a Nicoleena because of what she's made of the neighborhood here, Little Tanana.*

* * *

She whispered. "Husband, tell me the truth. Why are you taking him away?"

Unlike Jenda, whose large black eyes reminded people of the beauty of a camelid calf, the skin around Mala's eyes had hardened like clay. Joot never mentioned the changes to her, preferring to keep her happy in other ways. In the dark, however, Joot imagined her eyes as they had sparkled the first time he met her. Warming to the memory, Joot reassured her that it was the truth about his plan to leave Chebucto with one of his relatives.

"Why?" Mala insisted, "Has someone asked you to banish him?"

"No, my wife," Joot hurried to calm her. "It is all as I have said."

"I still don't understand why you must send him away," Mala hissed. "He could do a hunting vision here. You could teach him."

Joot shrugged irritably.

Mala bit her lower lip and fell silent. Joot, far more pragmatic than his wife, snuggled into her warm flesh and fell asleep without further worry, leaving Mala awake and restless. At first light Mala touched her husband's shoulder. He awoke instantly.

"Ssst."

Chebucto started and then nearly fell to the ground when a heavy hand clapped him on the back. He pulled himself together and whirled around. He had fallen asleep at the work place.

"Ready?"

Chebucto opened his mouth to speak but nothing happened. He tried again. "Aren't you going to sleep?"

"I did. It's time to go."

Chebucto stood. All his gear was strapped neatly in place along his body like his father's. Still stiff from lack of sleep, they trudged north through thick fog. Mala watched them. While the fog swallowed her husband almost immediately, Chebucto's oddly cut hair stood out for a long time against white tendrils of mist. She thought of the day Chebucto and Keyo had burst into her work area. They were proud and pleased about their hair.

"See, Mother," Chebucto had crowed. "We solved the problem."

"What problem," Mala remembered asking.

"You know the one braid for Hutlan, two for Tuudzaado, we solved the problem by cutting our hair short. Now we are just what we are, both Hutlan and Tuudzaado."

Mala hadn't known whether to laugh or screech at them for ruining their looks. They had simply hacked off big locks of hair without regard to anything but whether it could still be braided. Each head featured shafts of black hair that stuck straight off their skulls in all directions, they may have solved one problem but created another. After that day, absolutely everyone recognized them and almost everyone found ways to avoid them without being seen first. In another era people might have teased them, but their short hair simply emphasized a hidden hatred in the Dzagh—hatred of the first people, the tall Tuudzaado, even those who were only partly Tuudzaado. Even more, she thought, they hate it when we mate and bring out children like Chebucto and Keyo.

* * *

Deloo's arm flailed in the air, but she managed a perfect commune. *Baasee', what do you mean by hatred. If they avoided Chebucto, doesn't that mean they feared him rather than hated him?*

Baasee', your mortal is astute, but since I tried to change the ways people acted back then, let me answer this one.

Gladly, Grandfather, I replied.

Grandfather sent a beam of approval toward Deloo, swatted the air above her head. *Mortal, during that era our people seemed to have exactly four emotions: fear, hatred, love, and grief. When they were afraid, they hid in darkness until the danger past. So, yes, it might seem to you that avoiding being seen by Chebucto or me was fear, but not back then. Their form of fear was to be unable to move. When they felt hatred, they moved. Sometimes, people who hate avoid being seen, but not always. Since Tuudzaado people were much bigger than the small Hutlan, they were hated as dangerous beings, and Hutlans stayed out of sight.*

Deloo nodded. *I understand. I would hide from a grizzly bear out of fear and avoid Fat Jack, who always beat me up when we were kids. I hated him, but I didn't want him to see me, either. Is that what you mean?*

I beamed at Deloo and Grandfather and intoned with my usual Wise and Wonderfulness, *Excellent, Deloo. Let Grandfather tell us more of the story.*

* * *

Pushing memory of their short hair aside, Mala spent the morning feeling remorseful. She blamed herself for having been overprotective of her son. Perhaps if she had told him long ago to be aware of a sense of urgency about visions, he might have gone in search of a creature in need long ago. Now the bleakness of her empty household brought her thoughts toward Iglan and the emptiness on his side of the mountain. In hindsight, she realized that she should have acted immediately on her son's vision. Both should have left immediately to warn Iglan, or failing that, to follow the murderers and exact revenge.

It is not too late to do so. The words infiltrated her thoughts throughout the day, leaving her edgy and uncertain. At last she left her compound to visit Jenda. If nothing else, Mala could hold little Masito on her lap and pretend the world was warm and comfortable.

By the time the sun's first rays lightened the sky, the need to sleep weighed heavily on Chebucto. He found that walking with closed eyelids was almost as good as lying prone.

"My son?" The voice seemed familiar, but Chebucto couldn't place it and didn't try. Joot's voice continued more loudly. He could feel his father's warm breath on his face.

"In case anything happens to me and you must return alone, you should remember the trail. Look back often. Think about the way this cliff looms against the golden sky."

Chebucto opened his eyes, wondering where he was. His father waited patiently until he was certain his son was conscious. "We begin the descent now."

With that, Joot slid through a narrow cleavage between two sharp-edged rocks. If Chebucto had not been directly behind his father, he would have missed the entry point. As it was, Chebucto nearly fell forward and off the sheer face of the cliff below him when he emerged from the slit in the rocks. The ledge between him and eternity was barely wide enough to hold his foot. Air rushed out of his lungs and he thought his heart was bursting through his ribs at the shock of the sight below. Unhindered by fear, his father moved smoothly along the ledge beyond. His gray and black hair, plaited into a single braid according to Hutlan customs, glinted in the early morning light. Chebucto gathered his wits and pried up his right foot. He forced it to move through emptiness to find a landing on the ledge ahead. The foot reached safety as if by its own resources. Chebucto tested the ledge tentatively and then realized there was no room for him to shift his weight from the left to the right foot. There was no possible way to lean into the stones and then lift the left foot for yet another step. Chebucto couldn't breathe.

Ahead, Joot turned to watch his son's progress. Charged amusement spread slowly across the space between them. Joot's face, however, remained as immobile as the stone on which he leaned. Mixed fury and terror helped stir Chebucto's blood, he took the next step without thinking and was surprised to find himself already balanced for the third. He smiled tentatively at his father. Joot allowed his lips to curl upward before turning away.

"Don't forget to look back," Joot called over his shoulder.

Chebucto suppressed a moan, forced himself to take a breath, and waited until he could remember how to turn his head without moving his body. Even as he did so, relief flooded his being. He held the position for a long time, memorizing every detail of the crack between anonymous flat-faced rocks. When he turned his head back, he could not see his father. Carefully, he continued onward. Soon he saw his father's dark moschid-hide skin leggings swinging gently against a yellowish-tan slab of encrusted obsidian. Joot rested on a translucent spur of the stone. Chebucto wondered what had caused such a big fracture but put the thought aside rather than start his lively imagination again. He approached his father with caution.

"Father," he began, peering at his father's face for signs of rejection. Seeing none, he continued, "Why does Mother want me to marry? No one is telling Keyo to find a wife."

Joot stifled a sigh. "Keyo has a brother, a sister, a nephew and a sister-in-law. His mother has plenty to occupy her mind with all of them." Joot glanced at his son obliquely, carefully keeping his face pointed away. "You know that your mother works very hard to keep up with Jenda, but there are only three of us to the seven of them. That makes a difference. Jenda has more people to work on food and skins."

Chebucto pitched one pebble after another over the side of the cliff. Finally, he ventured, "But you seem to want me to leave home, too, Father."

This time Joot turned his head to stare at his son. "Leave home?"

Then he looked at the situation through his son's eyes. "Yes, I suppose it does appear that I am forcing you away from home, but the truth is just the opposite. Your mother and I need you—badly. We also know the choice, once you have finished your work down there, will be yours to come back to us or not. I hope you will want to come home, my son. Besides, your mother might kill me if you don't." They managed to come together with weak smiles. Then Joot chuckled. "Think of the positive part of all this. There is no marriage planned for you on this trip."

When they reached bottom, Joot shared the last crumbs of the dried meat. They found a protected place between rock outcrops. Chebucto thought he heard something moving in the tall grass. He alerted his father, who shrugged his shoulders. However, as a precaution, they decided not to make a fire. Chebucto entered the dreamless sleep of the untrained. His father slept lightly in the manner of a hunter.

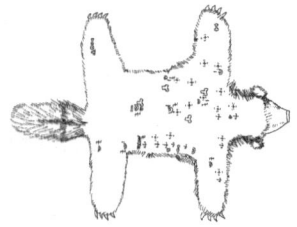

Seven

Aprimordial screech shaped thought, created awareness. Chebucto held himself still as he tried to remember where he was, why he awoke to a cold gravel bed. Memory of yesterday's traumatic rock face descent flooded his mind. Chebucto looked slowly around, trying to find the source of the scream. Rolling to his feet, he moved past his still-prone father to the edge of the stone sanctuary.

A golden tan giant stood in the middle of a thicket of new-growth aspens. Surrounded by tall grass, it was hard to see anything but an occasional glimpse of the animal's head and trees shaking wildly. Then Chebucto jumped to the top of a boulder and had a clearer view. He had never seen such a huge creature. It was a species of rhynchotherid, a distant relative of the mammoth. The rhynchotherid used his head to push through grass and other foliage to reach for the largest of the trees and then stepped into the open. Its enormous jaws were agape. With a mouthful of saplings, he turned his head to the side with an efficient backward twist. The aspen coiled in generous compliance to his tug. The rhynchotherid took a brisk step or two away from the stand to tear the trees out of the ground, roots and all. In the way of the dominant, he kept an unconcerned eye on the meal at hand, apparently eager to finish his snack before returning to the thicket for more. Unlike smaller creatures whose predators are many, the rhynchotherid made no effort to hide his presence or his preoccupation. The rustling of leaves and slender branches was loud as he chewed.

Perhaps it was the rhynchotherid's youth that left him so unvigilant. Chebucto could see that he had a stubby pair of tusks. By then, Joot had clambered the top of the rock and peered over Chebucto's shoulder. He murmured, "Within five or six years those tusks will twist into a single spiral above his snout. Right now, he's as tall as the tallest of our Tuudzaado men. When these rhynchoderids are full grown, they are about half again as tall as this one."

Chebucto wondered how to hunt such creatures and thought about making a deadfall, a thick jumble of dead trees covering a shallow depression in the gravelly moraine. He discarded the notion almost as soon as it entered his mind. *I wonder if I could go home if we killed it. Don't be silly,* he thought. By the time, he and Joot managed to construct a deadfall trap big enough, the rhynchotherid would be rotting on its feet as an elder of its kind. Chebucto almost snorted. Still, there was enough tender meat on this specimen to feed their entire community for a moon. Hope for such a wonderful resource evaporated as Chebucto noticed a dark shape skulking through the sedges on the far side of the rhynchotherid. In a few moments, the shadows took on the shape of a large dog.

"A peccary dog," Joot declared with satisfaction. "They are one of the plains' dogs. We call them peccary dogs because they usually follow the third largest of the plains peccaries. It's even bigger than a dire wolf."

Chebucto lifted his chin in acknowledgment. He watched closely. The peccary dog was ambitious. The rhynchotherid probably weighed ten times as much as the dog, and yet the peccary dog was huge, perhaps three times as heavy as Chebucto. Wondering how a dog, no matter how big, might kill the rhynchotherid, both men crouched down onto the stone hiding place.

Chebucto examined the stealthy peccary dog. Chebucto guessed this one to be a fully mature male, thickly muscled around the neck and shoulders. In comparison to the rhynchotherid's height, the dog stood about waist high to an average Hutlan man like Joot.

"Look at his hind legs," Joot remarked. "The peccary dog's hind legs from hip to toe are as long as I am. The stretch of leg gives this dog a spectacular advantage in both sprinting and leaping." Joot launched into a disjointed story about a peccary pack in his youth. As he spoke Chebucto watched closely and concluded that the dog's jaws might be its best asset. Massive, the peccary dog's jaws could crush nearly any size bone without bothering to chew. Five or six long creases in the dog's cheeks gave a false impression that the peccary dog smiled as he crept toward his prey. The creases were not about the animal's moods, but about leaving enough room for the jaws to maneuver around something as big as the foreleg of a rhynchotherid.

* * *

"Wow!" Deloo's uninhibited shout jarred my elegant spirit sense of peace. I glowered at her unseeing eyes.

Grandfather Kwaiikit, on the other hand, smothered a laugh, pleased that he had her full attention. *Have you heard of the rynchotherid, young woman?*

"Yes!" Deloo shouted excitedly. "There was an exhibit in Boston that had one."

Shush, I, the great Baasee' admonished. *You've already awaken people in North Pole.*

Deloo giggled, and asked our invisible selves, this time in the silent way, *is it true they could unhinge their jaws? The guide said it in a museum in Boston.*

Not this one, answered my illustrious grandparent, *because of his youth. His cartilage was still forming. To stretch it that way would hurt and cause permanent damage.*

Now, try to keep the noise level down, my Deloo, I, the brilliant Baasee' smiled.

* * *

The ears behind the peccary dog's long jaws were tiny by comparison. Short, round, and tufted from the inside, they stood straight out from the head, almost parallel to the ground, looking like the displaced wings of a moth. A white streak of fur between the ears reminded Chebucto of something. He struggled to recall what. The white topknot set off the dark fur around the muzzle as well as the spiny, gray bristles along the ridge of his neck. Like most of this species, the peccary dog was pure gray except for the muzzle and streak on its forehead. Then a memory flooded Chebucto's mind. There were three peccary dog pelts at home, all used as sleeping pallets. Mala had removed the stiff guard hairs to give the pelts more softness, but not enough for Chebucto. However, they were waterproof and Chebucto was too sensible to object to using them. Taking in the size and power of the huge dog wearing his sleeping pad gave Chebucto an odd sense of disquiet. He ventured a quick look at his father. An unfamiliar feeling of admiration or perhaps even awe welled in his young heart, knowing that his father had killed three peccary dogs, more than anyone else on the Dzagh, even Zaandan.

The dog made use of the rhynchotherid's noisy harvesting to move closer. Before long, the dog stood within easy eyesight of the giant. Seemingly gratified by a full chewing experience, the rhynchotherid didn't even flick his stiff, pointed ears. Suddenly the dog uttered one loud rasping cry and sprang with precision and power onto the rhynchotherid's immense shoulders. Using the talons of his hind feet to sustain his grip, he moved his front paws closer to the rhynchotherid's head and screamed into its ear. The sound stunned the huge beast. Instead of shaking himself rid of the attacker as he could have done with little effort, the rhynchotherid stood as if rooted by the very aspens in his mouth. The dog kept up a high-pitched rasping squeal into his victim's ear while he clung to the thick upper neck with his forelegs. Wasting no time to get a better position, he clawed the herbivore's neck in a frenetic running motion with hard rear talons.

Although the rhynchotherid's hide seemed tough, it was not thick enough to withstand the combined pressure and speed of the assault. In moments, the dog had opened a hole in the neck. Blood surged in a wide spray when the dog's talons struck an artery. Through it all the rhynchotherid stood unresisting, looking somehow at peace. Perhaps for him death was as easy as life. In a few moments, he slumped to the ground. The peccary dog sprang away from the carcass and emitted an odd, squeaky bark. The cry alerted the rest of his pack, and within a blink of an eye seven dogs were gorging themselves on the fallen rhynchotherid. Gigantic as the rhynchotherid seemed, the dogs appeared to be more than capable of eating all the flesh themselves. There would be nothing left for scavengers like Chebucto or Joot. In fact, it would be dangerous to move while the odor of so much blood filled the air, as the smell could awaken reckless violence in the minds of blood eaters. Maintaining a ready crouch, Chebucto settled himself more comfortably on the stone perch and took time to examine the surrounding area. Joot did likewise, pushing himself next to his son.

A shaft of sunlight fell across their two arms, so different in size and color. Joot's arm was more muscular but shorter than his son's. Chebucto was very conscious of the difference in skin tone. The skin of Joot's arm looked like granite, a dark greyish brown color, while his son's had a little of Mala's red-brown color. Nude, Mala could blend into a field of cranberries. Of course, other factors made it easy to spot her and Jenda, height being one of them. Mala said most Tuudzaado matched the red earth around the Red River.

Turning his attention to the gore, Chebucto's empty belly rumbled. He ignored it. His father always told him to eat little while hunting. Chebucto enjoyed hunger sensations, although he was skinny enough as it was.

Whoo whaaa whaa huhn.

"Teratornis!" Joot whispered. It was a sound Chebucto had never heard before. The giant bird's cry echoed along the hillside. A moment later he heard the creaking of pinfeathers squeezing against each other. Joot nudged his son, jutted his jaw to the left.

A teratornis male glided overhead. The females usually flew higher and slightly to the rear of their smaller mates. His wings, more than double the length of a bald eagle, could make turns that the females, with even larger wings, couldn't. The teratornis never hunted in the Dzagh where Chebucto was born it was easier and better for them to look for the abundant prey on the flat, warm plains. The teratornis arched his neck, extended his long legs downward and hovered over the gory scene. The tips of his right wing flirted with the winds. Banking the male brought in both wings as he approached a stony ridge just beyond the fallen rhynchotherid. His mate chose a cliff a short distance away and after landing, lifted her wings, flapping hard and fast, creating a thunderous noise and sent waves of an unfamiliar odor. The dog pack melted away. One of the largest carried a meaty joint between its jaws. Both giant birds settled onto the carcass. After a while the female teratornis, sated with the fresh meat raised her huge wings, the wind lifted her after seven lurching steps, nearly dropped her, then hoisted her higher. Staccato sounds from her frantically beating wings reached Chebucto's ears and carried with it the pungent odor of blood and urine.

When the ruckus died down, Chebucto turned to his father and asked, "Which of them peed?"

Caught off guard, Joot regarded his son with a blank stare.

Chebucto flared his nostrils suggestively and nodded toward the killing field.

"Hmm" Joot lowered his head to his chest. A small smile twitched his lips, but a light tap on Chebucto's head was the only acknowledgment he gave of his son's joke. "They left quite a bit. Why don't we check and see?"

Without wasting any time lest more predators approach, the two humans dashed toward the kill site. Joot cut some meat off one of the haunches and then helped his son cut as much of the golden-brown hide off the legs as possible. They raced back to their rocky lair. Chebucto cleaned the hides with a stone scraper while his father collected a pile of twigs and a thick bundle of dead grass. Using his fire drill, he lit a fire. Spearing pieces of meat on short, peeled willow sticks, they were soon eating charred rhynchotherid meat.

* * *

"Fire drill?" Deloo muttered, wrinkling her eyebrows.

Above her Grandfather Kwaiikit and I wrangled to be the one to answer. Grandfather waved permissively, and I, the fire-drill expert of my part of Zana, answered, *first, unpucker your eyebrows or they will become permanently wrinkled. I sent a fluff of calming light toward her. A fire drill is how we made fire by rolling a stick between our hands. Keep it next to some tinder so that the heat of twisting the stick will heat it and let you make a fire. Beginners used a stick with a hole in it for stability while you twist, but when you get better, you don't have to bother. The faster you roll the stick, the better.*

Thanks, Baasee', my glorious mortal thought/said.

* * *

Later they examined the three hides Chebucto had cut from the rhynchotherid. "I'll work with this one," Joot said. "You'll need the other two."

Chebucto looked at his father, feeling pleased with the unexpected gift, yet leery about his father's motives. "Don't you need this, Father?"

"Not as much as you will, Son." It was too dark for Chebucto to see his father's face, but he heard the pointed humor, and wondered again if his father expected him to come home.

"It's at least a day or two's journey to the old medicine man's home," Joot said at sunrise the next morning. They cleaned their fire site thoroughly, while Joot reminded Chebucto as always and yet perhaps for the last time—if his plan worked as he hoped, of the importance of leaving nothing behind to give predators or enemies an easy way to find them. Finally satisfied, Joot led them on a route that skirted most of the open areas. Every time he heard a noise, he paused to ascertain the source, constantly instructing his son on the dangers of this region. As they moved, Chebucto reveled in his father's expertise, wishing they could do this more slowly, be together a little longer. Nonetheless, every once in a while, Joot would eye his son with a look that reminded Chebucto of their purpose in traveling. Now, watching Joot moving swiftly away from him, Chebucto wondered what kind of reception they were going to find in this new world. Crossing the alluvial plains to reach the North Face had proven to be uneventful. It also proved that two men could walk for three days without food. Even though they saw edible prey and plants everywhere, Joot refused to let them stop to hunt or even to rest except at night. When they were a day away from old medicine man's Hutlan community, Joot selected a place to rest on the gravel moraine. This time the bed of sharp stones awoke Chebucto every time he moved, while Joot slept peacefully.

"Are we going to visit any of our relatives before we meet the medicine man, Father?" Chebucto asked on the third day.

"No," Joot responded. "I'll visit Lo's family. I'd like to talk to Reega and Chegwet, too. But I will do that after I have left you with the medicine man."

"Why can't I meet them?" Chebucto whined. "What if I want to visit some of my relatives while I'm here?"

"Son, you are here for a reason. Accomplish your training with the old medicine man and then you can do whatever you want."

"Who are Reega and Chegwet?" Chebucto persisted when he thought his father's shoulders looked more relaxed.

Joot signaled for his son to walk beside him. "First and foremost, she is Tuudzaado. She and Chegwet decided to tell everyone she is from the southwest of the glaciers where there are many different people, including the Dotson and people who resemble the Tuudzaado. Reega and her first husband came to the North Face about fifteen years ago to become the farthest north members of the Dire Wolf Alliance. They brought their only child, a boy named Ping. They built a sod house in the far west, way over there," Joot pointed toward the low line of blue mountains in the west. "That's where the glaciers are farthest from us. It's also the most dangerous place to live because of constant glacial flooding. They lived through three years of so much flooding they could not hunt. Then a group of Dotson death runners came through. They killed Reega's husband but she killed almost all them. Chegwet happened to be there and killed the man who killed Reega's husband. Afterward Chegwet took them to his home." Joot pointed north northeast of where they walked, "They've been together ever since."

"Is Chegwet a Tuudzaado man?" Chebucto asked, wondering if he, too, had changed his name to hide his heritage.

"No, he is a short Hutlan man married to a tall Tuudzaado woman just like I am." Joot smiled. "They have a son of their own. I think that boy is five or six years younger than you, but he looks something like you, so you would probably like him."

Chebucto's eyes brightened. "Are they our relatives?"

"Not direct relatives, but there are family connections here and there. I call him Cousin Chegwet even though we are not related."

Chebucto pondered in silence for a while. Finally, he asked, "Father, is it true that Uncle Zaandan has been telling Tuudzaado people not to be around us Hutlan people?"

Joot's shoulders sagged. He sighed and said, "first, you are not one of 'us Hutlan people.' You are one of the new people who are a little of both. And yes, Zaandan has been saying that on the Dzagh, but not for reasons that I understand very well."

"Father, his mother and father are Tuudzaado, and he was adopted by Hutlan people. His son, Kenduu, has married a Hutlan woman and Kenduu is Tuudzaado, not a, a new person." Chebucto rolled the phrase around in his mind, and then ventured. "How can he say such things?"

Joot uttered something like a snarl and wouldn't answer. Instead, he picked up the pace, rushing them faster than was wise considering that it as midday on the plains where the heat of the sun seems to go to the plains instead of to the Dzagh. Chebucto sweated profusely. After a while he realized how dry and big his tongue and grown in his mouth. He tried to say something about it to his father, but his lips cracked as he opened them and all he managed to get past his tongue was a hoarse squawk. Joot turned, saw what was happening, and handed his son a bag of berries mixed with moschid fat.

"Put some on your lips and hold it in your mouth until your tongue feels better," Joot murmured. "We'll stop here for a while until the sun is past second quarter."

* * *

Baasee', I'm confused. Deloo held hand to her forehead to prevent wrinkling, but I could see them form.

I was very confused myself, Little One, when I, Baasee' the Great Diplomat of Zana and Beyond, tried to make sense of it all. Just remember the handy word, cousin, and don't worry about whether they are Hutlan or Tuudzaado. Grandfather will finish his story quickly that way. I grinned at my regal grandparent and twirled away with a fake limp.

Right, very confusing. We go to another part of the North Face for the next segment, to continue the story of Rastuk, Grandfather Kwaiikit growl-thought and resumed his tale.

* * *

A giant salamander climbed slowly out of a shallow pool of water to bask in the midday sun. The tall grasses left little room for direct sunlight except at the edges of large pools of water. She favored the narrow band of white sand on the northern side of a certain pond. A northerly breeze brushed the top of her back as it crossed the pond and lifted the heavy sulphur atmosphere away. Her hide was feathery white. Vertical striations of gold and tan shafts of grass in combination with the white sand left the dozing salamander all but invisible. Rastuk and Ping burst through the dry grass and onto the tiny beach. A stinging odor very like the rancid oil of geranium reached Ping's nostrils. The reddish flowers filled sunny plains in summer, not the southern swamps of fall. He spotted the amphibian just as Rastuk was about to step on her. Ping jerked Rastuk backward and off his feet.

Surprised and impressed by the speed and strength of his assailant, Rastuk leaped to his feet and whirled around. Even as he turned, he saw the salamander twitch and Ping's finger pointed at her. The two men glared at each other. Rastuk slowed his breathing and smiled grimly. "Thank you. These creatures live in Dotshon, too. I have studied their habits."

"What have you learned?"

"A creature with no enemies never looks behind."

Together they watched the salamander as she made herself comfortable once again. Her head faced the other way.

Ping muttered, "even the short-faced bear can't afford to be so arrogant. We are fortunate that they don't live in other parts of Zana."

The pair continued until well past daylight. When Ping and Rastuk reached the outskirts of Falls Creek, Ping took the older man to a pile of rocks near the falls. It was dark, but both of them were used to maneuvering without eyesight. Ping lifted a large, flat stone away from the others, revealing a cavity he knew was just big enough to hold a full-sized man of Rastuk's size.

"Stay there or I will find you and kill you," he said in a flat voice.

Rastuk had been standing a little behind his Tuudzaado guide taking careful stock of the surrounding area. His alert olfactory sense picked out a familiar odor from a myriad of others. Suddenly cautious, Rastuk wondered if Ping had caught the smell himself. In his efforts to conceal the new information he almost missed Ping's instruction and tried to argue. Instead, he found himself propelled efficiently into the cavity by alarmingly strong arms. Rastuk wondered for the first time if he could defend himself against a Tuudzaado man like Ping.

"Whom are you going to meet?" he asked, as Ping lifted the flat stone into position.

"You'll know in a little while," Ping hissed through the stones. He placed one small stone directly in front of the flat one. It was too small to notice, but Ping would know instantly if Rastuk had left the enclosure if the stone was out of place. Ping scrambled to the top of a pile of nearby stones. From the top of the rock pile, Ping used a series of leaps and sidesteps to make pursuit as difficult as possible. Ping leaped from rock pile to rock pile until he was at the falls. Then he jumped into the water, pleased to find that it was barely below his own body temperature. *I'll be glad to move away from the northern glaciers,* he thought. *It's a lot warmer on this side of the Dzagh.*

* * *

Baasee' saw Deloo fiddle with the television's remote control and thought-asked, *do you wish to rest, my little one?*

Deloo looked up at the ceiling at a spot at least ten feet away from where Grandfather and I were floating, and smiled, *Of course not, Baasee', but I am a little confused about where everything is. Could you remind me?*

Grandfather Kwaiikit whirled around the room while I tried to figure out if Deloo was ready to turn in for the night. Suddenly he thought-muttered, *I have an idea. Granddaughter, your mortal is an artist. I could help her draw a map, if you think that would help. That's what I did, eventually with a few others. They liked it.*

Thus, Deloo, following Grandfather Kwaiikit's confusing instructions and my irritable corrections, came up with this map of Zana.

When we finished the map, it was obvious that the half hour of drawing had revived her spirits and those of my grandfather as well. He remarked, *let's continue. My granddaughter can help you figure out where we are on this map. The next part is about me and my mother, the Naan, as we all called her.*

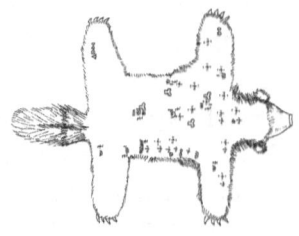

DIRE WOLF HIDE MAP OF ZANA

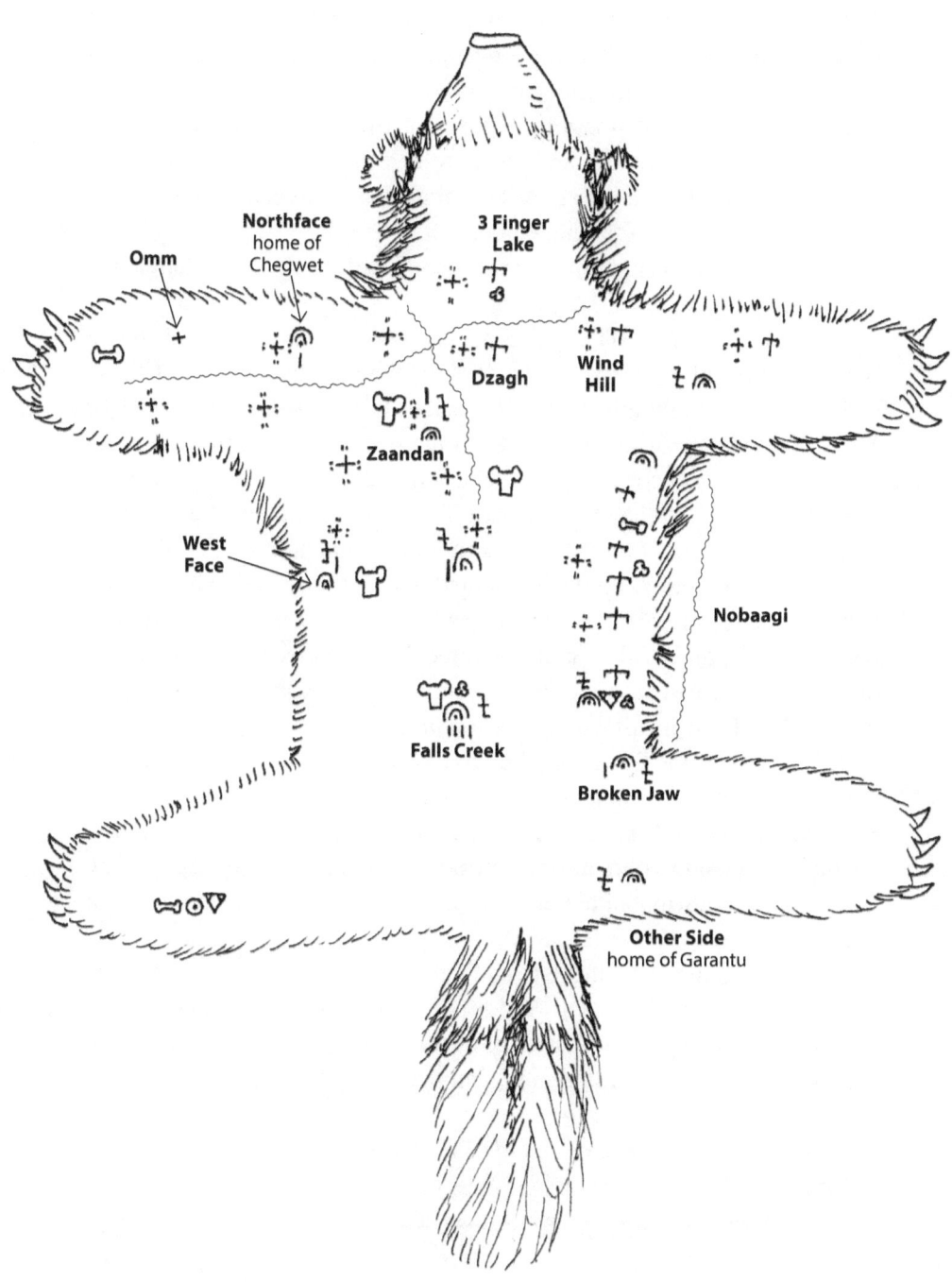

Eight

Kwaiikit arrived at the peak of the eastern side of the Gorge and waited for a signal in the late evening twilight. He had trained himself with the Naan's help to watch his own dire wolf shadow flare outward and disappear. It was a little different from hers in coloration: his came in colors of lavender and deep violet while hers was always brilliantly white. He was satisfied to see a brief flair of lavender followed by the hey-hey-hey call of the male nuthatch.

He queried silently in the most complex form of the silent language, *are you present, my friend Kejimkujik?*

Look to your left. The older man's response likewise was but a flicker of mental activity, far too fast for almost anyone except those gathering together on this quiet hillside. As they learned to do because of Mala's efforts, the original six council members still communed exclusively in the oldest form of the silent language to keep their conversations private. While they trusted their Tuudzaado relatives, they learned in those early years of the Alliance's formation that honesty, intelligence and discretion were skills to be learned and not assumed. The council had been together for twenty-four years, the year before Garantu was born. Kwaiikit and his late wife, Memree, had been teenagers, while the other members had been in their twenties. Now older and less active than he had been in his youth, Kejimkujik rarely left his home on the eastern slopes of the Gorge, so the Dire Wolf Alliance secret council, as they had come to know themselves, met there. None of them minded. Kejimkujik and the Naan fit the description of the mythical Nicoleena— people who give up all material comfort to help others. They also fit the mythical looks attributed to the Nicoleena, being taller and skinnier than other Tuudzaado.

Kwaiikit glanced to the left and saw a dark shadow emerge from some shrubbery and move toward him. Kejimkujik's long legs seemed even more scrawny than before. Kwaiikit cast back in his memory for the last time he had seen the man, and decided it had been nearly three years.

Who do you think sent us the message about Var? Kejimkujik communed.

I was hoping you knew, Kwaiikit replied.

I as well, volunteered the Naan, *hoped one of you knew who the messenger might be.* Her white dire wolf spirit cast the entire hillside into light.

The shimmering cobalt blue color of a blueberry spirit inserted itself between the Naan and Kwaiikit. The others greeted Garantu, Kwaiikit's older daughter and the Naan's great niece. After brief greetings, the four selected convenient places to squat, sit or stand as suited their needs. Garantu had brought as much trail food as she had available to share with Kejimkujik and the others. She often brought extra food to him whenever there was a little extra in her household even when there was no council meeting. For safety, none of them chose to be within speaking distance or within sight of the others. It was far simpler to use the rapid silent language while keeping watch. Within moment Kwaiikit solved the first problem.

We must meet him. I will be meeting your son, Zaandan, in a few days at our usual place. He paused for an affirmation from the Naan. *Do you want to join us?*

Not in person, she replied. *I'll wait at the base of your cliff to watch for the stranger's arrival. I want to see whomever it might be before we meet in person.*

What about you, my daughter? Kwaiikit queried of Garantu. He knew his son-in-law, a man far older than he, usually didn't notice if Garantu was present or not, but he had been oddly attentive of his daughter's whereabouts lately. Garantu told him about each of the senior Red Sun Warrior's attempts to take his oldest grandson into the Death Runners group. Each time it came up Kwaiikit had accused his son-in-law of becoming a Dotson, and Urd would put a stop to it. However, the two older boys, one eleven, the other ten, were eager to learn about the Death Runners despite all their training as Tuudzaado people. Since Urd was always too busy, Garantu had taught all the boys to hunt with Tuudzaado customs. The older two had surpassed the three main rules for becoming men and making their own choices. Garantu feared that now they wanted to be Dotson men rather than Tuudzaado.

Garantu paused to gather strength. *It hurts to tell you that I can't trust my sons anymore. They both tried to follow me here. I had to use both the power of water to hide my scent as well as the power of elevation to stay above the soil. Please confirm for me that I am correct in knowing that they turned back.*

The other three were silent for a while as each of them used their personal skills to ascertain the location of Garantu's sons. After a while, the Naan, who's ability to see others from afar was the strongest, announced, *they are all in Broken Jaw, including your youngest. The oldest is with your husband. Urd has always been a strong father to them. Don't worry.*

Hey-hey-hey-hey. The high nasal nuthatch call caused everyone to turn toward Kejimkujik. *They will wonder where you have gone, but you can claim your womanly need for a few days of privacy,* he communed to Garantu. *We need to know about this new Marten messenger first hand, and each of us must verify that he really has the high power of Marten. It could simply be a wonderful gift. I would go with you, but I foresee danger. It's served us well that I remain out of conflict to watch over and warn the rest of you of danger. Please go, young Blueberry.* Shifting slightly, Kejimkujik's shadowy form seemed to elongate toward the North Star. *Do any of us have any conjectures about the stranger's identity?* Kejimkujik asked.

The Naan hesitated before replying, then communed, *I think it might be Harbingeer's grandchild—Reega's son. I've heard he has great potential. It's odd to learn about him now, however, as Harbingeer has been dead for five years. I think his grandchild is well past twenty. If it is he, I wonder why Harbingeer didn't notify us of his grandson's ability.*

Kwaiikit offered, *it may not have happened before Harbingeer died. I was lucky. I was almost nearly seven when I saw the Naan's spirit force—yeege. Do you remember, Auntie?*

The Naan smiled in the darkness at the family endearment that Kwaiikit rarely used in public. *Yes, I do. It was a joyful surprise. I keep hoping that my son will do the same, but I doubt it will ever happen now.*

A soft hank-hank nuthatch call preceded Kejimkujik's silent words to the Naan, *I have been listening to terrible things about your beloved Zaandan. Are they true?*

The Naan sighed heavily and communed, *he hasn't divulged anything to me, but I have been listening to stories about a Dotson woman, and,* she coughed with embarrassment, *I have been following my son's activities with greater care. I know it's true. My nephew, Kwaiikit has worked on that situation with him. As to the stranger, tell me what he is doing.*

Kejimkujik communed, *we must ask him to avoid the grotto as well as Broken Jaw. I believe his life might be in danger, and there is no point in further endangering the lives of the youth we are trying to save.*

Kwaiikit cleared his throat before communing, *I'll be seeing the stranger in person very soon. Should I tell him?*

The Naan's dire wolf shadow flared again as she responded, *it will be better coming from me. I'll commune with him while you talk. Garantu and I will remain in a safe place close to the meeting place designated by the stranger. If Kejimkujik signals a yes, we will join you, Nephew, in meeting the stranger.*

If the stranger is protected by the Sacred Forces to have Tuudzaado power and is indeed Harbingeer's grandson or granddaughter, I would like to invite the individual to take the position left vacant when Harbingeer died, Kejimkujik communed, *even if he is not our late friend's grandson.*

Garantu and the Naan concurred and Kwaiikit asked, *do any of you know someone who could replace Var?*

Kejimkujik communed, *Var was a great Nightstalker; the Nightstalkers are our best defense against the Dotson. Thanks to Var, we could learn how many have invaded the North Face region.*

And thanks to Var, Kwaiikit remarked, *we know how many of the Nightstalkers have killed.* Because of their extreme secrecy, Nightstalkers were invisible to the Dotson, if not completely unknown. They had killed nearly fifty Dotson men. No one else had developed a better method of resistance. *We need to find a good replacement for Var as soon as possible.*

I have an idea, the Naan communed, *but it will require that we meet with him together.*

Intrigued, all of them asked, *who is he?*

My grandson by adoption. His name is Kenduu. My son adopted him after I found his parents — dead. His father was a Nightstalker. When I was in the Dzagh three moons ago, I saw him flare the Nightstalker yeege. Has either of you seen his yeege?

Kwaiikit thought about the last time he was in the Dzagh, and replied, *he was a little boy when I saw him last. I believe he is married now and has a son. Has he become a Nightstalker?*

Far from it, laughed the Naan. *I don't know if he's ever heard of the Nightstalkers. Until I saw him this past year, he hadn't exhibited any interest in either the Dire Wolf Alliance or the violence of the Dotson. He's a hunter and a family man. Zaandan has asked him to be the head hunter for their family. He's needed someone who could be at home all the time. That will change soon.*

Kejimkujik communed, *I'll join your meeting with the strangers with the help of the Sacred Forces. You are welcome to stay with me for the night.*

The others declined politely and without further communication, vanished into the night.

* * *

Zaandan moved quickly toward the base of a tall, narrow cliff a short walk from the rock pile in which Rastuk waited. He listened for other sounds, sniffed for other odors, and did not notice the call of an unfamiliar owl as a younger, less trouble Zaandan might have done. The base of the cliff was shrouded in vines inside a dense growth of aspens. He stepped around a pungent skunk cabbage, noting that it was still blooming despite the season. Pushing his way through the aspens he found the hand and toe holds that he had used for many years. Soon he reached the top of the cliff, not at all surprised to see his teasing cousin, Kwaiikit sitting before a tiny blaze. Kwaiikit, six years older than Zaandan, was at least a head taller. Kwaiikit took in his cousin's mood and health in a glance. Both knew the older style of the Tuudzaado customs thanks to Zaandan's mother and Kwaiikit's father, who was the Naan's brother. Zaandan's skill with the older language was not equal to Kwaiikit's, nonetheless, Zaandan relayed detailed information about events of the previous moon with competence unavailable to most younger Tuudzaado. He carefully omitted mentioning his prospective Dotson bride.

Jenda wants me to spend more time with my sons, especially Keyo. When I'm home I can't talk to him. He doesn't know either of our silent languages, since I use northern Tuudzaado and Jenda uses Datherd. Oddly enough, even though we raised him together, Kenduu's silent style is the odd Nightstalker dialect. I think all that leaves Keyo so confused that he speaks only Hutlan and doesn't want to commune with us. He spends all his time with Chebucto. What worries me most is that he is sixteen and still hasn't made a big kill. Between the boys who need help escaping from the Dotson and my own family, I don't know how to make decisions any more.

Kwaiikit added a stick to the fire and pointed to a shallow, dish-like stone that held a savory roast, wondering if it was the right time to ask about the rumors he'd heard about Zaandan's new Dotson wife. Deciding it was too soon, instead he communed, *Have some peccary.*

Garantu and I hunted this together today. It was the first time in years that she and I have spent that much time together. Kwaiikit handed a small flat wooden slab to his cousin. It was one of the many makeshift utensils that had accumulated on the cliff top from numerous hunters over the years. *You look hungry. This won't help you with Keyo, but you'll feel better. It's just as difficult with girls, especially after my wife died this past summer. Our daughter is tired of being cooped up all the time. She wants to run and hunt like other children. Memree wouldn't let her leave the cave, and now that she is gone, I forbid her to do anything without my permission.*

Are you still thinking of moving Garantu to the Falls Creek grotto? Zaandan communed. *I think the Dotson here are worse than those at Broken Jaw.*

The Dotson are bad no matter where they are, especially when it comes to women. They want a Red Paint Woman like my younger daughter. Clarvu is eleven years old now, and Garantu keeps reminding me that she will become a woman very soon. I used to think the claystone building would be safer for her, but now I'm not so sure. I hope you could tell me.

The question caught Zaandan by surprise. Zaandan recognized the moment of truth between had finally arrived. He had been stretching forward to capture a particularly tastylooking piece of meat and nearly fell into the flames. He recovered his balance, continued foraging for the bit of meat, and then chewed with gusty pleasure all the while probing the atmosphere for a hint of what to expect. At last he communed, *I guess you've heard about her, then?*

Kwaiikit nodded in the firelight.

Zaandan rocked on his haunches and communed the story about how easily a Red Sun Warrior had tracked him after a particularly difficult escape run two moons earlier. He had left the last of five former captive children at a Hutlan house in the eastern Dzagh when the Red Sun Warrior stepped out from behind some bushes directly in front of Zaandan. Zaandan attacked instantly, only to find himself wrapped between the man's powerful arms in a maneuver that stunned the taller man.

"I'm not going to kill you," the Red Sun Warrior had rasped, his Dotson accent so thick that Zaandan almost didn't understand him. "I followed you for a reason. I have a proposition to make."

Zaandan brought himself back from that moment and stopped

rocking. *Yes. It's true.* He described the Red Sun Warrior's proposition, which had been to marry his oldest daughter. *He convinced me it would be a good idea. I realize now that I convinced myself it was the best solution because I am a coward. I wasn't ready to die. Instead it seemed like a brilliant opportunity to bring all kinds of secrets to the Dire Wolf Alliance. Instead...*

Kwaiikit grimaced. *Have you told your mother?*

No. I haven't been able to tell anyone until now.

Someone is talking about it. I heard about it first when I reached one of the safe houses on the east side. What does he ask of you besides marriage to his daughter?

Zaandan shook his head repeatedly, stopping himself when an image of his head swaying uncontrollably floated into his mind. He laughed inwardly when he recognized the skill his mother had to send him intimate silent messages when he least expected it. He sighed, and felt better than he had for many days. The Naan knew him inside and out.

Mother, are you attending both of us?

Yes. Greetings to both of you, my son and nephew. The spirit force, or *yeege* of her dire wolf flared and disappeared.

Kwaiikit glanced sharply at Zaandan, trying to detect some sign that Zaandan saw his mother's spirit sign. Zaandan showed no such awareness. Perhaps he was so used to it, he didn't react any more.

Zaandan resumed his story. *He told me the only thing he wanted was that I instruct the Tuudzaado to stay away from marriage to Dotson people. Ha! I was shocked. I told him that I wouldn't. He reminded me how easy it had been to find me, and said the next person he would find would be my wife. He meant Jenda. He described our house, Jenda, Dagoli and Keyo, Duna and Masito all in detail. I should have accepted defeat at that moment, but I agreed. I did it. Everyone thinks I'm crazy to say what he told me to say, considering my own heritage.*

Kwaiikit stared into the fire. After a moment he communed, *I heard about your strange new message to people of the Dzagh. I also heard that people are accusing you of planning the ambush on Iglan.*

What?! Zaandan started rocking again. *I had nothing to do with it. I worked with Joot to arrange the marriage.* Zaandan emitted a low moan. *It's too obvious, isn't it? I would never have hurt my friends that way.*

The Naan interjected smoothly, *your friends defend you, my son. You have done nothing wrong.*

My son, I will join you in the morning. Under the circumstances, it is not wise for you to take any more children from the grotto. Because of what has happened, I want to spend time with you in the Dzagh to ensure your safety. Until tomorrow. I'll be with someone you know. A shadowy dire wolf suddenly bloomed into the night air and instantly disappeared. The shadow was always the Naan's signal of goodbye, seen only by the original members of the Dire Wolf Alliance. Kwaiikit looked at his cousin for any sign that Zaandan had seen it, again disappointed to see no reaction.

The two cousins communed about ordinary things for a while. Between comfortable silences Zaandan asked, *Is all well with your older daughter and her husband?*

I can't stand him, but everyone applauds his every word. Garantu does everything he asks. She is careful not to complain lest he allow her sons to join the Dotson Death Runners.

I don't know him. I've only met him once, and that was more than enough for me. Does he know how to use the silent language?

Yes, although he has never communed with me except with simple greetings. He does it the same way that Jenda and Mala do, that southern Tuudzaado style. My daughter avoids communing with him or her children, more to avoid prying outsiders than anything else. My grandsons don't know there is a silent language.

The shadow image of a marten appeared before Kwaiikit and disappeared. Kwaiikit glanced toward Zaandan.

Did you see that? Kwaiikit communed.

See what?

Kwaiikit thrust his chin to the side and shrugged. *I guess it was a bat. It's not there now.* Kwaiikit rose slowly to his feet and stretched. *I need to stretch my legs for a bit.* He sent an image of Skritforce, their ally at the Falls Creek grotto.

Zaandan frowned.

Aloud Kwaiikit murmured, "why don't you get some sleep here? I might be a while."

Kwaiikit had been coming to Falls Creek more often than he usually did, finally confessing three moons ago his growing interest in their mutual ally, Skritforce. Skritforce's late husband had worked with the Dire Wolf Alliance himself, and between them they had found a good way to sneak little slave boys out of the grotto and into safety.

You are right. I will be very careful. Without another word, he slid through the crack at the top of the cliff and disappeared.

Zaandan sank into a comfortable hunter's squat and cut another large piece from the roast with a slightly curved stone knife. The meat was delicious. The stones near the fire were very warm. Zaandan felt the need for sleep envelop him for the first time in two moons.

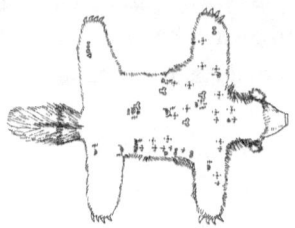

Nine

K waiikit hesitated at the base of the cliff, taking in every sound and smell he could, and then moved carefully to a secure spot between some tall boulders. It had two very narrow exit areas on the far side from which he could escape if needed. A zephyr touched his nose, bringing with it the scent of a human stranger a male, adult Kwaiikit estimated, in his mid-twenties. Kwaiikit turned toward the source and saw the barest glimmer of a marten *yeege* or spirit force dancing above a cast of boulders. Kwaiikit concentrated on his own dire wolf *yeege* or spirit force, and was satisfied that it appeared as he hoped. He had studied Kejimkujik's method of displaying the nuthatch *yeege* or spirit force, and suspected rightly, that Kejimkujik simply imitated the nuthatch call often. Shrugging, he sent a neutral greeting in the silent language and received one in return.

Come forward, Kwaiikit insisted, *and let me see who you are.*

After a long wait without response, Kwaiikit squeezed himself farther in between the boulders toward the nearest of the escape holes. He was nearly wedged in too tightly to get out easily when Ping communed, *where are you now?*

Kwaiikit considered the question carefully, then regretfully pulled himself forward, knowing the effort would damage both his tunic and some of the skin under it. He stepped out from the shelter of the boulders when he detected the strong odor of the younger man. As it happened, Ping had turned his back on the boulders in which Kwaiikit was hiding. He jerked backward when Kwaiikit murmured softly into the man's ear, "behind you." Both grunted when the top of Ping's head collided with the bottom of Kwaiikit's jaw. Kwaiikit's hands reached out automatically to steady the other Tuudzaado man. When Ping felt the touch, he sprang around to face his attacker and flailed wildly at anything in front of him. Kwaiikit melted into the crevasse and waited. As he knew what was bound to happen, Ping slammed his fist into solid rock and forced himself to swallow a loud squawk.

"Are you finished?" Kwaiikit muttered irritably.

"Who are you?" Ping snarled between clenched teeth.

"Let's start with you," Kwaiikit murmured while rubbing his tender jaw, "since you are the visitor here. What is your name and why did you come here?"

Ping sank into a squat and began feeling the ground near the base of a short spruce tree. His busy fingers didn't find what he wanted and continued prowling the area in frenzied jerks. When his hands touched the warm hide of Kwaiikit's moccasin, they paused momentarily, then dove suddenly between the older man's feet to snatch a small growth of club moss. Holding a patch of moss to his scratched knuckles, Ping scrambled to his feet and said, "my name is Ping."

For a few moments, the two men examined each other without touching, each aware of the other's many scents and pulsations that emitted from their minds and bodies. The odor of Kwaiikit's dire wolf pelt satisfied Ping that he had found a Dire Wolf Alliance man like his grandfather. Kwaiikit wondered how to prove the man before him was Ping. *Where is the man?* He communed.

"He's Tuudzaado on his mother's side," Ping said in a nearly voiceless whisper. "We'd better not use the silent method."

Kwaiikit tipped his jaw upward once and murmured, "Before we begin, please tell me something about your mother and father. Who are they?"

Knowing what Kwaiikit needed, Ping whispered a long seven-generation genealogy, including where each person was born and died and a little of their noteworthy feats during life. It would have taken very little time in the silent language, but Ping didn't mind. Reciting his family history aloud always brought him pleasure because many of them took part in important stages of Zanian history.

When he finished, Kwaiikit recited a much shorter, but equally impressive genealogy and added, "there are some things you should know about yet another recent massacre."

Ping's excitement was palpable. This was his first meeting with any of the core members of the Dire Wolf Alliance since he had spent most of his life on the North Face or moving through the Dzagh out of sight of others. His excitement turned to still horror as he listened to what happened to Iglan's family.

"My mother and I worked on creating that marriage, too," Ping mouthed. "Lo and her family live, or rather, lived near us. Tell me again when the ambush occurred. Maybe Rastuk had them killed as well."

"It happened on the twenty-first day of the Peccary Moon," Kwaiikit said, "five days before Var and his family were killed. I heard they might have had a Dotson man with them."

"Who?"

"I don't know. Do you know them that well?"

"I know of them, and some of the Hutlan women on the North Face have married them."

"Tell me what happened to Var and his family," said Kwaiikit.

Ping described what he had seen.

"What about Rastuk? Did he kill them?"

"His scent was only in their open area outside entryway. He didn't kill Kat or their daughter, Veetu. My men found Var's body and carried it back. As far as I could tell, his scent was not on Var." Ping pursed his lips. "There was nothing to indicate that Rastuk had anything to do with it other than being Dotson himself and having spent the night outside their sleeping house."

Kwaiikit made a low sound. "Wait. You said he was Tuudzaado. How do you know he is Dotson as well?"

"Ask him when you meet him. He's got the look of Dotson along with a big scar on his forehead. That's why I happened along." Ping told the other two about the old medicine man's vision. "He said the man who killed my father had that kind of scar."

Kwaiikit stared into space. "A Sun warrior. Black from the left, Red from the right. He is a Black Sun Warrior. I thought there are only seven other sun warriors in Zana. Most of them are at Broken Jaw. All but one are Red Sun Warriors. I've heard a Black Sun Warrior has arrived. He might be this Rastuk." He asked for more details about the West Face massacre.

Ping said, "There were five Dotson men. They were highly skilled in tracking. Var had been standing in the prairie grass about a hundred paces from his household compound. At least one of them had an extraordinary sense of smell and knew Var's scent. How else could you explain ever finding a Nightstalker. No one ever sees them. They surrounded him then beat him to death. Then they broke into the house and killed the women."

Zaandan asked, "Why did Rastuk want to come here with you? The Dotson have taken over the grotto below the falls. Is he part of that group?"

"He wants to go to the uplands."

"Why?" Kwaiikit asked.

"His mother's family is from the Dzagh. He said Var called it the uplands," said Ping.

"Where did his mother live in the Dzagh?" Kwaiikit asked.

"It's hard to tell from his way of talking. I don't recognize any of the names, but you might. Maybe they are people of your generation," Ping smiled into the darkness when he felt a throb of annoyance stemming from Kwaiikit.

"Watch your language, Infant!" Kwaiikit whispered into Ping's left ear. "You might find yourself walking too close to the edge of a cliff and never finding out what happens after your voice changes."

Ping snorted.

"How old is he?" asked Kwaiikit.

"He said he is thirty-five years old." Ping made quick hand signals—five fingers less than two full men.

"Hm. Six years younger than I. His mother might have known my parents. The Naan might know him" said Kwaiikit. "Why would it matter now? Why would his mother have planned to send him so long after her death?"

Ping said, "I don't think she sent him. I believe he's using it as an excuse. You'll know when you talk to him yourself. He's after something, but I couldn't get him to tell me."

"Where does he live now?" asked Kwaiikit.

"He wouldn't say."

"Has he been in Zana very long?"

Ping brightened. "He would not answer my direct questions, but when I talked about different places in Zana, he never had to ask me for directions. I think he's been here long enough to get to know the main trails. He didn't need me to lead him to Falls Creek."

Kwaiikit said, "It's got to be a trap of some sort. Whatever he wants is about today, not thirty-five years ago. It must be something else."

Ping said, "you might learn more if you talk to him yourself. He uses the silent language in the woman's way. I guess that's understandable. But he also has strange phrases that don't make sense. Almost a double talk."

"Double talk?" Kwaiikit whispered. "What do you mean?"

"It's hard to explain. I'll give you an example that really confused me," Ping said. "He said in the silent language 'I am the daughtered son of a woman not man who will give you my name."

Kwaiikit caught his breath and looked carefully around. Satisfied there was no possible way Rastuk could be near, he communed a quick phrase in Tuudzaado. "Is that what he said?"

Ping thought about it and said finally, "not quite. You are using the male style. Think of it in the female style and that's what he said."

Kwaiikit hummed tunelessly and then said to Ping, "She created a story around ordinary phrases. She knew he would have to tell it. She used a phrase from my grandfather's generation and twisted it just a little. I think she was saying through him 'my son is my slaughterer, but it could be something else." Kwaiikit added, "ordinarily I would kill him now, but I would like to hear what his mother was trying to say to us. We will learn from her. Child Ping, take me to see this half Dotson, half Tuudzaado man."

"Before you go, Nephew," whispered the Naan, "let me speak to this young man."

Ping swung toward the unexpected voice, shocked that his ordinarily highly trained senses had not detected the presence of someone else. He was even more shocked to see yet the *yeege* or spirit force another dire wolf looming above her. "Two of you?" he mouthed. "My grandfather said there were two in the Dire Wolf Alliance who had the power of the dire wolf. You must be Grandfather's friend, the Naan."

"Yes," intoned another disembodied voice, "that is who she is."

The third voice seemed to be on his left, and Ping turned his head slightly in that direction, then back toward the Naan when his nostrils finally found the scent of an older woman near that of a younger one. He opened his mouth to speak when a bright chimera lit the shrubbery for a moment. "Blueberry!" he nearly said the word aloud rather than in sotto voce. "I'm meeting the one my grandfather knew as the daughter of Blueberry. He never met you, but he knew your mother. I don't know your name."

The Naan kept the introductions brief with a curt, "Go now. When you have finished with the stranger, meet us beside the third knoll above." Kwaiikit knew the knoll, and projected his dire wolf toward them in acknowledgment. The two men whispered a quick strategy as they made their way quickly toward the Falls.

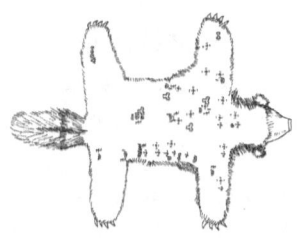

Ten

Ping returned to the rock pile where he had left Rastuk. The pebble was still in place, so he lifted the stone and signaled Rastuk to exit.

"My friend wants to meet with you."

"Who is he?"

"I will not tell you. If you continue to ask, I won't take you any further," answered Ping, inwardly sure he should simply kill the man now. Ping led the way to the falls and told Rastuk to stand next to him. They waited. Kwaiikit examined Rastuk as much as the pitch black of the new moon would allow. When he was satisfied, he approached Rastuk from the inner side of the falls. With the heavy sheet of water flowing between them the two men could not see or smell each other.

Using the Tuudzaado silent language, Kwaiikit asked the same questions that Ping and Var had already asked, and Rastuk answered them even more fluently than he had before. Kwaiikit was intrigued by several anomalies in Rastuk's wording and wished there was time to take each phrase apart. Time was too precious, so he thanked Rastuk and asked if the stranger had any questions for him.

Who are you? communed Rastuk.

"That I can't answer," said Kwaiikit, switching to the Hutlan voice language.

"Then where do you live? Here at Falls Creek?"

"I live in Zana," answered Kwaiikit, feeling both smug and oddly exhilarated. "There is probably nothing that I can tell you now. Ping, don't you think we should meet again during the season of 'Spring Water' to talk again?"

"Spring Water" was a code phrase asking Ping if he wanted to kill Rastuk immediately. The Dire Wolf Alliance had four Hutlan cues for simple messages. "Spring water" meant kill now, "Rainbow" meant follow and kill, "Blue Mountain" meant follow and observe, and "I've got a pigmy peccary" meant follow my lead. Context and using question or a command tone communicated even more. Use of any of these code words automatically meant, "We are talking to a dangerous enemy."

"Spring?!" Rastuk interjected. "I would like to talk to you again much sooner than that."

Ping intervened smoothly. "I agree with Rastuk. That would be like walking on a Blue Mountain. I will talk things over with our new acquaintance. Perhaps we can decide on a mutually agreeable time to meet in the future."

Kwaiikit heard "Blue Mountain" and slipped out of sight into the shadows. He watched Ping and Rastuk argue for a while on the other side of the waterfall. Finally, Rastuk shrugged angrily and stalked away. Ping ambled behind without a backward glance.

When they were completely out of his sensory range, Kwaiikit made his way to the third knoll as directed by the Naan. Still alert to the possibility that Rastuk understood more of the silent language than his vocabulary indicated, and aware that some Tuudzaado could "listen" to silent conversations between people who were more than a day's hike away, Kwaiikit continued to whisper to the others. "I think his mother taught him names of family members with the wrong relationship. Could any of you follow our conversation?"

Garantu shrugged and whispered, "no," while the Naan whispered, "a little."

"As far as I could understand, his mother named the people who died in one of the first big Dotson massacres on the West Face when I was just a boy of five or six. It was the first time I'd ever heard of the Dotson. I think she also planted phrases with a warning. She died twenty years ago, so the information is very old and I might not have asked enough of the right questions."

"Should we capture him to ask more?"

"No. In fact, one thing she made sure would come through in his phrasing was this: 'my son is being trained to be with Tuudzaado families.' I decided that it would be best if he never saw me or Garantu and especially not you. He might be looking for you."

"Ah," murmured the Naan, "Why didn't you kill him then?"

"I asked that of Ping," Kwaiikit said, reminding the Naan of the codes. "Ping said he would rather follow and observe Rastuk. Something must have triggered an idea. I hope it doesn't kill him, since if I'm not mistaken, he might be good on our secret council of the Dire Wolf Alliance. What do you think?"

Kejimkujik joined them by signaling a silent version of the nuthatch call. *I have been able to follow all that you as a group observed about the new Marten, and agree. If the others approve and he agrees, I suggest he be offered the chance to take his grandfather's place on our council.*

Kwaiikit returned to the cliff to await Ping. Garantu and the Naan went with him to talk to Zaandan. They agreed to meet at the same knoll before dawn.

* * *

Keeping his head up and rigidly facing the waterfall, Rastuk waited for a while in case Ping's so-called friend returned. He was intently aware of Ping's scrutiny. Under other circumstances one of them would have been dead by this time. From the time, he was wrenched from his mother's arms at age two, Rastuk had learned to meet hostile behavior with physical retaliation. Rastuk turned slowly toward Ping. It was impossible to see the young Tuudzaado man in the flat black, humid air, but he could smell Ping's rancid sweat.

Rastuk engaged one of his other Tuudzaado gifts, a gift he realized early that the Dotson men didn't share with him. He could sense the hidden thoughts of others, but they didn't seem to sense his. His mother had been the one person whose thoughts always remained untouchable. He supposed that as a Tuudzaado woman, she had a natural barrier, and that he did as well from her. He tried to talk to her about it but she refused to understand him. Standing next to each other, Rastuk tried using that ability on Ping. A burning sensation so intense he nearly collapsed swept across his head and shoulders.

Shame on you! Ping's amusement slid through the silent words. *Didn't your mother teach you not to do that? My mother insisted that I learn the rules of privacy the hard way. As you can feel, I learned to keep her away from my secrets, too.*

Rastuk understood but couldn't respond; it took all his strength to remain standing. Taking long, slow breaths, he was glad when the burning sensation calmed. At last he laughed. "That must have been something my mother knew would happen to me eventually."

"I'm sure she did," said Ping. "What would you like to do, now?"

"Now?" asked Rastuk. He hadn't planned on doing anything more with the annoying Ping. "I will rest here for the night and consider my options in the morning."

"An excellent idea. I'll do the same," smiled Ping as he leaned toward Rastuk. Rastuk wasn't used to anyone getting that close to him and his arm rose automatically to shove Ping away, but he was still too unbalanced to be prepared for the sudden twirling maneuver that brought Ping and his own arm together at Rastuk's back. Ping brought the arm upward with a fierce pressure and whispered, "it will be a pleasure to spend the night with you."

"I'll find my own place to rest," snapped Rastuk. "You should leave. There's nothing to keep you here with me anymore."

Ping laughed, the sound a seductive melody in the darkness. "I'm wounded that you no longer find me desirable. Don't concern yourself over my feelings. I'll settle nearby. If you need anything, just let me know."

* * *

My mortal up to this point had been patient, but now she couldn't hold it in. *Baasee', what's going on here. I got the part that Rastuk didn't get the lessons a Tuudzaado man would have taught him, but why did Ping still come on to him like that? I still don't get it.*

Both Grandfather and I chuckled. I communed gently, *It's simple. Rastuk's mother never punished him for what you sometimes call "reading" her and Hutlan, hence Dotson, people were never taught what the Tuudzaado "reading" sensations felt like. Maybe they didn't feel them, but since you do, it I think anything can be learned. Also, since Rastuk was sending his mental probes the woman's way, he didn't know that most Tuuzaado men would be offended, Ping is giving him a lesson that he should have got as a child. Now, sit still so Grandfather can continue. He might have made his point a little too hard for Rastuk's comfort.*

* * *

Completely baffled by the sudden change in Ping's behavior, Rastuk stalked away. It was dark. His body was tired from a full day of running. He tripped on something and fell hard on the stones. Ping sprang to his side and tenderly lifted the Dotson man to his feet.

"Don't touch me. Leave me now."

"My flaming ears! What a turn from the friendly way you have been for the past two days," exclaimed Ping, shimmering with laughter. "I suppose you must need a little privacy after so much intense Tuudzaado company. Let me help you find a comfortable place to rest."

Rastuk jerked his arm free.

"Over here," Ping continued, "atop that large stone is a place protected from the wind and rain. Why don't you take that place? There's another just over there that I will use." Ping thrust Rastuk gently forward. "Do you need my help finding it?"

Rastuk used a colorful phrase that Ping had never heard before. He laughed and seemed to dissolve into the night air. Rastuk spun around, searching for him. Already somewhat intimidated by the young Tuudzaado man, Rastuk was suddenly aware of how much he had always relied on his ability to sense the presence of others, even if they weren't close enough to touch. Ping had been touching him physically and mentally in a teasing way and then ceased both at once. Rastuk had unknowingly been arming himself in an untutored Tuudzaado method against mental contact, and the abrupt cessation was almost as unsettling as the burning sensation. Rastuk wondered why his Tuudzaado mother had not done something like Ping did to protect herself from all the people who tortured her. With that skill, she could have escaped both the Dotson and the west world that she hated. Is it possible she did it for me? He wondered.

Not far away Ping settled into a shallow rock indentation above the one he had suggested for Rastuk. He already knew that his shelter gave a better view of the surrounding area than did the other, and was also on the lea side of the northerly winds. He used his Tuudzaado awareness to follow Rastuk's progress to the other shelter. After a while he felt a shift in the atmosphere. Shrinking back into his enclave, Ping watched the older man slide quietly out of his shelter and examine his surroundings. Apparently satisfied that Ping was no longer there, Rastuk moved out of sight in the direction of the Falls Creek grotto where most of the Dotson lived. Ping waited a moment and then tracked him in the darkness. Concentrating on Rastuk, Ping was slow to react when a twig snapped just behind him. A heavy fist slammed into the back of his head.

Ping regained consciousness, careful not to move until he stabilized his senses and tried to recall as much as possible. Rastuk was nowhere to be found. Examining the surrounding area, Ping caught the pungent odor of another man, by the quality, he was older than Rastuk. He recognized the scent not only as Dotson, but also the person who had hit him. The residual thoughts and odor air were those of his assailant. Ping followed the older man's trail.

* * *

Deloo squirmed impatiently. *What just happened? I thought Ping was trained to sense everyone. How come he got ambushed like that?*

Grandfather answered before, I the Affronted but Ever Polite Baasee', collected my thoughts. He thought-said, *A steady breeze blowing away from Rastuk tends to cover thoughts or sensations emitted by others, and not merely sounds and smells. Ping should have worked in a stronger way with his guide, but both were inattentive at that time. They, the spirit guide and Ping, should have realized that the older Dotson man was far better at tracking than Rastuk.*

Ready Deloo, I asked with a toss of fake curls, *Grandfather, shall we continue?*

* * *

Within twenty paces, the older man's scent merged with Rastuk's. Both men continued south toward Falls Creek. Ping followed for a while, but stopped when the dense alder and jack pine ground cover thinned to swampy tufts dotted with single spruce trees here and there. On the far side of the swampy area he picked out the tumbled boulders marking the Falls Creek grotto in the grey light of predawn. Satisfied the two Dotson men had entered the grotto, Ping hurried toward the place he had agreed to meet Kwaiikit. They didn't know each other well, but Ping was so impatient to tell the dire wolf man everything, that he failed to notice Kwaiikit's wariness. For one thing, Kawiikit whispered in the Hutlan language.

Do you know this form of the language? Kwaiikit asked, using an older style of the silent language, not quite as quick or complex as that normally used by the council.

"Eh?" Ping muttered. Between the slight concussion and his excitement about following Rastuk, all he understood was that Kwaiikit were the familiar parts of Kwaiikit's question, and did seem to sense that it was coded.

Disappointed, Kwaiikit carefully phrased a simplified statement in the ordinary northern Tuudzaado silent mode. *Do you understand me now?*

Suddenly aware that Kwaiikit thought of him as under-educated, Ping retorted in an exaggerated simplification of the language, *Yes, Ancient Being, I un-der-stand you very well.*

Despite himself, Kwaiikit grinned and tried the older language again. *I mean this way, you imp. Do you understand this?*

Unabashed, Ping responded, *Ah, yes, Ancient One, my grandfather and I used this language a few times, but my mother prefers her method method.* Ping switched to a form of the silent language nearly identical to that used by the Dire Wolf Alliance secret council. *Do you ever use this form? My mother and I use it between us once in a while.*

Excellent, Garantu communed from somewhere out of sight. *Father, should we wait or ask now?*

Kwaiikit grimaced and replied in the same mode, *no, Daughter, we will wait as agreed*

Wait for what? Ping asked, sensing the invisible strange female's excitement.

I think you two are waiting for us, Zaandan supplied, ambling toward his cousin. Of the lanky Ping, he asked, *Who are you?*

Ping's dark eyes brightened as he took in the array of people suddenly standing before him. He didn't know which was more captivating, the beauty of the *yeege* (spirit forces) with each of the tall Tuudzaado men and women or the woman he guessed must be Blueberry. His eyes, of their own accord, elected to focus only on the young woman. She dropped her shoulders back a little and swaggered toward him.

Daughter!

Her grin widened and she communed, *I'm Garantu. Some call me Blueberry.*

And we will now visit my son's family in the Dzagh, interjected the Naan.

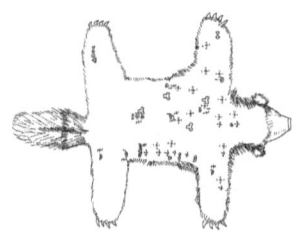

Eleven

B y the end of the second day of the Lone Wolf Moon, Chebucto felt as driven as his father and began to wonder why anyone ever bothered to eat. He felt perfectly clear headed and comfortable. Near dusk Joot pointed to his relative's house. At first Chebucto saw no house even as they were scratching on the side of an anonymous stone. He stood behind his father, amazed that Joot had perceived in this jumble of clay and stone out of a thousand other piles of stone a dwelling place. He continued to marvel even as a woman emerged from a crack between stones and flagged them to enter.

Once past the entryway, Chebucto was surprised to see the rocks piled beyond were disciplined into work areas, surrounds for small sleeping quarters, and shaped into a nicely ordered cooking area. An old man sat on a mat near the cooking fire. He glanced up to greet his guests. Even in the fading light Chebucto could see every feature of the medicine man's face as well as if the man had been standing in bright sunlight.

The aging medicine man looked at Chebucto without compassion and signaled to the two of them to enter a small dwelling beside the cooking fire. He listened in silence as Joot told their story. When Joot had been quiet for a few moments, the old medicine man asked some terse questions using words that Chebucto didn't understand. For the first time Chebucto realized that his father's people were not like the Hutlan on the Dzagh. Chebucto became acutely aware that his father belonged to this place rather than the Dzagh. His father's stories took on a layer of new meaning beyond the idyllic childhood adventures of an impossibly younger Joot on the alluvial plain, horrific glacial flooding, and his relatives "back home."

And what of your mother? A vaporous voice/thought intruded on his awareness. *Where is her home? How did she learn the tongue language?* Distracted, Chebucto tried to remember what his mother had told them just the night before. Meanwhile, there was a shift in tone and attitude between the two men. Joot's answers, crisp statements in the oddly familiar language grew in length. Joot's hands and shoulders moved in a mysterious dance, as equally incomprehensible as his words. Chebucto had an urge to flee. His heart leaped at the concept of running away, but even as the thought entered his consciousness, he snuffed it out. Instead, through narrowed eyelids he examined the old man's house. It was made of sticks and twigs woven into a tight mesh and held in place with white clay. As he learned later from his father, once hardened, the clay is nearly waterproof, but prone to crumbling whenever an earthquake struck which happened frequently. At home Joot smeared white clay on the dirt floor just as the old medicine man did here. Chebucto stared, torn between amusement and relief to find something familiar. According to Keyo, no one else in the Dzagh used clay to cover dirt floors besides Joot. Chebucto remembered defending his father: "You need a seal between the walls and floor to keep out wind and water."

"We don't," Keyo always protested with a smug look.

Chebucto took every opportunity after that to point out how dry his things were after a rain than were his cousin's, but Keyo only laughed. It wasn't a perfect solution in any event, since the white clay served as an inconstant protector against the weather. People in the Dzagh usually abandoned their houses during the worst of the storms for the caves that dotted the mountain sides. So, did Joot and his family. While they could make the caves endurable for a while, the airiness of a hide-covered house made life easier for the rest of the year.

Suddenly Chebucto wondered when and if they would eat. Joot and he had crossed the plain with no more to eat than the strips of rhynchotherid meat they had salvaged and roasted on the first night. Chebucto's suddenly greedy nose detected a cache of dried meat just behind the old man. While they talked, he tried to guess which basket held the delicious-smelling food.

"So, two Tuudzaado families have been butchered at about the same time by Dotson," the old medicine man said, his words suddenly perfectly clear to Chebucto. "Each family dwelt in an area so far not in use by the Dotson. I wonder if they have a new plan underway to destroy us even faster."

Chebucto stared at the two men, wondering about the second family. He wanted to ask, but his father's rules about courtesy were strict. He had to wait until the adults finished speaking.

"I didn't know Var or his wife," Joot said. "How long had they lived on the West Face?"

"I don't recall," the old medicine man replied. "Their daughter was old enough to walk when they moved. I think that about ten years ago."

"Do you think they were killed by the same people?"

"It's possible. From what you say about Iglan's family, they died first, then Var."

As their dialogue continued, Chebucto realized he understood almost everything the old medicine man said. He felt a small stirring of hope. Then the older men turned their attention toward him. The old man indicated with his hands that he wanted Chebucto to stand. The house was not very high, so Chebucto stooped to comply. As he stood in that uncomfortable position, the old man began to speak. His speech was long, but Mala and Joot had inculcated courtesy into their son's stance and face as soon as he could walk. Chebucto's neck was aching by the time the old man's speech ended. Even so, he maintained the position with increasing pride at his ability to endure. Unfortunately, the effort to endure impeded Chebucto's ability to comprehend the new dialect.

"He says he will keep you for one year as long as you are willing to hunt for him," Joot translated without giving his son permission to sit.

"A year!? But you said…" Chebucto squeaked.

"In exchange, I am to give him the amethyst knife as a gift," Joot continued as if his son had not spoken. He extracted the lavender blade from its sheath. In the firelight, Chebucto thought it pulsated with odd lights.

The Amethyst knife? Chebucto thought in amazement. After all the trouble it has caused? Chebucto forced his mind to leave the turbulent memories surrounding the knife and forced himself not to gape at his father. Instead he carefully lifted his jaw to indicate acceptance. He contemplated smiling, but quickly rejected the thought as impolite.

* * *

I, the Ever-Attentive Baasee', caught sight of a vibrant Deloo, arm raised in school-girl fashion. *Yes, my patient Deloo,* I intoned silently, sure that she wouldn't let slide something she had just seen earlier in the day. I was right.

Baasee'! Baasee'! Is the amethyst knife something like the women's knives we saw in that display case today? Deloo puffed out her chest, proud of the connection she had authored.

Grandfather Kwaiikit beat me to the answer. *Yes, Mortal. Your Baasee' has taught you well. She probably also pointed out the men's knives that were nearby: a little wider, used along with heavier adzes to cut bigger sections of meat. The amethyst knife that Joot gave to the old medicine man was made in a similar way, but never used in hunting.*

Joot was a good medicine man in the mountains. The old medicine man of the northern alluvial plain was better. What both of them knew and undoubtedly felt were the clear lines of power or energy that shot off the sharp sides of the knife. I saw it once. It was small, about six inches long and a couple of inches wide. The three sharp edges or what you'd call blades had been flaked out of the stone. Each of those provided the power that medicine men use to have a hunting vision. I didn't try to use it myself, but Zaandan did. He tried to buy it from Joot. Ha-ha! It was too valuable for that.

Deloo sighed a respectful thank you and I urged Grandfather to continue the story.

* * *

"If you are not successful in either hunting or otherwise satisfying his demands," Joot continued, "then I told him he could send you…" here Joot's voice cracked and he hesitated before continuing. "Back."

Chebucto stared at his father for a moment, not sure what "Back" might mean. Chebucto was certain that 'back' probably meant 'nowhere,' despite his father's pretense that this was not banishment. He suppressed a sigh, looked down at the floor and then lifted his head with false assurance. He jutted his jaw upward in a quick gesture of comprehension and assent.

The old medicine man allowed his lips to move toward a smile while his eyes remained stony. He did not offer them food. After a bit, Joot carefully placed the knife on the loosely woven grass mat that had become an impassable barrier between himself and the old medicine man. Once again speaking in the foreign language, Joot pointed to the translucent chipped stone. The old man regarded the knife without touching it. During the prolonged period of tense silence that followed, Chebucto wondered if he should do what he thought his father was afraid to do: remove the amethyst knife. Just as he tightened his right arm to reach forward, the old medicine man jutted his jaw upward. He said something in a very low voice and tipped his head toward the door. Joot reached for his knife, but the old man brought his hand up sharply, palm downward. They exchanged a few words and Joot turned toward his still-standing son. Even Chebucto, new at their coded silences, knew the old man indicated that Chebucto would survive if not succeed the training. Therefore, the old man took payment in advance for his services.

"Come, let us find a place to stay for the evening," Joot said. A few moments later, Joot introduced his son to the woman who had first greeted them.

She smiled cheerfully at Chebucto and said, "You should call me Cousin Agra, since he is my grandfather and…" She looked at Joot to complete the family relations, which he did at some length.

While his father narrated family history, Chebucto's mind collapsed inward. His father's voice stopped making human sense. Grasping for something tangible to help him focus, he watched Cousin Agra. She looked to be about Kenduu's age, around twenty. Chebucto guessed she was Hutlan by the way she encased her hair in a complicated knot of tethers. The woman chattered happily in a curious blend of words Chebucto recognized as well as many others. She invited them into her small household area on the other side of the cooking arbor. She put some dried fish into a woven basket, scooped some pemmican into a shallow wooden bowl and pushed both in their direction. Gratefully, Chebucto followed his father's lead by dipping a little fish into the fatty pemmican and chewing very slowly.

In the silent Tuudzaado language, Joot attempted to warn his son not to eat much. When Chebucto didn't react to his mental words. Joot whispered, "Remember, you have to let your stomach become used to food again. Wait before you take another bite."

Moments later Chebucto felt a spasm of pain in his midriff. He nearly dropped the tiny bit of fish he held in his hand and forced himself to sit still. Joot said something to their hostess.

She looked from one to the other with dawning comprehension and put the food aside. Speaking slowly in Chebucto's language, she said, "Do you wish to lie down on this bed roll?" She indicated a narrow mat near a lean-to.

Chebucto warmed toward her. He smiled and said "No."

"We've brought you some things from my wife," Joot smiled.

Chebucto had left all his belongings in their bags, belted around his torso always. His father would have done the same, but courtesy to their hostess had required finding the gifts that Mala had tucked into a myriad of empty spaces in his pouches. Not wanting to miss any of the small items, Joot had unpacked nearly everything, enjoying the suspense of discovery as much as his hostess did. As they retired for the night Joot murmured something to Chebucto to explain that it would have been rude to pack in front of their kinswoman.

Chebucto watched his father gather his few belongings into bags.

Each bag was secured to a separate belt of the many that kept his tunic closed and proof against wind and rain. Packing complete, father and son sat for a moment in silence, neither looking at the other. Finally, Chebucto whispered, "Father, how will I know if I can come back home?"

Joot lifted his jaw, somehow calmed by the nervous query. "If you have truly done everything that this medicine man asks, you will receive an answer to that question directly from the Sacred Forces." Joot smiled at his son briefly and tipped his head toward the old medicine man's house. "That is what he said."

Without further words, Joot left his son to wonder how to cope with a man who spoke another language. He didn't waste time, knowing that it would take nearly half the night to reach Chegwet's home farther east along the North Face. He walked quickly, feeling comfortable with the arrangements he had made for Chebucto. *The old man is tough. My son will return sooner than later. He just needs a little help to reach for the right kind of visions.*

When Joot reached Chegwet's house, he coughed politely outside their entryway. Chegwet lived in a stone and sod semi-subterranean house. It was a Tuudzaado style. Joot assumed that Reega built it herself when she and Chegwet married. It was so long before he heard a sound from inside, Joot wondered if they were both gone.

"Greetings, my friend," Reega said. Her odd way of twisting Hutlan words seemed more distorted to him than Mala's accent. When Zaandan and he made arrangements for Lo and Nazu's marriage the previous summer, Joot often wondered if he ever really understood her. Reega crawled out of the entryway. It was too dark to see her well, but in the dim starlight he saw her hand signal for him to sit on one of the mats near the fireplace. She sighed. "Thank you for coming to me. Lately I have heard so much bad news from the Dzagh and the West Face that I fear you have bad news for me as well."

Joot reassured her that his news was very ordinary about his son. "I simply wanted to express my condolences about Lo and her family. I know you were fond of her." Reega wept silently. "She was so kind to me," the Tuudzaado woman said. "Often I didn't understand the local customs. Lo would come to me even when she was a toddler. She always seemed to know exactly what to say to help me understand my younger son and my Hutlan husband. That's such a wonderful gift. I hate the Dotson for robbing us of her!"

After a while Reega recalled that Joot had traveled a long way and made him comfortable in one of their small sleeping quarters. "This is where Ping stays. You can stay here as long as you like."

Joot thanked her, grateful for a comfortable place to stay after such a long trip. "I will leave tomorrow," he assured Reega, and was asleep as soon as his head felt the thick sloth fur. Chebucto was not so lucky. While sleep came suddenly, it didn't come without the visions about yet another stranger.

* * *

A small woman stumbled toward him. Her arms sawed the air and she lost her balance. A line of men chased her. Chebucto tried to pull her out of the way but his legs would not move. Gasping for air he sat up and stared around him. There was no woman, nor were there any men.

Forcing himself to breathe slowly, Chebucto took in details of the strange place, gradually remembering the old medicine man and his father's final words. Chebucto sank back into the furs of his new world, wishing he could talk to his mother about the vision he just had. Very slowly he proceeded with an internal recitation of the vision just as he would have done at home with Mala. When he finished, he asked himself if he was called to the woman in the dream. Nothing happened. Nothing could happen since Chebucto had no idea who she was—or where.

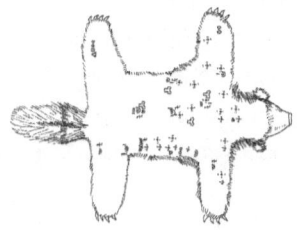

Twelve

Zaandan and the Naan led the way, with Garantu, Kwaiikit and Ping following in single file at a safe enough distance so that any watchers would see two different parties of travelers rather than one large group. Shortly after starting out, Zaandan spotted some caribou and asked if the rest could help him bring one home. After a successfully quick hunt, they divided the meat evenly between them all and continued their way.

They had been traveling for two full days with only one rest stop. Ping was surprised it took so long, since he had crossed the Dzagh several times to deliver messages from his mother's home to Iglan's compound. Iglan's compound was about halfway between Zaandan's compound and the Falls Creek grotto. The distance between his mother's and Iglan's homes was about twice the distance. Most of the time it took him two and a half days to get from one place to the other. During such trips, he rested frequently to eat or drink something, but never long enough to sleep. By contrast on this trip he was relieved when the Naan called a halt. He couldn't believe it when Kwaiikit shook his shoulder to wake him up. The rest of them looked at him with varying expressions of concern. He learned later that while everyone had slept a little, he slept twice as long and might have slept the rest of the day had he been alone. The Naan declared that she would walk beside him the rest of the way and entertained him with humorous stories in both the spoken as well as the silent language. If he failed to laugh, she would find a reason to stop and ask for his assistance in helping her tie a knot or repair something that obviously didn't need any help from him.

Why are you treating me like an invalid? He asked on the third such stop.

The Naan bent over slightly to peer into his eyes and answered calmly, *because of the way your eyes don't look right to me. They are so dark I can't see your pupils, but I can see the uneven way they are emitting this white flare. Can you see it?*

Ping couldn't see anything coming from his own eyes and tried to find some way to end the inquisition, when Zaandan came up behind them and said aloud, "look at the flare coming from my eyes. It should be easier to see."

Ping stared at the man's eyes, realizing for the first time that while Zaandan's eyes were green like those of other Tuudzaado people, he was a lot shorter than any of the rest of them. *Your father must be Hutlan,* he communed. *You have the same look around your chest as my brother does. A little thicker here,* he jabbed Zaandan's rib cage, *than the rest of us are.*

Zaandan raised an eyebrow and commanded, "look at my eyes, not my chest. What do you see?"

"Oh," Ping said with surprise, "it's like a ray of clouds. Odd I've never noticed that before on anyone."

"Everyone has them," the Naan said aloud, "just as you do. The problem today is that the ray from your right eye is short and drifting off to the right, while the ray from the other is like it should be. When we get to Zaandan's compound, I would like you to spend a day with me so that we can be sure you are healthy enough to climb down the north side cliffs without falling."

Ping tried to resist but the effort required too much strength, so he shuffled to his feet and began trudging after Zaandan. When they arrived at the compound, he was grateful to be shown a place where he could sleep, and did so promptly. The Naan woke him twice in the middle of the night to give him something to drink. Each time he swallowed obediently without tasting it or questioning the need to take her potion. When she awakened him at dawn he realized that she had been cradling him all night.

After drinking her potion yet again, he communed, *what is the matter with me? I've never been this ill before.*

Come over here, the Naan asked, *so that I can see your face in the morning sun.* She stared at his eyes, asked him to stand up, stand on one leg, and then asked him to recite the names of all his ancestors in Hutlan.

Ping stood up as directed and smiled. His body no longer felt too sluggish to move. He stood on one leg and continued doing so while reciting his long family history.

Kwaiikit smiled at him and communed, *welcome back to the land of the living. We were all worried about you.*

What happened to me? Ping asked again.

You were struck on the head; sometimes that causes people to want to sleep all the time. If you had, you might not have regained consciousness, the Naan communed. *That's why I kept awakening you. I didn't want you to get caught in the sleep of death as some people call it.*

Ping looked from one face to the other and communed, *thank you.*

"There are some people I'd like you to meet," the Naan said aloud.

Ping looked past her, grinned at Garantu, who had draped her arm around a woman with immensely sad eyes. "This is Jenda, my daughter-in-law. She made your potion," the Naan reached around Garantu to squeeze Jenda's shoulders. "I brought Jenda, her sister, and Kenduu up here after one of the most terrible and widespread series of Dotson massacres in Zana."

Ping regarded the Naan with curiosity while thanking Jenda for making such an effective medicine. The Naan continued to bring people forward, introducing Zaandan's large family one by one. The last person she propelled toward Ping didn't look like any of the others.

"This is my grandson Kenduu." A tall young man stepped forward. Ping knew at once he was not related to either the Naan nor her son, Zaandan. He recognized the distinctive Nightstalker *yeege* or spirit force that swayed above and around Kenduu. "I'm pleased to meet you," he said calmly in Hutlan.

In one quick look he took in the rest of Kenduu's features: taller than any of those present except the Naan, he was surprisingly full chested. His long legs seemed longer than those of any ordinary human. The most unusual detail in Ping's North Face experience was that he could see a living Nightstalker. He had known several, including Var, and while he always saw the Nightstalker *yeege* or spirit force above the grass or boulders in which the men sequestered themselves, he had never seen any in person. He wondered if any of them cheated on their commitment to the Nightstalker lifestyle in the intimacy of marriage. Ostensibly Kat never actually saw her husband, but he had picked up undercurrents of her knowledge of the shape of his hands and legs. Nothing specific or current, but enough to make him wonder.

When he was a little boy, Ping had asked his grandfather Harbingeer why they bothered to hide when anyone could see where they were because of the big spirit shade above them. His grandfather told him that only a few people could see the shades. Most people, including his mother, could not see them. Ping spent the rest of that summer testing others and learning that once again his grandfather was right. His grandfather explained to him that it was thanks to the Nightstalkers that there were so few Dotson on the North Face. Where there were more than one hundred of them in their training camp, Nightstalkers had killed nearly two hundred over the years. Their secret was knowing how to stay hidden even in open plains. They followed and killed their targets often without the victims knowing what had struck them.

"… Harbingeer?" Kenduu's face indicated he was questioning Ping.

Ping had been so distracted by the sight of the Nightstalker *yeege* that he hadn't been listening. "I'm sorry," he apologized, "could you repeat your question?"

Kenduu smiled gently and asked again, "I asked how well you knew your grandfather."

Suddenly caught by the peculiarity of the meeting, Ping stumbled through an answer when looking more carefully at everyone present. His voice drained away while Ping continued to wonder why they were all together. Zaandan cut through his reverie by explaining to everyone that he needed to speak with his friends in private. Jenda and Garantu embraced each other lovingly while Zaandan led the group to a place near the top of the drumlin that formed the west side of his stronghold. The five of them arranged themselves evenly across the western slope. Following the customs of the era, each carefully selected a position that gave him or her a different view from the others. At length Garantu separated from her cousin and joined the others with a sunny smile.

"Our mothers were cousins," she said by way of a casual explanation. She granted Ping an impish wink. Ping smiled hopefully, and she continued, "I haven't seen her in more than seventeen years. I should have come up here years ago; we have a lot of news to learn about each other," she beamed happily toward her father. "Maybe I should stay another day or so."

A nasal hank-hank nuthatch call preceded Kejimkujik's suggestion, *I think your husband and sons might miss you too much if you did so.*

If Kejimkujik had intended the voiceless thought to be a test, Kenduu passed it without any effort. *Who was that?* He communed, his head swiveling as he searched the underbrush for a sixth visitor.

The Naan smiled smugly at Kwaiikit and one by one the others turned toward Kwaiikit for a comment. Kwaiikit communed in the common level of the northern Tuudzaado silent language, since an evening of discussion had proven that neither Zaandan nor Kenduu had learned the high form of the language used by the council. *That, my friend, was Kejimkujik, an honored member of the Dire Wolf Alliance who can understand the communed thoughts of others who are more than two long days of walking from him. Yesterday my cousin revealed information to us that both Ping and our honored guest must learn.* Kwaiikit paused and then tried something he hoped would work. In the ordinary language, he invited Zaandan to repeat his words while in the high language he asked Ping if he would accept the position on the Dire Wolf Alliance secret council that had been empty since his grandfather's death.

Ping had perched on the edge of a solidly placed rock—a lucky choice, since a sudden bout of dizziness nearly sent him rolling down the hill. Hoping his grip on the stone looked casual, or at least covered the sudden quiver his fingers had acquired, he swallowed hard. He concentrated on Zaandan's silent words while he composed his response, and just as Zaandan ended an interminable and incomprehensible speech, he communed in his highest language, *I am honored to accept.*

A light nuthatch hey-hey-hey filled his senses, then he remembered this was Kejimkujik's signal of departure.

Kwaiikit smiled. He quick eyes had taken in the swaying torso and the quivering hand. He communed with a nod toward his cousin, *thank you, my cousin, for once again explaining your painful experience with the Red Sun Warrior. Zaandan, Kenduu and the Naan will work with the Hutlan and Tuudzaado of this part of the Dzagh to explain this new danger to everyone. For all of us, this means the end of Zaandan's many years of dedicated service to Hutlan and Tuudzaado people, but it is not the end of the Dire Wolf Alliance. Friend Ping, can you carry this message to your parents?*

One of Ping's skills was to be able to repeat to himself words spoken or thought simply by directing his attention toward the person or something the person had touched while saying speaking. He knew he could take time afterward to really "hear" what Zaandan had said. *Of course,* he replied with a smile toward Zaandan. *I am sorry this has happened to you. Do my mother or stepfather already know you?*

While Zaandan explained how he knew Ping's family, Ping caught a challenging stare from Kenduu. Wondering if he had offended Kenduu, Ping concentrated on understanding both Zaandan's words about the Red Sun Warrior as well as his last visit to the North Face.

I see, Ping lifted his jaw, *you were one of those who helped arrange the wedding between Lo and Nazu.* He lowered his eyes respectfully. *I hope we find Nazu soon.* A child squalling below them burst the morning air. Kwaiikit announced the end of the meeting, lifted a jaw toward his daughter, and communed generally to the group, *we'll be leaving now. How long will you be staying here, Auntie?*

Another day or two. Shall we go across to visit your Mala before you leave, Garantu?

The long-legged Tuudzaado family made the climb down the side of the drumlin seem like a two-step hop. Before he knew what had happened, Ping was alone on the drumlin with Kenduu and Zaandan. Zaandan stood and smiled ruefully. *I wanted to explain what has happened to my wife, but I see she has joined the others to visit Mala.* He drew in a long breath and added, *I will join them. I also need to speak to my old friend, Joot.*

Ping and Kenduu had both stood up when the others did. Now they turned, shuffled nervously and one by one sank into hunter's squats. They stared toward each other in silence. Ping could feel rage surging from the bigger man. He waited. Finally, Kenduu communed in an odd distortion of the common silent language, *they only met you a day ago. Why did they invite you to be part of the Dire Wolf Alliance?* He looked at Ping from head to foot. *You don't have a dire wolf pelt. I thought that was the way people were accepted into the Alliance.*

Ping stared at the other for a long moment and then answered using the same distortion of mental phrasing. *My grandfather didn't have a dire wolf pelt either,* "but we shouldn't use the silent language out of courtesy to your stepmother. I gathered from the others that she is not to know about this."

Kenduu ogled the other. "What do you mean?" he asked in Hutlan.

"I wasn't feeling well on the way up, so I might be mistaken. Isn't it obvious that we all came up here simply to meet you? The Naan could have talked to your father alone."

"To meet me? It didn't seem like it. No one said anything to me about it."

Ping shrugged and said kindly, "They didn't tell me anything about why all of them came to Falls Creek when I brought them a Black Sun Warrior. You learned about the invitation to me when I did, and that was fairly tricky, wasn't it?"

Kenduu snarled something impolite under his breath and then said in a slightly louder voice, "my father has always said that to be one of the Dire Wolf Alliance, you have to be chosen by a dire wolf pack. That's what happened to him. Dire wolves don't live up here and I probably will never see one."

Ping's eyebrows knotted, his face took on a comical look. Kenduu glanced at his face and chuckled.

"What's so funny?" The eyebrows danced, making an even more comic look.

Kenduu laughed out loud, the sound vibrated along the surrounding hills. His wife, Duna, smiled at him from below. His son shrieked, "Papa!" and made a wild lunge toward the drumlin. Duna swept him into her arms and waved at Kenduu before carrying the little boy to their sleeping area. Kenduu turned toward Ping with a calm smile and shook his head. "They couldn't have all come up here merely to see me and leave without saying anything. It doesn't make any sense."

Ping smiled. "They didn't say anything to me when they had a chance. I think they all needed to talk to each other before asking me to join them. That's what my grandfather told me once. He said the Sacred Forces created the Dire Wolf Alliance, but didn't choose the humans whom the wolves choose. It was a convenience, since four of the original six had wolf packs. The Dire Wolf Alliance secret council is different, they were brought together by the Sacred Forces. Once they met, they found out that each of them had the power to see each other's *yeege*. He told me there were only six people who had the power to see his *yeege* or spirit force, and I was one of them. Do you see mine?" Ping asked.

Kenduu looked at the side of Ping's head and responded, "if you mean the marten, yes. I see it. It's so big everyone can see it."

Ping's smile widened. "No. Not even my mother can see it, but Kwaiikit can. So, can the Naan, Blueberry, and now you. If Kejimkujik were here, I'm sure he would see it too. My grandfather said that there are two kinds of Dire Wolf Alliance members. Some are like your father who are dedicated to helping Zana. Others were chosen by the Sacred Forces. He called that the Dire Wolf Alliance secret council. Most of the people in the first group do not know of the existence of the second. Zaandan does because of his mother. If he had the power, he would be on the Dire Wolf Alliance secret council—but he doesn't have it."

Kenduu gazed off into the distance as if transfixed. Finally, he turned toward Ping and asked, "You named five people who can see your spirit marten," murmured Kenduu. "Who is the sixth person?"

Ping frowned. "He's dead now. The Nightstalker Var of the West Face."

"Nightstalker?" Kenduu twisted the word oddly. "My first father was a Nightstalker. He got killed when I was three years old."

A nuthatch called softly from a place between Kenduu and Ping. Both men started. *It's time to ask you,* Kejimkujik communed in the highest language, *in the mental presence of the entire Dire Wolf Alliance secret council, young Kenduu will you join our group?*

Kenduu gaped at Ping. Ping smiled calmly. *Do you understand the language this way too?* He asked.

Yes, responded Kenduu, *and yes,* he added in the high language, *I, too, am honored to join the secret council of the Dire Wolf Alliance.*

In quick succession, the two young men heard first the nuthatch, then saw two dire wolf spirits and lastly the typical hazy flare of blueberry *yeege*. The silence that followed seemed so loud that Ping's ears rang with pain. Kenduu rocked on his heels.

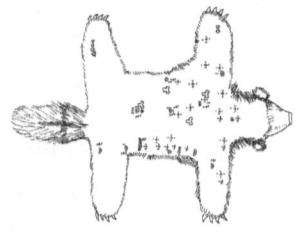

Thirteen

Chebucto's world centered on the old medicine man. He quickly learned the nuances of the new language, discovering that he simply needed to pronounce words differently. He didn't have a hunting dream but he did dream about the old medicine man. In those dreams the medicine man spoke to him, telling him things that Chebucto wanted to know. When he awoke, however, he couldn't remember any of what the old medicine man had said. Despite his failure to have a hunting dream, Chebucto found that hunting for small game off the alluvial plain was much easier than hunting on the glacial moraine where he grew up. Every day he brought back meat to the old medicine man and his gentle granddaughter. Every day he awoke glad that to see the sun shining instead of cloud cover, worried that his father might have got caught in a flood-bearing storm. He estimated his father would be safely home by the sixth day of the Lone Wolf Moon. Chebucto wished that he believed in the Sacred Forces enough to offer a prayer of hope. Instead, he spent a large portion of each day with the old medicine man who talked endlessly about the Sacred Forces much as his father always did. Chebucto soon developed an ear for the exact moment that he could shut out the old man's words and allow himself to dream about…

Snap!

The old medicine man had slapped the mat beside him with a dry stick. "You never listen," the old man growled. "The Sacred Forces have sent you many gifts which you do not acknowledge and do not understand. If you do not wish to be here, it is time for you to leave."

Chebucto stared at the old medicine man in shock. "What?"

The old medicine man turned away from him. "You heard the words. You understand the meaning. Go. Do not return."

Chebucto sat very still, hoping that the old medicine man would turn, laugh it off, and ask for more meat. Instead, the old medicine man kept his back toward Chebucto and maintained a solid wall of exclusion until Chebucto got to his knees. He looked about for the things that were his own. It wasn't much. Soon he found himself standing bewildered and alone outside the old medicine man's small abode. Chebucto wandered to Cousin Agra's household area.

She looked up at him with calm eyes. "He told you, then," she said. "I'm sorry we have been of no help to your father." She smiled and pushed a heaping wooden bowl toward him.

"You should eat this before you go." She helped him retie some of his tethers after he had eaten. Chebucto smiled hopefully, but she refused to meet his eyes. As he walked away, he thought he heard her voice.

"Beware of Three-fingered Lake."

Chebucto whirled around, not sure what she meant. His kinswoman was gone.

Nine short days had elapsed since he left home in the Dzagh. Now Chebucto didn't know where to turn. He couldn't go back home, at least not yet. He didn't know how to face his father. Chebucto had been satisfied with his hunting success even though he had only caught small animals and birds as always. He decided to go hunting and then think about what to do. He discovered a covey of ruffed grouse; before long Chebucto had three of them tied to his hunting belt. He walked to the area that had proven fruitful in the past several days, this time looking for a potential sleeping shelter. He ventured upland and found a quiet promontory and tucked himself into a shady spot to doze off.

Distant voices awoke him. As he looked around for the source, the sound escalated to a wailing scream followed by what sounded like low growls coming from multiple throats. Chebucto kept himself hidden while he peered around. Before long he saw them. A small woman was stumbling along the very trail he had used to climb to the promontory. He thought she was Hutlan from the way she used tethers to bind her hair against her head. Her arms were flailing as she tried to maintain her balance. He stood up to help her but stopped when he saw the line of men behind her. A sick feeling overpowered Chebucto. He sank to his knees because his legs no longer had the strength to hold him upright. He recognized her as the woman of his vision. His mother's voice echoed in his mind as he watched.

What keeps you from going to her?

Filled with mixed dread, fear and self-loathing, he watched as the men overpowered the woman. They circled her fallen body, kicking her as if to evoke more screams. Once she fell, however, the woman stopped making any sound at all. They, however, continued the odd noise they had been making. It was a frightening sound, a wordless chant. The Hutlan woman seemed to be beyond terror, she stared upward toward his promontory, her eyes bulging a bit from her face. Chebucto thought she could see him but then decided her eyes stared at something well beyond human awareness. One of the men sliced through the tethers around her waist. Her tunic, slick with blood, stuck to her skin except in one place, exposing her hips and belly.

A shudder flowed across Chebucto's shoulders. Something about the exposed areas seemed to rise toward him so that Chebucto could see details that he couldn't have seen unless he was touching her. The enlargement revealed jutting ribs and hip bones. The woman was so thin, Chebucto wondered automatically if she were married. A husband should have provided enough food for her. Suddenly aware that such a husband would also have wanted to protect her, Chebucto's heart pressed so hard against his own lean ribs that he could not breathe. He found himself praying to the Sacred Forces to help the stranger. Slowly he became aware of an odd tingle in his right leg near the foot; it crept up his leg. Father said that's the way the Sacred Forces acknowledge a prayer—with tingles from the earth. Hope streamed through him—without cause, however. After circling her for what seemed to be an eternity, one of the men lifted a large rock and struck her on the head. Blood splattered everywhere. Smelling it, Chebucto sagged back into the shadows. Although he was too far away for the blood to reach him he wiped away imagined traces.

You must not worry, a vaporous thought filled the air around him. *She felt nothing and has entered the First Walk of Death without fear. Your prayer helped her to do so.* Dully, Chebucto looked around for the source of the calm words and nearly gagged when he saw bright, black eyes staring at him from the edge of the promontory. He tried to get up but the bones in his legs remained as shapeless as water.

The stranger lifted his chin and held out a hand as if to invite Chebucto to sit. Chebucto could do little else, so he stayed where he was.

"Your first time?" the stranger asked.

"What?"

"Was that the first time seeing someone die like that?" the stranger clarified his query.

Chebucto stared stupidly at the man, then the meaning of his words came to him a little at a time. "Yes. No. I mean…"

The stranger settled into a hunter's squat beside him, looking at Chebucto more closely. "You're not from here, are you?"

"No." Thought ended abruptly at the edge of the word. Bit by bit Chebucto comprehended that the stranger had a single braid hanging from the nape of his neck. *Hutlan?* Chebucto clung to the thought while his eyes took in the length of the man's fingers. They were nearly half again as long as his own and probably twice the length of his father's. Tuudzaado fingers.

"Try breathing more slowly," the stranger said in a kindly tone. "That always helps." He waited until Chebucto's breath became even. "There, you'll feel better in a moment." The stranger shifted his weight so that he could see over the edge. Chebucto heard a moan that sounded like "go home," or "show me." The stranger sagged back onto the ledge.

"What's your name?" the stranger asked. He shifted his weight over his heels to retie a moccasin. When he glanced up, Chebucto felt captured as if in a dream. Chebucto watched the man adjust ties on his leggings. Chebucto wondered why he bothered with an ankle guard, since he tied everything to his bare ankle and then put the ankle guard into place with a pair of long straps. Mala always insisted that he put the ankle guard under his moccasin straps. He caught the man staring at him quizzically.

"I asked about your name," the stranger said with a smile. His skin looked dark in the shadow, but Chebucto's mind finally registered the reddish Tuudzaado skin color.

"My name?" Chebucto responded, knowing that he should be able to answer that question. "Oh, I'm Chebucto."

"And I'm Ping." *Do you understand me the silent way? Do you?*

Chebucto understood Ping but was paralyzed with shock. Until that moment, he had never used the silent language with anyone but his mother, Jenda and Zaandan. He thought the word "yes," but failed to use the peculiar mental twists of the silent language so none of it reached Ping.

Ping looked at him suspiciously and suddenly looked very weary. "I suppose you've never learned the Tuudzaado language. My brother doesn't even bother to try. Maybe it's harder for people who are only partially Tuudzaado."

No. I have learned. I didn't know what to say. Again, he forgot to use his mind correctly and nothing happened. "I'm not very good at it like my mother and Aunt Jenda are." Chebucto cleared his throat. "Have you been here all the time? Why didn't I see you when I came up?"

"You got up here before I did. I, uh, I knew they were coming," Ping tipped his head toward the edge of the promontory, "It's one of my favorite places to rest and take a bigger look at the world." Ping waved a hand toward the bright yellow sky. "Today I needed a different way to see things. That's when I saw you. You were asleep so I stayed on that side of the clearing to let you have peace."

Chebucto studied Ping carefully. Nothing much gets by him, I'm sure. Ping's eyes were deeply set into his face. Ringed by thick lashes, it was hard to see them, but when he looked straight at Chebucto, there was a piercing look to them. Like a fox, thought Chebucto. His eyes move like a fox's. He seemed older than Chebucto, but not by much.

"How old are you?" Chebucto blurted.

"Me?" Ping smiled at his companion. The lip movement removed clouds Chebucto hadn't noticed before. "I haven't been asked that in a while. Let me think." He dropped his head to his chest and pretended to consider the question for a while. Then Ping looked at Chebucto with a wry face. "I'm twenty-four, I believe. Rather old, don't you think?"

"Yes. I mean, no. I thought you were younger. My uncle adopted a boy who is twenty now, Kenduu. He was little when my uncle took him in. That was before I was born. I always think Kenduu is old, but he's really not." Chebucto smiled, relieved when he found he could move both of his legs again.

"And where is this ancient Kenduu?" Ping asked in a gently teasing tone.

"Back home," Chebucto answered, tipping his head toward the south. "In the Dzagh across the alluvial plain."

Ping had such a soothing manner that Chebucto found himself answering question after question about his life in the Dzagh without a thought about the woman whose life had been taken so brutally below. Then he saw a buzzard circling overhead and memory returned.

"Why did they kill her?" he asked.

Ping looked toward the ledge. He glanced at Chebucto and just as quickly averted his eyes. Chebucto thought he saw the glint of tears but nothing about the face seemed sad.

"Mysfet betrayed her family; because of her twelve people died in a massacre," Ping said after a lengthy pause.

Chebucto stared open mouthed, waiting for Ping to add more. The other man said nothing. Chebucto whispered, "There was a massacre in the Dzagh a few days ago. Is that the one you mean?"

Ping sighed. "Do you know Iglan's family, then?"

"Yes," Chebucto answered. "I met him a few times; my father knew them well. How did she betray them from way down here?"

"Mysfet helped a Dotson man go after them. He must have arranged for the other Dotson to find them. Were you there?"

"No. My father got there after it happened. He told us about it." Mala's criticism that Chebucto never tried to help the people in his visions spun in his mind. He should've gone to the young woman. Nazu would have done so. Angry with himself, he muttered, "I'd better go" and pulled himself stiffly to his feet.

"Go where?" Ping asked quietly. "You've been banished from your parents' home as well as from the old medicine man's house. As I understand it, you have no place to go."

Chebucto looked down at Ping, who was still squatting. "I can manage on my own. Other people have. It's time for me to go back to the Dzagh."

"You won't get there tonight," Ping said, standing up in a single, fluid motion. "Come. There's plenty of room where I live. You can meet my mother."

Chebucto stared at him. "No, but thank you. I'll stay here for the night."

"Nonsense," Ping said. "You must join me. My mother could use your help."

Instead of waiting for an answer, the man gestured with a tilt of his head and turned away. A series of emotions sliced through to Chebucto. All but one refused to leave: fear. Fear colors the skin, exudes foul odors, and stops the mind from working. A distant, uninvolved part of Chebucto's mind observed these reactions and did nothing. Chebucto's feet seemed weighted with a thousand stones. Ping was nearly out of sight when Chebucto's legs began to move after him. Chebucto remained unable to focus on a single cohesive idea; in that unwary condition, he simply walked. Ping stopped at a quiet place near the edge of a compound. A stranger waited for him there. Eventually Chebucto realized he might be intruding and turned to go.

"Stay," Ping stopped him with a reassuring touch, "I'll be with you in a moment."

The "moment" lasted quite a while. Chebucto kept himself occupied by rehearsing a greeting for Ping's mother. Eventually they reached her home. His mother was a tall woman with hair tightly bound in the Hutlan way. Ping introduced her as Reega.

"Whom have you brought with you?" Reega spoke aloud.

"This is Chebucto, he is from the Dzagh." Ping stunned Chebucto by providing a full and cohesive account of Chebucto's ancestry and accomplishments. Chebucto had never volunteered so much information, and he had never heard his mother mention anyone named Garantu. "He needs a place to stay for a while. Can you offer him help?"

Before she could answer Chebucto opened dry lips but didn't speak aloud. Instead he plowed through a series of brain-twisting leaps and turns to accomplish the greeting he had practiced. Mother and son stared at Chebucto for such a long time he knew he had got it wrong. He was about to try it again when Reega smiled and responded with a much shorter phrase.

That must be something your mother taught you to say to your uncle Zaandan, Reega added. *It's an old form of our language. I can tell how much you respect your mother, as you did that well. I try to teach my other son, but he isn't like* you. Reega waited for a response.

Chebucto smiled tentatively and lifted his chin. Reega lips parted in another stiff smile. *Normally you should use this phrase only for a man—not a woman—whom you know has proven medicine power.* She repeated a small portion of the greeting Chebucto had used. *That's how I know you have been taught to use this with your uncle.*

Relief washed over Chebucto. He tipped his chin again, remembering the morning he first stumbled through the long silent speech with Zaandan.

Since you don't know anything about me yet and probably little about my son, you should commune such a greeting like this. She communed an example and continued. *To greet me or another medicine woman, you should say it this way.* She communed a different phrase. Chebucto attended to her version and tried it himself, suddenly free of embarrassment.

Excellent! Ping slapped him on the back. *I thought you didn't understand me before. You must not practice the silent language with many people. Am I right?*

Chebucto tipped his chin upward and formulated a silent answer. *Only Mother communes with me. Aunt Jenda and the other Tuudzaado people around the Dzagh talk to each other this way but never to me. I think they all assume that a half Tuudzaado can't commune. I think it's true of some of us.* His mind lingered on Keyo for so long he didn't realize Reega was addressing him until he understood his father's name in the silent language.

Your father said you were going to be with the old medicine man for a while.

Chebucto hung his head but said nothing.

Reega stared at the spiky points of Chebucto's hair and tipped her chin upward.

Aloud Reega said, "you'll meet my husband and my other son in a while. This is where you can stay." She showed him a small enclosure made of stone with sticks and mud wattle holding everything together. Turning to Ping, she said, "I see you have something there. Is it for me?" She glanced at her son through half closed eyes.

Ping dropped a bulging hunting bag onto the mat beside her. She quickly examined the contents and looked up. "It's good. Will you stay while I cook it?"

Just at that moment Chebucto recalled the three grouse he had killed and offered them as well. She smiled and put them with the Ping's bag. Ping excused himself and disappeared. Chebucto offered to help Reega prepare the meal. After a while, the familiar tasks of cutting strips of meat and roots and wrapping them with leaves and sheaves of grass calmed Chebucto's worries. He told Reega what the old medicine man had said before sending him away.

"Ah," she murmured but said no more.

Chebucto felt his shoulders relax when she didn't offer any advice. After a while Ping returned with two men. Reega introduced them as Chegwet and Yon, her younger son. Chebucto and Yon stared at each other with open curiosity. By the time Reega pulled the savory meats from the roasting pit, Chebucto's youthful appetite was fully restored. He devoured nearly half the food without realizing the others were eyeing him with expressions varying from Ping's humor to Yon's irritation. Fortunately, there was more than enough for the five of them. After they ate Ping disappeared with Yon and Chegwet, leaving Chebucto to help Reega clean the cooking area.

"I'm sorry I ate so much," Chebucto said in a subdued tone. "I didn't eat much at the old medicine man's house. I wasn't hungry there. I don't know what happened to me."

Reega folded some roots into a woven mat and inserted them into a storage area. When Chegwet offered to make her a house, she had chosen a home site along the bordering alluvial plain where she knew the ice was close to the surface at a convenient distance from the house itself. Roots and meats froze quickly in her storage pits.

"Do not be concerned," Reega murmured. "You were afraid of him. He is the greatest medicine man in the area." Reega stretched her lips into a thin smile. "Sometimes he frightens me." In the silent language she communed, *I always use a phrase like the one you did whenever I see him.*

Reega busied herself with household tasks while Chebucto watched and tried to help. After a while she sent him away, so Chebucto made himself comfortable in the small space she had allotted him. His mind immediately returned to his biggest problem: what was he to do now that he had been banished twice? He contemplated some of the caves he knew in the Dzagh. Perhaps the best thing to do is to go back there and live on my own.

"Why don't you stay here for a while?" Reega stood outside the tiny structure and spoke aloud. Chebucto wondered if she had been heating his thoughts and didn't answer at first. She repeated her invitation.

Finally, Chebucto said, "Do you really mean that? I won't eat as much. I'm good at hunting for small game. I'll do whatever you tell me to do." Words tumbled out of his mouth.

Reega's was not adept at laughing. The sound she produced was more of a squawk than a chuckle, but Chebucto understood. He smiled timidly.

"You can stay as long as you work as hard as I do," Reega said calmly. "Perhaps one day the old medicine man will let you try again. I know your father would want you to do that."

Chebucto sighed, feeling relief flood his body thanks again to Ping's mother. *Thank you,* he communed. Chebucto fell asleep before Ping and the others returned to their household.

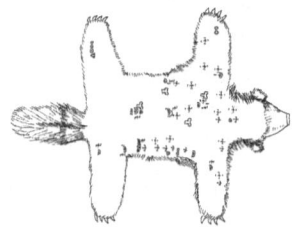

Fourteen

I*'ll find Kwaiikit. He will help us.*

We don't have much time. Black Sun Day is not very far away.

Chebucto rolled over, comforted by his mother's incessant silent chatter with Jenda. Their silent conversations had flowed across his mind since before his birth. When he was very small he had tried to make sense of them but eventually realized doing so was nearly impossible. A sharp stone cut through the lynx fur, awakening him enough to remember that his lynx fur was back at his home in the Dzagh. The fur Reega lent him was the badly worn pelt of a giant beaver. He felt his skin where a sharp stone had scratched his skin, although his nose already told him the blood was minimal.

Son, he didn't have a scar. I saw him several times.

Startled, Chebucto tried to respond to his mother's words, but in his sleepy state he couldn't remember how to do it.

From the left side of his hairline to between the eyebrows, Mother. I saw it.

Chebucto froze and then slowly relaxed. *That must be Ping,* he mused, then mentally muffled himself in the odd way he had learned to do before the age of two. His mother and Aunt Jenda, each on different sides of the ravine, had slapped little Chebucto sharply with mental probes. The sting had been painful. Whenever he was physically close enough, Zaandan always swathed toddler Chebucto in a mental cocoon. Inside the cocoon, Zaandan communed, *Stay this way. They won't hurt you if you stay this way.* It had taken a few more harsh mental slaps from Mala and Jenda before little Chebucto perfected the art. He often wondered why Zaandan had not taught the same skill to Keyo. Maybe Jenda was worse than his mother. Maybe she avoided doing such painful things to her son when Zaandan was home. Keyo had learned to loathe the mental language and Chebucto didn't.

Knowing he was being rude, Chebucto tried to understand what the mother and son were communing so rapidly to each other but soon the effort became too much and he drifted back to sleep.

Two nights after the strange silent conversation Chebucto awoke. Sweat bathed his upper chest and back. He gasped for air as if he had been running but his legs were trapped by enormous jaws. He looked over his shoulder. He saw the face of the man who killed Iglan.

The face had no scar. The man's arms were raised, holding a club. Chebucto made a superhuman effort to get out of the way and hit his head on the cold stones of his lean-to. Pulling the thin beaver hide around his shoulders, Chebucto sniffed the surrounding area carefully to make sure there were no strangers. A little at a time memory flowed into his mind and Chebucto remembered he now lived on the North Face. He caught a glimpse of the moon through the opening at the front of the lean-to. The moon was nearly at full. He sighed. This was his seventh night in his new home. Slowly trusting his senses, he allowed himself to rearrange the big beaver hide and fall asleep again.

* * *

"I get it," Deloo muttered under her breath, "some of us get more of one side than the other. Maybe not knowing anything about my dad's side made both me and Mom look only at the Athabascan in me. That still doesn't explain everything, though." Suddenly remembering her silent voice, she communed to me, *Right, Baasee'?*

Some of your gifts came from your father, my dear. Your mother has told you she never learned to climb trees like you, I, the Masterful Outdoors Spirit Guide Baasee' replied with a peek at Grandfather Kwaiikit. *I apologize, Grandfather, for my mortal's rude interruption; please continue your fabulous story.*

But, wait, there's something I don't understand. How could Chebucto see a face when he was awake. I thought visions only came when people are asleep.

You're right about the changes going on in Chebucto, Mortal, Grandfather Kwaiikit supplied calmly, *his power over visions is starting to grow here. Some of it has to do with his motivation. Seeing that woman get killed shocked him as much as the old medicine man's rejection. He's growing into his power because of need than because of his parentage.*

* * *

The following night, Chebucto was admiring the light of the full Lone Wolf Moon when Ping appeared out of nowhere. For the first time since they had met, Ping appeared to be irritable. He huddled with his mother for a long while before turning to Chebucto.

"I saw you at Three-Fingered Lake today," he said, voice clipped.

Puzzled, Chebucto relived his day and replied peaceably, "I was there but I didn't see you. Why didn't you call out to me?"

Ping stared at Chebucto in silence for an endless moment. Chebucto, confused about his friend's strange attitude, was about to ask more when Ping turned on his heel and walked away without another word. Chebucto stared after him and then turned toward Reega. "Did I do something wrong?" he asked.

Ping's mother frowned pensively but didn't reply.

"He seemed angry with me," Chebucto pressed, "do you know why?"

She kept her face down and murmured something in a low voice.

He moved closer. "I'm sorry. Could you say that again? I thought you said something about Dotson."

The woman sighed and looked at her guest. "They don't like anyone to go near the Three-Finger Lake. It's where they meet. I think the time has come for you to leave, you'd better go tonight."

"What?!? Why?"

She sighed and indicated with a hand for him to move into the shadows beside her. "Don't speak. They might be watching."

Chebucto gaped at her. He was now sitting so close to her he could smell the deer fat from the hide she was tanning. A tremble vibrated the air between them.

"My son has learned…" She stopped.

Chebucto waited, tingling with mixed anticipation and dread.

"He said there might be a death run tonight. You've got to leave now!"

In the shocked silence that followed her statement, Chebucto heard a sound in the distance. It was an almost rhythmic tone that might have been thunder, but in a moment, he recognized it: a chant he had heard in the distance every night he had been in Reega's household. It sounded a little like the one used by the Dotson on the day he met Ping.

The woman nudged him. "Go!"

Chebucto was out of her household area before he realized he had moved. He paused to pinpoint the direction of the chanting as well as to conjure up his newly acquired knowledge of the surrounding area. He rejected the first few hiding places he recalled when an image of an oddly shaped rock formation appeared in his mind. Like any hunter of the Dzagh he could run in the dark, but tonight he was glad for the pale light of the full moon. Using all his senses, he plotted his course without effort. He reached the leaning boulder that had served him as a direction marker during the past few days. He stopped briefly to listen. He no longer heard the chanting but he felt a nameless urgency to run—and did. When his feet encountered a rivulet of water that had not been there a few days before, Chebucto's thoughts seemed to explode into meaningless shards. As always, he remained in fear of the fabled glacial floods. Forcing himself into a state of calm, he squatted beside the narrow stream of water and watched it twinkle in the moonlight. A memory of his father explaining the horrors of flooding on the northern plain presented itself.

"Sometimes you have no warning but vibration in the ground beneath your feet. If you are lucky, it will be a herd of peccaries, no matter what, pray that the waters go in another direction. The old people say that there was a flood once that filled the whole northern plain, but that hasn't happened for a long time. Most of the floods are quick, thick with rocks, mud, dead plants, animals, and ice. They don't have a fixed course like the stream in our ravine. They go wherever the ice is pushing. Most of them appear out of nowhere, stay for a day or so and then disappear. Others happen like the floods in our ravine. The ravine fills without warning, killing anything that happens to stay in the vicinity. We are lucky that the sides of our ravine are so hard and high. There are only two ravines on the North Face, both near the edge of the glacier." Joot's voice faded in Chebucto's mind, and with it his sense of panic. Chebucto breathed a sigh of relief. This must be one of the small floods and this water will take away my scent if I walk in it. He made his way in the streambed for a while before turning toward the far side.

Thank you! He communed generally and stepped toward the water's edge.

No. Go farther, came an unidentified instruction. Chebucto didn't question it. He kept stumbling and splashing along the unexpected creek bed, musing on his changing attitudes about the source of the perplexing thoughts that came to him in this way. Two or three moons ago a much younger Chebucto would have refused to follow the advice, stubbornly sure such ideas came from his mother, now he welcomed it with eager obedience.

Thank you for covering my scent, he thought again, wondering distractedly if he addressed the rivulet, the old medicine man or Ping. *Maybe they won't find me.* When he reached the rock formation, he fumbled for the place he had explored a few days earlier. Two craggy stones at the base of the formation hid a series of flattish rocks that led to its summit. He knew by the pungent smell of cat urine about halfway up that no other creature than some kind of feline had ever used it. He reached the top and pressed himself into a narrow space between two rocks. From that position, he could listen for the death runners. At first, he heard nothing but the harsh rasping of his own breath and the racket of his wildly pounding heart. He forced himself to take slow, even breaths. It took a while before his heartbeat slowed. Finally, he could hear beyond the edges of his body. At first there was nothing but the gentle sounds of insects and bats. Then he heard the chanting again, he could tell they had reached the stream because the tone of their chanting changed. The new sounds arranged themselves into words.

"Other-side-other-side-other-side." These were answered by "Nothing-here-nothing-here-nothing-here." The second set seemed to be moving toward him. He hoped he had stayed in the stream long enough. If not, it would take them no time to find the rock steps to his hiding place. In rising panic, he edged out from between the two rocks in order to make his way back down to the bottom. He didn't know where he might run, but his legs insisted on flight.

"Go-back-go-back-go-back."

At first, he thought the rhythmic words were in his skittering mind. He fought the urge to move and stopped to listen again.

"Up stream-up-stream-up-stream," he heard them chant.

By the decreasing level of sound, Chebucto realized with tenta-tive relief that the death runners had turned around and were searching in another direction. He settled back into his hiding place. There was nowhere else to run, anyway. He strained his eyes to look for them. By the sound of the chanting, the death runners were not very far away. They moved steadily upstream and away from him. Then his heart stopped beating when he spotted a flicker of movement somewhere to his left. Clouds moving rapidly in the night sky darkened the place he thought he had seen it. He stared at the spot, hoping for another shaft of moonlight.

Just enough light filtered through a break in the clouds to reveal the outline of a man. Chebucto stared in horror. The man stood still, appar-ently not concerned if he could be seen. His back was toward Chebucto. Hutlan? The wind was blowing in the wrong direction to bring Chebucto his scent. Chebucto hoped the wind was equally kind to himself. The man turned his head just as a bright ray of moonlight bathed his face. All Chebucto could see was a quarter of the man's profile and the short, stiff shape of a Dotson braid. Not enough to form a complete picture, but enough so that he imagined he recognized him as the man in his visions—the man who had killed Iglan. Chebucto felt a sudden, inexplicable urge to shout but fortunately something seemed to seize his throat. Then clouds moved in again, this time they were so thick he couldn't see the man at all. Chebucto widened his nostrils as much as possible, hoping that a vapor might tell him more. He waited, but neither wind nor moon helped him any further. In a while the sounds of the death runner's chanting faded and disappeared completely. Chebucto waited until night was in its final quarter before moving. By that time he had formulated a plan. In absolute silence, he retraced the path that led to the stream.

Without stopping, he entered the rivulet and continued walking through the cold glacial water until he passed the place the Dotson death runners had made their final crossing. Chebucto kept walking in the stream until dawn. By the time the morning sun was warm enough, he dragged his numbing legs out of the water. He walked steadily until he reached his destination.

* * *

Baasee', Baasee', Deloo commune-shouted, *was that Dotson man Rastuk? Was he the guy who murdered the groom earlier in the story?*

Deloo, Grandfather and I are happy you are excited about the story. Let Grandfather finish it before you interrupt that way, I chided in my usual superior spirit guide fashion and nodded sweetly to my grandfather.

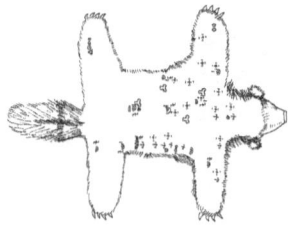

Fifteen

"**P**lease, Uncle," he pleaded, "I beg you to teach me to have a hunting vision."

"Stay out." The old medicine man's steady voice stopped Chebucto as harshly as if it had been the screech of a giant night hawk, Zana's most feared nocturnal bird. Chebucto hesitated, hardening himself against the hollowness of his chest.

"I will do everything as you say this time, Uncle," Chebucto called, his voice more of a whisper. In the chilly silence, Chebucto explained what had happened to him. "His name was Ping," he let his voice trail away, sure that the old medicine man was not listening.

"Then what happened?"

Chebucto whirled around. It was Cousin Agra. He attempted a smile, but his lips quivered so much they couldn't hold a shape. The young woman dimpled and lifted a finger to her own steady smile. She pointed at the door and motioned for Chebucto to stay where he was. Chebucto shuffled awkwardly, shoulders slumping. "The death runners followed me for a long way. Then I saw the man who killed Iglan. I knew him from the vision. I am sorry for not paying attention before."

Chebucto wavered, then took a deep breath and while his voice continued begging the old medicine man for mercy. The old medicine man remained silent. Eventually Agra told him to go hunting and pointed to an uncomfortable place on the outside perimeter of the compound that was sheltered from the wind and rain, but not inside the old medicine man's domain. Later that day, Chebucto brought Cousin Agra a brace of five grouse. She traded them for a bundle of dry meat and a bone awl.

Chebucto smiled at the awl. He had been worried about the one he brought from home, as lately it seemed to give a little when he used it to poke holes in his hides. Chebucto's tunics were layered, with the one under all of them being the oldest and thinnest. Before leaving the Dzagh, he had taken all the scraps of hide he could find in his mother's discard pile and wound them around his innermost tunic to use as the need arose. One of the most pressing needs was to cut more moccasins as the constant walking over the stony alluvial plain had ruined three of his existing pieces of footgear. Like all people, male or female, of his era, Chebucto was adept at cutting hides to the right pattern shape for his feet and weaving long strips of narrow hide through the small holes made by an awl to strap the parts together. Making a new moccasin took very little time as long as there was enough deer hide available to make it. Chebucto checked those remaining, and realized that he would need new deer hide in less than a moon. He wondered how much grouse his kinswoman would take for a big piece of deer hide—if she had any available. With considerable consternation Chebucto realized how much he had depended on his father's hunting ability to supply him with moccasins.

Chebucto went to the old medicine man's door and asked again for forgiveness. He heard a cough but no words. After dark fell, Chebucto left the side of the old man's house to find the space allotted to him.

* * *

A dark shape separated itself from the blackness around it—A man, familiar in some way. Chebucto sniffed for scent, stunned to detect nothing in the environs. Loss of the sense of smell meant death in Zana. Chebucto jerked awake, breathing hard. He stared into the darkness but saw nothing. Eventually his nostrils took in the familiar smells of charcoal from the fire pit.

An opossum wandered close by, and Chebucto eased himself into a squat. Loosening his bola, he listened for the soft scrabbling sound of the clawed feet, pleased to hear them just at the place he knew they would arrive. By the light of the moon he began swinging one end of the bola in preparation. As if sleepwalking, the opossum moved toward Chebucto. When it was within two arm's lengths, Chebucto propelled the hide and stone weapon in a perfectly shaped arc. The opossum squealed when the stones swirled around it, but the creature's shock was brief. Chebucto followed the bola with a swift blow to its head.

Chebucto took the dead animal to Agra's fire place to look for a wooden bowl or trough. She had heard the commotion and emerged from her sleeping quarters just as he reached her cooking area.

In a low, sleepy voice she asked, "Do you want to cook it now or trade it for something?"

"Do you have any hides for moccasins?"

"Mmmm. That's too much. I'll cook it for him and share the blood with you now."

Chebucto thought about the exchange. It seemed very fair to him. The blood was the best part of a small kill like the opossum. "Why not give him the blood, too?" he asked.

Agra thought about it and said, "He needs to sleep."

Without wasting more time, she made a couple of deft cuts around the neck and handed the opossum to Chebucto. He held the rodent so that its blood drained into a large wooden bowl. In a little while she handed him a second bowl and took the carcass from him to store in her work area. Chebucto poured some of the blood into the second bowl and left the majority for her. When she returned, he lifted his bowl toward her and waited for her to do the same.

"May the Sacred Forces protect the *yeege* of the opossum," she murmured. Together they drank deeply of the warm liquid. When he finished, Chebucto handed her his bowl and returned to his sleeping area. He heard her moving quietly in the cooking area, but didn't return to help. By the rules of Zanian household trade agreements, the opossum no longer belonged to him but to her. When his granddaughter offered the cooked rodent to the old medicine man in the morning, it would be her gift to him and not Chebucto's. Chebucto smiled. His father would be proud of him for figuring all that out by himself instead of waiting for the usual quick rap on the head and a not-so-gentle reminder of how to be courteous.

Chebucto wriggled until he found the least uncomfortable position. It wasn't cold—yet, but in another moon, he would need a fur or two to keep out the chill. As sleep tugged at his awareness, he wondered who the man had been in his dream. A hazy sense of seeing a zigzag nearly jarred him into wakefulness but failed. Chebucto slept until dawn.

A couple of days passed in the same way. Chebucto would start the day with by waiting outside the old medicine man's private domicile. When first quarter crossed to the second, he would go hunting for small game. In the late afternoon of the nineteenth day of the Lone Wolf Moon he returned with one game bag filled with prairie hens and another with a wild turkey. These he traded to Agra for small, precious items: a waterproof bag made from the carefully cleaned and tightly sealed stomach of the opossum he had killed, a tightly rolled coil of dried grass that he would use to tie things into bundles, a small pouch filled with opossum fat, and a meal of dried meat and mustelid fat served on a wooden platter.

When he finished eating, he went to the old medicine man's doorway and again got no response. As before, Chebucto settled outside the doorway until dark, then went to his sleeping area when darkness fell. His eyes flew open when he heard voices. Taking careful stock of his surroundings without moving his body, Chebucto realized the words were in his mind rather than in the air around him. He closed his eyes to concentrate.

A man squatted beside another who stood. The squatting man said aloud, *He is the son of an ordinary man.* The standing man moved a short distance. The squatting man turned so that Chebucto saw the zigzag scar on his face. Then the standing man turned. He was younger and Chebucto thought he looked like the Dotson man who had killed Iglan.

The vision faded. *Am I the son of the ordinary man?* He wondered. Chebucto sat up and stared at the moon for a while, hoping for more but nothing happened. Finally, he settled down and slept until he felt the light of dawn on his eyes.

* * *

Joot hesitated before entering his compound. He could see Mala bent over her a pile of grass in her lap. Ever since she told him about the Dire Wolf Alliance he had felt a stirring dissatisfaction. Why should his wife be the one to understand that he could never harm a dire wolf when he hadn't known it himself? He thought taking his son for training at his kinsman's home would restore his sense of equanimity. Instead, his dissatisfaction had grown stronger, gnawing at him both day and night. He sighed and entered the compound. Mala's hair shimmered in the sunset light, glowing a soft orange on the outer curves, a shadowy black on the inner curves. Joot focused on her hair, forcing away the image that continued to haunt him: Lo's tiny body so slimy with blood that it had taken two people to lift her onto the pyre. *Why can't I become a member of the Dire Wolf Alliance?* He wondered despite himself. *Why can't I be called by the dire wolves?* I want to be called to help in these horrible moments. Lo's image faded, and Joot moved to Mala's work space. He squeezed himself between her shallow pile of damp grass and her bony hips. Mala grunted and shifted to make room for him.

"Why do we keep trying?" he moaned. "I learned today another Hutlan family was ambushed, this time in the valley just north of Broken Jaw. Everyone was killed."

Mala froze and turned toward him. "Not again," she whispered, torn between horror at the news and nagging doubt about Joot. She pushed her doubts away and leaned into her husband's shoulder. She plucked the grass out of her mouth. "It's got to stop sometime, but how? The Dotson lose when we Tuudzaado and you Hutlan work together but nothing has changed. Something will come along one day to guide us."

Internally Mala pondered an odd but small incident in the afternoon. Dire wolves did not roam in packs in the Dzagh, but female solitaries often climbed to the higher land to give birth alone and raise their young during the first year of life outside of the wolf pack. Mala had seen one such dire wolf several times ever since Joot and Chebucto left for the North Face. Mala and the female dire wolf had stared at each other for so long that her back had knotted with cold. Finally, the wolf broke eye contact and trotted away. Mala hoped the wolf had been examining her as a potential human pack assistant. She shivered, unsure, excited. She wanted to consult the Naan. Mala, needing something to calm her, searched for her bundles of sweet grasses. Now that she had confined several rows of grass into a new order, she felt better.

Joot rubbed her back, and tweaked a lock of Mala's silky hair. "I hope so. I want to help but don't know how. I wish I could be guided to do battle against the Dotson."

"I wish I could kill the Dotson!" Mala said, her voice even and low. "All of them."

Late into the night they finally finished their daily work and crawled into their sleeping quarters. "I miss him, don't you, my wife?" Joot mumbled from his side of their sleeping area.

"Yes, but be patient. Too many thoughts coming from others, good or bad, can flood the mind, fool the dreamer, and bring confusion to those around the one we wish to protect."

Joot snorted in irritation. Sometimes his wife's aphorisms made so little sense that he wondered if she made them up as she spoke.

* * *

Baasee', if they missed their son so much, why did they send him away? Deloo asked the kind of question dozens of others had asked me before, and I used the same explanation as I had with them.

Little One, you broke your mother's heart when you went to school in Arizona and again when you married Arthur. Even though you hurt a lot when Arthur was killed less than a year later, it still didn't occur to you that your mother felt joy when you came home to her. You were busy growing into the second phase of adulthood and she was facing the fact that losing you meant that her own second stage in adulthood was ending. Of course Joot and Mala missed their son, but both of them understood the absolute importance of his becoming a man. Sometimes I, Baasee' the Truly Wise, felt brilliant.

* * *

Asleep in his small sleeping area, Chebucto felt hot, foul-smelling air on his face. He flailed the air despite himself, then forced his arm to be still. As Chebucto calmed himself, a vision formed in his mind. It was the same man with a zigzagged scar on his face. The man was snarling, exposing a black hole near the front edge of his lower teeth where at least one tooth had been. His mouth moved energetically, but Chebucto heard no words. After a while the vision faded.

* * *

The old medicine man rejected Chebucto for eight days. At dawn of the twenty-fourth day of the Lone Wolf Moon, the old medicine man shouted through the thatch walls of his house, "Nephew, bring me deer meat from the plain beside the two crooked rocks. You'll find one of the large prong-horn deer there. A buck. Bring me that buck."

On hearing the old medicine man's words Chebucto scrambled to get ready. In a little while he found the two crooked rocks as instructed. The large prong horned deer he saw beside the rocks was an animal he knew well on the rocky glacial moraine but had not seen on the grassy plain.

How is this teaching me what a hunting vision truly is? Chebucto suppressed a sigh. This is my only chance, he thought, the awareness suddenly filling his senses with sadness. Please, he thought in a general direction of his feet, please help me. I need help, please.

The large buck stepped into the open. It looked from side to side as if mystified, then its eyes locked on Chebucto. Something odd happened. The large brown eyes of the deer seemed to empty of life, its yeek [breath spirit] is gone! Chebucto thought, awestruck. The deer remained still even as Chebucto approached within an arm's reach. Chebucto dragged his spear into position with heavy arms, then thrust it into the neck of the buck with an unexpected feeling of reverence.

When it was over, Chebucto used a hand ax to cut two large alder trees into poles. When he was satisfied, he lashed the deer between them, using six of his precious tethers to do so. He looped a seventh, somewhat wider tether around the front ends of each pole. This became a forehead pull by which he dragged the deer back to the old medicine man. He was so excited about his experience that he walked faster than usual, yet felt none of the weight of the deer on his forehead even though the deer outweighed Chebucto by almost double.

Agra greeted him with a big smile, and between them they gutted and cleaned the deer. She teased him about the deep crease in his forehead caused by the weight of the deer. Afterward she began cutting it into strips to hang on the rack in her smoke house. Meanwhile, Chebucto went to the old medicine man's house to tell him what had happened. He scratched on the wall beside the door and waited. In a moment, he heard a rustling.

"Come!"

Chebucto entered, and stopped in shock. Did he look as sick as this before?

The old medicine man appeared too weak to sit and too listless to try to talk. Covered with furs, he motioned for Chebucto to sit on the dirt floor beside him. Chebucto settled into a cross-legged position near the old medicine man's head.

"Uncle," he began tentatively, "I didn't realize you were so ill."

A sound something like a dry leaf being crushed between two fingers escaped the old medicine man's lips. "There's nothing for you to do. I am dying and looking forward to the stillness. I am hoping that the First Walk of Death doesn't actually call for walking."

Chebucto snorted and tried to stop the sound by sucking in the air. A hiccup rose out of his chest instantly followed by another. "I'm [hiccup] sorry, [hiccup] Uncle."

"Why be sorry? You have pleased me. I was hoping that my jokes were still funny." He stopped talking for such a long time that Chebucto was tempted to leave. Then he remembered his father's rules about talking to older people. Leave only when you are dismissed, and not before. Chebucto held himself still and waited. At long last the old medicine man spoke.

"Tell me about the deer."

Chebucto needed no further invitation and babbled without stopping, providing every detail of his morning. He dribbled to a halt, eventually aware that the old medicine man seemed to be sleeping. He waited in silence, wondering what his father would say about sleeping elders.

"Good," the old medicine man said at last. "Tonight, you will sleep inside my house—there, near the door. When you have a vision of your own, I will be near you."

Chebucto slipped outside the old medicine man's house to tell Cousin Agra about the new arrangements. She smiled, ducked into one of her many small, thatched lean-tos and brought out a small, stiff segment of a mammoth hide and a soft lynx pelt. He breathed deeply of the lynx pelt, thinking of the one he had at home. Suddenly he knew that he still had a home. He smiled at Agra, and murmured his thanks.

"Now you may sleep in more comfort." Two playful dimples danced at him in the firelight. Her fingers brushed lightly against his when she placed the hides in his arms. Chebucto felt an alarming sensation in his groin and other reactions that startled him. She smiled at his confusion. Chebucto stepped backward, tripped and fell on the gravel that served as their common ground. Embarrassed, he picked up the pelts and scuttled out of sight. He thought he heard a soft giggle behind him.

On the following day, just after the sun set, the old medicine man called Chebucto to him. "We will begin your lessons now."

Chebucto stared at the old man, uncertain about what he was expected to do. On the mat between them were five objects. The first item was a short, brown, stone knife. The second was a small yellow stone that glimmered in the twilight. Chebucto recognized its odor. In sunlight, the stone would look grey and rough, but in this light, it seemed smooth and yellow. The third object was a small skin pouch without decorations. The fourth object was a single dried leaf of lobelia. The last object was a short strand of Chebucto's hair. Chebucto couldn't remember giving his hair to anyone. The glowing coals of a dying fire crackled as a bit of charred wood rolled to the side.

The old medicine man picked up the stone knife and without looking at Chebucto, began intoning a low note. Chebucto's shoulders twitched despite himself, at first simply compliant, and then with growing curiosity, Chebucto followed the old medicine man's brief instructions with precision. In turn the old medicine man handled each object, then directed Chebucto to do likewise. Finally, he lifted the lock of hair and handed it to Chebucto.

"Put this in the fire while you repeat the prayer, when the hair is no more, go to your bed and sleep."

Chebucto accepted the lock of hair and did as he was told, careful to avoid thinking critical thoughts of his mentor. A memory of himself and Keyo jeering at Kenduu in a moment of prayer curled through his mind. Chebucto forced the thought away before he succumbed to the temptation to laugh again. When the acrid smell of his burnt hair finally dissipated, Chebucto stood. Instead of reclining on the mammoth hide bedding Chebucto left the old medicine man's house, moving slowly. The old medicine man leaned back onto his bedding and using only his mind, found Chebucto, already some distance from the house, spear in hand. Time passed.

He believes in the power of his visions about human actions but not the power of the Sacred Forces over the rest of nature, the old medicine man mused. He is desperate now, maybe this time he will follow my rules.

The old medicine man continued to wait, soon the images became clear. The old medicine man could see Chebucto moving as easily as if it were daylight. Although his steps were even, Chebucto moved like a sleepwalker. The old medicine man watched Chebucto stop beside a low juniper tree. Beyond him was an opening between dark boulders and a grove of short, bare branched alders. The old medicine man's vision wavered, then cleared again. A prong-horned deer entered the glade beside Chebucto. As he had seen them do hundreds of times for other hunters, the deer stepped closer to Chebucto and stopped. The old medicine man's power let him see the peculiar glow around the deer that meant its *yeege*, a spirit force, was with it. Then the tension in the deer's body seemed to flow outward. Having a deer with *yeege* was better than a deer with only a *yeek*, its breath spirit. Chebucto moved forward, slowly drawing his knife along the lower side of the neck of the ruminant, the deer fell in its tracks. The old medicine man waited patiently for Chebucto to return. Although the old man insisted that he no longer slept, he was chagrined when Chebucto awoke him the following morning. The smell of deer hide filled the small chamber.

The old medicine man said, "well done, Nephew."

"It wasn't like what you told me would happen," Chebucto said to the old medicine man after he butchered and helped Agra hang strips of the deer meat over the smoke rack. "It wasn't a dream. The deer walked in front of me, so I followed it. And the deer I followed was bigger, fatter' and kept looking at me. It stood beside the little deer while I killed it. Then the big deer disappeared."

"What you saw was the deer's *yeege* walking before you to guide you to the deer it had selected for you," said the old medicine man.

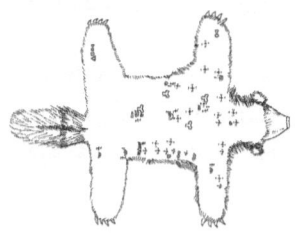

Sixteen

Days flowed by in a blur. Chebucto was shocked that it was already the second day of the Teratornis Moon. Cousin Agra wanted to celebrate his hunting success on that day, but Chebucto refused because he had not yet had a hunting vision of his own.

"Besides," he said, "those Dotson may still be looking for me."

A shadow crossed her face, taking her dimples with it. She looked down, saying nothing for a long moment, then she burst out, "Yes, it's true. They killed my husband because he was a Red Paint Man; they hunted him down until they found him."

Chebucto stared at her in shock. He knew that a Red Paint Man was born on summer solstice and that the Dotson believed they had to be sacrificed to the sun. "When did that happen?"

"Five years ago. We were both fifteen, married less than a year. He was the first Red Paint Man of North Face to be killed on Black Sun Day." Her face puckered.

Chebucto reached out to her automatically but she shrank away from him. "I lost my baby that day, too," she said in a voice so low that he wasn't sure he heard her correctly. Chebucto knitted his brow. "I'm sorry." Chebucto considered asking her why they wanted to kill him at winter solstice instead of summer as they did in Broken Jaw, but it occurred to him that she was too upset to talk about that. Instead he asked, "What about the red ochre mark?" Most people in Zana made use of family markings. Chebucto had his was his father's bola cross. Although he envied the most precious markings was a single vertical line drawn with red ochre, it was reserved for Red Paint people, only they could mark their belongings that way. Chebucto wondered if his cousin Agra had inherited the right.

She shrugged. "I burned everything my husband owned because of those marks, all of his tools, all of his tunics—all of it." She looked away. "When we married, I was so proud to have a Red Paint Man. I wanted to mark our house with the Red Paint sign as well, but he laughed at me." She burst into tears.

Chebucto stared at the ground, wondering what his father would have done comfort her. He finally said "I'm sorry this has happened to you. My family worries about one of our relatives who is a Red Paint Woman at Broken Jaw."

"Broken Jaw?" She looked at him in horror. "She'll never get away from them there. That's where they all want to be, even Jis."

"Jis?" Chebucto repeated.

"He's a Dotson death runner who married a Hutlan woman from here, her name is Mysfet. Broken Jaw is where all the Dotson wish to be because it is as close to the sunrise as anyone can be."

* * *

As midnight approached just before the birth of the second day of the Teratornis Moon, Chebucto awoke to a hunting vision. When it was over he coughed loudly to awaken the old medicine man.

"Uncle," he whispered.

"Tell me," the old medicine man demanded, needing no further explanation.

Chebucto described the deer, a white buck with large pale yellow patches on each flank. "It stands beside a pile of three stones. The center stone is dark green quartz; the other two are speckled and flat, and the green stone is big and jagged. The deer is not like any I've seen before. It doesn't have any horns, but I know it's a buck. It has a dark brown line along the bridge of its nostrils. Do you know that kind of deer, Uncle?"

"Yes. They are bigger than the plains deer, and you will have trouble carrying all that back with you. It will help if you use my old swing board. Tell my granddaughter; she will know where it is. I'll show you how to use it in the morning. You'll have to go north, into the moraines along the edge of the glaciers. It will be cold up there, but you probably won't feel it this time." The old medicine man emitted a dry cackle and choked on a cough.

"Get some sleep, Nephew," he said. "You must leave as soon as you get the swing board."

Chebucto left just before dawn, so excited he only half understood the old medicine man's instructions about how to use the swing board. The old medicine man shook his head in frustration after repeating the instructions twice and sent Chebucto on his way. Chebucto turned north, traveling easily toward the rocky moraines at the base of the glacier. His feet seemed to know exactly where to step, which direction to turn, how high to climb, so when he felt them come to a halt, he relaxed into a hunting squat. Turning lightly on the balls of his feet, he rotated less than half a circle when he stopped. There before him were the same three stones he had seen in his vision. He remained squatting, and from that position prepared himself. The wait took longer than his knees could stand, but that made no difference once the deer stepped into view. The white deer looked about, saw Chebucto, and its *yeek* died in its eyes. Chebucto approached the deer with a sense of deep quiet. Unlike before killing the deer gave him a deep sense of shock and shame. He had brought the dragging poles with him, and lashed the deer carcass to it as quickly as possible, surprising himself with clear knowledge of how to use the swing board. The swing board prevented the ends of the poles from digging into the earth. Dragging the deer to the old medicine man was almost easy.

Later that night he described his experience to the old medicine man. "It felt easy, Uncle, but something feels wrong, too. Why do I feel that way, Uncle?" he asked.

"I wondered how it would be for you, Nephew," the old medicine man responded. "Each hunter reacts to the hunting visions differently. You are one who understands that you can give nothing in return for the life you took. For you there will always be a sense of obligation when you have a hunting dream. Tonight, you must ask the Sacred Forces how to repay that deer."

Later that night Chebucto awoke to another vision. When it faded he coughed tentatively.

"What did you see, Nephew?"

"Kenduu." Chebucto answered. "My uncle adopted him when he was a little boy." Two arm's lengths separated Chebucto from the old medicine man, but he could feel the older man's shudder as if it had shaken the earth. "What is the matter, Uncle?"

"I do not know, Nephew, except to warn you that it will not be easy for you to honor your debt to the deer."

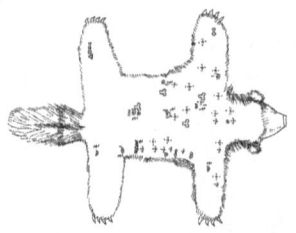

Seventeen

On the thirteenth day of the Teratornis Moon Ping heard the call of the nuthatch, recognizing it as the signal from Kejimkujik of the Dire Wolf Alliance's inner group. Now he that he'd been accepted into it he felt the nasal vibration lift his mood and empower his legs. Without knowing exactly where he was to go, he left his home on the North Face, traveling toward Falls Creek. Unaware of Ping's movements, Kenduu loped toward Falls Creek as well knowing only the call of the nuthatch was not to be ignored. The nuthatch did not live in the upper Dzagh any more than it lived on the North Face.

* * *

Baasee' is that Dire Wolf Alliance like a club? I don't like clubs. Why'd they choose the nuthatch as a mascot? Isn't that one of those small bird with a trill call. I always thought our Alaksan nuthatches had a high-pitched call. Deloo was obviously bored enough to pester my non-stop. I used my mothering powers to stop her prattle.

Sh, Deloo, don't interrupt Grandfather Kwaiikit. Remember that we are thousands of years old and you are not even twenty-two yet. The nuthatch came to Kejimkujik as one of his spirit animals. It was handy for the group because it fit easily into forest settings without being noticed. In other words, Kejimkujik could make the sound himself when he wanted to announce himself.

Yes Noisy Mortal, my grandfather interrupted me when I, Baasee' the Great, was about to launch into a great talk. *The Dire Wolf Alliance helped us, the wolves and other species to try to keep order in Zana. Ultimately, it didn't do any good since the floods drowned those of us who hadn't drowned already. It wasn't a club.*

Deloo stared in consternation at the ceiling, obviously suppressing a dozen more questions. Finally she said, *Baasee', thank you both.* With a finger to her lips to signal her silence, I smiled at Grandfather Kwaiikit to continue.

* * *

When Ping reached Falls Creek, he let his feet do the guiding. He found himself staring at a thick growth of aspens. With a little patience, he discovered the hidden way upward and he climbed. When Ping reached the top of the cliff, he made himself comfortable. Soon images came to him of Kwaiikit and Kenduu. Ping turned his attention toward Kwaiikit. He saw him with a small girl. They were in darkness except for the dark red vertical *yeege* that played above the girl's head. Ping felt a chill along his shoulders.

"A Red Paint Woman," he muttered.

"That must be his daughter, Clarvu," Kenduu murmured beside him. Ping started violently, he had been so mesmerized by the vision, he had forgotten where he was. He turned to glare at Kenduu, who sent a playful image of a dead marten to Ping. After calmer greetings, they tried to locate Kwaiikit again to no avail. Silently the older man climbed up to take his place beside them on the cliff ledge. He was alone. Soon the three were communicating at the highest level of Tuudzaado language. Ping repeated all his conversations on the North Face; they demanded details and Ping supplied them.

Kwaiikit pondered the situation, and said, "We have heard there were two Black Sun Warriors at Falls Creek. We believe Rastuk is one of them. I'd like to find out if Black Sun Warriors are friends or enemies of Red Sun Warriors, and I have come up a plan."

The three of them communed at length before Kwaiikit left them. The younger men remained to rest before traveling north.

* * *

Chebucto stared at the Teratornis Moon. A night away from its full state, it was so huge, it seemed to press onto the earth and everything that dwelt there. It never looks this big in the Dzagh, Chebucto thought, I wonder if it's different this year. He was at the top of the moraine over-looking the old medicine man's compound. Down below he could see everything in the odd silver light of the Teratornis Moon. All the other moons of the year bathed the earth with shades of lavender or gold, but not the Teratornis Moon. Chebucto began the descent, trying to avoid the tiny bolts of painful shocks that scorched him every time he touched something. He felt warmth from the stones with each footfall. It seemed to him that the earth pulled his feet while the moon created the shocks of light through his fingers. He had been meaning to talk to the old medicine man about these experiences, but his mentor tired more easily with each passing day.

"Tonight, you will have a vision of your own." The words were spoken so softly that Chebucto wasn't sure the old medicine man had said them. The old medicine man didn't speak again and Chebucto didn't want to leave his side. At last Cousin Agra scratched on the wall and invited him to have some deer meat.

"Give this to him before you eat," she said, handing Chebucto a wooden bowl with a small amount of finely cut meat floating in a savory broth.

The old medicine man was awake when Chebucto returned to his side. He indicated he needed help to sit up. Chebucto tipped him forward and propped a big role of fur behind his back, and held the bowl for the old medicine man. In a still moment, Chebucto absorbed the reality of the old medicine man's coming death, oddly without fear or uneasiness.

"Thank you, Nephew. You have done well."

Sudden tears clotted Chebucto's throat, preventing him from answering.

"Go now. Tonight, you will have a vision. Be ready for it."

Chebucto awoke. An opaque blue light filled the space. *Hootlyeets,* Chebucto thought in amazement. He had seen it only once before near the house where a Prayer Woman had died. The light near the dead Prayer Woman's house had been a lot like this, but a different color. Hers had been light green. His father told him *hootlyeets* were the spirits of the sun, wind, and the earth. The old medicine man had spoken of *hootlyeets* as well. He said it was the light of the spirit world. Chebucto could see things by the light, but not easily. He sought the old medicine man, satisfied he could see the smooth rise and fall of the single skin blanket.

The old medicine man spoke. "Nephew?"

Chebucto drew himself into a sitting position and looked intently at the recumbent form. The old medicine man's face was perfectly visible in the strange light. His eyes were closed and so was his mouth. Chebucto looked around the tiny interior, wondering if he had imagined the voice.

"Nephew." Chebucto turned back to the old medicine man even as the word was uttered. The old medicine man's dry, thin lips remained closed. "I am speaking to your mind as well as to your ears. Listen closely."

Chebucto felt a chill begin on his arms and flow through his entire body. He dared not move a muscle. This was nothing like the silent language of the Tuudzaado. Chebucto had learned the Tuudzaado way that called for making bodily sensations to emanate from the head along with projecting visions and thoughts. The old medicine man's way was gentle and easy to understand.

"When you awaken in the morning, I will be dead. You are a man now and not a boy. You will seek your vision's destination. There you will be offered choices. You are to work within the rules of your family and not the rules of other people. Remember this and your choices will be obvious to you."

Chebucto remained still, waiting for more, but there were no more words. After a long while, the blue light faded and Chebucto felt pulled back to his place near the door. With heavy limbs, he felt himself collapse but had no sense of falling asleep. While lying there, he became aware of voices murmuring gently in the background. He understood what he heard and allowed the information to flow through him. Then he remembered that he was to get his brother. He began to panic because his brother needed his help. He tried to get up to run to his brother, but his legs would not respond. Slowly he remembered he didn't have a brother and wondered if he was having another strange vision or dream.

"Nephew!"

The sound bewildered him for a moment, and then Chebucto recognized the old medicine man's voice. He sat up and stared around. It was the fourteenth near-day of the Teratornis Moon and its eerie light penetrated the gloom of the house. Memory of the bright blue light trickled back, but not the light itself.

"Uncle?" Chebucto responded, but there was no answer. Slowly, Chebucto relaxed, recalling there had been people speaking; recalling that he had understood them when they spoke, but now couldn't recall a single word. He lay in the dark, mystified by an odd sense of simultaneous fear and comfort. Gradually he became aware of the voices again. This time even as he heard them and comprehended them one word at a time, their meanings slipped away. He tried to sit up but his body did not obey him.

Then he saw a face. He knew the face, knew the eyes, and more, he knew what he needed to do. Even as he relaxed with the certainty, he could not remember who it was. The face dissolved before he could fix it in his mind. He sat up again, and this time he crawled over to the doorway to look out, wondering if the person with that face might be outside, looking in at him. He stood up and walked forward a bit, stumbling on things that he couldn't quite see. Then he saw the face again—just ahead of him, just beside a cluster of aspen trees. Chebucto rushed toward the face and stumbled again, this time falling to one knee. When he picked himself up, the face was gone. He looked for the trees, but could not see them. Turning, he was relieved to see his little lean-to across from his parent's sleeping quarters. He took a step toward it and it vanished.

Chebucto cried out softly, the sound surprised him and then he realized that he was outside the old medicine man's house. The eerie light of the Teratornis Moon distorted shapes so much that he couldn't trust his sense of sight to find his way. Inside the old medicine man's house, the darkness was so intense that he could see nothing at all. Memory of the old medicine man's words came to him first. Then he recalled fearing for his brother. He struggled, angry and fearful, to remember his brother; then it occurred to him again that he didn't have a brother. Chebucto sighed, and pushed the borrowed soft lynx pelt out of the way and remembered his own lynx pelt was still on the Dzagh. He heard something slide onto the dirt floor and felt for it.

The amethyst knife.

Chebucto held it up to the light, taking a moment to admire the way light changed and shifted on it. He hadn't seen the amethyst knife since the night his father gave it to the old medicine man at the beginning of the Lone Wolf Moon. Chebucto glanced toward the old medicine man. He is far too weak to move this, Chebucto thought. Filled with dread, Chebucto put the knife on the mammoth hide and crawled over to the old medicine man. He knew even as his hand touched the withered cheek that his teacher was dead. As light penetrated the gloom, the old medicine man's still-open eyes startled him.

Chebucto thought the eyes glittered with rage. He heard a loud choking sound and thought it was the old medicine man's death rattle. Then he recognized the choking sound as his own voice. Battling an urge to flee, Chebucto forced himself to examine the old medicine man's face more carefully. A softening glow from the eastern sun displayed a small smile lingering on the old medicine man's face. Chebucto understood that the old medicine man's final emotions must have been sweet recognition of something or someone. When his hands stopped shaking, Chebucto opened the pouch he always kept at his neck and smeared yellow powder on the old medicine man's forehead. In the emptiness of the small hut, he whispered "May your First Walk of Death be easy and without the pain of walking, Uncle."

Later than morning Chebucto and Agra began the painful effort of sorting through the old medicine man's belongings. Careful not to touch his sacred tools and garments, she kept her usually cheerful face averted from Chebucto. In a few moments, they squatted across from each other inside the small house. Three small piles separated the young man from her. With her head lowered just enough, Agra surveyed Chebucto through lowered eyelids. His looks pleased her. The North Face had hardened his face and roughened his hands. His shoulders had been thin when he first arrived so little time ago. Now they filled his tunic. She liked his eyes. Large black eyes. Not like Ping's, but... A silence, momentarily companionable, lengthened uncomfortably.

Chebucto wondered if he should ask her to become his wife. Formal customs didn't quite cover their situation, nor did emotion impel either of them to obvious action. After he returned from Reega's house, Agra had playfully introduced herself as his teasing cousin, but the old medicine man had stopped the mild, one-sided flirtation with curt words. Chebucto wished his father were there to advise him. Chebucto was still uncertain of his welcome at home. Except for the Dotson, the North Face was a quiet world. He liked it. As the tension between himself and Cousin Agra increased, he swallowed experimentally to determine if he was too nervous to talk. Releasing a soft cough, he glanced quickly at her and caught a look of intense speculation in her eyes. Unnerved, his energy receded, his shoulders sagged.

Agra glanced at the largest pile between them. Four bags of dried berries and bundles of grasses stacked on top of two baskets filled with smoked deer meat lay under eight small sacks of dried herbs. A frozen leg of deer lay pillowed between other cuts of meat. Chebucto had brought it to her when he came to announce the death. A sudden memory of the day her husband died brought tears to her eyes. The aching pain of missing her husband sometimes sent hot shafts of lust and panic through her entire body, but that happened less and less often. The old medicine man had counseled her through those days of sorrow. If Chebucto stayed, she would be forced to take him as a husband. A momentary burst of humor lifted her mood, quickly squashed by thinking of her mother's request to come home to help with her ailing father.

If she took Chebucto she would have three people in need of a lot of help. A small rip in Chebucto's outer tunic caught her eye. If he asked for another, she would feel compelled to delay her plans to make a ceremonial tunic for herself. Another flash of humor brought her dimples into action. She smiled at Chebucto. He is too young to be First Husband in my future household. I need to look for an older man, then later a strong, handsome one like him. A decision made, she cleared her throat and transformed her smile, achieving a look of graceful hurt.

"I think you'll want to take this," she said, pushing a small orange quartz knife toward him. "You could use it just to scrape hides. He did."

Chebucto lifted his chin. He said nothing, recognizing her statement as an unspoken declaration of their mutual freedom from each other. He covered a quick shaft of remorse by studying the knife with more care than it needed. He had seen the old medicine man using the surgical knife several times, once on his own groin. Chebucto had watched the procedure with alarm and curiosity. He tucked the knife into a sheath. Chebucto knew Agra was twisting the truth about the orange quartz knife a bit. Like his father's amethyst knife, this short blade may have cut flesh for medicinal reasons, but it had never sliced meat or scraped hides. He turned his eyes back to Agra, anticipating her next comment.

"You should take it with you. He would have wanted you to have it," she said. Chebucto hesitated. The words made it final. He was to go rather than to stay. Agra insisted, "he used it to cut meat. It's not a medicine knife like your amethyst knife." She kept her face down as she spoke. "And these," she pointed to a small pile of bags, "are for your family from me."

After an internal debate, Chebucto lifted his chin, and slid the orange quartz blade into one of his pouches.

"Shall we begin," he murmured.

Together they moved food bags to her house and placed the bundles of dry grass into the entryway of the old medicine man's house. Shortly before sundown Agra brought a burning stick from her cooking fire to the house. Chebucto stood to the side as she touched the grass with the fire. In moments, the house burst into flames. The two watched, one on each side of the dwelling. No one else joined them, although several people had stopped to speak with Agra over the course of the day. When the fire was completely dead, she walked back to her house. Chebucto wondered if he would ever see her again. He spent the night near the smoldering coals. In the morning he examined the ashes, careful not to touch them. When he was sure that none of the medicine man's bones could be seen, he turned toward the south and walked away.

Late in the afternoon two days later Chebucto came upon the place where he and his father had watched the killing of the rhynchotherid. Although it was still early, he decided to spend at least part of the night where he had been less than two moons earlier. He tried to remember what he had been like then.

My father wanted me to learn to use hunting visions and I have done so. I'm glad for those lessons. What I don't know is whether they come to me for a reason or if I simply happened to have those visions. I don't feel different.

As Chebucto ruminated over the nature of the visions, his mother's words echoed in his mind: When the Sacred Forces give us visions of people in danger, they look for the person to offer help.

Chebucto fidgeted nervously. He had seen a Hutlan woman in a vision before she was killed by death runners, and he had done nothing. What was I expected to do for her? Those men killed her because she planned a death trap for her own relatives, including her father and sister. She was in danger, I didn't know what she had done. What of the men I have seen in visions? They looked like men who have caused a lot of trouble. How can I find out? What good are these visions?

Annoyed with the Sacred Forces for neglecting such an important part of his training, Chebucto stood and walked away from the rhyncho-therid site. He was too restless to sleep and home was far from where he was. He took one step when he heard an unfamiliar sound. Freezing in place Chebucto peered around. Even daylight during Teratornis Moon was strange. Everything glinted in the intense brightness. Chebucto squinted to avoid the painfulness of the glare. Most of the time the soft glow of the amber sun soothed his eyes. Sunlight in Teratornis Moon cast dark shadows with hard edges. Strangest of all was the color of the sky during a Teratornis Moon. The sky behind the occasional clouds was brilliantly blue, Chebucto wished he had waited until the Long Winter Moon arrived. Then the sky would return to normal.

Brawwwk!

The sound jarred him out of his reverie. What is that? He wondered. Then he saw a movement between two stands of tall prairie grass. A large brown creature moved awkwardly from the grass to a patch of sand not far away. Chebucto knew it must be a giant toad. He studied the toad while he culled his memory for what he had learned. It's poisonous. He remembered his father saying one touch by the toad's long tongue could kill a child.

The giant toad, about twice as big as a rabbit, used its lipless mouth to carry a long blade of grass onto the sand. Using the weight of a front foot to hold an end of the grass in place, the toad broke a segment of it with a deft biting motion. The cut piece fell to the ground. Twisting slightly, the toad brought more of the grass into its mouth and repeated the cut. In moments, the toad cut a stack of grass sticks, each the length of Chebucto's forearm. The toad stood over the grass. At first Chebucto didn't notice the rhythmic distensions of the toad's throat until a thick fluid began to dribble onto one end of the grass sticks. The toad moved away from the grass with great care. Chebucto stared at the grass with surprise. The ends of the grass that had been wetted by the toad's saliva were bright red.

The toad, apparently satisfied with its work, picked up one stick in its mouth and with a quick maneuver of its front feet and mouth, shoved the yellow end of the grass into the sand. The stick remained upright as the toad moved back to the other sticks. The toad placed each stick in the sand. When every stick was in place, the toad backed away to survey its work. The red tips glowed in the last light of the day. When Chebucto returned his attention to the toad, the brown creature was no longer in view. Chebucto settled down to watch the sticks for a while. There seemed to be a haze around the sticks. As Chebucto crept toward the sand to get a better look, as the haze took shape as a swarm of flying insects. One by one as they touched the sticks, the insects fell to the ground instantly. The swarm never seemed to dissipate, although Chebucto saw a growing pile of dead flies. Then a large vole scurried toward the sticks and entered the maze without hesitation. The vole reached the center before the poison took effect. Its short tail twitched once and the vole collapsed in death.

Chebucto had seen several patches of such grass sticks during his short stay on the North Face, but none with red tips. He supposed the color faded with time. Just yesterday he had seen a patch and nearly stepped into it when he pulled back because he thought the sharp points might cut through his moccasins. Now he was glad to know what made them. As Chebucto walked away, he wondered why the toads didn't live in the Dzagh. Maybe Father will know. The thought of being able to ask his father lifted his spirits.

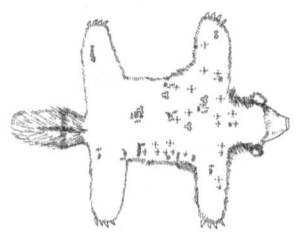

Eighteen

Chebucto climbed steadily, keeping his eye on the shape of the cliff that he had memorized two moons earlier. Everything seemed to be as he remembered until he pulled himself over a ledge and looked up to a completely different skyline. He was lost. Heart thumping with more than exertion, Chebucto slowly turned to look at the broad alluvial plain below. Forcing himself to be calm, he found the place he had seen the rhynchotherid, then he found the place he had watched the toad. He visualized himself looking at both places nearly two moons ago and could not. Then he caught a glimpse of bright orange quartz and smiled. A younger Chebucto had tried to pry it lose during the climb down until he learned it was part of the stone face of the cliff. Moving closer, Chebucto tried loosening it again. Satisfied he was in the same place; Chebucto squatted beside the quartz and tried to picture the way the cliff had looked when he was climbing down, once again trying to follow his father's advice.

There's only one way to go, he thought irritably. Up. How can I get lost? So, saying, he looked for the best way to go upward. He got to a place that not only looked and smelled completely foreign, but offered no likely hand holds above him. Waiting until his heart slowed before lowering himself again to the ledge of the orange quartz, Chebucto felt a buzzing in his head, and his vision blurred. Pressing himself closer to the cliff face, he pinched his eyes shut until the buzzing stopped. Then he opened his eyes to clear vision, he moved his right foot experimentally until he found a foot hold. Little by little he made it back to the orange quartz. Once there he realized it was nearly midday. A breeze tickled the back of his neck, Chebucto looked beyond the alluvial plains to the darkening clouds in the northeast. He forced himself to breathe slowly while he considered the next place to try an ascent.

Again, he felt a buzzing in his head, but this time he felt an odd warmth on his chest. His hand went to the area and felt an unfamiliar shape. Chebucto traced the hot object and recognized the sheath of his father's amethyst knife. He reached into his tunic and extracted the knife from the sheath. A flame sparked between his finger and the blade, the blade felt hot but not enough to generate flames. Chebucto caressed the length of it to make sure. As he did, he saw a contour of stones in his mind. Looking around he saw the same contour off to his left. Chebucto sheathed the knife and stepped toward the contour. It looked like a good place to try, so he did. With relief, in a few moments he found himself on another ledge a little higher up. He looked back over the plain below and recognized several of the places he had tried to memorize on the way down.

Chebucto touched the knife sheath, wondering if he should make a prayer of thanks. Words vanished, so he looked around for another likely way up, and soon found what he needed. Before long he reached one of the stones against which his father had leaned while waiting for him. Chebucto took a long breath and looked at the narrow ledge he had crossed. From where he stood the slit in the rocks was not visible and the ledge itself didn't seem very long. Wishing his father could be there to see him, Chebucto forced his right foot onto the ledge. He stopped, planted his hands firmly on the same hand holds he had used before, and dragged his left foot around the right. He almost wished it couldn't find a place to land, but it did. Chebucto propelled his hands toward another hand hold. It seemed to take all winter, but in fact when Chebucto squeezed through the welcome slit between the rocks, he noted that day's third quarter had barely started. He felt so light that he nearly catapulted to the top of the cliff. Chebucto found a good place to perch and looked back in comfort toward the North Face. He thought about himself the morning he and his father started the trip and felt a smile grow across his face. Even I can feel myself mature, he thought. Even I can tell I am no longer a child; the memory of each horror, fear, and triumph he experienced came to him as he studied the terrain below.

It's amazing how much more has happened to me in the past two moons than all the rest of my life, Chebucto mused. His back felt stiff and Chebucto realized he had been ignoring an increasingly cold northerly wind. He studied the position of the sun. Day's fourth quarter had come and gone. Nightfall was nearly upon him. In the brief twilight, Chebucto found a shelter on the south side of some aspens.

On the following morning Chebucto watched the sky darken into various shades of gold, orange, and deep purple as the wind pushed clouds along the eastern side of Zana. Relieved the rain would pass by him, Chebucto set about exploring the cliff top. The feeling of omniscience enthralled him until he thought of the many Dotson raids in the Dzagh. They have passed this way, too, and they have seen what I'm seeing now. This would be an ideal place to build a camp to watch over the North Face, they must have made plans to take over the Dzagh. As Chebucto contemplated the logic of such an idea, he suppressed a shudder. They are probably already up here just waiting for the right moment to strike, he thought. Chebucto spent the night beside the cliffs, in the morning of the twentieth day of the Teratornis Moon he retraced his steps toward the main path that led home.

* * *

"How about camelids?" Chebucto heard his father say. He scratched again, but the sound was overpowered by his mother's voice.

"No. Jenda doesn't have time to go with us. I don't want to go without Jenda if we go after camelids."

"You don't have to come with Zaandan and me," Joot objected. "I've done it before without you, and you haven't complained about the hides I bring back."

"I haven't complained about the hides that you let me keep," Mala said in a rising voice, "because I've always been able to work with the skimpy pieces you've brought back. We haven't talked about the one I didn't keep."

Joot interjected quickly, "My wife, I have apologized for that. Please believe me that will never happen again."

Chebucto scratched again, this time a little louder, but continuing noise inside his parent's small sleeping quarters deafened their ears to the outside. Chebucto opened his mouth to call to his father.

"No!" Mala's voice, even louder, filled the night air. "I don't want to discuss camelids anymore."

"Maybe we should hunt for rhynchotherid, then," Joot said. Joot's heart always beat a little faster when he tried to outwit his wife.

"Rhynchotherid?" Mala repeated, her voice suddenly rich with humor. "You idiot. Are you trying to deceive me about something?"

Chebucto recalled how he and his father had scuttled around the rhynchotherid carcass on their way to the North Face. His father told him that only a fool would waste time hunting for something that big when there were plenty of smaller animals around. Chebucto closed his mouth and listened intently.

"Me? No! I just wanted to include you in my plans, my beautiful wife."

"Hmmm."

"It's been a while since I have hunted on the northern plains," Joot began.

"You want to go visit our son!" Mala said. "You've always told me that neither the father nor mother should interfere when their son is receiving training from a medicine man. We can't go there."

Outside their door Chebucto paused, waiting for more, then decided against it.

"Father? Mother? It's me. I'm back."

Silence punctuated the air. No one moved. Chebucto coughed nervously.

"Father? Mother? Is it all right for me to stay here again?"

There was a scuffling sound inside the low-ceilinged abode. Joot succeeded in wrestling his wife out of the way to poke his head out of the doorway first.

"Son! You were supposed to stay for a... Ooomph!"

Mala shoved her husband unceremoniously out the door and stormed over his prone body. "Chebucto!" She engulfed her son in a deep embrace, drinking in the smell of his hair.

Joot picked himself up and asked, "What happened to you? Did my relative die?"

Chebucto managed to extract himself to lower his head in silence. He said in a hushed voice, "he was expecting it."

Mala announced, "I'll prepare something for you to eat. My son, you are too thin."

Joot went to light a fire in the cooking arbor while Mala went to a storage pit. He glanced uncertainly at his wife's foot, the only part of her anatomy that remained visible. She had crawled into one of their many storage pits. I wonder where she keeps the dried deer meat. Oh, I remember, he thought, and handed the fire drill to his son while he went to the cooling larder where they kept smoked meats.

"What are you doing with my cooking stone," Mala demanded irritably when she pulled herself out of the pit. "No one touches my cooking stone." The wooden slab they normally used to serve dry food materialized in her arms, and she quickly placed all the dried meat onto it. She removed the cooking slab with a dark look at Joot. "This doesn't need to be cooked."

"I want to know what happened on the North Face, my son. You have changed in a lot of ways," Joot persisted.

"I have?" Chebucto glanced down at himself, "how?"

"Your shoulders are bigger, for one thing," Joot said.

Chebucto was pleased. "What else?"

After a little more banter, Joot asked key questions about his time with the old medicine man, and Chebucto filled in as many details as he could remember, building to a dramatic flourish with each new vision. He stopped short of the final experience of the night the old medicine man died.

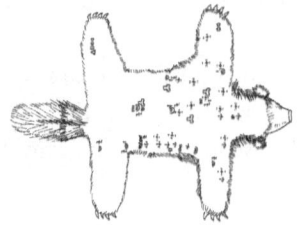

Nineteen

In the morning, Mala was outside and already busy before anyone else got up. By the time Chebucto joined her she had made plans for a celebration of his manhood.

"Come," Mala said comfortably. "I noticed some items in your gear to store in the pits."

"I forgot!" Chebucto said, suddenly a boy again. In a few moments, the pair of them were examining the many gifts he had brought for her.

"Our kinswoman sent this to you," Chebucto said, showing her a thick roll of grass willow fronds.

"Oh!" Mala exclaimed aloud. "This is perfect. I'll soak it in the spring," she said. She tipped her head toward the rill of water that edged the east side of their compound. "When I was, young I made baskets all the time with these grass willow fronds." The fronds were too dry to unfurl, but Mala didn't need to do more than smell them to remember their durable fragrance. "I'll be able to twist some good, waterproof baskets with these."

Mala pressed her face into the grass willow and murmured, "Your father told me she is a very attractive young woman." She eyed her son through the cracks in the frond and smiled when she saw his deep blush. Silence louder than a glacial flood filled the small area. At long last he muttered, "She didn't want me."

* * *

That's what this was all about, wasn't it Baasee'. In the old days, people on the Yukon River traveled for days to get to trading festivals. Children were shown off, and marriages were arranged by everybody but the kids. At least that Chebucto guy got the idea all by himself. And she said no. That's the way to go, I think, Deloo pronounced, looking important.

Yes, my wise one, but sometimes young people don't make good decisions, often ending up with lazy husbands or ignorant wives. In my day, we had a combination of both ways, I retorted, struggling to prove I was right. Grandfather looked questioningly at me, and I continued, *Grandfather is ready to start the story again. Ready?* Deloo nodded silently, her mind swerving away from the idea of the four stages of life, marriage usually the trigger to begin the second stage. I signaled Grandfather to continue.

* * *

Mala took stock of her son. Eventually, she touched him gently on the hand. "I wish that one day you will be as lucky as I have been with your father."

As if just awakening, but literally because he had been listening for the right moment, Joot emerged from the sleeping structure and bid them both good morning.

"Father," Chebucto smiled. "I have something for you." He held out the amethyst knife, and told them the story about the old medicine man's death. "Our kinswoman gave me this one." He brought out the orange quartz knife. "He used it to make cuts for healing. Would you like it as well, Father?" Chebucto extended the orange quartz crystal knife to his father.

Surprised, Joot removed the amethyst knife from its sheath and examined it. "Thank you, Son. I never expected to see it again." He restored the amethyst to its sheath and looked at the orange quartz crystal. "This is beautiful as well. Keep it in memory of our kinsman." Chebucto smiled and reclaimed the orange quartz knife.

Later that day the three crossed the ravine to visit Jenda and her family. On the way, Chebucto noticed Duna walking along the path. Her parents accepted her marriage to Kenduu they had made the day Duna was born. Chebucto enjoyed admiring her face, and took time whenever possible to speak a few words with her. She was walking quickly in the opposite direction, so Chebucto stayed with his family.

A noise near the rear of the compound entryway attracted Chebucto's attention, and he headed toward the noise. Keyo and Kenduu were huddled over their work area, each busy with a separate task. They looked up with smiles when they saw Chebucto.

"Tell us about the deer, Cousin," Kenduu said. "Your father told us you have become a great hunter."

Chebucto flared angrily at his cousin's tone of voice, then recognized the banter as something he had long envied. His father and Zaandan often teased each other that way. Abashed by what seemed like a sudden change in his status with Kenduu. Chebucto smiled timidly and began his story. Kenduu and Keyo prompted Chebucto for exact details about the vision and his white deer. Chebucto enjoyed his audience, embellishing the size of the white deer just a little. He continued with other elements of his visions, excluding the final one, the vision about Kenduu. He thought of the old medicine man's words about his debt to the deer and glanced at Kenduu, unable to understand why his debt to the deer involved his older cousin.

Kenduu tipped his chin upward and said "Good for you, Cousin. Now it's time for you to go after a truly dangerous predator. Have you ever hunted the scimitar cat?" Kenduu asked.

Shocked by the unprecedented turn of conversation, Chebucto couldn't speak. Finally, he took a deep breath and shrugged.

"Neither have I. Would you like to try it?"

Chebucto smiled in awe and said, "Yes, I would."

"Do you mean it?" Keyo piped up in a squeaking voice.

Kenduu turned to his little brother. "About the scimitar cat hunt? Of course. You can't really become a man until you have hunted a creature that would be happy to hunt you first."

Scimitar cat! Chebucto gawped at his cousin, suddenly aware of the horror of what he had agreed to do. Kenduu had never asked Chebucto to go hunting with him.

Chebucto asked, testing the sincerity of the invitation, "When?"

Kenduu thought about his obligations toward his larder and else-where and said pensively, "I'm ready now. We could leave in the morning if you are ready. Are you?"

Chebucto paused. "I should ask my parents if they need anything first. Maybe I can borrow some things from my father, since I've never hunted such a large predator."

"Good. Let me know as soon as you can," Kenduu said to his cousin, "When you are ready, come back and stay the night with us. Bring your gear. If you don't have what you need, I'll find something here. We will leave the morning afterward."

"What about me," Keyo burst out, "I want to go, too."

Chebucto looked uncertainly at Keyo, but Kenduu intervened quickly. "Brother, in the Dzagh a man proves his worthiness in steps. Chebucto has completed the first step by having a hunting vision, and the second by finding and killing the right deer. The next step is to hunt a predator like the scimitar cat. You must test your courage in all ways and wait until you either have had a hunting vision or pull the animals toward you."

"Father doesn't have hunting visions and I don't either," Keyo flared at his brother.

Kenduu responded calmly, "Father has told us both that hunting visions do not come to everyone. That doesn't mean you shouldn't try to have one. That's why Father expects us to learn bring the game animals to us. Haven't you been practicing?"

Keyo dropped his gaze, but not before displaying an extended lower lip. "I pulled an opossum toward me just after Chebucto left at the end of the Peccary Moon," he muttered.

"And," Kenduu prompted, eyebrows arched.

"It got away," Keyo confessed, chin on his chest.

Chebucto looked at his cousin in awe. "Really? You actually felt yourself pulling it?" He prompted for details, Mollified, Keyo told his story.

When Chebucto told his parents about the invitation a little later that day, Joot burst out, "Son, you are behaving as if you have suddenly become the greatest man in Zana. Do you think you are ready to hunt one of the most terrible of our predators? You should wait until you are sure of your hunting skills before tackling such a creature."

Shocked at his father's harsh rebuke, Chebucto scowled. Pent up rage prevented him from speaking. When he did, his voice refused to cooperate, and the words came through both his mouth and nose as squeaks and hiccups.

Mala laughed. Chebucto whirled around to face her. She swallowed the sound and tried to look noncommittal.

"What did Zaandan say about this idea?" Joot asked.

"He hasn't returned yet," Chebucto answered.

"You should wait for him to return. If anything should happen to either of you, they will be left without a hunter."

Stung by nameless feelings, Chebucto felt trapped in a shell of childhood. Mala seized the silence to ask Joot to take a walk with her, something they used to do in their early days of marriage. Chebucto watched them leave. In a rage, he paced the length and width of the compound several times. Finally, on his third pass by his parents' sleeping quarters, he ducked inside. In moments, he found himself outside their quarters holding the amethyst knife in his hands. Ignoring all wisdom gained from the Old Medicine Man who had returned to amethyst knife to him, Chebucto jammed the knife into his inner tunic and took a walk himself. When he returned home, darkness had fallen. He knew Mala and Joot were home by the smell and feel of the compound. Instead of signaling his presence, he crept to his lean-to and pretended to sleep. It was only when he pulled the sheath of the amethyst knife out of his tunic and tied it to a tether that he then looped over his head that he fell into a doze.

When he heard, his father moving around in the morning, Chebucto got up as well. They pretended to ignore each other at first. Then Joot took a deep breath and said, "Go if you think you are ready."

Chebucto kept his back turned but answered, "I will. I'll get some things together today and spend the night there."

Joot glared at his son's back. After waiting uselessly for Chebucto to face him, he muttered, "fine. I'll lend you one of my bigger spears." They examined Joot's spears in silence. Joot selected a spear.

Chebucto thanked him woodenly and said, "I'll be going now."

From the shadows of their sleeping house, Mala watched with a sense of deep dread.

* * *

Six Dotson men struggled up the steep trail that led into the Dzagh. The six were used to northerly glacial winds in Dotson. The northeasterly winds that blew off the ocean seemed colder, but they did not complain. The wind pelted them with occasional pellets of ice along with sleet. The ice made the climb almost impossible, but to Dotson men pain meant nothing. They permitted themselves to feel only one sensation: successful muscle control under all conditions. When they reached the high point of the trail, Jis called a halt. He found shelter below a tumbled mass of boulders protected on the northeast by a thick growth of short aspen trees. Calling them with a whistle, he gave the signal to build a fire.

"We'll shelter here for the night. We'll find them in the morning," he said.

* * *

Working alone in his stepfather's compound on the other side of the ravine, Kenduu checked his own spearheads and then examined each spear shaft for straightness, and then tightened or replaced bindings and generally made sure that he would be completely ready for his hunt with Chebucto. When he was finished, he looked around the compound.

Something was missing.

A zephyr passed Kenduu, bringing the familiar scent of his wife. He saw her in the distance. She was carrying a bundle, her steps slow and even. She seemed to be alone. Kenduu's heart made a tiny leap as it always did whenever he saw her. Alone? No. Another shape entered the narrow path, merged with Duna's and then pulled away.

A shiver of something like shock made Kenduu's right foot stumble on a pebble. The offended stone skittered away, struck another, and together the two small rocks created a shower of sand and stone that fell along the sloping path.

Duna's shoulders jerked. She spun around. Kenduu could see the perfect circle formed by her lips. A loose braid slid along her shoulder while the other remained obedient in its binding at the top of her head. The figure beside her receded into the shadows of large boulders.

"Husband!" Duna breathed, approaching him rapidly. "What are you doing here? Is something amiss?"

Kenduu's tongue failed him. He stared at his wife, unable to think of how to say the words that jammed into his throat whenever he saw her with another man. He wondered why she had left their household when there was so much work to do. He suspected her abrupt departure had something to do with his stepmother. Jenda had come to their work area early. She often did. Kenduu had seen his wife and stepmother in conversation and saw his wife's spine stiffen. He wondered then if he should intervene. However, at that moment the binding on his spear shaft accidentally snapped open and the sudden unraveling distracted him. Now facing Duna, he wanted to talk about his compassion and understanding of her life with his family. Instead he reached for the sleeping toddler on her shoulder and bent his head to breathe in the sweaty smell of his little boy's hair.

After a while he murmured, "I saw you on the path. Why did you leave?"

Duna's face darkened to nearly black, or so it seemed in the eerie dusk of the Teratornis Moon. "I needed to stretch my legs a bit," Duna said, her words sounding odd in the electric air between them.

She shrugged her shoulders and peeped upward at her husband. His long Tuudzaado body always thrilled her. A small smile creased her face. She thought, he is so handsome.

Aloud she uttered, "I feel better now."

Kenduu shifted Masito to a higher position on his shoulder, very aware of the smile and the promise it seemed to hold. Other thoughts came to him, quenching his body's hungry reaction to his wife's shadowy eyes.

He said, "I saw someone with you."

Duna peered over her shoulder then at Kenduu. Their eyes met and held. Duna smiled and tugged suggestively at a strap on his tunic. "Yes. It was my brother. He came by to visit."

"He should have stopped to say hello to me as well," Kenduu remarked and slid his free hand toward her belly. Their next child greeted him with a high kick. Duna grunted absentmindedly.

"Ready to go home?" he said aloud.

"Home?" Kenduu could feel Duna's shoulders droop. "All right."

"Chebucto and I have planned a hunting trip," he said. "We will be gone for a day or two. You could always go visit Mala, if you wanted to get away for a while. I don't think she ever gets visitors."

Duna touched her belly. "I don't think I can manage the ravine now, but it would be nice to go visit Aunt Mala." She glanced toward the east, and added, "Or my mother. She's closer. I'll visit them while you are gone."

A sudden gust slammed Duna against her husband. He tightened his grip on her and moved a little more quickly. "There must be a storm brewing on the North Face," he murmured. "I guess winter is finally upon us."

"Will you still go hunting?" Duna asked, hoping he would stay home a little longer. "Our larder is very full, thanks to you," she smiled into his face.

"This will be a special hunt for Chebucto," Kenduu replied, and decided he might as well tell her the whole story. "I invited him to hunt for a scimitar cat."

"A scimitar cat? That's too dangerous! We have a baby on the way. What are you thinking?"

Kenduu looked a little shamefaced at her reminder about the timing then smiled. "Don't worry. I'll just be there to watch. This is Chebucto's hunt, not mine."

* * *

Jis waited for the couple to pass before he joined the others, recognizing Kenduu and envying their conjugal intimacy. Jis tightened his resolve. He was a Dotson death runner. Mysfet, although Hutlan, would have expected no less of him that to complete this mission. He approached the place he had left the others and signaled his arrival by moving upwind of them. He entered their bleak shelter after hearing what passed for a welcoming grunt. There was barely enough room for all six of them among the boulders, but it was adequate cover to protect them from wind and discovery by the Tuudzaado below. The wind and sleet had been rough along the southern plains. The worst of it had not yet reached this part of the Dzagh, but Jis knew it was coming soon. The others had gathered wood. The warming fire surprised Jis. He had not until that moment realized he was cold. He pressed as close to it as he could. While none of them permitted cold to interfere with their carefully cultivated image of strength, Jis couldn't quite get past a greedy need for heat even in summer.

"We will wait. Tomorrow we watch and by evening I will tell you my plan," Jis murmured. The others lifted chins of assent. None of them broke from the tight formation. Soon each of them found ways to stretch out on the bare ground below the boulders to sleep.

A small glen separated the boulders from Zaandan's family compound. On the following day, the Dotson men took a careful look at the compound. No one entered the compound during the first half of the day. The sun was in its third quarter when they saw someone approach. They watched the newcomer with mixed feelings. Because of his short, spiky hair, he looked like one of the other occupants. The newcomer stayed in the compound. They watched him talk with the one Jis identified as Kenduu.

"I'll take these two with me tomorrow," Jis announced, pointing to the Dotson men he had selected. "We will wait for the one we want."

His companions grunted. The sound crackled across the freezing ground.

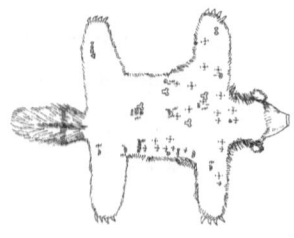

Twenty

"Since this is your first scimitar cat, we must prepare with great care," Kenduu said. "If you haven't eaten today, do so now, for we will not eat again until after we have returned. Let us burn lobelia to purify our minds."

Kenduu opened one of the pouches hanging from a belt inside his outer tunic. He extracted a pinch of dried lobelia leaf and began working his fire drill. In a moment, a spark ignited a corner of the lobelia. Chebucto watched as a flame flickered and went out. Soon a trail of smoke emerged from the leaf, filling his nostrils with its familiar scent.

"May the Sacred Forces guide our thoughts, our feet, and our arms tomorrow as Chebucto and I face the courageous scimitar cat," Kenduu whispered. "May we return to our homes in safety, secure in the knowledge that my brother, Keyo, is here to help his mother and my wife." The words soothed Keyo's mind. The three young men watched as the lobelia leaf disintegrated into a silvery ash, leaving nothing unburned — a comforting sign that Kenduu's prayer had been received by the Sacred Forces.

* * *

Lobelia! My Deloo interjected. *Isn't that the flower they plant in Anchorage along with some yellow flower?*

Indeed, I responded with some irritation. Grandfather had barely got into the most exciting part of the story. *It's also called Indian tobacco and parts of it are used as a medicinal plant as well as a smudge for prayers.*

Isn't it poisonous? Deloo asked, remembering something vaguely notorious about the bright blue flowers.

Sighing, I Baasee' the Eternally Patient, answered, *yes, if you shovel in the entire plant, but the people in Anchorage use it without concern because most plants can be poisonous if you eat them without learning more. In flower pots along Alaskan streets it stands for the blue and gold of Alaska's flag, remember?*

Right, Deloo subsided and waited for more of the story from Grandfather Kwaiikit.

* * *

After a while, Kenduu left and Keyo grudgingly invited Chebucto to share his small shelter. Chebucto, unable to suppress his glee, chatted endlessly about the hunt. Torn between bitter envy and natural buoyancy, Keyo slowly relaxed, caught up by his cousin's excitement. The two had always been close. Kenduu, twenty and married, fell into the category of old men, while Chebucto and Keyo often considered themselves still boys in need of games and fun. Moreover, neither Keyo nor Chebucto forgot that Kenduu was not really related to either of them.

Before dawn Chebucto slid out of Keyo's shelter to wait for Kenduu. The pair walked for nearly half a day until Kenduu stopped at a jumble of rugged boulders. Neither noticed the three men following them from afar.

After a quick inspection, Kenduu said, "We'll use this as a trap. Notice the narrow passage here. It's flanked on both sides by rocks that are steep and flat. If we put the bait in there, the scimitar cat will be trapped by its own greed. Its haunches will be exposed to whatever comes along—meaning us." Kenduu grinned at Chebucto.

Chebucto lifted his head in solemn assent.

Kenduu explained what he wanted: two or three birds or ground squirrels to use as bait. "We will splatter the blood around to attract a cat and leave some meat over here," he said, pointing to a place about ten strides away. "The cat will stop to eat. We will already be in position up there." Kenduu pointed to the top of the boulders with his chin. "We'll put more meat into that crack." Kenduu pointed to the darkest part of the stones. "Let's wedge it in with a rock so that the scimitar cat has to push itself in as far as possible and work to get at the meat."

Kenduu started prowling around the boulders. "Here's one." He turned toward Chebucto. "Help me move these rocks to the front of the trap." As they rotated one of the big stones into place, Kenduu continued, "This way the scimitar cat has to jump out of here before it can attack us. Father says they can't do both at once."

Chebucto looked puzzled but rotated a stone toward the trap anyway. "What do you mean by 'both at once'?"

"They can't jump up and over something as well as attack us at the same time," Kenduu explained. "They aren't birds." In a few moments, they had a big pile of stones blocking the way into the trap.

"This will make it more of a challenge to the scimitar cat," Kenduu said to his young relation, one side of his mouth querying upward. "It will give me a chance to jump out of the way. You, I'm not so sure about," he said, eyes dancing.

Chebucto grinned, awkward, uncertain.

Kenduu examined the boulders for places to hide while waiting. He pointed out two or three that were at the right level—about shoulder height above the trap. "We'll have to put our spears up here first, then climb up after them. When the time comes, I'll jump onto its shoulders and spear it in the neck." He turned toward Chebucto, whose small stature suddenly struck Kenduu as too scrawny and insufficient to cope with a predator as big as the scimitar. "You'll have to aim for the under parts. When you strike, keep your mind on the bait, not on the scimitar cat. If you do it that way, the scimitar cat won't sense you are there."

They went in opposite directions to hunt for small game to use as bait. When Chebucto returned with a wood pigeon, Kenduu was already at the site with a dead rabbit that he shoved into the back end of the trap.

Kenduu said, "splatter the wood pigeon's blood on the rocks farther away. We'll leave it as additional bait."

Examining the area, Kenduu tipped his jaw upward in satisfaction and then opened one of his smaller pouches. He tore off a piece of its contents, dried lobelia leaf, and carefully placed a tiny bit on the ground in each of the four primary directions, starting with the east. When he finished, he glanced at Chebucto expectantly.

Embarrassed, Chebucto stammered, "I, uh," Chebucto's throat tightened convulsively. "I don't have any," he croaked, almost blurting out that he had always sneered because his father made so many prayers with dead leaves. Instead he said lamely, "My father does all that when we go hunting."

Kenduu turned toward the shorter man as if seeing him for the first time. Chebucto lowered his gaze while Kenduu continued to stare. Kenduu broke the silence by saying, "the Sacred Forces are here to help and protect us, Cousin. They can hurt you if you do not respect them."

Chebucto kept his face lowered and fidgeted with one of the belts laced on his outer tunic. He sounds like a grandfather already, Chebucto thought with mixed humor and bitterness. Sighing, Kenduu directed Chebucto to climb to top of the steep boulder on one side of the trap. Kenduu leaped to a place on the opposite side. Each of them hunkered down to wait.

The wait was not long a long one. A male scimitar cat approached. It was not as big as they'd hoped. A yearling, muscles already thickened, but not quite as tall at the shoulder as he would be given a year more of life. The scimitar cat turned his face toward Chebucto and tilted his chin upward slightly. His nostrils flared.

Chebucto forced himself to remain calm even though he could feel his leg muscles burning with an urgency to run. The scimitar cat's mouth opened slowly. The upper fangs were at least as long as Chebucto's index fingers. The lower fangs were less than half that length. He hoped the scimitar cat could not see him. Like other cats, the scimitar cats were excellent trackers. Their eyes were powerful tools for hunting in both night and day. Like most cats, the strength of their vision depended on detecting motion, distance, and certain qualities of life-giving energy. Left out of this complex were details of shape, especially shapes that didn't move.

The young scimitar cat did not seem to sense them and turned to inspect the wood pigeon. He mouthed it gently and then swallowed it whole. His nostrils twitched and he turned back toward the rocks where the two men waited. This time he focused on the entry to the trap and started to move forward. Without warning, the cat stopped and looked upward. Chebucto was crouched as far back as possible, partially hidden by a larger rock in front of him.

The tip of the cat's tail twitched once, then stilled. The scimitar cat's eyes were focused to the right of Chebucto, whose heart came to a halt.

He thought, it's my spear.

Indeed, his spear point, on his right, glinted in the sun. Opposite him, Kenduu directed a wordless prayer toward the Sacred Forces and waited, breathing stifled. As if hearing the suggestion, the scimitar cat's ears twitched, his nostril's swiveled. Then, steps dainty, the scimitar cat moved in grace, gliding over the stone gate in one precise leap. Chebucto heard the scraping of hide against rock and hoped the scimitar cat was wedged in tightly enough. He was not quite prepared for the shock of hearing Kenduu shout.

"Aiieee!"

Kenduu was on top of the scimitar cat. One part of Chebucto's mind sent shafts of lightning throughout his body, while another dispassionate being inside himself analyzed Kenduu's foolish leap.

Is Kenduu showing off because I am here, Chebucto wondered irritably.

The scimitar cat's scream shattered Chebucto's focus and everything seemed to swirl around him, especially Kenduu. The scimitar cat's back rolled like flood waters, but the high rocks pinned the cat into the trap. The scimitar cat's screams filled the small space. His heaving back soon forced Kenduu to find another way to keep himself from falling into the trap along with the furious animal. Kenduu's feet slipped but he could get a grip on a jagged spur of granite a little higher up. Using the spur for leverage, Kenduu tried to find footholds in the sides of the rock above the scimitar cat. Nothing held him. Finally, the cat jerked upward and dislodged one of Kenduu's slipping feet. With a desperate twist, Kenduu flung himself backward to the ground behind the cat. His spear, clean of blood, fell beside him. Kenduu jumped to his feet.

Moving as if driven by demons, Chebucto leaped without thinking onto the scimitar cat's back. Ear-splitting screams ripped out of the cat's throat as it continued to writhe and heave. One of the scimitar cat's rear legs found freedom on the outward side of one of the rocks the cousins had rolled into position. Chebucto could feel the panting cat's muscles contract into a tight mass as he prepared to leap backward out of the trap.

Chebucto's left arm was wrapped convulsively around the cat's neck. He worked the knife free of its sheath with his right hand. Under him the scimitar cat exploded into a leap. Chebucto almost dropped the knife, but managed to swing it around to the neck. Plunging wildly, he slashed the cat's throat once, twice, perhaps three times, each time unaware of the blood that gushed forward into the trap. The cat collapsed. Chebucto's left leg was wrapped around the still belly, while his right leg was pressed into his own chest cavity. Chebucto's head had collided with that of the cat. The two fell together, one still breathing, waiting for the lungs of the other to expand, to take in life-giving air. He heard someone speaking, but couldn't understand the words. He prodded his companion, the scimitar cat, in the ribs, but was too exhausted to ask it to repeat himself.

"Chebucto?"

A loud buzzing prevented him from hearing more words and he was too tired to try. A hard thump on the buttocks jolted him to consciousness. Kenduu's rough hands yanked him off the cat and lifted him away from the rocks.

"Get up!" Kenduu's voice was terse. "We've got to get out of here before a bear comes."

Chebucto pulled himself to his feet and gazed in amazement at the bloody pool below the cat's head. He glanced at his own hands, both of which were soaked in blood and then saw the knife in Kenduu's hand. Without a word Kenduu handed him a lavender-colored crystalline knife. Joot's amethyst knife. Chebucto took it meekly.

Kenduu and Chebucto worked quickly to cut off the head, the feet, and the tail. They stowed everything into their hunting bags. Kenduu reached for the spleen and raised an arm of protest when Chebucto tried to take it away, but there was no time for squabbling. Each of them cast nervous glances around, glad that they had selected such a protected site. Scavengers would be there soon. They cut and tore off a hindquarter. Then they wrapped the raw ends with pieces of the scimitar cat's skin they had pulled from its flanks.

Chebucto contemplated the heart but discarded the idea when he realized that Kenduu was already running silently toward the base of the steep outcropping that they had selected earlier as their campsite. Near the top, a shallow indentation offered minimal protection from the winter winds.

Before he started running himself, Chebucto stripped off the blood-soaked wrist guards that covered his arms from the base of his thumb to his mid-upper arm. He inspected his feet, wondering if he should leave his bloody leggings behind. He was glad he had opted for moccasins instead of taking his one good pair of boots. He didn't have a way to replace those until he got another deer.

A sharp whistle brought him back to the present, and he broke into a run to catch up with his cousin. His moccasins left red footprints on the cold ground. Shards of ice caught and highlighted red droplets. That's when he noticed the tops of his leggings were stiffening and cold. He flared his nostrils inquiringly. He wondered why he had missed such a strong odor before. Then he recognized the smell of his own urine.

Carrying the hindquarters of the scimitar cat prevented them both from clambering up the icy rock face as easily as they had done earlier in the day. Neither of them was adept at balancing dead weight on their living shoulders while defying gravity. Fear, however, helped, and soon they leaned against safe stone walls to catch their breath.

Kenduu was the first to speak. "Why did your father let you take his amethyst knife?"

Chebucto covered his surprise with heaving breaths. "Not exactly."

"You stole it!" Kenduu said, horrified.

Chebucto's throat squeezed into a tight knot. He stared at his cousin. A feathery image came between himself and Kenduu. It was the old medicine man. In his mind Chebucto could hear the old medicine man's words. *I warn you that it will not be easy for you to honor your debt to the deer.*

Suddenly the events of the day drained him of strength, leaving him angry and uncertain. There was not much room in the tight enclosure, but he managed to squeeze his narrow frame past Kenduu. He pressed his share of the cat's remains as far into the rear as possible and squatted beside it. Chebucto felt a draft edging along the top of his wet leggings from somewhere behind him.

Kenduu continued to stare at him. With a deep sigh, Chebucto pulled the amethyst knife from the stiffened leather sheath at his belt. He held it toward the light. The gesture reminded them both of Joot's great pride in showing it to them. Chipped from a large amethyst crystal, the knife was a little longer than the full length of Joot's hand. Each young man knew about the knife from different sources.

Kenduu had heard the story from the man who made the knife. Over a year ago Joot had traded a full camelid hide for having a good knapper shape the raw amethyst crystal into a dagger. News of the trade had circulated throughout the community. For over a moon, people stopped by to visit Mala to see how she was reacting to Joot's trade. Camelid hides were always thought to be the property of women. No one had ever heard of a man trading his wife's waterproof, prized, but ultimately utilitarian, camelid hide for something as impractical as a ritual dagger. Moreover, most people would have taken the stone to Zana's best crystal knapper, a Hutlan man who lived near Broken Jaw.

Mala held her head high through all the interrogations, pretending to one and all that it had been a mutual decision. Joot, on the other hand, told the knapper that he had had a vision. In the vision, he was called on by the Sacred Forces to give up the camelid hide to create the blade.

"It took no more than a half-day to find the amethyst and camelid. I already knew," he said to the knapper. "It was in a place on the alluvial plain that I had been once when I was a child. I saw a camelid. It was at the bottom of a stone basin, unable to clamber out. Near it was the amethyst. In my vision, I saw first the camelid, then the amethyst, then your face."

Chebucto, on the other hand, heard about the knife and vision directly from his father. He went with Joot to the stone knapper's home. When it was completed, he watched in awe as Joot wrapped the handle in a long strip from the underbelly of a peccary dog. Joot made the handle himself from the foreleg of the same dog. The entire project had taken most of a day. Joot had held the blade aloft and said, "If the Sacred Forces are with me, this handle will hold its place on the knife forever."

Joot's words echoed in Chebucto's mind as he contemplated the crystal knife.

"You've got to clean that strap," Kenduu warned his cousin. "Don't you know that getting blood on the handle can stop its power?"

Even as he said it, Kenduu wondered how anyone could use any knife without getting it bloody, but Chebucto looked stricken. His hands fumbled for the knife's sheath. He lifted it so Kenduu could see it as well.

"It's soaked," Kenduu stated the obvious.

A thin stream of water trickled across the face of the stones at the back of their stone shelter. Chebucto leaned toward it with Kenduu bending over his shoulders. The only way to get water to the handle was to press it against the rock. Chebucto held it in place for a while, then turned the blade over. After a while Kenduu moved away to rest while Chebucto soaked the handle in the dribbling spring. The sun was well into its last quarter when Chebucto finally gave up in defeat.

"It's never going to come clean," Chebucto whispered to Kenduu.

"What are you going to do?" Kenduu asked.

"Mind your own business!" Chebucto flared back. They didn't speak again. When Kenduu awoke just before dawn the next morning, he saw Chebucto lifting his half of the scimitar cat onto his back. Without a glance at Kenduu, Chebucto slipped out of the narrow passage and disappeared. Only Chebucto's blood-stiffened leggings remained, tipped against the stones where Chebucto had slept. Kenduu laced his share onto his pack board and left.

Jis and his death runners had positioned themselves carefully on the western side of the ravine. Chebucto took the trail on the eastern side of the ravine as it was the shortest way to his home. Kenduu followed the western path, the same trail they had taken the day before. As Kenduu made his way through a dense grove of short junipers, he imagined the tirade he would deliver to Chebucto. The passion of his thoughts distracted his usually watchful eye. Kenduu was caught completely unaware when someone grabbed his left arm and yanked it upward behind his back.

Kenduu's pack blocked some of the attacker's effort, and Kenduu twisted out of the grip. Whipping around, he caught and slammed the attacker into a nearby spruce tree. A solid blow to the stranger's jaw dropped him. Kenduu turned back toward the trail, only to come face-to-face with another leering stranger. Kenduu feinted to the right and kicked the man in the groin with his left foot. Another kick to the head stilled the second attacker. Kenduu was reaching for his knife when a blow to the back of his head knocked him to the ground, unconscious. Jis tossed aside the stone he had just used and tied the young Tuudzaado man to a stout scrub pine tree trunk. He was finished when his companions regained consciousness.

"What about the other one?" asked one.

Jis glanced toward the east and shrugged. "This one is the one we want." As he spoke, he picked up Kenduu's pack, sniffed it, and dropped it back onto the trail.

"I could use this for my ceremonial regalia," murmured one of the men.

"Leave it!" Jis snapped. "Scimitar cat scent will attract wolves or giant sloths. We have enough to do without inviting that kind of trouble."

The other man asked, "shall we wait for Tavo?"

Jis looked toward the west where he imagined the other Dotson might be and answered, "They know what to do. Let's go."

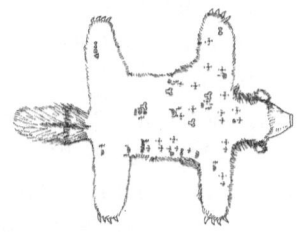

Twenty-One

Chebucto was already too far away to have heard or seen anything that happened to Kenduu. When he got home, he showed his mother his portion of the scimitar cat. Her hands were completely immersed in the blood and guts of a fat hedgehog. She continued working with a quick glance at his hunting bag.

Lifting a skeptical brow, she asked, "Who killed it?"

"I did."

"Your father will be very pleased."

"Where is he?" Chebucto asked, hoping his face revealed nothing of his anxiety.

Mala said, "He went hunting for ground squirrels."

Chebucto lifted his chin and deposited the scimitar meat into one of their storage caches, a deep hole in the ground covered by a flat rock. Then he put the scimitar claws and his gear into his sleeping hut. After donning dry clothing and boots he said, "I'll look for Father."

Mala watched him leave, trying to understand the feeling of dread that she had felt ever since her husband and son quarreled. Seeing her son again increased her worry. It was very unlike him to search for his father when he should have taken time to clean and dry the meat before storing it. He was fastidious about his hunting gear and the game he brought home. She watched him select an empty hunting bag and pick out his squirrel hunting gear. He strode in the direction of the ground squirrel colony near their house.

When Mala finished cleaning the hedgehog, she rocked back on her heels and crossed her arms over her chest. Something was wrong. She wrapped the meat in dried mint leaves, tying the bundle with dried grass. After she deposited it into the ice storage larder, she cleaned herself with a scrap of hide dipped in a thin poultice of mint and water. It was a while before she felt clean. When she finished, she followed her son.

Chebucto, meanwhile, had located his father long before his mother finished wrapping the meat. His heart jumped at the sight of his father's single braid swaying gently along his back. Joot had not yet reached the best hunting area. Chebucto hesitated before signaling his presence.

On hearing Chebucto scrape a pebble softly on juniper bark, Joot turned and looked into his son's eyes. Neither smiled. Neither moved until Joot lifted his chin. Only then did Chebucto walk over to his father.

In silence, a peaceful hush from the viewpoint of the elder, agitated secrecy from the perspective of the younger, the two strolled among the ground squirrel burrows and separated as was their custom. Chebucto continued stewing over the knife as he walked toward the right.

Chebucto's thoughts shied away from the events that laid blame on himself and explored other possibilities, such as his father's long-ago theft of his mother's camelid skin, and his mother's unreasonable desire that he, her only child, marry. In a while he convinced himself that the fouled amethyst knife was yet more evidence of the cruelty of his parents.

* * *

"Is he serious, Baasee'?" my judicious Deloo asked aloud. *How can he blame his father for his thievery?*

I knew she had heard many of her friends blaming their parents for something they had done, and the same was going on with Chebucto thousands of years earlier. *My dear mortal, there's no simple way to learn to take responsibility for your actions. Today's very full prisons are proof. Just be glad that you have learned what many can't. Grandfather, could you go on with the story, please?*

* * *

In this disquieted state, Chebucto nearly missed the bright eyes of a ground squirrel peering at him from under a short, roughly plaited bridge that spanned the entrances between two burrows. Bringing himself into focus, Chebucto walked a step or two more, pretending not to see, pretending to keep his mind on his own misfortune. Unwinding his bola, Chebucto watched the ground squirrel out of the corner of his eye. He tinkered with one of the knots and then allowed one of the bola's stones to swing ever so slowly from his idle hand. The ground squirrel's curiosity bloomed. A thought entered Chebucto's mind, transfixing and binding him to the squirrel.

Sometimes the urge to die is irresistible. Sometimes the urge to kill is overwhelming. Sometimes victim and killer come together as if of one mind.

Disquieted by the alien words, Chebucto eyed the squirrel with altered interest. As if to Chebucto's mind, the ground squirrel moved toward him, one tiny step at a time—nose twitching inquisitively. When the squirrel was two arms' lengths away, Chebucto floated the bola up and outward. The bola settled gracefully around the ground squirrel. Stunned, the small animal remained pinioned for the split second it took Chebucto to strike it with a short lance.

A few moments later, Chebucto tucked the limp body into his game bag. He unwound a tiny length of woven grass from one of his pouches and placed it on the ground near the nettled bridge where he first saw the animal. The squirrels used such gifts to reinforce their bridges, doorways, and underground passages. He groped for the pouch of rye grass seeds that he normally gave as tribute to the ground squirrels. It wasn't there. A shiver of raw anger came from nowhere to race across his shoulders and flow downward along his spine. To rid himself of the uninvited mood, Chebucto took a deep breath and remembered his pemmican. Relieved, he tugged at a gelatinous pouch and scooped out a bit of moschid fat and blueberry mix.

They don't like it on the matting, he remembered.

A quick glance around him revealed a tiny wedge of flat slate. He smeared the pemmican onto the stone and tucked it next to the scrap of matting. Then he thought his way through a prayer of thanksgiving, hoping he gave it some level of credibility: *May you receive this gift in heartfelt gratitude for the life of your brother.*

Even as he tendered the tribute with one part of his mind, his practiced fingers cast the bola again and caught another ground squirrel. He stepped into a lunge as his father had taught him to do, unaware of his gracefulness. Even as he squeezed more pemmican onto a convenient stone and removed a second fragment of woven grass to offer the ground squirrel's relatives, his mind sought and discarded one excuse after another about his father's knife.

Chebucto then searched for his father who had also caught two ground squirrels. Each of the squirrels provided about half of the energy that active people need each day. Between them, the two men had a little more than enough food for themselves, but not yet enough for Mala. Chebucto used the opportunity to tell his father about the scimitar cat, leaving out everything that happened after the cat died.

"Good," Joot said, allowing a small light to brighten his eyes.

Momentarily unburdened, Chebucto felt optimism lift his feet. He was confident that after a good meal Joot would understand and laugh his son's troubles away. Chebucto had no sense of how wrong and yet how right he was.

* * *

At sunrise, earlier that same day the boredom of inactivity had churned Keyo's youthful energy into a whirlwind of barely suppressed urges and nervous twitches. His father was gone, as usual, and Keyo wanted to go somewhere. When grey skies gave way to orange and rose, he bid farewell to his mother and promised to be back soon to help cut and smoke meat with the rest of the family. Jenda smiled helplessly and turned back to her own endless work.

Tavo and the other two men who had watched the northern Tuudzaado compound for a full day observed the slim figure walk toward the east. On Tavo's signal they followed Keyo, choosing a course that took them a little farther to the south than they anticipated. It was a while before they discovered their quarry again. Keyo's distinctive uneven, sprigged haircut reassured them that this was the youth they had targeted.

Unaware of the Dotson, Keyo enjoyed the edgy feel of chilly wind on his face. This was his favorite time of year, his favorite kind of weather. He breathed the fresh air with keen pleasure, glad to be alive and in the Dzagh. He examined the hilly drumlins dotting the area, thinking of himself as the only person in the world. His illusion was dispelled by the sight of three strangers. A sudden tightening gripped Keyo's abdomen. Without thinking he ran, stumbling on the icy, uneven stones. He was suddenly sure they were Dotson.

One of the men stayed where he was while the other two moved toward Keyo. Keyo's view of them was blocked by a tight cluster of spruce trees. A light breeze brought their scent, fresh and immediate, toward his nostrils. He stopped in his tracks.

They are after me, Keyo thought, trying taking stock of his situation.

The snap of a brittle spruce bough breaking somewhere close forced him to run, once again without thinking of where he was going. His long legs covered more ground than those of his followers. After a moment, his initial panic gave way to a kind of deadly force of thought. Keyo took a sharp turn toward the right, a route that would lead him up a steep hill, toward the ground squirrel colony that spanned the western side of the ravine, just opposite its twin colony on Chebucto's side. If the Sacred Forces were with him, his pursuers would stumble in the burrows, slowing them even more. Keyo looked over his shoulder and tripped. One of the men was only ten strides away. As he righted himself, Keyo could hear the man's labored breathing.

Good. He is tiring. I should be able to gain some distance on him up this knoll, Keyo thought, getting to his feet and lengthening his stride.

Keyo aimed for the pathway he had used most of his sixteen years to get to or from Chebucto's house. The path was well worn, and Keyo had no trouble finding the rock and root indentations they used as steps. He was halfway up when he heard another branch cracking in the crystalline air.

Not far away Keyo's mother, Jenda, sat on the comforting softness of a muskrat blanket. As Jenda scraped fat and other tissues from moschid skin, a mental image of her son's face appeared before her. Jenda paused, waiting for the vision to reveal itself in full. She saw Keyo running. He was below a cliff. In a moment, the vision narrowed in on the sheer face of the cliff, and she recognized the pinkish sugar quartz as the place that Keyo and Chebucto used as a shortcut. A narrow path led up the side of the cliff to Chebucto's house, forming a nearly impassable ledge.

Jenda waited to see if there was more. Just as the vision seemed to end, she saw a man's face, saw that he had nearly caught her son. The vision ended.

Jenda leaped to her feet and communed to Keyo.

Son! Are you safe?

She knew he couldn't always understand her use of the Tuudzaado language. She blamed it on his mixed heritage, while her husband, Zaandan, blamed it on himself for not requiring his youngest son to learn the silent protocols. Jenda conjured up the beginning of *aahntaan*, hoping it would work even when she was so agitated. Luckily, Zaandan caught her appeal and responded.

Aloud, Jenda called to Dagoli as she slid through the gateway to the compound herself, "Dagoli, my daughter, no matter what happens, do not follow us." *Stay here until we return,* she finished in the silent language.

Dagoli lifted her face from her sewing in the far corner of the work hut and said with knotted brows, "Yes, Mother."

When her mother was gone, Dagoli put on her outer gear. Slowly, watchfully, she left the work area and crept to her sister-in-law's house on the far side of the cooking arbor. After scratching on the side of the doorway, she ducked to enter. Unlike Keyo, Dagoli used the Tuudzaado language competently and had understood Keyo's plight. Duna, a Hutlan, didn't know any of the Tuudzaado language. Dagoli told Duna what she knew.

"You must stay here," said Duna. "We'll find out what is happening soon enough."

Keyo scrambled the rest of the way up the knoll and glanced around.

There were two more hillocks and then the sheer face of a cliff between himself and the other ground squirrel colony. He ran, trying to project that information toward his parents. He heard the man behind him shouting something indistinguishable and forced himself to move even faster.

Father!! Mother!! Keyo communed, impotent, afraid. *Help me!*

Still unaware of Keyo's plight, Joot and Chebucto came to a hillock overlooking the valley. Chebucto saw something moving on the hillside across the ravine. As Chebucto stared, he picked out Keyo's ungainly way of running. Another movement farther away caught Chebucto's eye. A man. No! Three men. Another movement caught Chebucto's eyes. Zaandan ran to the edge of the cliff and stopped.

"Father!" Chebucto shouted. Joot glanced at his son. Chebucto pointed toward the place he saw Keyo.

"Dotson!" Chebucto whispered.

"What? Where?" Joot asked, squinting. His eyes were too weak to pick out distant features.

"Dotson," his son repeated. He pointed to Keyo. "See? They're chasing Keyo."

Joot stared at the scene below, lips compressed.

"Who is that?"

Chebucto gasped, "That's Uncle Zaandan. He was over there a moment ago." Chebucto pointed to where he had first seen Zaandan. "Look at him move down the face of that cliff!"

Beside him Joot murmured, "did you see him jump off that last ledge? He looked like a bird twisting in midflight. That's Zaandan! He always runs without any regard for his own safety."

Zaandan didn't think about anything but Keyo. He simply leaped into space, grateful that his legs moved without having to be directed. He found himself springing from one icy rock ledge to another with absolutely no sense of the impossibility of his actions. By the time, he got to the bottom of the cliff he had almost reached Keyo, but nothing could undo what was happening to his son.

"Come, Father!" Chebucto shouted. "Let's get down there."

"Stay here, Son," Joot said, his voice constricted. He caught his son's shoulders in a hard grip. "We don't have wings and we are not as fast as your uncle."

Chebucto caught a glimpse of Keyo's bobbing head. It seemed as if his cousin was out of reach of the pursuers. Chebucto felt a spurt of exhilaration. He thought, he's going to make it!

Then Chebucto's groin tightened as he watched one of the men take an inspired shortcut by which he got in front of Keyo. Chebucto shouted, but those below didn't respond. An odd pressure cupped Chebucto's head and blurred his vision. Keyo's legs seemed to warp. Chebucto's chest tightened. He couldn't breathe. Keyo was now two strides away from the tall spruce where the man hid. Chebucto lurched forward, unsure of what he planned to do. Joot's arm clasped his son tightly.

"It's too late," Joot said. "They caught him."

The hidden Dotson man struck Keyo a glancing blow on the head as he passed the spruce tree. Keyo struggled, but the other two caught up. There were too many of them. Keyo was down but not dead. Chebucto could see Keyo's arms writhe, his back arch. Using their feet and cubs, the men battered his cousin.

* * *

Why did they want to kill Keyo, Baasee'? He didn't do anything to them, Deloo's mind reeled with shock.

I asked Grandfather the same thing at the time. I think he should answer.

Grandfather Kwaiikit started with a spray of calming feelings over both me and Deloo. *Poor Keyo was caught in the larger Dotson ambitions to take over all of Zana. Keyo was known as the son of one of the important Tuudzaado people. We learned eventually that they knew about Zaandan's connection to the inner circle of the Dire Wolf Alliance. They knew they could stop Zaandan if they killed his family and better yet him. That's why they killed Keyo.*

Thank you, Grandfather. Those were terrible years for all of us, I, the Penitent Baasee' communed to him.

* * *

Chebucto heard nothing: no screams, no sounds of bones breaking. He was too far away, and Keyo had never been one to express fear or pain with noise. From where Chebucto was, the attackers seemed to move in peaceful respect around the boy, almost as if they were trying to help him.

Zaandan reached them just as one of them turned to go. Without a pause in his stride, Zaandan struck the man with all his body weight, his hands automatically reaching toward the man's neck. The man fell instantly and didn't move again. One of them jumped Zaandan from behind, but Zaandan seemed to have eyes in his spine, for he turned away just in time and kicked the man savagely in the head. Zaandan didn't wait to see if his second attacker was dead or alive. He turned to the remaining man and sprang toward him. The man tried to move out of the way, but Zaandan's long legs brought him face to face with the other before he could do more than twist his torso. Using the momentum of the man's turning shoulders, Zaandan grabbed him by the neck and rammed his head into a sharp-edged rock. Blood spurted onto Zaandan's leggings and tunic. When the third Dotson slumped to the ground, Zaandan's steaming energy left him and his legs felt too heavy to move. Zaandan forced himself to walk back toward the place where his son lay.

Sensations of hot and cold coursed through Chebucto's head and chest as he gawped at his cousin's bloody remains. An odd feeling of being replaced by someone or something else flooded through him. He felt his other self detach from his body—incurious, aware, waiting.

Keyo is dead.

The thought floated through Chebucto, past him, misunderstood and unwanted. His legs moved as if someone else lifted them.

Joot went to get help, instructing Chebucto to wait beside his uncle. Joot returned in a little while with a handful of Hutlan men. Zaandan stood over his son's body. His green-brown eyes were vacant as if he were somewhere else. After an awkward moment, Joot brought out a pouch of red ochre and knelt in the blood to smear some on his nephew's forehead.

"May the Sacred Forces avenge your death, my nephew," Joot murmured. It was a modification of the Hutlan prayer for the First Walk of Death intended to guide Keyo onto the path toward the unknown, the same prayer that Joot had said over the bodies of Iglan and his own relatives.

After he stood up, Joot glanced obliquely at Zaandan, then at his son. He touched Chebucto on the arm. Dark glazed eyes stared back. The Hutlan men who had come to Joot's call moved restlessly. Some of them studied their feet, giving every appearance of wanting to turn and go. Suddenly Chebucto realized that they were waiting for him to take his part in the death rite. Taking a deep breath, he tugged at his string of pouches, feeling for the one he needed. Then he knelt beside the body and applied a dab of yellow powder next to his father's red in the prescribed manner. If he had any words of prayer, his mind refused to give them up. Instead, he heard a strange sound coming from somewhere close and then realized it was his own voice.

Joot put an arm around his son's shoulders to steady him as Chebucto stood up. One by one, the others in the group knelt beside the body until Keyo's forehead was coated with red and yellow powders. Someone brought grass matting. With gentle hands Keyo was rolled out of his blood and onto the dry mat. Joot untied two of his straps and, with help from the others, bound the matting.

A gentle rustling erupted around them as more people moved toward the body. Chebucto saw the distinctive face of his aunt, Jenda. Her eyes, as always, caught attention. Symmetrical, their shape was well marked with prominent upper and lower bones that arched away from her nose. Her eyes were hidden in shadow except for a flicker of light on lash as her eyes darted from one face to another. Zaandan encircled his wife's shoulders with his left arm, and with his right hand held her so that she couldn't grab their son's body. Four or five other Tuudzaado people joined them. Moving stiffly, the Hutlan men who carried Keyo's body laid it gently on the ground before Jenda and Zaandan. No one spoke. After a disquieting pause, the Hutlan men backed away. Without a word, one of the Tuudzaado men lifted Keyo's remains and led the way along a trail that would take them onto the glacial moraine where they would build a funeral pyre.

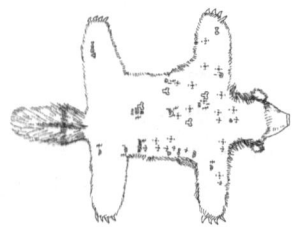

Twenty-Two

Joot found a juniper branch on which he rubbed his hands free of Keyo's blood. He craved the sound of the haunting Prayer Women's dirge to cut through the pain that dragged at his body. However, the Prayer Women sang only for Hutlan funerals. Joot heard a soft grunt. Chebucto nudged his father. Together they watched Mala merge into the group of Tuudzaado people who walked with Jenda and Zaandan. Mala enfolded her sister in a long embrace and then released her to Zaandan. As she extracted herself from Jenda, Mala turned her head and locked eyes with Chebucto. She moved toward him.

"Where is your cousin?" Mala asked.

The question demolished what little remained of Chebucto's self-control. He felt a tremor in one leg and stepped backward to prevent himself from falling. Once again Joot steadied his son.

"Where is Kenduu, Son?" Joot asked in a quiet voice, hoping not to attract attention from the small funeral procession.

Standing in a clot of his dead cousin's blood, Chebucto worked his way through a choppy narrative of his night together with Kenduu. With each attempt to hide the truth, one or the other of his parents caught nuances of deceit and dug for details. By the time, they demanded to know the reason for the argument, Chebucto gave up his last fragment of dignity, burst into swelling sobs, and fell to his knees on the bloody soil. Both parents stood their ground, forcing each other to remain aloof from their crumpling son until he had told them everything. A sudden burst of nameless rage helped renew Chebucto's energy as he described using the amethyst knife and of Kenduu's uninvited and self-righteous accusation that he took it.

"I know I ruined it!" Chebucto shouted, his voice suddenly an unfamiliar, nasalized honk. "I'm sorry, Father," he added, dropping to the blood-reddened ground. "I'm sorry. All of this is my fault. I don't know what happened to Kenduu. I don't know what came over me. If I had stayed with Kenduu, we could have fought these attackers together. Even if we had lost the fight, I would be with him now. It's just what the old medicine man told me. He said I would have trouble honoring my debt to the deer. He was right."

Mala and Joot looked at each other with raised eyebrows. "Debt to the deer?" Joot prompted. "What do you mean?"

Chebucto looked up in surprise, and then breathed more easily. He told them about the old medicine man's prophecy and hung his head. The earth seemed to swallow him. "I am ashamed of myself, and I don't know how to make this up with Kenduu or anyone."

Joot tightened his grip on his son. "We have customs that take in the needs of those left behind when someone dies or disappears. Duna is pregnant with her second child. If Kenduu doesn't come back, it is your responsibility to support Duna and her children if you live. On the other hand, if Kenduu comes back, you must ask him what he will receive from you in payment for what you have done. You will be glad to do whatever he asks."

"I will," Chebucto said. Joot felt a shudder reverberate across his son's shoulders. "That is what the vision means. I will be glad to see him and I will be glad to do everything he asks."

After a brief silence Mala announced, "I'll stay with Jenda while you two go to find Kenduu. If you are not back by the time the funeral pyre has finished its work, I'll search with you." Her lower lip quivered a little as she shifted the wording in the last sentence from "searching for" to "searching with."

Joot moved closer to his wife and wound a lock of her hair around one of his stubby fingers. He pulled on it gently. She nudged him with her shoulder in a feigned gesture of irritation. The playful tug had become the only act of intimacy between his parents that Chebucto could tolerate as his adolescence progressed. Even yesterday he would have pretended not to notice, but now as he looked up at them from his position on the ground his eyes hungered to see all their tender gestures.

Joot glanced at his son and tapped him with the toe of his moccasin. "Get up! Your leggings are soaked."

Chebucto sprang to his feet and looked down. Multiple dark patches saturated his leggings. He caught a whiff of Keyo's blood and staggered back. As before, Joot caught his son by the shoulders and turned him toward the north. Prodding with the heel of his hand, Joot steered his son in the direction of the shallow cave where Chebucto had last seen Kenduu.

"We'll be back," Joot murmured over his shoulder.

Mala lifted her chin in quiet assent. With a sigh, she turned to join the procession. The Naan had been watching the trio from a knoll a short distance to the west.

Too late!

Throughout her life, the Naan had suffered continuous visions. Many times, she had been able to use her cryptic knowledge to save lives but not this time. After taking a small group of freed slaves to safety from Falls Creek, she had hurried to the Dzagh, knowing her grandson was in grave danger. Now that she was here, too late, the Naan pondered her choices: Joot or Zaandan. She chose Joot.

Her long legs closed the space between herself and her quarry with little effort. Following the custom of Zana, the Naan circled silently around them and stopped in an open area to give them an opportunity to see her before they were close enough to speak. It would give the two Hutlan men a chance to deal with their surprise before they confronted her. Her sharp ears picked up the sound of halting steps and a jumble of noises. Then Joot rushed forward.

Chebucto, trailed behind his father, far less sure of his standing with the Naan or the rest of the world. The Naan had tied a coiled dire wolf pelt against the nape of her neck. Tethers dangled from each end of the roll, allowing her to unfurl the pelt with little effort. Chebucto saw that it could be easily used as a head covering as well as a bed roll. Instead of a tunic, endless tethers bound a wide hairless length of hide around her torso that extended from her armpits to her knees. Upon closer examination Chebucto saw that it was the doubled-over waterproof hide of a camelid. As he considered the practicality of the Naan's apparel, Chebucto missed most of the conversation.

"Son! Put your eyes back into their sockets and come with us," Joot muttered to Chebucto, rolling his eyes upward and then meeting The Naan's eyes with an apologetic expression.

The Naan smiled and pointed with her chin toward the north. "I'll go with you to search for my other grandson."

They went first to the place where Kenduu and Chebucto had spent the night. Shortly after midday they found the place where Kenduu had been abducted. The Naan spotted Kenduu's pack. She picked it up and attached it to one of her belts.

When his elders stood side by side, Chebucto saw the remarkable differences between his Hutlan father and the gaunt Tuudzaado woman. Joot was at least two heads shorter than the Naan. His stocky body displayed his well-developed musculature even through heavy clothing. The Naan's willowy body, on the other hand, was so narrow that she could easily hide within a leafless stand of winter-barren willows. Her face, while evenly shaped and attractive, was difficult to appreciate by ordinary standards, both because of the unusual color of her copious body hair as well as because of her extraordinary height. Chebucto touched his own hairless face, wondering why most of the Tuudzaado people he knew, including his mother, seem to have little body hair.

The adults found the scent of the Dotson. The Naan recognized two of them as Dotson men she had seen at the Falls Creek slave grotto.

"I think this scent comes from the man who killed Iglan," Joot said abruptly, "Do you recognize it, Mother-in-Law?" he asked.

The Naan sniffed, and agreed. Until that moment, the amethyst knife had been quiescent, but as soon as his father located the scent it had begun to burn. A vision formed in Chebucto's mind, and he felt himself impelled toward the spot. Chebucto sniffed carefully and whispered, "Father, this is the scent of the man who chased me on the North Face." Between them they told the Naan about it.

When they finished looking at the place Kenduu was captured, they followed the trail for a while. "Do you know why they abducted Kenduu, yet killed Keyo?" The Naan asked the others.

Joot said after a moment of silence, "It seems to me that they would have taken both, not just Kenduu. In fact, it would make more sense to take Keyo, since he was a lot smaller."

The Naan replied, "I agree. Let's go back to where my grandson, Keyo, was killed."

When they returned to the site of Keyo's death, each of them took care to examine the men whose bodies had been left unceremoniously to scavengers. "I think I know this one," Joot said, "I saw him last year when I was visiting my relatives on the North Face."

They inspected the other two bodies. The Naan nodded toward Tavo. "This is a man who has caused a lot of hardship among us. He didn't hunt for slaves. He hunted for Tuudzaado—to kill them."

"Did you know him yourself?" Joot asked.

"No, but I have found his scent whenever there's been a massacre, including Iglan's."

They made their way to the preparations for a funeral pyre. By the time Joot and Chebucto reached Mala, the pall of shock had been displaced by the warmth of the fire. Joot saw Jenda and Zaandan sitting together, wrapped in a short-faced bear hide.

My brother-in-law has aged over night! Joot studied the haggard lines etched in yellow by firelight that creased and shadowed Zaandan's face. Even in the darkness he knew his oldest and best friend was no longer a lively, handsome man. Joot walked toward them and was a few strides away when he saw Dagoli's small head poking out of the shadows between her parents. Duna and her son, Masito, sat behind them under a separate pelt. The Naan reached them before he did and crouched beside her son. Joot could tell by the expressions on their faces that she was telling them what happened to Kenduu. Jenda began to wail, her voice ringing ever more loudly with each breath. The Naan lifted her chin toward Zaandan. He drew Jenda out of the bear rug and took her toward their family compound. The Naan picked up the fallen bear skin and trailed after them.

* * *

Jenda's mind spun in dark circles blurred by images of Keyo. Only by throwing herself into the frenzy of planning could she stop the ringing peal of his final words: Help me! Between them, the Naan, Jenda and Zaandan made some key decisions. Then Zaandan insisted that Jenda take a sleeping potion.

"You have to be strong for Dagoli and Duna," he said.

"I don't want this, Husband. I want to go with you to find my son," Jenda protested, but gave in to the pressure from both her husband and mother-in-law. Jenda had always treated Kenduu as a son. Kenduu's mother died in a brutal ambush by Dotson men when her son was barely three years old. With no one in his household to take care of the active boy, Kenduu's grandmother tended him, but the effort exhausted her strength and resources. She was sad to lose him, but relieved when the Naan offered to take him. Then the Naan had brought Kenduu, Mala and Jenda to her son's compound. Zaandan leaped at the chance to offer a home to the little boy and to give his new son a mother. No doubt he felt the comfort of the Sacred Forces when Jenda's beautiful eyes and face aroused feelings in him that he hadn't felt for his first wife, the aged widow of one of his Hutlan uncles. Although Kenduu had missed his late mother as much as any toddler can, it wasn't long before stepmother and stepson became inseparable. Soon Jenda called Kenduu her son, omitting the linguistic distinctions that others might enforce.

Zaandan said, "If Kenduu manages to escape and return here, he is going to need your help. Moreover, he will want to see that both his wife and his mother are safe."

Responding to the wisdom of his words, Jenda gave in to the strong sleeping potion and sank into the folds of their ermine wedding blanket, a gift from her Hutlan grandmother-in-law. With fading awareness, she pulled her husband toward her, hoping to lure him into the warmth of the luxurious fur. Zaandan slid skillfully out of reach.

"As we decided, my mother will stay here for a day or two to search for the Dotson. I must go soon, although there is something else that needs my attention here," he said.

Almost slumbering, Jenda managed a comforting "mmm."

Regretting having given her the potion so soon, Zaandan communed more forcibly, *my wife, don't fall asleep yet. We must decide what to do about Duna if our son does not return.*

Jenda's body tightened. She responded, *what do you mean 'do something about Duna?'*

I mean that in the conventional way of things I should take her as another wife if Kenduu doesn't return. If you have any objections whatsoever, then we must decide what else we could do to provide for their care while Duna's children are so young.

The calming effects of the herbs vanished. Jenda lay rigidly still as she contemplated her husband's words. After a great while she replied, *but surely that is Chebucto's obligation.*

Yes, but Chebucto is young and obviously not very responsible, Zaandan answered. *He has an obligation to support Duna, but he is not yet capable of raising a growing family. Much as I know you cherish Mala, do you want your sister to take our grandchildren away from you and away from our household?*

Jenda absorbed these thoughts, then quickly rolled away from Zaandan's long reach. She pushed herself into a sitting position.

You must tell our daughter-in-law that she is to become your second wife and Masito is to become our son. Masito will replace the son I don't have anymore. I must have him in my arms and in my heart, Jenda communed decisively. *Husband, you must tell her before you leave.* Her body radiated tumultuous energy, assuring him that the sleeping potion had lost control of her.

Zaandan searched for Duna in her house. She wasn't there. He prowled around the compound and found her seated on the dirt floor of a work shed, apparently sorting through a pile of things. He wondered if she had better night vision than he, for all he could see were heaps of grey bundles.

Not that it matters, he thought. She's probably as worried and restless as I am.

Zaandan shuffled nervously from foot to foot. A cough erupted from deep in his chest, shattering the calm of the night. A mild congestion that a day ago would have disappeared by evening now seemed to have taken control of his normally healthy body. Head held at a stiff angle, Zaandan clenched his jaws and forced himself to say in the Hutlan language, "My daughter-in-law, I'll be leaving soon to search for your husband. My mother will stay for a day or so in case there's more trouble. If all goes well, Kenduu and I should be back here in a few days. However, you and I both know that it's possible Kenduu might not return."

Zaandan stared at the dark night sky, finding it easier to talk to a star than to the young woman in front of him. With his voice tight and cracking, he continued, "Daughter-in-Law, you are an important part of our family, as well as the mother of my grandson and future grandchild. It is my obligation to find another husband for you if Kenduu doesn't return. Jenda and I have spoken, and we would like you to..."

Zaandan's throat clamped shut. He struggled to swallow. The fever in his lungs hurt, but Zaandan was less aware of it than the discomfort of speaking with a woman whom Zanian protocol required he should avoid. Forcing himself to breathe evenly, he continued, "Daughter-in-Law, I would be honored to know that you would accept me as a husband if something should happen to my son."

While Duna listened to her father-in-law she kept her face downcast in a posture that had become customary for Hutlan women. Zaandan suddenly realized how well the custom allowed her to hide all emotional reactions. For whatever reason his normally keen intuition deserted him. After a while, Duna peeped at her father-in-law and quickly glanced down again.

"I am aware of the custom, Father-in-law." Her voice was tiny. "I am sure you will bring back my husband. If not, my parents told me it was also my right to return to them if something should happen to Kenduu." Duna ventured a glance at Zaandan's face but it was too dark to see his expression. Unable to think of what else to say, Duna, simply sat on the cold ground, staring at her feet. When he didn't leave, she collected her thoughts and said in a frightened voice, "I thank you, my father-in-law. I will consider your words and discuss it with my father if it happens that I should need to make a decision."

Zaandan smiled, relieved. "You speak the formal language very well, my daughter-in-law. I am proud to be your father-in-law."

Duna smiled, forcing back tears. Getting to her feet, she left without speaking. He heard the soft crackle of hide on bark as she opened the stiff hide that covered the entryway to her small house.

Zaandan returned to Jenda and described their daughter-in-law's ambivalent response. "Maybe an eighteen-year-old woman thinks a man of thirty-six would make a repulsive husband," Zaandan said aloud.

Aroused by the odd twist he gave spoken language, Jenda smiled into the darkness and reached for him. "I won't give away your secrets, my husband. I was only fifteen when I married you. At that time, I was very sure that a man of nineteen was too old to breathe."

Zaandan let his wife pull him closer. He cuddled her for a while, hoping she would sleep. However, fatigue overpowered him instead. He dozed off. Jenda wrapped her arms around her husband and lay in an uncomfortable reverie, wishing that everything that had happened was all part of a strange and horrible story told by someone who had accidentally used their sons' names. Nearly convinced of the unreality of Keyo's death, Jenda fell into a state in which she was equally asleep and awake. Her arms remained locked around Zaandan.

The Naan entered the sod house just when night was beginning its third quarter. She roused her son with a gentle nudge. Zaandan, fighting both grogginess and a twisting headache, forced himself to awake.

My son, the Naan urged, *the sooner you find the men who have taken him, the more likely you are to find our Kenduu still alive. Also, I think you should consider my grandson's murder sufficient reason to break your agreement to marry a Dotson wife. Agreed?*

Yes, Mother. That agreement was broken the moment my son was attacked.

Jenda awoke just as Zaandan tied the last of the straps that held his gear in place and headed for the southern trail leading toward Falls Creek. In the glimmering light of the waning Teratornis Moon, Jenda watched his long legs gliding along the trail until she couldn't distinguish him from the rest of the landscape.

* * *

Just after daybreak of the last day of the Teratornis Moon, Mala, Joot and Chebucto quietly entered the compound. The rustle of their leggings was enough to arouse Jenda. The Naan joined the group from the shadows of the drumlin.

"Is this yours?" The Naan asked Joot.

Joot glanced the pile and said, "Mother-in-Law, you know that I would have brought my sister-in-law food at a time like this, but this is actually from Chebucto. He has expressed his grave concern about Kenduu and acknowledges with this food his intentions to repay you for the loss of your grandson."

Chebucto stood up straighter and shuffled his feet nervously. "What happened to Kenduu is my fault," he said. "I want to do what's right and this is not enough."

The Naan looked at her great-nephew and smiled. "It's not your fault that Kenduu is gone. He might have been abducted whether you were there. Thank you for this, as it will make it easier on everyone to know my family has food for many days."

Joot and his family left shortly before the day reached its second quarter.

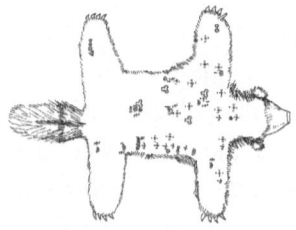

Twenty-Three

As Chebucto recalled it, his life began that day, the twenty-eighth day of the Teratornis Moon. In the early morning light of that day, Joot, Mala and Chebucto crossed the ravine separating them from Zaandan's compound. Bound into their private thoughts, each walked unmindful of the others or anything around them. Of the three, only Joot thought of Keyo. He thought of the happy grin on the boy who took such joy in small things. The boy who, but for the fact that he decided to take a solitary walk, would have greeted him at the entrance to his father's compound. Joot glanced at Chebucto's buttocks in front of him. Chebucto's best friend died the same way his own childhood friend had died so many years ago, and like he did, Chebucto would mourn his friend for the rest of his life.

Is this going to continue with every new generation? he wondered. Why haven't we done something about it? Even as the thought burst forth, Joot realized that some people, namely those in the Dire Wolf Alliance, were doing what they can. Why can't I join the Dire Wolf Alliance? I need to do something. He thought about the day Zaandan had asked for help with the escapees. At the time Chebucto was only two, and Joot was reluctant to bring his wife or son any closer than they had been to the brutality of the Dotson. When he explained his reasons for saying no, Zaandan had looked disappointed. That was the only time Zaandan ever asked him for such help. Joot wondered if saying yes back then might have prevented Keyo's death now. Confused about his feelings, Joot looked around for Mala. He nearly stumbled at the sight of her. Except for the sheen of sunlight on her billowing hair, the woman behind him was a stranger. Her dark eyes stared at nothing.

"Mala!" he whispered, "are you with cold?"

If his wife heard him, she didn't react. Joot reached for her hand, hoping the strength and warmth of her long fingers coiling around and into his would revive her—or him. The hand he grasped lay passively in his. Joot looked at it, surprised to see for the first time that his wife's hands were calloused and hard. Refusing to lose contact with her, he said, "I want to do something more than offer food."

The words filled a void in his chest. As Joot contemplated the peace that came with them, his left foot tangled with Chebucto's. All three of them fell, arms and legs striking each other. When they reached the bottom of the ravine, Joot was the first to pick himself up.

"What did you say?" Mala whispered, shaking off dust from her tunic.

"Me too!" Chebucto said, his voice oddly flat. "I'm going after him."

"After whom?" Mala asked, looking from her husband to her son with dawning comprehension. "Kenduu?"

"Yes," Chebucto replied. He touched his tunic, and said, "I have to go. The knife won't stop moving. I see Kenduu and I see the man with the scar. I have to go after Kenduu."

"What knife?" Mala asked, now more irritated than confused.

Joot helped his wife to her feet. "The amethyst knife," he explained. "Our son took it and still has it." He gave a sketchy explanation of how their son got the knife.

Chebucto removed the knife from his neck and handed it to Joot. "I'm sorry Father. I meant to give this to you earlier, but I forgot."

Joot held the knife in his hand and stared. It glowed and moved on Joot's palm. Joot tried to clench his fist around the knife, but his fingers would not close. Suddenly the knife soared out of his hand and dropped on the ground in front of Chebucto. When Joot could speak again he said, "No, Son. The Sacred Forces have given the knife to you. It's your responsibility now."

* * *

Deloo squirmed in her mother's comfortable chair, and mumbled to herself, "Let him ignore the Sacred Forces now!" She looked up toward a placed she imaged as my lair in the ceiling, *Baasee', did Checbucto ever figure things about those Sacred Forces? Like me?*

Like you, Mortal? Grandfather's attention was caught now. I smiled and reminded him about trying to teach her about the four stages of life and its responsibilities.

Yes, my beloved Deloo. He is at this time in his story younger than you are now at twenty-one. Like you have done in coming to terms with your late husband's sudden death, so did Chebucto have to learn to understand that something beyond him has more to say about life and death than we do.

Deloo stared down at her hands. *Yeah. I don't have as much to take on. Not like Chebucto did back in your era. I don't have to adopt entire families because Arthur died, but I want to. I want to help Great Aunt Pauline. She's like the Naan, isn't she?*

I shimmered toward Grandfather Kwaiikit, for whom the Naan

had been like a mother. He nodded, and communed to my Deloo, *Yes, Mortal, your Great Aunt Pauline is very much like the Naan.* He continued telling the story.

* * *

Mala glanced at each of them, her eyes unreadable. "So, you want to do more," she tipped her head toward Joot, "and you want to go after Kenduu." Getting two lifting chins in response, she added, "I, too, want to do more. I can't live in fear of the next Dotson who storms through here. Jenda and I spent our early lives cringing from the Dotson. I used to help the Dire Wolf Alliance when I was in Broken Jaw. Now all I do is hoard food and try to impress our Hutlan neighbors. I am disgusted with myself."

"Son," she said, turning her eyes on Chebucto, "your father and I talked quite a bit while you were gone. He helped me understand that I have been wishing for something that doesn't match reality." Mala sighed heavily, and continued, "He helped me to understand that I have always envied Jenda and all she has without thinking of what she does not have. And now she does not have Keyo. I always thought that Jenda was content," Mala tipped her head toward her husband, "but long before yesterday's horrible events, your father saw the burden she carries in her marriage to Zaandan. She has two grandchildren, a stepson and two daughters remaining to her—and a constant fear of the vengeance of the Dotson for all of my early work with the Dire Wolf Alliance as well as the work Zaandan is still doing for them."

Mala reached toward Chebucto's short hair. "Keyo was not as mature as you were even before you went to the North Face. He needed to be guided by a firm hand. You needed that kind of guidance for a long time as well. All that has finally changed for you. I am proud of you for wanting to go after Kenduu."

"So am I," Joot said. He clutched Mala's hand, but her fingers slipped away from him lifelessly. He looked at her, torn between petulance and fear.

Mala continued speaking in a toneless voice. "I am proud of you, Son, but it's probably too late. Kenduu is probably already dead. You could have saved him. I suspect that you could have done something to save Keyo. You watched it happen. Both of you watched it happen."

Chebucto froze in horror. She was right. He had simply watched. He remembered feeling his father's arms pulling him back and opened his mouth to say so. The amethyst knife burned on his chest, and he touched it again.

"You are right, Mother. I should have run to him. I was closer than Uncle Zaandan and younger. I knew what they were and did nothing to help my cousin. I will never let that happen again."

Joot sank to the ground, "My wife, do you remember when years ago Zaandan asked me to help him in the Dire Wolf Alliance. I refused him. Now I want to ask him or the Naan to let me help. I feel a huge need inside me to help in some way."

"Us," said Mala with quiet authority. "Inside us, my husband, we can do a lot to help."

Chebucto touched the amethyst knife, once again tied to his neck. It moved gently. He said calmly, "We should talk about this at home while I get ready to search for Kenduu."

The three resumed their struggle up the side of the ravine. When they reached the edge of their compound, Mala refused to enter. "This home that your father and I built is a horror to me now, I can't live here anymore."

"What?" Joot stared at the stranger who had just spoken. "My wife, this is our home; we can't leave it just because one person has died."

"It's not just one person," Mala responded, unmindful of the tears flowing from her eyes. "There's Iglan and his entire family. There's the family who were butchered on the West Face. My mother and all my relations were murdered at Broken Jaw. I am a strong woman, just as strong as Zaandan, but I've never lifted a finger to help anyone. I can't go on being that person, I won't go back to that life and I can no longer live in this home."

The shocks of the day had taken away Joot's sense of reality. Mala was taking away his life. He stared at her soundlessly.

Mala said quietly, "I've been thinking about this ever since you and I had that long talk," she lifted her chin toward her husband. "Now I am sure, Husband, that it is just as you told me. I have been trying to help others by becoming wealthy with extra food and all our things. You helped me understand that I have deceived myself, all I wanted were these things. Helping others with our extra food was an easy way to satisfy the *hootlyeets* that haunt me. As you said to me so many times, the only way to be of genuine help to others is to become free of all this. I want to ask the Naan if I am ready to become a Nicoleena."

Joot couldn't recall a single time that he had urged her to give up their compound and everything they had done to create it. "Do you mean you want to abandon me as well as the compound?"

Mala's mouth quirked downward. "I treasure our place, but you taught me to think about what I really want." She considered her husband's face. "You made it for me and I treasure anything you do, whether it is for me or other people. I don't want to abandon you, but a Nicoleena usually works alone like the Naan does."

Joot was flabbergasted, he looked at the compound helplessly. He and Mala had built every part of it together. It represented his entire life. "Why?"

Mala dropped her chin to her chest. "It is too close to them," she said, nodding her head toward the area to the north where most of their Hutlan neighbors lived. "It is on a main trail. Everyone passes here if they are going south or coming in from either the southern or eastern trails. If we had escapees, they would be scented right away. We have to protect them."

Chebucto looked at his mother with growing comprehension. With a broad, suddenly boyish smile he said, "You mean it's too exposed to be a safe house! Keyo talked about the safe houses. The Dire Wolf Alliance has about twenty of them around Zana. Is that what you mean, Mother?"

* * *

Deloo waved her arm in the air, completely captivated. *She wants to be just like Great Aunt Pauline. Pauline gave up having a life of her own to take care of my mother and later me. Now she takes lots of people. Great Aunt Pauline is a modern day Nicoleena!*

Glowing benignly at her, I agreed with my beloved Deloo and asked Grandfather to continue.

* * *

Mala tipped her chin upward, looking at Joot with appeal in her dark eyes. "Yes, that is what I want to do. At least it's part of want I want. I also want revenge against them for everything they have done to us."

Joot turned and gazed across the ravine. Chebucto stared wordlessly at his mother. He realized suddenly how different she looked from the day before when he brought his scimitar cat hunting bag home. *Her eyes have a look I've seen somewhere.* He stared at his mother until it came to him. When he was seven, his father had taken him to see Falls Creek, while there they encountered a hunting pack of dire wolves. The leader of the pack had turned and stared at Chebucto. It was the same look that he now saw on his mother's face. *She has the look of a dire wolf. A look of someone who could kill without mercy.*

He turned toward his father, wondering if Joot saw the change, but Joot stood with his back to them. After a long silence, Joot said, "So it's time, then. I knew this moment would come as soon as I saw those twelve bodies piled on Iglan's funeral pyre. I didn't want to admit it then, but it's obvious that unless we do something now, we might as well cut our own throats to save the Dotson some time." He turned and stood beside his wife. "We can't leave it like this," he said after a hesitation. "We have things to take with us and we have to hide the rest so no one will be able to use it unless they belong here."

Chebucto watched his mother's face come to life. He took a deep breath. "I'm going to find Kenduu, dead or alive. I'll kill every one of the Dotson men who took him, whether he's dead or not." Chebucto stopped, surprised at the force of his voice.

Joot had walked into the compound and picked up Chebucto's hunting bag with the scimitar claws inside. He pulled out one of the claws and turned toward his son, an odd look on his face. "I think you are finally ready for that kind of work, my boy."

Chebucto took one of the claws from the bag and wound a narrow strap around it. As he knotted the strap to the sheath and looped it around his neck, he asked, "What about you, Mother? What are you actually going to do once we have got this place ready?"

Mala answered, "The Dire Wolf Alliance needs safe houses, but a safe house is only safe if no one knows it is there."

Chebucto responded by lifting his chin. "I want to join forces with Dire Wolf Alliance," he said, "even if I don't have a dire wolf pack."

"I agree, Son," Mala said with tight lips. "I believe the only way to do that is to become a Nicoleena."

"Like the Naan? I don't understand. How can you become a Nicoleena if you aren't born that way?"

* * *

Deloo sagged back into her chair, *what does it mean to be born that way? Was Great Aunt Pauline born to make Little Tanana out of this little neighborhood in Fairbanks. Does it take knowing you're that way from birth?* She looked for me, Baasee' the spirit guide hiding in my ceiling hole.

No, Deloo, the people who become great leaders or behind-the-scenes-helpers like your Great Aunt Pauline or Mala in this story are touched by great forces in their lives. Often those great forces are obvious, like taking care of your mother, Tally, was to her Aunt Pauline. Mala and the rest of her family were touched by something even greater than that: they were guided by the Sacred Forces. That's why you are excited. So are you. Grandfather Kwaiikit and I, Baasee' the Awestruck, were used to helping people understand what they could do when they were grabbed by the Sacred Forces.

* * *

Mala stared into space, her mind racing.

Joot wandered slowly around the compound, touching things as he passed. He stopped at his work area and examined the lean-to that held all his tools in neatly strung containers dangling from makeshift pegs. He pulled out one of his longer hand axes and caressed it with his finger. Finally, he turned toward Chebucto and said, "Being a Nicoleena is more than powers and appearance, Son. It means having nothing. The Naan has nothing except what she wears," Joot said, unable to keep a mournful tone out of his voice. Even as he spoke, he thought of the amazing number of pelts and tools she kept dangling around her lanky body. In the summer, she changed the camelid robe for a lighter deer hide. He wondered if she had a place to keep extra things after all.

Mala said, "A good hunter makes do with what he's got." She smiled, remembering how often she heard Joot say that to Chebucto. "That's what a Nicoleena is."

Joot looked at his wife with something between fright and loathing. He sighed. "I wanted Zaandan to ask me again. I don't have the Naan's power, but I am ready to do my part in fighting the Dotson."

"Before we do anything else," Mala said, "we need to agree that this compound is no longer to be used like a home. If we can't agree on that, then it's time for me to say goodbye to both of you."

Chebucto stared at his mother and father, he waited for Joot to answer. Joot strolled around his compound as if no one had spoken, he stopped in front of his tall wife. "I agree," he said simply.

Mala released a huge sigh and smiled hopefully. She reached toward him, but Joot kept his face averted from her and studied the compound. Without a word, he went to his working area and lifted a spear point. "I guess I'll start here," he said. "All of our stone tools will be stored here," he pointed to the back side of the compound. "We need to place a slab of slate on top of them. Then we'll be able to come back for some of these things when we need them."

Hurt, mystified, yet oddly detached, Mala followed his directions. She said nothing as she observed her husband searching for spear points, bola stones, axes, burins, mauls, and other stone tools. The two placed each item with precise care into a shallow pit. She helped them cover the tools with a thin layer of sandy loam. Between them, Chebucto and Joot carried a big piece of slab to the tool pit and covered the pit.

* * *

I don't understand, Baasee', why is Joot taking over when it was Mala's idea in the first place? My wonderful mortal twisted a nonexistent ring where her wedding band had been throughout the past year. I had encouraged her to remove it a few weeks ago to symbolize to others that she was ready to move on.

I took a big breath into nonexistent lungs, and communed, *Grief does odd things to people, my Deloo. Remember how it was for you shortly after Arthur died. That happened to all of them, and also, Joot is trying to show his wife that he will go with her wherever she goes. It's a gesture of the strength of his love for her.*

Deloo felt a shiver go through her body and she smiled, *I wish I...* She patted her ring finger and swallowed. *Thank you, Baasee'. I'd like to hear the rest of the story now, Grandfather Kwaiikit. I'm sorry I interrupted.*

* * *

Mala had never liked Joot's tools, but now that they were buried and no longer his, she wanted to shriek with horror when Joot came up behind her and encircled her waist with his arm. Mala first tensed and then relaxed against her husband. Together, they walked slowly around the compound they had built together. Thinking he needed to give his parents a little privacy, Chebucto contemplated taking a break to visit Keyo and looked for something to clean the dirt from his hands. He saw a piece of hide, stepped toward it and suddenly remembered.

Keyo wasn't there anymore.

Chebucto was still in his lean-to when Joot and Mala returned. They heard his loud snuffling and left him in peace.

Twenty-Four

Like Broken Jaw, the Falls Creek region was warm in winter and hot in the summer. Where their earlier journey toward the Dzagh had found them battling icy winds, the three Dotson were now unpleasantly aware of the muggy warmth of the Falls Creek valley. Unlike the Dzagh where the constant wind left a hardened surface that made walking easy, they now had to navigate a combination of ice-laden muddy slop and sharp-stoned gravel trails. Their way led past one side of the sprawling claystone buildings to reach the grottoes. Despite the cumbersome weight of Kenduu they arrived at Falls Creek near dawn, a day after the capture. They kept listening for Tavo to catch up with them, but were not concerned that he had not yet arrived.

Kenduu was not tied to the pole. Rather, his hands and feet were bound tightly together and the scrub pine trunk had been slid between his body and the bindings at ankles and wrists. Most of Kenduu's weight suspended from his wrists. Every time the carriers jostled the pole, pain shot through Kenduu's arms and shoulders. His wrist guards prevented the skin from bleeding. Kenduu wondered whether if leaving the wrist guards in place was an oversight or an inadvertent kindness that they might rectify. He concentrated on his shoulders and back. By spreading his elbows, a little and pushing his focus carefully along his spine, he could spread some of the drag on his wrists to his ankles. It relieved some of the pain and kept his mind away from the larger problem of how soon they planned to kill him.

"Ho!" The snarl startled Kenduu. He cracked his eyes open and peered around. Facing backward, Kenduu could see they had emerged from the scrub brush of the Dzagh and crossed a narrow strip of grassy open land. He turned his head cautiously and closed his eyes against the burning brightness of a white stone nearby. Using his nose, ears, and skin, Kenduu explored the new environment carefully, hoping to plan his escape. He brought in air slowly to sort out the different scents.

All men. Not much information and certainly not a surprise, but Kenduu was satisfied he could make plans even though he couldn't see anything. He let the air out quietly and took in the various sensations on his exposed skin. In moments, he had a clear idea of where each man stood. Heat from on one side of him compared to the cool air issuing as a draft from the other gave him the cardinal directions of East and West.

It was early morning, and the hot lowland sun already radiated from the stones to the west, stirring a mild current in the colder air on the east. There he sensed the rocks were larger and probably shaped into some sort of wall.

Someone greeted his Dotson captors with a cheerless grunt. Through half-shut eyes, Kenduu studied the new arrival. Short, rough hair sprang away from his brows as if to greet the sun. He muttered "So you finally arrived. I was expecting you five or six days ago. Do they want us to take him as well as the other one?"

The men holding Kenduu muttered, "What other one?"

"The Tuudzaado man I've been keeping here. They said someone from Broken Jaw would come to get him. Isn't that why you are here?"

The other Dotson men stared at each other and shrugged. One of them said, "I don't know anything about the other one. Ask the Black Sun Warrior."

"The Black Sun Warrior?" The guard shook his head. "I don't want to ask him anything."

"Where shall we take him?"

The guard reached out to touch Kenduu.

"Careful," someone muttered, "he's a fighter."

After more arguing, the guard pointed the way to a big slab of wood leaning against the side of a boulder. Two men lifted Kenduu and deposited him on the ground. They waited while two other men rolled aside the wood. The men who brought him wanted to drop Kenduu inside with his bonds intact, but there wasn't enough room for the long pole nor room to let anyone as big as Kenduu to lie prone.

"You're going to have to untie him," said the guard.

Kenduu was waiting. As soon as his legs and arms were freed, he began flailing the air, landing a resounding blow on at least two people before someone struck him on the back of the head.

When he awoke, Kenduu sat against the far wall. At least he thought it was the far wall. Regaining consciousness didn't come with his normally acute sense of direction. In the intense blackness of the cell, he couldn't tell which way was up, let alone whether he was close to the opening. Eventually he discovered the splintery texture of the old wood that had been used to block the entry. A few experimental shoves against the stones near it convinced him that there was no way out in that direction. He explored the wall to find out what else was there, his hands touched something warm. Kenduu jerked back and then reached out again, it was the dormant body of another person. He felt along the body until his hands distinguished the head from the rest. He determined that it was a male, and by the size of him, probably a very young one. He shook the youth with determined vigor until the other person moaned.

"Be at peace, my friend. I won't hurt you," Kenduu said.

"Who are you?" a soft voice asked.

In the quiet time that followed Kenduu learned his companion was ten years old and had been in the cell for three days or so.

"No one lives more than three days in here, and I'm still alive," he said.

"Why did they put you here?" Kenduu asked.

In a detached voice, the youth said, "this is the dying cell." After a long silence, he asked Kenduu to try to get word back to his father about what happened to him.

"My name is Aadso'."

"How did this happen to you?" Kenduu asked.

"I was hunting in the lower reaches of the glacial moraine with my oldest cousin. Strangers attacked us. Dotson. They tied my arms behind my back and forced me to walk. I don't know what happened to my cousin. He was older than me. He's probably dead."

They took Aadso' to the slave grotto. Day after day he was forced to pick clams and crabs off the beach.

"They made you a slave, then." Kenduu said at last.

"And you as well," Aadso' responded.

Kenduu recoiled. After a while he asked, "How did you become so weak, my friend?"

"They give us rotten shellfish to eat. I can't keep it down. It makes me sick," Aadso' said.

"Did they put you in here when you first arrived?" Kenduu asked, intending to follow the question with an estimate of how long they would be there.

"No, this is the dying cell. At first I was placed in one of the grottoes."

"They went to a lot of the trouble to capture me," Kenduu said. "Why put me in here to die without getting the work out of me, too?" Kenduu puzzled.

"You must be strong and big," Aadso' whispered. "I saw them put a few other big ones in here. This place is for fighters and the weak ones like me. I got too weak to dig for clams, but I was still strong enough to try to escape if they let me sit outside. If you're a fighter, they might let you out of here." Despite the words, Aadso's voice carried no hope. After a long silence, Aadso' asked, "How old are you?"

"Twenty," Kenduu answered. After a moment he added, "I'll be twenty-one in the next Glacial River Moon. My wife will give birth to our second child in the spring. We already have a son who is two-and-a-half years old."

Kenduu stopped as he realized that he might never see the unborn baby. Suddenly all the strength drained from his body and he nearly collapsed when the enormity of his situation came to him.

He felt Aadso's thin fingers stroke his head. When the fingers reached the back of his skull, Aadso' tensed and stopped.

"Blood," he whispered. "They hit you very hard."

Kenduu reached up himself and felt the wound. He could tell by the tackiness of the blood that the main bleeding had long stopped. Under the wetness, he felt the swellings and soft scabs from the wounds he got the day he was captured. He explored the new injuries carefully and tried to pull out what seemed to be dirt or dead tissue.

After a while he muttered, "It won't kill me. I've survived worse than this." Dropping his hands to his lap he asked, "will they let me out?"

Aadso' waited before he answered. "They might let you out if you are still alive when they come again." He stopped and then added in a lower voice, "I won't be alive. Maybe they will force you to eat my body."

In disbelief, Kenduu rebutted, "No! They can't do that to us."

The boy didn't respond, and after a while Kenduu asked how long he had been enslaved.

"I'm not sure. My cousin and I were attacked on the night of the sixteenth day of the Camelid Moon just after it was full."

"Camelid Moon. Last summer," Kenduu murmured. "I think today is the twenty-eighth day of the Teratornis Moon or it might already be the first day of Black Paint Moon. That's almost four moons since you were captured."

Aadso' responded, "Others say that one or two moons are all they expect out of a slave." His hollow laugh sent a shaft of fear through Kenduu's belly and groin.

In a while, Kenduu asked about Aadso's family, taking care to memorize the details in the dim hope of meeting them one day. As the boy spoke, Kenduu realized that he could see a thin band of light around the entry way to their prison. He kept his eyes on the light until it faded completely.

Aadso' had fallen asleep before the last bit of visible light seemed to slip out of Kenduu's grasp. Kenduu kept his eyes open as long as possible, but eventually awareness slipped away from him as well.

Kenduu wasn't sure what awoke him. He noticed an odd white haze around him and fought the urge to sleep to locate the source.

Are you there?

Kenduu started. The silent language was different from anything he knew. He waited.

Are you the Tuudzaado man they brought in? I have information for you.

Kenduu used his private thinking mode to consider the question and questioner. The language was that used by the Naan, but in some ways, it seemed like that of his stepmother, Jenda. Jenda's parents were from some distant place called Datherd. What it didn't feel like was the style of language used by the Tuudzaado women of the Dzagh. Then he remembered Rastuk spoke with the woman's language. Maybe.... Overwhelmed by the possibility that the Sacred Forces had brought him exactly to where Kwaiikit wanted one of them to go, Kenduu felt a thrill of victory. Kwaiikit's plan had begun. Because of that, Kenduu suddenly felt an immeasurable surge of hope. Then he wondered if Kwaiikit was there, too. Using his mind to probe for the presence of familiar Tuudzaado people, Kenduu had no sense of Kwaiikit's presence. Then he reasoned, maybe I am too weak and confused to pick out his location.

Are you there?

Pulled back to the present by Rastuk's second query, Kenduu tried to remember everything the four of them had talked about upon the cliff top so close to where he was now. Then he thought of the strategies that he and Ping created as they hiked together. Ping and he had communed and whispered continuously, each by turns offering a phrase or technique to pry as much as possible out of Rastuk. The long hike up a difficult mountain trail slipped by as if they had been sauntering on soft grass. The two young men also marveled to each other about the sudden, easy way they were now part of the Dire Wolf Alliance. They discovered they thought alike about almost everything that had to do with the Dire Wolf Alliance. At the time, they were sure it would be Ping who would meet Rastuk again, since Kenduu could imagine no reason to return to Falls Creek. Between them they devised several imaginary conversations by which they thought Ping would extract all the hidden information Rastuk's mother had sent them through her son. Now realizing that it was he rather than Ping who was talking to Rastuk, Kenduu felt fear that everything would fall apart because of this glitch in their plan. He took a deep breath and remembered how often his father had faced death and outsmarted Dotson men to save so many lives. Kenduu had envied his father's strength and resolution all his life. Now it was his turn.

I was captured by the Dotson. Who are you?

Rastuk introduced himself as a woman named Roseau, and provided the same ancestry that he had used with Ping and Kwaiikit. Kenduu asked the questions everyone mentioned and others, surprised that "Roseau" seemed so willing to answer and added even more information without being prompted. After a while Kenduu realized "Roseau's" willingness to talk came with quite a few of "her" own questions. Kwaiikit knew what kind of information Rastuk would be seeking, and gave instructions a set of fabricated facts and names about places and people in the Dzagh. Very soon Kenduu found himself revealing everything Kwaiikit invented that night. As they thought, "Roseau" needed a lot of information about the history of each family. Kenduu tranquilly supplied a myriad of useless information about his invented family. In return, "Roseau" willingly provided a lot of information about Dotson, especially details about people of a long time ago. "Roseau" repeated a story about someone called Sloth Herder so many times, Kenduu found himself dozing on and off during the recitation. Kenduu cast aside all worries that "Roseau's" information was as false as the facts and figures he was supplying when he recognized the peculiar word patterns that Ping mentioned. Gradually Kenduu began to doubt that Rastuk's mother had encoded any secret messages. After a while Kenduu decided to test his new theory that what Rastuk said was true and asked more questions about Sloth Herder and some of the other names. Finally, it occurred to Kenduu that Rastuk was not only telling Slana's story about the massacre of her family, but a lot of other information.

What did you come to us now? Why so many years after this Sloth Herder betrayed you?

Without warning, "Roseau" ceased communing. Feeling dazed, Kenduu looked around and saw a pale streak of light across from him. It took a while to orient himself to the idea the light came from the crack between the top of the wooden slab and the rocks above it.

Twenty-Five

Hundreds of miles away in the Dzagh, Kwaiikit's aunt, the Naan, listened Tuudzaado style to the peculiar conversation between her great-nephew, Kenduu and the woman who called herself Roseau. As one of the few members of the Dire Wolf Alliance who had known Rastuk's mother, she felt it her duty to find out what her son was doing in Zana. She'd listened to Ping's story with growing concern. Why was he there? Was he there on behalf of the Dotson or as he claimed, to find out more about his Tuudzaado heritage? Why had he claimed to be a woman rather than a man as he had with Ping. It was obvious from his story, that he was telling it as he'd told it to Ping, but with a pretense.

Sloth Herder? The Naan dangled the name in her memory, feeling something come forward and then retreat as quickly as it occurred. She glanced toward the hide-covered doorway of Jenda's house, feeling trapped by the stone surrounding her as well as by her inability to extract the elusive phrase from her distant memory. By the greenish gray light at the bottom of the hide, she knew dawn was close. She felt among the nearest of Jenda's household tools for something to do while she thought. Her fingers touched the shallow hollow of a stone bowl. *A lamp!* the Naan smiled inwardly.

Jenda awoke to the sounds of the Naan striking a flintstone against another rock to start a fire and tried to open thick eyelids to see what her mother-in-law was doing. It was too dark in the windowless dwelling. One eyelid stuck to the painfully dry surface of her eye.

I'm trying to light your lamp, communed the Naan, aware of Jenda's unformulated query.

What? Jenda responded in a somewhat blurry Datherd silent way.

Oh, sorry, the Naan adjusted her phrasing to suit her daughter-in-law's style. *I figured out where your camelid oil is and found some cotton grass for a wick. Now I'm trying to make a spark to make it brighter in here.*

Jenda rolled over under the ermine blanket, tempted to blot out awareness, but the force of youth returned to her and she pulled herself to a stand in one fluid motion.

Here, let me help. It works best if you put a pinch of this yellow powder on the cotton grass.

"Ah." Sulphur.

Jenda lifted the moss. "We need to keep a little moss out of the oil." she mumbled. Jenda fussed for a few moments and soon there was a yellowish light in the house. It wasn't bright, but she squinted anyway.

The Naan chuckled, delighted with the lamp. *I've never used one of these. Too heavy and bulky for someone who does as much trekking as I do,* she communed. The Naan examined her daughter-in-law and lifted her chin in satisfaction. *You're stronger, my dear.* The pair sat in silence for a while, then the Naan communed, *my daughter-in-law, like most of us Tuudzaado in Zana, I've always called the place of your grandparents "Southern Tuudzaado." I don't recall ever hearing what you or your family call it.*

"Mmmm," Jenda pondered the question for a while. *Odd you should ask, Mala asked me that a few days ago. Neither of us ever lived there, it's too far away. Father said it took our grandparents six moons to make the trek with so many children.*

They were driven out, communed the Naan. *Do you remember who your enemies were?*

Yes, Jenda communed, *it was the Dotson. Father said they came from some place far away to the south. They stole land from us. That's why my grandparents had to leave. They were lucky to find Zana.*

The Naan tucked her chin onto her and thought about what Jenda had said. She arose onto her haunches, still in a crouch because Jenda's stone house was too low to allow her to stand. *Daughter-in-law, it's time for me to go to Broken Jaw. I need to talk to some of your relatives.*

After the Naan departed, Jenda collected some projects that needed work, and surveyed her home. When her daughter came in, Jenda assigned her the job of fixing a ripped tunic while she worked on a pair of torn moccasins. Duna scratched on the door and entered. Her son, Masito, bolted between Duna's legs. Jenda smiled and handed her daughter-in-law one of Keyo's old tunics.

"I want to turn all of his older clothing into hunting bags but it's too painful."

Duna made a dutifully sad expression and took the tunic. "I understand, Mother-in-Law. I'll do these for you."

After the three of them had settled into a soothing pattern of chitchat intermingled with complaints about working in such a darkened room, Jenda said to Duna, "My husband told me that he offered to take you as a second wife. I suppose I should say his fourth wife, since I am his second wife and we all know he now has a third wife."

The tunic fell out of Duna's hands, in bright light Jenda would have seen her hands quivering. Without that advantage, she plunged forward.

"What are your feelings about that, Daughter-in-Law?"

Duna took a deep breath, forced herself to smile, and opened her mouth to speak, only to discover that her teeth were rattling. Her daughter, Dagoli, giggled. When Jenda recognized the sound, she put down her own sewing and scooted over to where her daughter-in-law sat.

"I'm sorry, Daughter-in-Law," she murmured, tentatively grasping one of Duna's hands, very aware that in more than three years of being together, she and Duna rarely touched each other unless there was a medical reason. Duna's hands shook so much that her initial jerk at Jenda's touch went unnoticed.

"Daughter-in-Law, if the idea of being my co-wife is too terrible for you, please say so. It was my idea. Zaandan won't object if you want to do something else." Jenda's smile was genuinely caring.

Duna lifted her head and squinted at her mother-in-law. Duna had known Jenda all her life and used to think of her as a gentle, caring person until she married Kenduu. When she moved into the Tuudzaado compound, she discovered a new Jenda, a woman who demanded hard work of anyone who seemed idle. The results were a compound filled with sturdy dwellings and tidy work sheds, neatly stored tools and clothing, as well as food preserved in containers that reviled all pests. A hidden result, at least it was hidden from Jenda, was a daughter-in-law who detested her as an overbearing invader of every detail in the not-so-private dwelling Duna shared with her husband. As she looked at Jenda, Duna felt a tiny ray of hope pierce the wall she had built around herself.

Choosing every word with care, Duna said, "I was honored by your husband's generosity, Mother-in-Law, but not prepared to lose my husband so soon. The mere thought makes my hands shake, as you now know."

Jenda rocked back on her heels and smiled encouragingly. "Yes, I feel them. It's best to face harsh realities before they occur. For my part, I want you and your children, my grandchildren, to be safe and well nourished. I am relieved that Chebucto is taking his obligation to you so seriously. You will be able to count on his support for the rest of your life—or his."

Duna picked up Keyo's tunic, hesitating. Finally, she said, "just before coming in today, I told my parents about Zaandan's offer." She paused to look for Jenda's reaction.

Jenda settled onto a nearby mat and contemplated her daughter-in-law. For the first time, she saw the youngster as an adult, worse, as an adult of an enemy force—the Hutlan. Duna's father had permitted her to marry a Tuudzaado man first because of a sense of obligation to Zaandan's father and because Duna was nothing but a third daughter. It mattered to only Kenduu that Duna had begged for the marriage.

"What did they say about it?" Jenda prompted.

"Father thinks it is a good idea to have a second marriage, but he wants me to marry a Hutlan man. He told me that Zaandan has been telling people that Hutlan and Tuudzaado should stay apart. He's concerned that Zaandan, whose father is related to my father's sister, would criticize his own parents and his own son, my Kenduu, in that way. It bothered me, too."

Jenda studied Duna, sensing that Duna was not as concerned about Zaandan as she was about something else. "What is it, Daughter-in-Law?" Jenda asked at last. "What are you afraid to tell me?"

Duna looked at her mother-in-law's beautiful eyes and began the carefully crafted tale about missing Kenduu. It was true that she missed her husband, but she had other problems that diminished her personal desires. "It was a mistake to talk to Father," Duna said at last. "He wants to arrange a marriage between me and a Hutlan man in the west country, someone I've never met."

Shocked, Jenda said "Who is he? What kind of hunter is he? Has he ever been on a big hunt alone?" Jenda paused, sensing Duna closing away from her. "I'm sorry. I'm sure you have thought of these things."

Duna slowly relaxed. "Maybe. There's one issue that marriage to a Hutlan man cannot resolve." Duna clutched her little son tightly and fell silent.

Jenda watched the gesture and let her head drop slowly to her chest. "I understand," Jenda said.

The Hutlan man and Duna's family would expect a widowed Duna to become his primary wife and live with him in his west country household. If that happened, Duna would take her children with her, thus bringing Tuudzaado children into a Hutlan household. In an earlier era when the two groups were friendlier, the only problems would have been in adjusting to the customs and personalities of the new family. That blissful time had faded not simply with Zaandan's new attitude, but because of other harsh realities of the present era. Jenda suppressed a shudder, knowing of Hutlan families in which Tuudzaado children were fed less and never allowed new clothing unless they had the skin, sinew, needles and awls to make it themselves. They were not allowed to visit their Tuudzaado relatives.

"What is your thought about my grandson?" At the word, the little boy twisted out of Duna's grasp and crossed over to Jenda, arms extended. Always ready to oblige Masito, Jenda pulled him into her lap and held his bony head against her equally bony chest. Jenda adjusted her clothing to create a cushion along her sternum.

Duna said, "I told my father that I would tell him my choice at the end of the Moon of Starvation. By that time, they should be back...."

Jenda tucked her chin more tightly around her grandson's fuzzy head. In a low, slow voice she echoed Duna's last words, "they should be back."

Dejected by the unsettling discussion, the two women folded away their sewing projects and talked about Duna's pregnancy, a subject both found fascinating and warmly companionable.

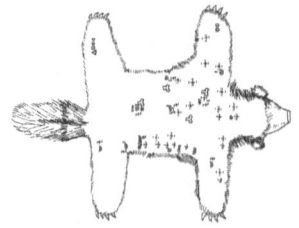

Twenty-Six

"Friend?" The creaky voice awoke Kenduu at some point in the blackness after his conversation with Rastuk. Aadso' reached for Kenduu's hand, clinging to the older man as if to keep his mind in focus. Although Aadso's voice failed him several times, he was determined to give exact information. Aadso' described every possible escape route that he had discovered, all of the people he had seen, including the small children who were required to hang seaweed on the drying racks in the grotto area.

"The best chance for escape is to become one of the filth slaves. These are slaves who clean feces and other kinds of decay left by both the living and the dead. *Dinjiidra'*, they are called," Aadso' said.

* * *

"Gross!" Deloo piped up from the softness of her easy chair. *Baasee', that's the worst thing anyone should ever have to do!*

I, the Impervious-to-All-Grossness Baasee', suppressed a chuckle. *Don't worry, Deloo. You'll never be made a filth slave by Grandfather or me. Now, back to the story!*

* * *

"They need lots of *Dinjiidra'*, but if you don't understand their dialect, you might miss your chance. How well do you understand their Dotson words?" Aadso' had wheezed.

"Not well, but I know a lot of jargon for feces and rot."

Aadso' managed a weak chuckle and said, "their term for the job is Dinjiidra'. Say it."

"Dinjiidra'," murmured Kenduu, squeezing the young man's hand a little as he said it. "Thank you, my friend. I will follow your advice."

Kenduu wanted to ask more, but stopped when the boy's hand dropped away from his. Kenduu placed the youth's head on his lap and cradled him until Aadso' died. The Dotson men had stolen Kenduu's prayer pouches. In view of his current situation, the loss of the powder was small, but in that moment Kenduu fought a rising panic, irrationally certain that red ochre was the only way to guarantee Aadso' would be brought safely along his First Walk of Death. Kenduu prayed for extra help for his friend and carefully removed Aadso's clothing following

Hutlan customs. Smoothing Aadso's clothing as best he could in the dark cell, Kenduu placed them in a pile near the wall opposite the drifting light. He then lifted the body onto the pile, trying to create as much of an illusion of a funeral pyre as he could. Then he readied himself by straightening his own apparel, and after some thought, tightly plaited his hair into the single braid of the Hutlan instead of his habitual double-braid Tuudzaado style. Then he sat cross-legged beside the head of the dead boy.

At home, the Prayer Women would have sung their strange songs while members of the Hutlan sang a set of funeral dirges. Despite the many Hutlan funerals he had attended over time, Kenduu had never memorized the songs. Opening his mouth to try any way, Kenduu was surprised and gratified when the first of the series of chants swelled out of his throat as if brought to him by the spirits of all who had protected their son, Aadso'. While he chanted, he silently prayed to be able to avenge this youth and all others who had been abducted and enslaved. He prayed to be allowed to work for the Dire Wolf Alliance on the West Face, as Kwaiikit desired.

When he finished chanting, Kenduu's mind turned obsessively to the whereabouts and wellbeing of Chebucto. Maybe his cousin had been taken to another part of this slave encampment. Maybe he was dead, Kenduu supposed Joot's beautiful amethyst knife was now in the hands of a Dotson man. A smothering depression filled the tiny cell; Kenduu found himself pressing against the wooden plank that kept him a prisoner. In a mindless state of shock and exhaustion, Kenduu didn't recognize what was happening until he fell backward.

Someone was opening the cell. The effort took just enough time for Kenduu to stage his innocence. He lay on his side and pretended to be too weak to sit. A man prodded him with a stick, and Kenduu produced a weak groan. The man likewise prodded Aadso's body several times to make sure he was dead. During this process Kenduu remained inert and silent, Aadso's counsel had led to his planning exactly what to do when this moment arrived. Aadso' told him that there were always at least three guards to get slaves from most of the slave cells. Escape was impossible. They both hoped that methods differed for the dying cell, but no. By the odors and sounds coming to Kenduu, the dying cell was just as tightly supervised. Using every sense but sight, Kenduu checked the surroundings, trying to put Aadso's words together with everything he heard, smelled and felt.

The first problem was the location of the dying cell. Aadso' said it was too far from the skimpy tree-covered area for escape, and Kenduu was now too weak to do much running. Everything now depended on which of the jobs they assigned to him. He hoped they would not put him in the fishing zone, although there he would have access to nets and weirs. Aadso' had warned him that the fishing job offered relative independence and better food, but the Dotson demanded a high quota in fish every day. Aadso' said they beat the fishermen often and fighting back had only one reward: The dying cell. Aadso's final words rang in his mind.

"Try to become a *Dinjiidra'*."

Kenduu was impatient to play out the role and worried about the Dotson dialect. At first, he didn't understand them, but soon he began to make sense of what the men were saying to each other. Kenduu thought they were debating between themselves about who would dispose of the dead man. He decided to take a chance and volunteer for the job.

"Me," Kenduu said, coughing, hoping that his cough would keep them from being suspicious about his potential for escape. Kenduu feigned weakness as he pulled himself up to a straighter posture. Gasping theatrically, he reached over and caressed the dead man's face. "Please," Kenduu looked up at one of the guards.

They looked at each other. The tall one grunted and turned away. The other said, "Take him out of here."

Step One of Kenduu's fragmentary plan was accomplished — permission to do the funeral process for Aadso'. The plan had two steps. Step two was to become a Dinjiidra'. After that there was no plan.

As he moved out of the dying cell, wind tore at Kenduu's clothing and exposed skin. Is an ice storm coming? he wondered. Ice storms were bad in the Dzagh. His father told him they were far worse along the coast and in the area between the Red River and Falls Creek. It wouldn't be possible to see much of the area until the wind abated. Almost as if the Sacred Forces heard his thought, the wind abated, a momentary lull.

Kenduu sent a quick prayer to the Sacred Forces and turned toward the body. Careful to continue the illusion of weakness, Kenduu made a production of pulling the body slowly and tying Aadso's tunic and leggings together for a makeshift litter. Once out of the cell, the first guard showed him which way to turn. He kicked Kenduu in the buttocks, more as a display of force than as a punishment. Kenduu contemplated how to move the body. Dragging it behind himself would allow him to look around and get a sense of the terrain, but Kenduu quickly dismissed the idea as impractical. Aadso's tunic was too short to be gripped that way. Instead, Kenduu bent to lift Aadso's narrow frame and found that it was much heavier than he expected. Three days of immobility and starvation had taken a toll on Kenduu's normally powerful muscles. Kenduu took a deep breath and lifted the body over his shoulder. Righting himself painfully, he started moving in the direction indicated. He noticed that only one guard followed.

As Kenduu moved toward the edge of the claystone structure, he tried to look around but the light was too bright. He squeezed his eyelids to a narrow slit and kept his head down. He tried to estimate the time of day by observing shadows, but there were none. A gray day, Kenduu thought, with heavy ice, but no fog. Fog would heal my eyes, not hurt them. This light is sharp. A high layer of clouds must have just blown in—trapping light and cold under its weight. As he moved, Kenduu's eyes relaxed, and in a while he found he could open them fully. He examined what he could see of Aadso's body. The youth's emaciated corpse was scarred with cuts in various stages of healing and rotting. Kenduu noticed the boy's childlike lips, so much like those of his own son's mouth. Kenduu was overcome with sorrow and an even greater resolve to avenge him.

He began singing in a low voice the funeral dirge he had sung earlier, moving his feet in rhythm to the chant. With each repetition of the chorus, the guard dropped farther away from his side, so that by the time they reached the western end of the claystone building, the guard was two full strides away. At the corner of the claystone the guard pointed toward the jumble of huge boulders ahead.

"Keep moving," the guard said.

Kenduu nodded and looked at a jagged spill of red boulders leading up an incline. They glistened with ice. Kenduu could see nothing beyond it. Although there were no shadows, Kenduu recognized the languorous sheen of water entering a freezing moment and guessed it was midafternoon. Most of the walk was partially protected by huge overhanging boulders. Kenduu moved one step at a time and continued singing the funeral dirge. The guard stopped when they reached a fully exposed, large flat-topped stone. Kenduu stepped up onto the boulder, nearly losing his balance on an unexpected bit of ice. Keeping his mind on his footholds, he did not try to identify the creaking sweep of a teratornis wing until, looking up, he saw the huge bird, wings flapping as it lifted off the edge of the nearby claystone building. Kenduu wasted no further time. He dropped Aadso's body and slipped-scuttled back to the shelter of the stones behind him. Together they watched the giant bird settle on the corpse.

Kenduu observed how the boulders spilled downward toward a dribbling glacial stream--Falls Creek. He remembered its rocky shores, twice daily the river filled to the place Kenduu stood, judging by the mineral stains on stones. In the early spring Falls Creek, he knew would become a raging torrent filled with ice bergs, boulders, and broken trees from the rush of melting glaciers. Kenduu suddenly felt overwhelmed with the exhaustion. He no longer had to feign weakness and could barely stand when so commanded by the guard.

"Come," the guard snarled. "Eat."

The man led him through icy mud toward a protected area on the western wall of the claystone ruins. Through narrowed eyes, Kenduu saw the guard's increasing lack of vigilance as well as a couple of promising places to try for an escape. Yet even as he tensed himself to make the move, something stopped him. Each time a distant voice breathed toward him, *you can go, or you can stay to avenge Aadso's death. It's your decision.* Kenduu decided to wait.

They made their way to a dilapidated thatched awning where the guard pointed wordlessly to a pile of bark platters. The man added something else in the Dotson jargon and laughed as if at a lewd joke. Kenduu wisely ignored the hostility and moved toward the awning. There wasn't much, as whoever had been cooking there had abandoned the area for shelter when the wind blew up. What Kenduu wanted and needed was something to suck. After so many days without food, the only thing he could consume safely was the saliva his own body would create if he sucked a bit of dried meat or even a smooth pebble. After his stomach had accepted that small amount of liquid, he would be able to eat a little solid food. He found a pile of what looked like dry fish and chose a piece. Glancing at the guard, he sat on a rock to try the fish. The taste was unfamiliar, but the process of sucking was successful. Breathing evenly and deeply, Kenduu sat up straighter and willed the fishy fluid to slide farther. Concentrating on the painful process of ingestion, Kenduu failed to notice the approach of other guards. One kicked him savagely. Kenduu fell, lost consciousness, and then slowly became aware of his surroundings again. The ordeal of swallowing fish oil and saliva had left him with a craving for death and no interest in how that happened. Kenduu lay still.

"Can you stand up?"

The effort to analyze meaning took more strength than Kenduu had left. The guard repeated the question. Kenduu drew a deep breath and gathered strength toward his legs. He closed his eyes as he forced himself to stand without reaching out for support. Once upright, Kenduu had to take a moment to stabilize himself.

"Yes," Kenduu answered, using their phrase. "I can stand," he added.

The first guard contemplated him for a long moment, seeming to assess him for both truth and vigor. After a while he said something that ended in "*Dinjiidra'*."

Since he appeared to be addressing Kenduu, Kenduu responded, "yes, *Dinjiidra'*."

The tall guard smirked at the others, said something with a sneer, and shrugged. With a curt nod at the man who had been with him all along, the tall one left.

Kenduu looked at his guard and asked, "What did he say?"

"You are now *Dinjiidra'*," the man answered, adding the Hutlan term, "a slimer."

Kenduu nodded without expression, Step Two was accomplished. Kenduu sat again and tried more fish. Just thinking about it brought on a cramp. His body ached to be horizontal, but he forced himself to sit up straight. He didn't notice the absence of cloud cover until a ray of sunlight began warming his thighs. The heat felt so good that he imagined squeezing himself into as flat as being as possible to take in all its warmth. The tiny playfulness of the moment gave way to dawning awareness of the direction of the sun, it was nearly sunset. Kenduu sucked the bit of fish. He swallowed easily. Then, as soon as the sunlight had given him warmth, the wind whipped up from the east. Kenduu tucked the dried fish into a fold in the tunic near his armpit. He would eat it later. Hands free, he hunched his shoulders against the wind and looked around for the guard, who was huddled in a dim corner with a larger man.

Kenduu tried to get a better look, the man with the guard looked a little like his father, but the illusion faded as soon as the stranger turned his head. The man glanced once at Kenduu and strode quickly away. Kenduu saw something above the man's eyes but the man was gone before he had a chance to examine it. The guard noticed the searching eyes and came toward him. Some extra movement of the Dotson man's neck and shoulders radiated brutality. A stab of terror ricocheted through

Kenduu but he forced himself to remain still, forced himself to look the man in the eye. Something passed between them. The red light of belligerence in the Dotson man's eyes dissipated, a play of humor seemed to replace it, then opacity.

"Come," he said in the Dotson dialect. A slight movement of the head and eyelid said the rest: get up, go that way. Kenduu took this as a sign that dinner was over. He tried standing and doubled over with an intense abdominal cramp. The man waited for Kenduu to recover, and then kicked him savagely. Kenduu slumped, face forward, unaware of the icy mud until his nose was in it. He tried moving his head himself, but it was too heavy. Pain gave way to the inertia of being horizontal at last. This is dying, he thought without caring. Suddenly he was on his feet, or at least one of them, without any sense of transition. A clawed fist stabbed at his neck and shoulders to keep him from falling.

"Move!" the man hissed in his ear. Without warning the guard released him. Kenduu lurched forward one step, then another. Freezing wind cut through his tunic. He tucked his hands into his armpits for warmth. Finding the piece of dried fish he'd put there earlier offered him a moment of hope.

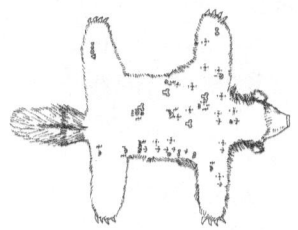

Twenty-Seven

Mala awoke. Something troubled her. She searched for a pattern by feeling for the usual sore spots on her body and found nothing amiss. She curled a finger experimentally. It bent without pain. Taking a deep breath, she rolled over to inspect her husband. His back hunched away from her. She remembered.

They had moved through yesterday as if in a nightmare with no escape. Once or twice they had come together almost as if nothing could tear them apart. When he broke down over a forgotten stone point in his work area, she held him until his breathing calmed. Later she started screaming with no end when Chebucto picked up her cooking stone, and Joot pulled her to their tent and cuddled her. Those small moments made the work endurable. When they were too tired to keep working, they went to what remained of their sleeping area. Mala knew nothing would be right again. Joot turned his back on her and rolled to the edge of their bedding so none of his body touched hers.

Mala could feel the tension in him and knew he was awake as well. On another day, some prior day, she would have been able to slide across the fur to envelop him in her arms. Experimentally, she moved an arm toward him but stopped when she felt his shoulder stiffen. Pulling back, she whispered, "I'm sorry for what I have done, Husband."

* * *

Baasee', why is Joot acting that way? He was so full of himself the day before, I thought he wanted to be a Nicoleena. Deloo stared at my imaginary ceiling lair in consternation.

Hiding my amusement about her slippery grasp on maturity, I gathered my impressive self together and sent a little love-puff of lavender to her. *Deloo, my dear you have gone through horrific shock when your husband of just a few months died. Joot and Mala had those shocks, too. Now they are facing the more painful losses of losing the small things that made up huge parts of themselves. The pain of discovering each and every part that has to go is often worse. Much worse. You'll understand later. Let's find out how Kenduu is doing in Falls Creek.*

* * *

Kenduu awoke in the dim light of dusk, rocks jabbed him in the face. Slowly he took in his surroundings. Voices murmured nearby and unfamiliar. He didn't want to know more and turned his attention toward oblivion, but it was too cold to sleep. He reached for a fur to cover himself but his arms wouldn't move. A sudden thought inspired him, he rolled toward his wife and her warm belly, swollen now with his second child. Instead of finding Duna, he rolled onto something sharp. He eased away from it and in so doing recalled where he was. A grotto; he and a small group of boys had staggered into a grotto framed by huge granite boulders on the west side of the claystone buildings and near the eastern bank of Falls Creek. A guard had walked behind Kenduu, alternately prodding or lifting him. When they got inside the grotto, the guard gave Kenduu a final shove and left. Kenduu had a vague memory of hitting the ground. Now that he was awake again, he contemplated this new prison. His body urged him to seek warmth. Only one source presented itself, and the other slaves were already making use of it: their own bodies huddled tightly together, he crept toward them. He picked out their individual odors, and sensed their wariness. The smallest one moved a little.

"My name is Kenduu. What is your name?"

No answer.

Kenduu tried again, still no response. Finally, one of them said something to the young slave. The boy nodded but said nothing.

"His name is Stal," a boy said. "He is from Falls Creek. Born a slave, half Dotson. He speaks, but he is shy." The speaker introduced each of the others and stopped. He didn't identify himself.

"Who are you?" Kenduu asked, trying to see the youth man in the gloom.

"Nazu."

"Nazu!" Kenduu brightened. "I'm so glad you are alive, I am sorry about what happened." Kenduu recalled his only meeting with Nazu more than a decade earlier. He reached toward the youth.

Although there was little room for movement, Nazu pulled away from Kenduu's extended hand and said nothing.

Kenduu hesitated and began to commune details of his heritage in the silent mode.

Speaking aloud, Nazu cut him short. "Don't do that. There are spies. They listen for Tuudzaado speakers. Someone keeps trying to talk to me in the Tuudzaado language, but she doesn't do it right. I don't converse with her." Without another word, Nazu turned away.

Kenduu decided not to reveal his conversation with "Roseau" and said, "I apologize. I should have known better. My father says it's dangerous to use the Tuudzaado language in this area because that." Kenduu waited for a moment, and then began again to tell them about his heritage as was proper in all of Zana. When he finished, no one spoke. "What about you?" he asked after a while.

Just when he was sure Nazu would never speak again, he heard the soft slur typical of Tuudzaado speech when struggling with Hutlan pronunciation. Zaandan spoke like that, as did Mala. Jenda had learned the Hutlan tongue much better than either of them had done. Kenduu thought of a day in his childhood when he overheard a Hutlan woman criticizing Zaandan about his inability to talk right. Zaandan, tall and handsome, was not present, at least not then. Because of that day, Kenduu had forced himself to learn the tongue language perfectly. When he slipped, Duna reprimanded him sharply. Bringing himself back to the present, he listened to Nazu's introduction of each boy in turn. The other slaves included a Hutlan lad of about eight years who had lived in the slave compound since he was two or three years of age. Next to him was another boy of mixed Dotson descent who had been born to a slave woman approximately nine or so years before. The third was a boy who spoke a language that no one else knew. Nazu called him the ocean boy and thought he was around ten.

"He's got that bump on his hand," Nazu muttered. "You know, they call it the Nobaagi Bump." He held up the boy's hand for Kenduu to inspect. Kenduu felt what seemed to him like a partial finger.

The fourth slave either couldn't or didn't speak. Nazu called him the West Face boy. After the introductions, the boys began to talk. Kenduu tried to listen to their chatter, only comprehending a word here and there. He felt too sluggish to piece anything more together and slept until he heard Nazu say "we are all *dinjiidra'*."

What about you? Kenduu asked, unintentionally slipping into the silent mode.

Nazu closed away again and he didn't say anything for a while.

"Please tell me about yourself."

Nazu said, "I am Iglan's son. They captured me and killed my father and my wife to be on the twenty-first day of the Peccary Moon. I am alone now."

"What do you mean?" Kenduu asked.

"Our *aahntaan* is gone, I know they are dead."

Kenduu sat very still, and then said, "I know what you mean. I have tried to reach my father through our *aahntaan*, but something interferes. My wife is Hutlan and we can't do *aahntaan* together. I don't know what has happened to my family. I want to know if my wife and son are still alive, they should know that I am alive."

Kenduu reached out once more and brushed against Nazu's hand. The youth yanked his arm away but not before Kenduu felt the rough scars and lumps on Nazu's hand.

"What happened?" he asked.

"They smashed a rock on my hand after I got here. It doesn't hurt much anymore, but I can't move any of my fingers."

"Both hands?" Kenduu asked, appalled.

"No. Only the right."

A sudden, stiff breeze brought the temperature down considerably. Stal began to shiver. Kenduu put his arm around the small child. Soon all of them were huddled together at the base of a protective overhang on the eastern side of the grotto. Three large gypsum rocks formed a short wall on the south, leaving them exposed on two sides. Kenduu lay next to Stal with his back against a gypsum boulder. Unable to sleep, he thought of escape plans. Kenduu had puzzled for years about slavery. He had asked his father why slaves didn't simply leave. In Nazu's case, it was simple. He couldn't climb with a broken hand. A corner of Kenduu's mind remembered the way he had shrunken inward, tense, fearful of another kick or beating when they took him out of the Dying Cell. Kenduu reveled in the thought of fear; it's not exactly fear, but a holding, as if I was holding myself still to keep what was left safe. And yet, he explored the idea a little more, I am still Kenduu still the man who has pledged to avenge Aadso'. I will find a way to get out. 'Us out,' he amended, thinking of Nazu and the boys he had just met.

* * *

The last quarter of the first day of the Black Paint Moon ended. Chebucto looked around in despair. The compound was a jumble of loose objects strewn into every possible place. He was sweaty with exertion and no closer to leaving the Dzagh in search of Kenduu than he had when he first awoke. Worse, his parents behaved as if they had never met each other. Whenever one had a question about something, she (when it was Mala) crept up behind Joot, or he (when it was Joot) would ask loudly of the air. Chebucto dashed between the two, trying to help carry the heavy objects from one place to another. When the day started, he had been aware of a plan unfolding. Now he wondered what that plan had been or if there was anything left to eat. He looked in some of the likely places, nothing. He checked another place and still found nothing. Discouraged, he gazed around the glooming compound and spotted his father chewing something. He crossed the short distance between them, nose twitching the entire way. It was dried moschid meat. On another day, he would have continued looking, but not now.

"Is there any of that left?"

"Sorry. I'm eating the last of it."

Disappointed, Chebucto turned away. Just as he turned his sensitive nostrils caught the alluring smell of cooking meat. His mother's cooking area was a shamble and she was not visible. Chebucto prowled through the compound and found her cooking over a low fire near the back side.

"What's that?"

"Moschid meat, it's the meat I didn't cook last night." Mala had resurrected her cooking slab by putting four stones around the fire and placing the slab on top. The meat was searing on top of the stone. Chebucto waited hungrily for his mother's signal. He saw a promising slice brown to perfection and well beyond. He decided to take it without permission and speared it with a short willow stick. He glanced at his mother with concern. Despite the darkness, he spotted the sheen of tears coursing along her cheeks. Spearing the remaining cooked meat, he slid it into a ready basket and put more of the moschid meat onto the slab. While it cooked, he observed his mother and communed. *Mother, why are you doing this if it makes you so unhappy?*

Mala stirred herself, looked at the meat in the basket and on the slab, and communed, *I have to do it, Son. It's the Sacred Forces on one side of me and my own past on the other.* Mala glanced at Chebucto and communed, *Thank you, Son. You've been very helpful today.*

Impatiently, Chebucto peered through the twilight to see if Joot was still there. He caught a glimpse of movement in the farthest corner from them. *Shall I ask Father to join us?*

A loud sniffle was the only answer he got.

Stifling a sigh, Chebucto walked over to his father and said in a voice that stunned him with its newfound authority, "Father, Mother is crying again. I want to talk to the two of you, if you don't mind."

Joot grunted and didn't move.

"Now, Father. Please join us at the cook fire."

Ordinarily, Joot resented his son speaking to him in such an unmannerly way but he didn't have enough energy to feel resentment now. He trailed after his son obediently.

Chebucto pulled three of Mala's smaller baskets out of the stash she had created behind her and arranged meat on each of them. Handing a basket to each of them, he ate while they did nothing.

Clearing his throat softly, Chebucto spoke into the night air. At least he thought it was he who spoke, but as the words flowed from his mouth, he began to wonder how he had become so intelligent. He felt the amethyst knife burn and roll on his chest, and knew the words came from it. "Mother and Father, I beg of you to listen to me. We are destroying our home and you are destroying each other. I think we are making a mistake by not talking about what is happening to each of us. In fact, I think we have even lost sight of what we are trying to accomplish here."

It was too dark to see much of their reactions, but Chebucto could tell from the quality of the silence that they were listening.

"It will help us all if each of you will reach toward the other. Touch each other as you have done for so many years."

"Son?" Mala's voice was barely audible. "Is that really you speaking?"

As if answering her, a wind swished leaves in a nearby tree, while nothing else stirred in other trees. The amethyst knife roiled on his chest and out of his tunic. Although still attached to his neck, it lifted itself upward and glowed. Joot gasped.

Chebucto's mouth moved and words in a strange voice floated into the air, "Mother, it is I only in the sense that this is my body. If Chebucto doesn't understand the words or approve of them, I will not allow them to be uttered. That which controls the words is the *yeege* who abides with the amethyst knife. I, that guide, am here to help the three of you through this difficult transition. Please listen to me."

A spark of fire spat into the night, illuminating Joot's roughened features. He stared at his son in amazement.

"Please, Mother and Father, clasp each other's hands and become more comfortable. I will guide you both through an easy way to understand the other. It must be done now or you will lose each other forever," stated the *yeege* via Chebucto.

Chebucto stared at his parents, wondering if this had ever happened to either of them. He watched as Joot settled onto the grass mat next to

Mala, Mala leaned into him.

"Thank you, parents of Chebucto. Now I asked you, Joot to express your thoughts to your wife and son about what you have decided to do with the rest of your life," intoned the *yeege*.

Joot coughed and looked first at Chebucto and then sideways toward Mala. He coughed again and said timidly, "I am going to become a Nicoleena—I want to be able to help others without concern for my own comfort and safety. I have envied The Naan's freedom and her ability to help others. Now I am going to do as much as I can to help her accomplish her goals."

Chebucto felt his mouth open and heard more unforeseen words escape. "Mother of Chebucto, please tell your husband and son your thoughts about what you have decided to do with the rest of your life."

Mala opened her mouth, coughed, and tried again. "I want to go back to Broken Jaw or somewhere around there and find the Datherd man who has betrayed his own people. I think I must have come close to finding out who he is when they captured Jenda and me. I want to find him and torture him like he did us. I want to kill him slowly for everything he did to my father, my mother, to Memree, to Jenda, and to me."

The words hung in the chilly air. No one moved or spoke. Chebucto wondered if he was supposed to figure out what to say next when he felt his spine stiffen and shoulders relax.

"As you have heard, you each have different goals. Now it is time to hear about your son's goals," remarked the *yeege*.

Chebucto felt the strength leave his shoulders and wondered what he should say. The silence spread throughout the compound. Finally, Chebucto spoke, knowing it was only he is speaking. "I want to join Zaandan in working with the Dire Wolf Alliance. I thought that was the same goal as Father had. I might kill Dotson men when I see them as well. I want to kill the men who killed Keyo and stole Kenduu."

"Now family, you have heard each other. Of the three of you, Mother has the strongest and most daring goal. I would like Mother to express herself again. Is there a way your goals can become more like the goals of the other two?"

Mala's hand was clenched Joot's knotted fist so hard that Joot hoped she would not break any of his bones. He didn't try to loosen her grip, hoping that his silence would encourage her to speak her mind honestly.

"I've never talked about those years of my childhood to anyone up here except my husband. Jenda doesn't want to remember. My son never seemed interested until this past year. I was part of an important group, one that formed what's known as Dire Wolf Alliance, but that's not what they were at the beginning. There's a secret council that included my cousin, Memree, Garantu's mother. I was included in some of their work, but not all. I don't have what they do. They told me if I couldn't see mine or theirs, then the Sacred Forces hadn't chosen me." Mala paused to clear her throat. When she continued, her voice was raw with rage. "But ever since Jenda and I were captured, I've known differently. The Sacred Forces did choose me to help them, I am a helper of a different sort. If I manage to rescue an escapee while doing so, I will. Please help me." Mala fell silent, her heart pounding hard and fast as if she had been running.

The guide continued relentlessly, "Father, you have heard your wife speak the truth, how do you respond to her?"

"My wife has told me about the secret council and what she did. She knows things I don't and can't know to do. I want to be part of the Dire Wolf Alliance, but I thought it took belong to a dire wolf pack; even so, I have the same hatred of the Dotson that she does. I can't stop seeing my nephew's dead body; I also want to be with my wife more than anything else. I want the Sacred Forces to keep us to be together."

Mala's hand relaxed but she clung to him. "Me too, I need you, my husband."

Joot reached for Mala's hand with his free one and pried her fingers loose. "Please don't crush my hand, Beloved," he whispered back. "I might need to save your life one day from all of the Dotson men you plan on killing." He felt her shoulders shaking and wondered if she was crying or laughing.

She released his hand and tapped him on the head. "You always make me laugh."

"Family of Chebucto," Chebucto felt chills streaming throughout his body. "Your lives are going to change in all ways. Now that you have reassured each other of your common goals, please reassure your son of your goals toward him and his toward you."

What followed was something that Chebucto would never forget. They talked until the Opossum Constellation indicated it was nearly night's third quarter. At peace with each other, they went to their sleeping places and slept until the sun was nearly at its second quarter.

* * *

The grotto was near the rocky bed of the stream that edged Falls Creek's western side. Kenduu listened for the sound of running water, not expecting it but hoping to complete his mental map of the grotto. The enclosure's steep sides formed a natural prison of quartz, feldspar, granite, gypsum, and other colorful stones. He noticed the flaring glow of a soda lite cobble that projected from the bottom of the short southern wall. The eerie stone emitted a weak phosphorescent white light; not enough to reveal things around it, but useful in night shadows. Kenduu glanced at the moon, observing that it was past the darkest phase. Kenduu remembered his father prefers to rescue escapees at new moon. The four days ending one and beginning another moon was the best time for escape because of the dark. He examined the moon and position of the stars more carefully to confirm his sense of time and place. Kenduu sighed, remembering the private meeting between himself, Kwaiikit and Ping on the cliff top a few days ago. He thought, I must find a way out of here to tell Kwaiikit what Roseau told me, even if it turns out to be false information. The more I think about it, the more I believe what she or he communed that night.

The Dotson guard had brought Kenduu to the grotto by way of a winding, narrow trail that was loosely covered by a series of large, flat pieces of granite. The entryway was so narrow that those entering had to go in single file. The stone sides of the passage were not very high, in some sections only slightly above Kenduu's head. Even in the grotto the boulders were not more than twice his height.

An agile person could scramble out with help from the others. Many slaves must have escaped without the help of the Dire Wolf Alliance. Kenduu mused about other possibilities besides the inconstant vigilance of the slave guards. An adult like me, a man trained to hunt in both night and day, could get out with little difficulty, he thought, but some of these boys have never had a chance to acquire those skills.

An image of his two-year-old son came to him along with a gnawing pain. At this time of night, he would chat with his wife in the flickering light of a camelid oil lamp, each of them busy with small tasks, such as repairing snares, moccasins, or cutting new garments. In those cozy moments, he liked to tease Duna about her tanning, as he was usually repairing something that she had tanned and he had torn. She would allow him to insult her skill only so long and then would challenge him about his clumsy style of making nets or mats.

Why not leave now? Kenduu thought. I'm weakened, but not as weak as I will be in this place. Just at that moment Stal's leg twitched, and the little one moved himself closer to Kenduu. Kenduu tightened his grip on the boy's shoulders and cast a glance at the small brood near him. He thought about Aadso'. I will get us all out of here, Kenduu affirmed. I'll find Aadso's family, too.

* * *

Chebucto finally saw the pattern underlying his father's organization. Satisfied they had a plan for everything littering the compound as well as themselves, Chebucto told them he would leave in the morning. When the sun was in its third quarter, the family crossed the ravine again to present Jenda and Duna with two more travois of stored food and other goods. They explained their plans.

The Naan listened, giving words for their half-formed ideas. She helped Joot understand that he could easily contribute to Mala's renewed spying by simply being an ordinary Hutlan man who fit in with the other Hutlans at Broken Jaw. "A real Nicoleena might work alone, but I don't. Neither should any of you," the Naan repeated constantly. "You should work together. You love each other and I brought you, Mala together with you, Joot for a reason. I don't like it when young folk disobey me." She gave them a stern look that dissolved when she saw their guilty expressions.

"Just stay together, please. You'll be very important as a team. Son-in-law, you will never be noticed the way your wife and I are seen in Broken Jaw," the Naan assured him. "We need that. It will be important to always be on the alert so that our Mala is never captured again."

Sitting on the side, it finally occurred to Jenda that her sister was planning to leave her. Appalled, she flared the Tuudzaado way, *No, Sister, I need you here! Please don't do this. Please do not become a Nicoleena.*

Talking to the Naan had given Mala a vivid shape to her future. She encircled her sister in warmth and long arms. *We will always be together, Sister,* she reassured Jenda in thought. *You and I have even more reasons now to use our aahntaan every day. We are going to stop those evil creatures ourselves. You know it's no longer safe here in these compounds. The Dotson found you. The Naan showed me the place they waited for Keyo to leave that morning. It was over there, on the other side of those rocks. If we had been more vigilant, we would have seen them before it happened. I must go back. The time is right for me. No matter what, you and I always have aahntaan.*

Jenda looked at her sister, doubt filling her luminous eyes. Glancing toward the rocks where the Dotson men had waited, her shoulders sagged. In private *aahntaan* she communed to her sister, you *are right. They come after us with relentless ferocity, but my grandchildren are too young to take away from here.* In the open Tuudzaado silent mode she continued, *I'll commune with my husband to plan. I want to do my part as well.*

The Naan had been following their silent Tuudzaado conversation. Communing rapidly, she interjected, *Life is going to change for all of us. There are rumors the Dotson have something terrible planned for the North Face. They are determined to kill all of us, including their own relatives, the Hutlan. We must find a way to stop them.*

Joot suddenly looked confused. He could understand most of what they had been saying to each other in the mental way, but The Naan's last phrase alarmed him. "What do you mean, they are planning to kill your Hutlan relatives. Do you mean me and Duna?"

Four pairs of baffled eyes turned toward the short Hutlan man in their midst. Chebucto understood more quickly than the others and corrected his father's interpretation. The Naan looked pleased and said, "You will be our most secret weapon at Broken Jaw. It's time to go. Your son must move quickly to find Kenduu. You, Chebucto, will travel fastest if you follow Zaandan's tracks." In the mental language, the Naan then gave him specific details. After a few questions, he was ready. Joot and Mala walked with him a short way along the path, but held back when it became clear that his focus was on his future rather than his past. Instead, they followed their son at a short distance behind, knowing they were simply delaying the moment of separation.

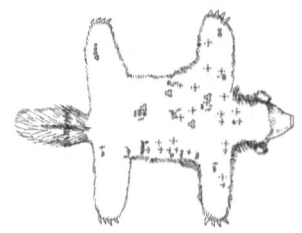

Twenty-Eight

Kenduu woke the boys before dawn's first light. With Nazu's dispirited help he explained his determination to get them all out of Falls Creek. "It's going to take a few days," he said. "Tonight, when we return here we must make a better shelter inside this grotto. A storm is coming, and we have to find a better way to keep dry."

Six pairs of sleepy faces eyed him without interest. Finally, Nazu said, "No one escapes. They hunt for the runaways and kill them. We've seen the bodies. They make sure we see the bodies."

Kenduu looked at the small faces and thought about the number of escape stories his father had told. "Haven't you heard of the Dire Wolf Alliance," he asked. Nazu's mind blazed outward toward Kenduu.

"The Dire Wolf Alliance? Yes, of course, I know of it. My father thought I should become a part of it."

"I hope to do so as well," Kenduu assured him. "My grandmother was part of the group that started it. One day I would like to go back to my birthplace on the West Face to create a network of safe houses on the West Face. I've always wanted to join my father in rescuing captives, especially since he can't do it anymore. I'm starting here and now with all of us." Nazu explained in the boys' pidgin language. They seemed to understand that Kenduu was serious, although it was hard to know if either the ocean boy or the West Face boy understood him. Eventually, Kenduu understood that they didn't seem to want what he had to offer. He wondered how his father managed to get such apathetic escapees to leave Falls Creek.

"I want you to look for some things." Kenduu wanted materials for bolas, hand axes and lots of straps. He looked at their ragged tunics, and said, "We need clothes to keep you warm."

Nazu looked at Kenduu with consternation. "I can't do any of that with his hand. I won't be of any use to you at all."

Kenduu didn't have time to respond. Two Dotson slave guards had rolled away the large stones.

The Dotson guards herded them to the wide field where Kenduu had eaten the day before. There was no opportunity for them to work together, as the Dotson guards forced each of them to go in separate directions. Halfway through the morning, waves of ice-laden wind slammed into the slave area, knocking over people and fish racks. Kenduu watched as the Dotson guards ran for cover without regard to the slaves they left behind. Kenduu's heart soared, he looked for his companions and gathered them together.

"We should go now!" he shouted to Nazu.

For an answer, the youth tipped his chin upward once and made a hand gesture to the other five. Soon all of them were headed toward a nearby rock overhang on the south side of the field. Kenduu ran quickly to catch up with the others. The older Dotson boy pushed his way farther and farther into the stones. Soon they led him to a covered space that seemed to be completely enclosed. Kenduu felt a current of warm air coming from somewhere beyond and laughed when he smelled sweaty steam lifting out of his own wet garments.

"Where are we?" Kenduu asked.

"It's an old house" one of the boys answered. "There's not much left of it."

"Best of all," Nazu said, "the Dotson guards don't know it's here."

Without waiting to see if Kenduu would follow, he and Stal dashed into the darkness where the ancient walls of the claystone building seemed to be nearly intact. Kenduu looked at the spot where the boys were and realized that he was alone. All of them had melted away. He walked tentatively toward the place he had seen them go and sniffed for their scents. The mute West Face lad came to his aid, sliding a small hand into Kenduu's and leading him through a pile of huge stones. The stench of smoke and dried seaweed mixed with other odors was suffocating. Kenduu had forced himself to suck on the dried fish throughout the night despite rising bile with each painful swallow. The smell of seaweed and smoke brought on another urge to vomit. When they reached the other boys, Stal crowded against Kenduu's legs and wrapped one arm around the tall man's left thigh. The contact restored Kenduu's sense of balance, he fingered Stal's springy Dotson hair and followed the others to what seemed like a solid wall. His young friends moved easily beside and in front of him.

The older of the two Dotson boys emerged from the dense air and located Kenduu's free hand. Tugging at the tall man, the boy guided him along a narrow, low-ceilinged pathway. It was too low for Kenduu, who gave up standing and dropped to his knees. The Dotson boy simply bent over a bit and maintained his grip on Kenduu's hand. At some point Kenduu's fingers discovered the stones became clay and that there was more room overhead. Awkwardly, Kenduu pulled himself upright, amazed that a man of his height could do so. It was obvious the clay-stone building had been built by some very tall people. Kenduu could not quite touch the ceiling. He sensed by the rustling behind him that the others were close. Stal pressed himself tightly against Kenduu's leg. A draft of fresh air from the storm cooled Kenduu's face. He drew in deep gulps of air to dampen another wave of nausea.

"It smells as if someone has been cooking in here," Kenduu remarked.

"Yes," Nazu answered, "the Surf Clam people live inside. They use this space occasionally to smoke dry fish and seaweed. They have a better place on the grotto side."

Kenduu frowned. His father had talked about Tuudzaado people who lived in the claystone building. Now that he was inside the famous build-ings, Kenduu couldn't imagine living in rubble like this. It was too dark and airless for his comfort.

"Who are they?" he asked.

"They are Tuudzaado people I think, I haven't met any of them. They don't talk to us. I've heard they may be Nightstalkers," Nazu said. "You are so tall, you must be a Nightstalker. Are you?"

Kenduu shrugged and said, "I might be. I think so, but my first par-ents are dead and I was adopted by Zaandan. I don't know anything more—yet."

Stal peeled himself away from Kenduu's leg, maintaining his place by a tight grip on Kenduu's legging. The older Dotson boy said, "the tall men get angry if we use the halls. And the cerdocyon dogs bite."

Kenduu relaxed. His father had mentioned the small cerdocyon dogs who lived in and around the claystone buildings. Zaandan said the cer-docyon are considered pests, and they did their best to get rid of them. Likewise, the Tuudzaado who used the dark halls did their best to rid the old building of the cerdocyon dogs.

Stal clamped himself back onto Kenduu's leg, Kenduu could feel the boy shivering.

"Let's build a fire. There must be plenty of dry grass, twigs and other things to burn," he murmured. "Quickly, bring me firewood." All the boys except Stal scattered while Kenduu felt for grass at his feet. Soon his questing fingers found enough to get started. He felt for his fire drill that he kept in the large, flat pouch covering his abdomen, amazed the Dotson didn't take it, too. As he worked the fire drill, the boys placed hand a full of dried grass and twigs beside themselves. Soon they were crowded around a cheery fire. It didn't provide much heat because draft from the ice storm crossed overhead, taking heat with it. Looking around in the firelight, Kenduu saw a better place for the fire.

"Let's move it over there," he suggested, and showed them what he meant. Once out of the draft, the warmth from the fire began to make itself noticeable. Stal still shivered on Kenduu's right side. The older Dotson boy didn't shiver but like Stal, burrowed into Kenduu's side for warmth. Kenduu listened to the howling of the wind.

"How long do these ice storms last?" he asked.

"Four days," said one.

Another said, "five days."

Nazu sneered, "I think they mean that it will last more than one day. My father said they are called ice storms because the rain turns into sheets of ice that fly at you from the side. It's not a blizzard of snow and sleet like we get in the Dzagh."

Kenduu said, "What about the Dotson guards? Are they going to come out during the storm?"

"No one goes out in an ice storm," the Hutlan boy assured Kenduu. "No one!"

Kenduu thought about the racks of food and other materials that he had seen the day before. "What about all the dried fish on those racks out there? Is anyone going to collect it?"

"The slave women will get some of it. The guards will get some, too," Nazu said.

"Why don't we get some?" Kenduu asked.

Nazu looked at the others doubtfully. Kenduu smiled. Like himself, Nazu had become a center pole for two of the boys. Only the West Face boy remained apart.

"I'm hungry," said one.

"Me too," said Stal.

"Then let's get some food," Kenduu said. "You two," he said, pointing to the smallest, "stay here and keep each other warm. Don't let the fire go out, the rest of us will get things from the racks." Stal slid next to the other boy obediently. Their springy hair mark them both as having Dotson heritage.

Kenduu felt the Hutlan boy resist, but Nazu overwhelmed them by standing up and removing himself as a heat source. Nazu led the way through the rocks, they paused under the cover of a rock table formation. Kenduu could barely see through the sheets of rain and ice. If there were any racks in the open field, they had all toppled over and become part of the landscape. Nazu nudged him and pointed. "Over there, see? There's a woman collecting some of the seaweed."

"Yes," Kenduu said after an intense effort of squinting. He looked around at the boys. "I want you to collect as much as you can." He took off his outer tunic and spread it out on the ground beside them. "Let's run out there and pick up as much as we can, no matter what it is, and put it back on this. Then go back again for more." He got tipping chins from all but one of them. The ocean boy looked confused, but smiled pleadingly. "Ready?" Kenduu asked, and then said, "Go!"

The five of them burst out of the shelter and streaked toward the woman. She must have seen them but gave no sign of interest at their presence. Four of the five racks had collapsed under the force of the wind. He dashed to one of the racks and picked up an armload of dried fish, along with as much of the rack as he could hold without droppin any. He ran back to the rock shelter and saw the pile on his tunic was quite large. Seeing that it held almost more than seemed possible, Kenduu said to the two Dotson boys, "Take this tunic to the fire." Pointing to Nazu and the ocean boy he said, 'we will go for more and then join you." Kenduu showed them how to carry the tunic without dropping the fish. Turning to the older boys, he said, "this time I want you to look for mats and straps, we need clothing." He pointed to the straps on his second tunic.

They ran back to the demolished food arbor. It took more time, but Kenduu picked up plenty of matting and straps, all made of various materials. Then he spotted what he thought was the best find. The roof of the central cooking arbor had broken into three parts. He watched as one of the biggest pieces skittered across the field to land directly in front of the rock table. He didn't have to call the others to join him. All three of them dashed toward the roof before it got any farther. Kenduu was delighted to find that it fit under the rock table. After dumping their combined scavenged goods onto the ground under the rock table, the three of them shimmied and shoved the piece of roof under the big stone.

With a satisfied grin at the other two, Kenduu said, "we can use this for firewood and other things."

He picked up as much of their find as he could and waited for Nazu to lead the way back to the fire. Once there, Kenduu told the boys to spread the mats and straps on the stones beside the fire. Then he looked at the food. The boys had left it on his outer tunic. All of them ate greedily except Kenduu, whose stomach still rejected company. He busied himself by creating a makeshift rack out of the sticks he had scrounged.

Soon he could take the remaining food off his outer tunic and arrange it on the rack. He sat back on his heels, comforted by having accomplished so much in such a short time.

"You'd better eat something," Nazu said behind him. Kenduu's stomach roiled when Nazu pressed something flat and crisp into Kenduu's hands. When his stomach stopped cramping, Kenduu sniffed the substance tentatively. It smelled pleasantly salty.

"What's this?"

"Porphyra," Nazu replied. "Eat some."

In the opinion of all the boys, the Porphyra had been smoked to perfection. Unfamiliar with seaweed, Kenduu tasted without interest. In a moment, he noted that its salty sweetness calmed his upset stomach. Later he would learn that Porphyra was yellowish green when still alive and dark green when smoked. Kenduu took another small bite and knew he had recovered from the worst phase of starvation. In a moment, he noticed that two boys had something else in their hands, one pressed a piece into Kenduu's hand. In the dark he felt nearly crisp, ruffled edges. He let his tongue explore what he learned later was the yellow-brown kelp called Laminarian, sugar wrack.

"This is good," Kenduu murmured. "Thank you."

They sat in collective silence, each of them wrapped in private reverie. After a while Kenduu contemplated the appalling state of the boy's clothing. He was shocked that Stal wore only a single grass-weave tunic with nothing under it. Worse, only one rawhide tether belt kept the sides closed from drafts. The older Dotson boy wore two layers of a woven tunic, each made of a different kind of vegetation, each woven or twined differently. Wiser than Stal, he had tied five or six woven tethers over the topmost tunic to keep its sides together. Through the loose weave of the upper tunic, Kenduu could see that four other tethers held the inner layer in place. The West Face boy wore one legging and a single grass-weave tunic like Stal's. Several hide straps bound his tunic in place to provide a little more covering. The Hutlan boy wore an odd assortment of ragged tunics. Kenduu counted four layers, one of an unfamiliar skin, the others of badly torn woven grass. He fastened each layer by strategic use of scrap hide tethers. Kenduu counted at least twelve such bits of hide. Except for the West Face boy's one legging, none of the younger four wore leggings or moccasins.

The ocean boy and Nazu had two layers of skin tunics apiece, each layer was held in place with a variety of straps and large pieces of hide.

Both wore skin leggings. Like Kenduu, Nazu wore gauntlets on his upper arms as well as wrist guards. Nazu's leggings were held in place with thigh guards as well as shin and ankle guards. The ocean boy had seal fur leggings that he held in place with hide straps. The hide at the lower end of each legging was worn, dirty, and clearly in need of ankle guards. He had no arm coverings. Of all of them, only Kenduu had a shoulder cape to cover the upper portion of his tunics. The cape was partially fitted over his upper arms to better protect him from the wind.

Nazu glanced around the group and asked, "Now that you see us in daylight, do you still think you can get us out of here?" His face was twisted with a blend of worldly sarcasm and pinched hope. Kenduu was grateful to see hope.

"It will take more effort than I thought to get ready, but yes. I know we can do it."

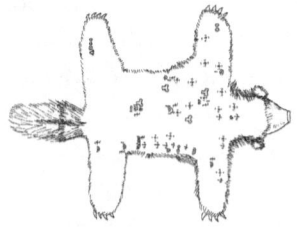

Twenty-Nine

When morning came Chebucto looked at his father as asked, "where shall we find each other next?"

Joot covered fleeting shock with a wry smile. "Let your knife guide you to us, Son. It's been doing good job for you so far."

They stood facing each other awkwardly until Joot reluctantly turned away. Chebucto stared after his father's retreating back and turned away himself. He didn't know the trail to Falls Creek beyond the highest point of the trail, which was as far as he had ever gone without Joot. He and Keyo used to explore the caves along the eastern trails just below the peak, but Falls Creek had been forbidden territory to both. Chebucto followed Zaandan's fading scent, comforted by the occasional, but faint, presence of Kenduu's scent as well. At the first trickle of a mountain spring, Zaandan's scent disappeared. Stymied, Chebucto studied the main trail where he eventually found the combined scents of Kenduu and his captors. Occasionally, he thought he detected Zaandan's scent, however, like any good hunter, Zaandan had walked on the side of the trail to avoid detection. Chebucto decided to follow Kenduu's stronger scent. Despite the strong odor of the men ahead of him, Chebucto lost their scent each time they forded a stream, something they did constantly.

After a while Chebucto caught Zaandan's scent again and followed it and soon he realized his uncle had turned east rather than heading in the direction of the grotto. Chebucto was tempted to follow Zaandan, thinking his uncle knew a secret route to Kenduu. However, when he turned in that direction, the amethyst knife churned angrily on his chest and Chebucto received a vague image of Kenduu stumbling on a pile of stones. Very uncertain, Chebucto at last decided to trust the knife and turned toward the grotto.

In a few moments Chebucto was relieved to find Kenduu's trail mixed with the stink of many strangers. He was contemplating the direction taken by the strangers when the sting of an ice-laden gust of wind cut through his outer tunic. He pulled a wide piece of hide that hung from his belt and tied it over his head. A look at the dark clouds racing above warned him to look for shelter. When shards of ice struck his face, he rushed toward an aspen stand. From the protection of the aspen he saw better cover among some dense willows on the leeward side of a huge boulder. He dashed to the boulder, hoping he would have time to select a decent covering before the storm hit.

* * *

Baasee', what does leeward mean? She had stood up and was pacing around her mother's small living room. She'd been riveted to the story for over an hour, and I swirled some energizing invisible coils around her legs as she walked.

Leeward refers to the side of a hill that is away from the wind. It's warmer there, I, the Eternally Wise Baasee' answered. *Please continue, Grandfather.*

* * *

Chebucto noted gratefully that there was a shallow overhang of rock on the western side of the boulder. Stiff willows pressed into the stone, leaving him little room to squirm into their midst. Once there, he used his hand ax to dig as fast as he could. He was still digging when he heard ice pummeling the far side of the boulder. He stopped digging and covered his head with whatever his hands found. Chebucto buried himself in sand, leaves, bark, twigs and mud. Then he placed a large piece of bark over his face and waited. The wait was not long. Most of the sleet was stopped by the boulder and dense leaves of willow that clung to the branches above him. Nonetheless, he heard heavy drops fall on the bark over his face. By whatever Sacred Forces that found time to protect him, Chebucto remained dry. He slept. When he awoke, he heard the wind lashing overhead and explored his body for signs of wet or freezing. His feet felt slick with mud. Walking the trail had dampened them long before the storm began.

Chebucto felt for the pouch of dried meat he had placed close to his chest on the inside of his outer tunic. He extracted a piece and chewed slowly. He slept again, trying to keep track of the number of times he awoke but gave up. Each time he awoke, he explored on each part of his body for wetness or numbness. He noted only two changes; the first was that he was more comfortable than he expected possible, considering that he couldn't stretch or roll over. The second was that the sound of the howling wind provided a strange sense of well-being. It was far easier to eat a little and fall asleep than to worry about Kenduu.

* * *

Kenduu looked at his little group of slaves huddled beside the fire and said, "Let's get to work. Nazu, could you take those two back to the rock table?" he indicated the West Face lad and the ocean boy. "I would like you to bring that piece of thatched roof in here." He pulled out a hand ax—a prize he had found in the grotto. "Use this to break it into smaller pieces."

Nazu lifted his chin and signaled to the others. When they had gone for the roof piece, Kenduu turned to the other three. "You need better tunics." He picked up his outer tunic and judged its weight and size. The fire had dried it completely. He enjoyed the warmth on his fingers. Of his three tunics, it was made of the thickest hide. Kenduu decided to keep it for his own safety. He undid the ties to his second tunic and tied his outer tunic back into place, binding it from armpit to hip with all his straps. With boys helping he spread his second tunic across the rocks. If it hadn't been for the neck hole, he could have made three smaller tunics from it. As it was, he cut the tunic in half with his curved hand knife. The two pieces would be long enough to cover the legs of the Hutlan boy, and too long for Stal. In addition, the pieces were too wide for any of their skinny bodies. He sliced the excess skin from the sides of each hide, and then cut a length from the main piece he reserved for Stal. After slitting neck holes in the two big pieces, he slipped one over Stal's head and the other over the Hutlan boy's head. Using two of his own straps, Kenduu tied the tunics at the waist of each child. Stal's new tunic reached nearly to his feet, while the Hutlan boy's new tunic reached to below his knees.

"Bring me some more straps from those we brought in earlier," he told them. "You each need at least three more for the tunics."

Kenduu took the segment of hide he had cut from Stal's tunic and murmured, "there is enough here for two leggings and a couple of ankle guards." So, saying, he cut leggings and guards for Stal, along with several narrow tethers. He sliced three short gashes along the long sides of each legging and three short gashes along the upper side of each. He inserted short tethers in the slits along the leggings, and slide two long tethers through the top gashes. When Stal returned, Kenduu attached the leggings to Stal's inside belt with the long tethers, fitting the length so that they reached Stal's feet and stretched to mid-thigh on each side.

Then he tied the back sides together with the short tethers. "When we get more bindings," Kenduu said, "we'll make you some thigh guards. For now, these ankle guards will have to do."

When Kenduu was satisfied with his knots, Stal twirled around in front of the others. Crowing loudly, he did a little dance around the fire.

"Now let's make yours," he said to the Hutlan boy. When he finished the Hutlan boy's new tunic, leggings, and ankle guards, he pointed to the remaining hide.

"I am going to make leggings for you," he tipped his jaw toward the bigger Dotson boy who had been trying to hide a trembling lower lip when saw that he would not be given a new tunic. "I'm sorry I don't have enough for a new tunic for you, but you've been smart in collecting all of this to cover yourself." Kenduu picked up his shoulder cape. "Try this on. I think this will help keep you even warmer." Kenduu watched as the Dotson boy tied on the shoulder cape. It was so big, it drooped past the small boy's hips. The trembling lips gave way to a damp smile. Kenduu remembered that the bigger Dotson boy, like Stal, had been born to a slave. He had known no other existence than this, and probably had never been clothed with as much warmth before.

One legging remained after Kenduu finished tying the bigger Dotson boy's leggings into place. He had it ready for the West Face boy when three others returned. The West Face boy, silent as always, smiled in gratitude to have not just one, but two leggings again.

Nazu examined Kenduu's work and said in a low voice, thick with emotion, "thank you. What can we do next?"

Kenduu had been wondering about that himself. "Let's eat more of this strange seaweed and talk."

The lads each selected a piece of seaweed or fish and clustered around the fire. Kenduu saw a scurry of movement to his left but when he turned he saw nothing.

"What was that?" he demanded.

The ocean boy said, "sir lion."

Everyone looked at him and Nazu laughed. "He means he saw a cerdocyon dog." He pointed to glinting eyes between two rocks. "There it is. It's probably after our fish."

Kenduu spotted the eyes while his fingers tugged at the slip knot that held his top bola in place. He tossed a fragment of dried fish toward the small cerdocyon dog. The fish landed a short distance from where the eyes peeped. Kenduu began spinning his bola in slow, neat circles. As he hoped, the cerdocyon dog emerged from the rocks to grab the fish. Just as the dog's fangs pierced the fish, Kenduu's bola encircled its body. Startled, the cerdocyon dog tried to escape, but the four tethers of the bola had it trapped. The ocean boy, who was closest, grabbed a convenient stone to club the dog, ending its fear and pain with quiet efficiency.

"Headgear," Kenduu murmured. "We can skin it and use this hide for ear coverings. Do you think there are more of them around here?"

Nazu, excited, took the cerdocyon carcass. "Yes," he said. "They live in these rocks. There is probably a dozen of them trying to get enough courage to steal our fish from us." He avoided looking at Kenduu. "I'd skin this for you—but…," he lifted his right hand.

Kenduu looked thoughtfully at the boys in the dim light. "Do any of them know how to skin an animal?"

Nazu's eyebrows and chin lifted simultaneously in comprehension. "I'll take the three youngest with me, I think the other two already know how." Nazu led the way toward the edge of the rocks where volumes of freezing rain and ice would clean the butchering area.

While Nazu taught the young ones to skin a cerdocyon dog, Kenduu searched through the materials they had salvaged. He began tying knots and wrapping pebbles, showing his bola pattern to the ocean boy and West Face boy. The ocean boy learned the technique quickly and squawked in pleasure. Eyes bright, he began to make a bola himself. Soon they had seven bolas ready to show the others on their return.

"Nazu, can you use your bola with your left hand?"

Nazu lifted his chin upward. "Father insisted that I learn to do everything equally well with both hands just in case." He lifted his mangled right hand. "He knew what to teach me."

"Good. I want you to train our West Face boy on his bola." Kenduu said after a moment. He turned to the ocean boy, "You teach this Dotson boy how to do it." With a few hand signals to reinforce his meaning, Kenduu turned to the two smallest boys, the Hutlan boy and Stal. "Come, I want to watch you two do it."

It took the balance of the day of practice before the inexperienced slaves could cast a bola well enough. Once they learned the best flick of the wrist for their own bolas, they became lethal rock killers. It was the older Dotson boy who surprised the rest with the first live catch with a bola.

* * *

I know how to cast a bola, Baasee'. I learned in the museum last year. They call them Eskimo Yo-Yos. Isn't that what a bola is? Deloo was nearly dancing with amusement, making small circles with her fists to cast imaginary bolas.

I watched with approval. When I'd noticed the announcement in the campus electronic news, I'd encouraged her to go and try it. I glanced at Grandfather for approval.

She's good at an ancient tool, Granddaughter. You should be proud of your mortal, Grandfather Kwaiikit remarked, showering me with golden light. *May I continue?*

* * *

"Whoo-aah!" the ocean boy shouted, jumping up and down and pointing at his pupil. Kenduu hurried to where they stood and made shushing noises.

"Don't let the guards hear you. That was so loud, you could be heard at the top of the Dzagh," Kenduu warned.

Then he saw why the ocean boy was grinning. The older Dotson boy's bola was wrapped around the struggling body of one of the still-living cerdocyon dogs. Kenduu was impressed. Before he sent them to skin the cerdocyon, Kenduu tried to explain that they needed to make a small offering to the rest of cerdocyon for the lives of their brothers.

The ocean boy understood and dug into his tunic where he had hidden a small pouch. Kenduu was pleased to see it, as he thought that none of them had any extra gear. The boy extracted a bit of smoked seaweed from the pouch and displayed it for Kenduu's approval. Kenduu lifted his chin and brow. It was dark by then, but the ocean boy stood and signed to his Dotson pupil to follow. The two made their way toward the rocks where most of the cerdocyon prowled. In a moment, they returned without the seaweed.

"Where did you find the pouch?" Kenduu asked while they shared charred bits of cerdocyon meat.

With hand signals and marks drawn in the sand the ocean boy explained that he had taken the pouch from a Dotson slave guard when the man was not paying attention. Kenduu was having trouble grasping the story when the West Face boy added another piece of driftwood to the fire to give more light to the marks. The West Face lad studied the diagram and then added a deft scratch or two in the sand to the ocean boy's marks. Suddenly Kenduu understood. The picture showed the pouch attached to a loose belt around the Dotson's waist. The mute West Face boy had drawn a knife slicing through the belt.

When darkness filled the enclosure, Kenduu covered the food with matting. Directing the small boys to sleep around the coals of the fire, he, Nazu and the ocean boy took positions at three sides of the food cache. The fire made the fourth side. During the night Kenduu awoke several times when he heard scuttling sounds but he didn't smell the tell-tale odor of cerdocyon. Listening to the howling wind in the dim light on the following morning, Kenduu murmured, "I guess you know the weather. This storm seems to be here to stay."

The older Dotson boy snickered. "Yes. It will be over in a couple of days. What shall we do today?"

Kenduu chuckled. "You need to practice your bola. I am going to make a new knife." He lifted a piece of sugar quartz he had selected the day before. It was a flat piece of pinkish orthoquartzite which was easy chip to create sharp edges. While the others practiced using the bola, Kenduu impressed himself by flaking a knife, albeit a crude one, in less time than it had ever taken him before. Kenduu had created a simple hand ax. He held up his newly flaked sugar quartz tool and showed it to the ocean boy. "Do you know how to use this?" he asked and panto-mimed a slicing motion. The entire group gathered round. He showed each boy how to use it for slicing, chopping and other tasks. From that moment onward, the seven worked steadily to get ready. Kenduu hoped to leave as soon as the storm let up. The following day he trained the younger boys how to see in the dark, how to listen and how to climb rain-slick rocks in both light as well as dark. The younger boys were more than willing, but exhausted by the time night fell. Nazu had been afraid to try rock climbing again with his mangled hand. He was proud to be the first to scramble up to the top of the rocks in the pouring rain.

On the evening of the third full day of the storm, Kenduu said, "It's not as noisy as it was. Be ready for the first moment of quiet. That's when we will leave Falls Creek."

* * *

Deloo had resumed her place in her mother's soft chair, and observed *Kenduu is the one with a son and a child on the way, isn't he? Seems like he's become the father-figure to all of those boys.*

I, who never had children of my own, but had helped raise fifteen orphaned children in Zana, agreed. *We needed to be parents for both boys and girls back then. Grandfather and his cousin, Zaandan went in search of them as often as possible. That was one of the primary func-tions of the Dire Wolf Alliance. They'd find homes around the Dzagh where widows needed a hunter. There were many widows, and even children as young as this make good hunters in desperate times. Kenduu proved to be a welcome addition to the Dire Wolf Alliance.*

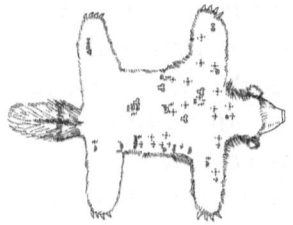

Thirty

The Naan left the Dzagh much later than she had planned. To avoid upsetting her daughter-in-law any further, she elected not to tell Jenda that she would travel directly to Broken Jaw rather than to Falls Creek. Instead, she crossed the ravine and told Mala, *it is no longer necessary to go to Falls Creek. My grandson is a strong man. He will bring himself back. Chebucto will be safe.*

Mala agreed. *The sooner you get to Broken Jaw, the better it will be for everyone.*

After a long embrace, the Naan left Mala. She blackened her white hair when traveling at night, one of the many precautions she took to vouchsafe the safety of the Dire Wolf Alliance. She took the only route heading south from the upper Dzagh. At the highest point of the Dzagh the trail forked and she veered east rather than continuing south. She didn't use the main trail. She traveled along its general direction, aiming toward Broken Jaw and her son.

* * *

Chebucto awoke to a heavy dream in which he and Keyo were struggling to climb the side of a mountain. In the dream water erupted all around Chebucto, while Keyo seemed to reach the top with no trouble. Struggling to get away from the water, Chebucto clawed at his face. Mud clung to his cheeks. He was soaked to the skin. His dirt shelter had become a death bed. He leaped up and stared around, wondering if Keyo was somewhere near. Gradually memory of Keyo's horrible death came to him. Chebucto made his way out of the muck and sat on a nearby rock. It was still night. The wind wasn't strong and the rain felt warm to the touch. The ice storm was over, but not the rain. Chebucto had memorized The Naan's instructions on how to get to the grottos of Falls Creek, but she had given him visual and olfactory clues that had made sense in the clear air of the Dzagh. The ice and rain had washed all such signs away.

It doesn't matter how. I know I will reach them, he reassured himself, *I must get to Kenduu one way or another.* Leaving his flimsy shelter, he made his way to the trail that he had skirted earlier. Rain pelted him. There was no division between drops of water. Instead he felt pools of warm liquid being flung at him from somewhere above. He was surprised by the warmth. In the Dzagh, rain was always cold. Chebucto approached the north end of the claystone building. In the dreary moonlight, he could just make it out.

Stay close beside it, the Naan had warned. *Go only at night. You'll see the field to the right of it. There should be racks of drying fish in the field. Stay away from those, as Dotson guards are often prowling around the food. You will come to a huge heap of boulders. Walk on the right side of them. You'll come to a narrow where you will see the first of the slave women's houses also on the right. Straight ahead you'll find the grottos. You'll have to climb the rocks at that point to be able to see down into them. Remember. Do this only at night.*

Concentrating on her description, Chebucto was relieved to see the huge tumble of rocks and boulders just as she described them. His sharp eyes picked out the shape of a small dwelling off to the right in the field but he saw no fish racks. He felt the amethyst knife writhe against his wet skin and stopped, waiting for some sort of signal. Nothing happened. There were no mental images and he couldn't smell anything. Then, despite the pounding rain, he heard voices. Straining, he determined there were two sources: one to the right and the other to the left in the rocks. Chebucto pushed himself into the shadows and waited. Two things happened simultaneously. The first startled him so much he nearly jumped. A figure emerged from the rocks on his left, barely an arm's length away, while on his right Chebucto saw a man moving stealthily toward the rocks. At first, he thought the man on the right was moving toward him, but then he assumed by the angle of his movement that he was aiming for the man on his left. Chebucto tried to keep both men in view, but they were too far apart. The man on the right aroused his suspicions, so Chebucto kept his attention focused in that direction. As a result, Chebucto didn't see the man on left move farther away from the rock pile. More importantly, he didn't recognize him as Kenduu. If he had, he might have called out a warning. Instead, he saw the figure on the right separate into two men creeping steadily toward the rock pile. Chebucto was almost certain they didn't know he was there.

Then Chebucto heard a wailing child's voice followed by a familiar voice say, "Quiet!"

Kenduu! Overjoyed to find Kenduu so unexpectedly, Chebucto almost stretched out to him mentally but stopped. The Naan had warned him of the spies. One of the men on the right kicked a stone accidentally. The sound was muffled by the rain, but Kenduu heard it and ran back to the rocks and pushed the boys back into the shadows.

The Dotson guards on Chebucto's right picked up their pace, now moving with less caution. They came close to Chebucto, who cast a bola at the closer man's legs, he felt the heat of the nearest Dotson man and caught a whiff of his scent. The man went down with a thud. Chebucto had the second bola ready and hurled before the other Dotson man knew what happened to his companion.

Cousin! Come out! Chebucto ventured a quick commune to Kenduu. *Hurry!*

Kenduu and the boys spilled out of the rocks and ran. Chebucto didn't recall picking up a rock, but he did. Chebucto leaped onto the man nearest him and smashed his head with a rock. He felt a satisfyingly sluggish resistance as the skull split. Hot blood spattered into the rain. Chebucto would have struck again, but his legs had a mind of their own. He sprinted to the other man, who wrenched the bola off his legs and lunged for Chebucto. They tumbled together on gravelly mud. Chebucto rolled out of the man's grasp and found himself poised with one leg on the ground, the other leg waited for its moment and brought Chebucto into position against the man's back. Chebucto yanked the springy Dotson hair back hard and fast with his left hand and struck the man again and again with his right fist. When he stopped, he found himself kneeling in the second man's blood. The amethyst knife twisted. Chebucto didn't need a vision to tell him what to do. He got up and ran, knees high. He caught up to one of the little boys.

"Run!" he shouted. The boy ran harder. Together Chebucto and the boy caught up with Kenduu. Chebucto shouted to Kenduu. "Stay to the left of the trail. Stay left. Don't go on the trail." Chebucto didn't remember that the Naan had told him to stay to the left of the field. The amethyst knife urged him to stay beside the buildings and he obeyed. Before long they entered the underbrush to the left of the trail. Chebucto glanced over his shoulder. He could see two more Dotson men running after them, one closer than the other. Chebucto took a moment to look for others and saw none.

Chebucto shouted, "Keep running! I'll try to stop them."

Beside him Nazu said, "I'll help you, Chebucto."

Chebucto glanced once at the dark Tuudzaado form and recognized Nazu with a surge of emotion. He saw the bola in Nazu's left hand and asked, "Do you have any more of those?"

"Yes," Nazu responded.

Together they pushed themselves a little further into the under-brush and found a small opening between two jack pine trees. They moved into the cover of the trees and waited. In a moment, a Dotson man stormed through the underbrush, aiming straight for the two trees where Chebucto waited. Chebucto stepped out of the shadows to give the man a point of focus. Beside him, Nazu waited for the best moment and hurled his bola at the man's legs. The man fell on his face. Chebucto leaped toward the man's head, grabbed his thick, short braid, and yanked upward. He pulled the amethyst knife out of its sheath and slid its sharpest edge along the man's throat. He felt hard pulsations of blood bursting from the man's neck and dropped his head.

Chebucto pulled out the third of six bolas. Another man was already through the underbrush and nearly upon them. Nazu threw a bola and missed. Chebucto's aim was better. The man fell on his side, bellowing angrily. Nazu didn't have a knife and didn't need one. Pent up rage gave his arms and one good hand a power he had never felt before. He twisted the Dotson's head hard and sharp to the side. Chebucto heard the bones crack, but Nazu didn't stop. He started pummeling the dead man in a whirl of pent up rage.

"Stop!" Chebucto yelled, "You did it. Let's get out of here before any others come out."

Even as Chebucto shouted, they both heard an angry outcry in the grotto area. Nazu leaped off the Dotson man and dashed after Chebucto into the spruce forest. They just made it to a stand of scrubby blue spruce when there was another shout, much closer. More shouts followed but the two young men did not wait to hear more. Soon they caught up with Kenduu and the others. A boy just behind Kenduu stumbled, and some-thing broke beneath his small body with a loud crack. Nazu paused to haul the boy to his feet. The boy sobbed once, then regained his com-posure, unable to move. Nazu didn't waste time. He lifted the child to his shoulders. By that time, they were far behind the others but Nazu found the free soil of the woods a welcome change from the grotto. His legs flowed into the stride that worked best in tangles of roots and dead branches and soon he caught up to the others.

Chebucto took advantage of the stillness to move into position alongside Kenduu. When his breath slowed, he said, "They got Keyo."

Not able to stop, Kenduu twisted sideways to stare at his cousin. "Got Keyo? What you mean?"

"It happened the same day that they got you, they killed him." The noise of shouting behind them grew louder. Chebucto looked over his shoulder toward the grotto and said to Kenduu. "Don't worry. I will lead them astray."

Kenduu hesitated, wanting to know more, wanting to go back with Chebucto to cover the trail as well. Then he heard Stal whimper and said to Chebucto, "Catch up with us afterward."

"I can't. Your father left home a couple of days ahead of me. I don't know what happened to him. I'm going to find him as soon as the Dotson give up the chase for you." Chebucto laid a brotherly hand on Kenduu's shoulder. "He will be glad to know he doesn't have to marry Duna."

Kenduu caught on instantly and offered a weak smile. "When you find him, tell him it was I who talked to Rastuk, not Ping. I'll tell him more when he gets home."

Nazu interrupted them, "I hear them!" A distant voice shouted somewhere to the south.

Chebucto said, "I'm going now. May the sacred forces be with you all."

* * *

In the grotto Jis was trying to bring order to a milling group confused and angry Dotson. Pointing to each in turn, he selected ten men. "You— follow them." The ten left without a demur. Jis selected another group. "You! Go to the trail that leads to the Dzagh and stop at the highest point of the trail. Be ready for them to come through the pass."

After the two groups headed out on their assignments, the Black Sun Warrior grabbed Jis by the shoulders. "What happened to him?"

"He got away," Jis replied, "with the other Tuudzaado man."

The Black Sun Warrior threw Jis to the ground and stood over him with a foot on either side of his chest. "I want them both, don't leave it up to these fools! Get them yourself. Don't come back without them." Without waiting for an answer, the Black Sun Warrior strode away.

* * *

Chebucto positioned himself a little to the east and south of the first of the pursuers. He looked around for a convenient noisemaker and spotted a dead spruce tree not far away. With as much noise as possible, he broke off a branch. Without looking to see if he got the man's attention he moved silently toward the east, counting twenty strides before he stopped.

"Go east," he said loudly to invisible people. Moving quickly toward the south, Chebucto paused and then began running noisily toward the east. When the amethyst knife moved on his chest, Chebucto stopped and moved silently toward the west. He pressed himself into a small copse of aspens and waited. As he hoped, Chebucto heard crashing as men ran awkwardly toward the east. Chebucto didn't waste any time. Running silently, he made his way toward the north and then around them toward the east. It was easy to determine the location of the Dotson by their loud movements through the scrub brush. It was still raining lightly as he circled around them on the south and shouted. Continuing to circle toward the west as quickly and quietly as he could, he found another place where he could pause and shout. In this manner, he continued to circle the small group of men and shouting from key points in each direction, keeping out of reach, he led them toward the grotto. When they were almost back where they started, he left them.

Chebucto headed toward the trail to the Dzagh. There he found several convenient hiding places and chose one that gave him a good view of the distant grotto. Just as he settled himself, he heard the uncanny sound of Dotson chanting.

"Not-here-not-here-not-here."

Chebucto counted ten Dotson men running in single file. When the last one past him, he slid out of his hiding place and squealed in a very good imitation of a dying opossum. The man at the end of the line stopped and called to the others just as Chebucto hoped he would. He recalled this part of the trail vividly because he had nearly fallen over the edge and into the deep canyon below. Chebucto selected one of the places where the edge of the ravine was hidden by a pile of sharp boulders. Standing, he shouted as loud as he could and dashed toward the boulders and ducked behind them to jump to the narrow ledge below. Then he pressed against the stone wall of the canyon, hoping that he couldn't be seen from above. Just when he thought his plan had failed, he heard a shout and caught the terrified eyes of a Dotson man as his fell to his death on the steep canyon floor below. Three others screamed as they too tumbled to their deaths. Chebucto knew better than to remain where he was. Turning to face the stones, he worked his way along the ledge until his grateful feet found a widening that led to the forest soil. As Chebucto crept away from the edge of the canyon, he could hear the Dotson men calling in vain to men who had fallen.

He didn't waste time finding out what they would do next. Moving as quietly as he could, he looped around to the south and went back to the glade where he had left Kenduu. When he neared the glade, Chebucto heard rapidly approaching noises of the second group from the grotto. He began to break off spruce boughs with each stride he took, making false trails. He used his collection of broken spruce boughs to create the appearance of five trails leading in five completely different directions from a central glade. The first of the Dotson pursuers reached the glade and spotted the first trail of trees with broken branches. The tracker shouted, waited for the others to catch up with him, and the entire group ran along the trail toward the southeast. Chebucto, who had positioned himself on the north side of the glade, watched them all file down his first false trail with a feeling of awe that his strategy worked. He smirked, thinking of how irritated Keyo would be when he heard he had missed the fun. Chebucto almost sobbed when he realized that he could never tell Keyo about this day. His despair vanished when he felt heat rising on his chest. He touched the amethyst knife and immediately saw a vision of a man with a zigzagged scar on his forehead. The hackles on the back of his neck lifted. He stopped and turned around. The rain had stopped and the black of night had shifted to the gray light of predawn. A Dotson man stepped into the glade Chebucto had just left.

Jis recognized the man he had chased on the North Face. Remembering the bulging eyes of the woman the death runners bludgeoned to day, he snarled, and readied himself for battle. Against his better wishes, Chebucto entered the glade. The two men eyed each other silently. Jis, older, was more muscular but shorter. Chebucto was surprised the Dotson man didn't have the zigzagged scar he was expecting. Jis, on the other hand, was consumed with overwhelming hatred toward everything he had done to cause him to lose his precious Mysfet. He no longer saw the man in front of him as anything other than the Black Sun Warrior he had been hunting. He shouted and charged Chebucto, who feinted toward the left. Chebucto felt the amethyst knife guide his steps through a maze of contortions and turns that helped him avoid the murderous blows of his opponent.

Suddenly Jis found himself on his back. Meanwhile, chest heaving, Chebucto willed his legs to stop quivering. The power of the amethyst knife drained away from him. Am I supposed to kill him? Chebucto wondered. Jis recognized the doubt and rolled into Chebucto's leg. Chebucto toppled. Keyo's ruined body suddenly filled Chebucto's mind with wild fury.

He leaped to his feet so fast that Jis fell backward. Chebucto could not remember later when he slid the amethyst knife out of its sheath. Never to leave him was memory of the harrowing cry the death runner made just before the blood surged forward. He envisioned the woman who had betrayed her Hutlan family by marrying a Dotson man, and the same vision showed him Jis. It came to him that this was the Dotson man she married, and the feeling was confirmed when he shouted.

"Mysfet!" Jis' howl filled the surrounding hills.

Chebucto waited in the glade, feeling uneasy around the Dotson body still in a pose of disordered death, he used rain water to clean himself. All he accomplished was to smear malodorous muck evenly over everything. Chebucto studied the body and after some hesitation took a bit of yellow powder from his pouch. He dabbed it on the man's forehead, wondering if he should close the eyes. The man's face, so terrifying in his vision of Iglan's death, looked small and out of place. Chebucto doubted the man ever felt comfort from the Sacred Forces. *He must have called it the Sacred Sun.* Still bending over the corpse, Chebucto pondered the unexpected thought. *I've always been filled with doubt. The old medicine man and the amethyst knife have changed some things, but what is it that makes me doubt there are Sacred Forces? Will that ever leave me?*

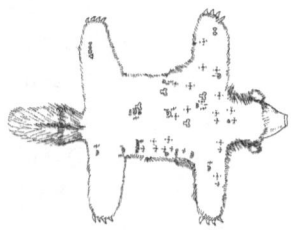

Thirty-One

The hey-hey-hey of an unfamiliar bird call brought him back to the moment and he muttered toward the body, "may the Sun guide you on this your First Walk of Death." Standing, Chebucto gazed at the glade and caught a glimpse of movement to the east. A Dotson man entered the glade. Chebucto gasped when he saw the zigzagged scar. He reached for the knife. The sheath strap broke. The sheath dropped to the ground. Chebucto grabbed for it, but his hands closed on nothing.

Chebucto was surprised to see how large the man was, and as the gray light brightened, a zigzagged scar, just as he had seen in the vision. Below the scar, black eyes locked eyes with his own. Just as Chebucto tried to gather the strength to fight a much larger man than he was, he felt the amethyst knife twist. It came to rest when a flash of light lit the Dotson man's eyes. He was not surprised, then, when he felt the mental vibrations of awkward Tuudzaado speech.

Tell Ping that you saw me, Rastuk, leaving Zana. I sought explanations of who or what I am, and did not find anyone who could help. All of my mother's family are dead, killed by my father's kind. There is nothing more for me to learn, and I will go back to Dotshon where I was born. They will not accept me there, so I will go beyond there. I will never see you or others of your family again. Goodbye. The man turned to the west and strode away. Chebucto watched, wondering who he would tell. Then he turned north to find Kenduu.

Meanwhile, Kenduu was struggling with the cluster of boys he'd amassed. When he was sure they were beyond the immediate reach of the Dotson guards, Kenduu called a halt to see how badly injured the Hutlan boy was, the fall had been as bad as it sounded. The boy's leggings were torn and askew. Bending over him with Nazu on the boy's other side, Kenduu adjusted the Hutlan boy's leggings and saw blood clotted along the inside of his thigh. Removing the legging, they saw that something had gouged a long tear on the inner side of the leg from mid-calf to mid-thigh. The leggings were bloody and the boy was too weak to stand. Using his nose to lead him to the right species, Kenduu found some medicinal moss and told the wounded boy to hold it in place while he made some bindings to wind around his leg.

"There isn't much we can do now except to reattach the wet legging and hope for the best," Kenduu said. "When we get farther away, we'll do more."

Nazu tenderly lifted his small patient and they walked until the Opossum Constellation was at its peak, signaling that night was nearly over. The dark was no longer as black as it had been. Kenduu stopped at the base of a glacial isolate, a huge boulder left in the wake of a glacial flood in the middle of the scrub forest. Beyond them were more gigantic boulders scattered here and there. Kenduu saw the sheer face of a cliff. He lowered Stal for a moment, grateful that the rain had stopped. Kenduu waited until they are all assembled and led the group through the maze of tumbled glacial stones and finally around to the base of the cliff. When they were on the other side, facing north, the sun was just rising. They saw a wide forested valley below them, on the far side was a rock table formation he remembered from previous treks. After all the rain, Kenduu was pleased to see its highest point bright in the sunlight, although most of the stones were still in darkness.

"That's where we are going," Kenduu said to the others.

The sun suddenly broke free of clouds. It was nearing day's second quarter when they reached the table rock formation. The Hutlan boy was feverish and had lain passively across Nazu's shoulder most of the way. The morning sun had blessed them with warmth throughout the entire climb, but they had a northerly ascent into the Dzagh and cold, Dzagh weather on the other side of the rock formation. Kenduu looked around for a shelter. The table rock was too exposed to unwanted surveillance. They could only rest there for a moment.

The West Face boy was alert. His intelligent eyes met Kenduu's in comfort and confidence. With a lift of his chin, he pointed to the Hutlan boy and made a motion that clearly implied, "put him down." Kenduu smiled wearily and signaled to Nazu to place the unconscious boy on the ground near the rocks that served as table legs. The soil was dark brown loam. Kenduu thought, *Mud. It's cool and damp, perfect to bring down his fever.* When he looked up, the West Face boy was nowhere in sight. Kenduu stood up in alarm but Stal inserted his hand into Kenduu's, holding the big man in place.

Stal smiled and said "shelter" with a wise nod.

Then Kenduu realized the ocean boy was also missing. Nazu shrugged. Kenduu looked around and found the older Dotson boy sprawled on the sunny side of the table formation. Kenduu couldn't help grinning at the boy, remembering the child had been born to a slave woman. He had lived his entire life in slavery and this was his first day of freedom, he lifted himself to the flat stone surface and smiled at the child. "You'll be able to sun yourself later. It's time for us to go." The ocean boy glared at Kenduu for a moment, then grunted and reached for Kenduu's right hand. Together they leaped from the table rock to the hard earth below.

Just as the group was about the head north, Kenduu saw someone moving steadily toward them. Something about his gangly figure seemed familiar, and then details of Chebuto's face became clear. They regarded each other warily for a moment, until Chebucto announced, "I came after you cousin. I've told my parents that I owe you everything to pay for the way I have been. I owe you and Duna all of my future hunting success." Chebucto stopped, studied the many faces gathered around and grinned, "I think I will start by helping you with your new family."

Kenduu introduced the boys, including Nazu, and then explained, "I thought my father would try to find me, but he wasn't at Falls Creek. Do you know where he is?"

"I followed his tracks until he headed east." Chebucto pointed toward Falls Creek, "I followed your captors. I don't know where he is."

Have you tried to reach him this way? Chebucto added in the silent language.

I tried, but someone at the Falls warned me not to use the silent way. Nazu did as well. Kenduu turned anxious eyes at Chebucto.

"We're far enough away," reasoned Chebucto. "Let's try now."

They tried the regular way with no results. Then Kenduu said, "let me try the high Tuudzaado language. I've never used it before, but I understood Father when he did."

Zaandan responded immediately. *Son, I have been in a shelter from the storm. It's about a half day's walk from Falls Creek. I'll join you soon.*

Excited, Kenduu beamed at Chebucto. *Father, we're north of Falls Creek. Maybe you should...*

We're on the east side of the trail that you used from the Dzagh, Chebucto interrupted, *I think we're close the place where your father turned east.*

Nazu, meanwhile, was waving at Kenduu and pointed wildly toward the east side of the rocks. "Is that him?" He shouted.

Indeed, it was Zaandan. If they hadn't tried the silent language when they did, they would have missed him. As it was, Zaandan joined the group, embraced his son and awaited introductions to the boys. It took a while to get everyone arranged with smaller boys riding the shoulders of the larger rescuers. While unburdened travelers could make the climb from Falls Creek to Zaandan's compound in two days, the ragged troop with Kenduu took four. On the way, they made contact with several members of the Dire Wolf Alliance. Well before they reached the upper Dzagh, Kwaikit found a Nobaagi family near the eastern coast who wanted an extra hunter to replace a son who had been killed by the Dotson. Likewise, the Naan had two families in the area north of Broken Jaw who wanted to take any one who knew how to do small game hunting, and orphan boys would be welcome. They made arrangements to meet the group at a place near the foothills of the Dzagh where they would take the three children from Kenduu.

Zaandan, meanwhile, was certain of placing Nazu with a Tuudzaado woman whose husband had been killed a few months earlier. She had three children with a fourth expected soon. Nazu volunteered to take the boy of Dotson heritage with him to help the Tuudzaado widow. Kenduu was sure that Stal would make a good older brother to Masito, and hoped that Duna would accept him as well. By the time they arrived at Zaandan's compound, Jenda had explained all of the adoption plans to the expecting widow, who was desperate for help. They agreed that the Nazu and his two new "sons" would spend the night with Zaandan before meeting her.

Chebucto, satisfied that they had settled the former slaves with new families in the mode of the Dire Wolf Alliance, *Cousin, I would like to begin repaying my debt to you by hunting for a deer tomorrow.*

I will go with you, Cousin, responded Kenduu.

No, Cousin, you have been gone too long from your wife. Allow me to do this now. Afterward, I will travel toward Broken Jaw. I hope to find my mother and father to make sure they are well. It will take me away from your compound and my debt to you.

Zaandan overheard them and joined them. *Chebucto, may I go with you. As Keyo told you many times, I don't have hunting visions. What happens to me is deer of all species notify me in their way that they are ready to offer themselves in exchange for healing a younger member of their herd. A moschid called to me a short while ago. It's a herd I've worked with often and they have three females in need of help. He has offered his life and that of another old moschid in exchange for helping them with their assorted ailments. I need help to carry all of that meat. It's something your father would have helped me to do, and now I'm asking you to go with me now. As to visiting your parents, do so after you have helped me bring food back to all of these new faces. They will need your help as well. I'm sure that with them you will find a more suitable way to repay your debt to my family.*

* * *

So that's what your Dire Wolf Alliance was about. Were you accepted as a member when you grew up, Baasee'? Deloo asked. You must have been perfect for them.

Grandfather Kwaiikit intercepted the question by communing, *your spirit guide, Baasee' was one of the best of the Alliance. She not only took care of many orphans herself along with several other women who lived north of Falls Creek, she was our best hunter and child rescuer. She was always there to bring widows and orphans much needed food, especially in winter, but all of that is another story.*

Deloo beamed at my secret ceiling spot, and I obligingly moved to it giving her my best Baasee' the Great grin.

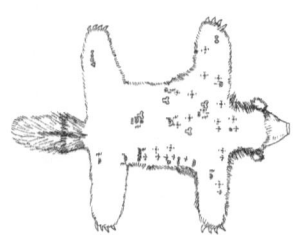

ABOUT THE AUTHOR

PHYLLIS ANN FAST, winner of the North American Indian Prose Award, is an artist (painter) and a woman of mixed descent (Tleeyegg'e hʉt'aane, which is also known as Koyukon Athabascan and white American). She was born in Anchorage, Alaska in 1946 to Elsie and Oscar Fast, graduated from East Anchorage High School in the year of the 1964 Alaskan earthquake. She earned a BA in English from the University of Alaska then centered in Fairbanks, later an interdisciplinary Master of Arts from the University of Alaska Anchorage, and concluded her education with a PhD in Anthropology from Harvard University in 1998. After teaching at the University of Alaska Fairbanks and the University of Alaska Anchorage, she retired Professor Emerita in 2014, when she turned to writing fiction. She now lives in Washington state.

Please visit her website: PHYLLISFAST.COM

REVIEWS

Half-Bead of Fundy — Native American Paranormal
5 stars (Amazon)

"A 5-star blend of cultural interfaces driven around in a used Passat by a young Native American woman who hears a 'voice'. The 'voice' belongs to Deloo's metaphysical spirit guide Baasee'. Then there is the Chinese connection, the Cuban spirit healing, the Canadians, the Boston Brahmins and the Harvard alums. All told with a Native American curved story line involving murder, cross country chases and scaling tall buildings while dodging bullets. It would take a Native American anthropologist with a Harvard PhD to make it work. So it does.

"For readers interested in Alaskan Native American culture there are words, references and philosophy that all add to the telling. The most intriguing part, for me, was the relationship and machinations between Spirit Guide and guided mortal. Is this the author's vivid imagination or does she have a special connection? Is a chance meeting a coincidence or a connection? We may find out if there are sequels.

"While the author avoids any form of clichéd cliff hanger there are hints of further adventures of Deloo and Baasee, perhaps on the metaphysical side. I've read several other 'paranormal mysteries' but this is the first that provided me with more than just a glimpse of how paranormal may work. I look forward to future, hopefully far reaching, adventures of Deloo and Bassee." –DL, 2016

Half-Bead of Fundy
5 stars (Amazon)

"A must read Mystery. Entertaining and elegantly written. The story races along with passion between the mystical spirit world of Baasee and the Koyukon Athabascan, Deloo, to unravel the twists and turns of this thriller!" – JH, 2016

Half-Bead of Fundy
5 stars (Amazon)

"Fast has created an engaging mixture of mystery and humor. The narrative, told from the viewpoint of Deloo's spirit guide, swings through maritime Canada to Boston as the young Athabaskan solves the mysterious death of an innkeeper." – JKR, 2016

OTHER BOOKS BY THE AUTHOR

These three are also available as ebooks.

Fiction / Native American & Aboriginal

Half-Bead of Fundy

First in the Native American Mystery series

Deloo had always welcomed the pull of a myriad of oddball spirits. ~Pull a 180!~ Baasee' shouted into her head. Deloo wasn't used to spirit guides like Baasee', but the crazy people following her didn't know or care. They wanted her beaded jacket at any cost. It was up to Alaska Native, Deloo Goode, to figure out what was so important about her mother's beading—or else be killed like the innkeeper at the Secret Spirit Inn.

270 pages
ISBN 978-0-9974977-2-4 (trade paperback)
ISBN 978-0-9974977-0-0 (ebook)

Midnight Trauma

Second in the Native American Mystery series,
sequel to *Half-Bead of Fundy*.

Someone has killed a teenager at a bead shop in remote Fairbanks, Alaska. Moreover, the owner, Earlene, is missing and the shop keeps getting broken into. Deloo Goode and her mother try to unravel the mysteries surrounding the bead shop. Luckily, Deloo has an invisible weapon: her playful spirit guide Baasee', who can see things others can't—sometimes. Will they force the murderer into the open? Can they untangle the clues and surprises before anyone else gets hurt?

252 pages
ISBN: 978-0-9974977-3-1 (trade paperback)
ISBN: 978-0-9974977-4-8 (ebook)

The Dire Wolf Alliance

A Native American Saga
Prequel to the Native American Mystery series

The prehistoric story told by her spirit guide Baasee' and her Grandfather Kwaiikit, helps Deloo, the protagonist of *Half-Bead of Fundy* and *Midnight Trauma*, come to grips with her own recent widowhood.

"Go where?" Ping asked Chebucto. "You've been banished twice. You have nowhere to go." Growing up, no matter the era or place, can be terrifying. Chebucto understood what the medicine man told him to do, but couldn't do it by himself on the ancient northeastern coast of North America. Meanwhile, adults in a local group called the Dire Wolf Alliance, tried to rescue and find homes for widows and orphans traumatized by the violent Death Runners bludgeoning their way through Zana.

260 pages
ISBN: 978-0-9974977-6-2 (trade paperback)
ISBN: 978-0-9974977-7-9 (ebook)

JUVENILE FICTION / Animals / Deer, Moose & Caribou

Tepi, the Girl Who Helped the Deer

Story and illustrations by Phyllis Ann Fast

Tepi finds herself in communication with a deer spirit who wants her to go into the forest and help an injured deer in need. This is the story of how Tepi found her calling.

66 pages, full color

Trade paperback

ISBN: 978-0-9974977-1-7

JUVENILE FICTION / Animals / Elephants

Brella and Her Umbrella, A Baby Elephant Story

Story and illustrations by Phyllis Ann Fast

Brella, the baby elephant, is so curious that she dreamily follows a pretty bird. She wanders away from her family and is suddenly LOST! Her spirit guide, Umbrella, attempts to keep Brella safe from danger.

68 pages, full color

Trade paperback

ISBN: 978-0-9974977-5-5

Available at Amazon.com and other retail outlets.

Northern Athabascan Survival
Women, Community, and the Future
(North American Indian Prose Award)

by Phyllis Ann Fast

The Northern Athabascan peoples of the Alaskan interior and the Yukon have survived centuries of contact and attempted domination by outsiders. Their lives today are rich in meaning and tradition yet are also complicated by numerous challenges such as poverty, alcoholism, domestic violence, suicide, and troubled leadership.

Combining scholarly analysis, first-person accounts, and her own experiences and insights as a Koyukon Athabascan artist and anthropologist, Phyllis Ann Fast illuminates the modern Athabascan world. Her conversations with Athabascan women offer revealing glimpses of their personal lives and a probing assessment of their professional opportunities and limitations. Also showcased is the crucial but ambiguous role of Athabascan leaders, who are needed to champion reform and social healing but are often undermined by conflicting notions of decision making, personhood, and leadership in Athabascan society.

A troubling observation of this study is the vast extent to which addiction—manifested as both substance abuse and economic dependency—pervades Northern Athabascan society and threatens to curtail its cohesion and aspirations. But Northern Athabascans are far from victims. As Fast discovers, Northern Athabascan men and women are well aware of these widespread social problems, and many have undertaken initiatives to deal with and heal them. Rigorous and compassionate, *Northern Athabascan Survival* provides an uncompromising view of a remarkable and troubled world.

When Spirits Visit
A Collection of Stories by Indigenous Authors
Compiled and Edited by MariJo Moore

WHEN SPIRITS VISIT contains stories centered on spiritual visitation – animal, bird, and people. Some are fiction, some non-fiction, and some faction. Discernment is left to each reader.

Writers included are: Susan Deer Cloud, **Phyllis A. Fast,** Gabriel Horn, Amy Krout-Horn, Evan Pritchard, Jim Stevens, MariJo Moore, Sean Milanovich, Clifford Trafzer, Dawn Karima Pettigrew, Lois Red Elk, Willliam Yellow Robe, Jr, Dean Hutchins and Denise Low—all respected published authors in the Native American realm of literature.

This book is unique in its presentation of the fact that "...many of us do believe in the mysteries of the universe, even if they cannot be 'proved' mathematically or scientifically. There are spirit beings who help us, who guide us, and there are spirit beings who can confuse us as well. Spirit beings are all around us at any given moment. These spirits have their work to do in helping us, so they need us as much as we need them."

www.ingramcontent.com/pod-product-compliance
Lightning Source LLC
Chambersburg PA
CBHW031311170626
46807CB00001B/379